"YOU'RE

Lorena said against his neck. She sensed that he smiled.

"Yes, I know, little one," Clay said into her hair.

"A horrible monster," she added.

"Yes, a horrible monster."

"How could you be such a beast?"

"It couldn't be that I was provoked at times, could it?" he asked in mock wonder.

Lorena's senses reeled when he captured her lush lips in a sweet embrace.

"You are so sweet, my Lorena."

He could not get enough of her, could not get her close enough. He turned to lay her on the bed and mold his hard, lean body to hers . . .

IN DESIRE'S HEAT, SHE WOULD BLOSSOM . . .

Desert Rose

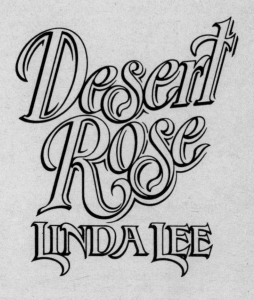

Desert Rose

LINDA LEE

DIAMOND BOOKS, NEW YORK

DESERT ROSE

A Diamond Book / published by arrangement with
the author

PRINTING HISTORY
Diamond edition / August 1991

ISBN: 1-55773-548-4

Diamond Books are published by The Berkley Publishing Group,
200 Madison Avenue, New York, New York 10016.
The name "DIAMOND" and its logo
are trademarks belonging to Charter Communications, Inc.

PRINTED IN THE UNITED STATES OF AMERICA

10 9 8 7 6 5 4 3 2 1

1

Paso del Norte, Mexico, 1830

HER EYES OPENED SUDDENLY. THE MORNING SUN had filtered through the glass-paned window, casting rays of golden light around the room, forcing her from her dream-filled sleep. Her surroundings slowly came into focus, and she remembered the sandstorm that had plagued the Paso del Norte area, leaving no possibility of going outside. With a sigh and a punch straight to the center of her pillow, Lorena flopped over on her stomach and burrowed back down into the bed.

As the sun rose higher in the sky, light streamed boldly into the room, making it impossible to sleep. The warmth pulled Lorena up from the folds of her bed to the realization that the sand-laden wind had gone, replaced by the shimmering sunshine of a clear spring day. A smile spread across her face. "Heavens above!" she cried as she threw the covers off and leaped out of bed. "I can hardly believe I'm finally home!"

Lorena Cervantes didn't bother with a robe or slippers. She ran to the window, pulling it open with more excitement than strength. The precious glass panes some long-ago ancestor had imported from Spain rattled loudly in protest as they banged against the thick adobe wall. With an excited squeal, she twirled away from the window and bellowed a few bars of an unrecognizable tune.

1

* * *

Startled by the sound, all those within the walls of the hacienda Cielo el Dorado paused abruptly. Indians and outlaws passed through their thoughts before the off-key melody filtered toward them, carried on the slight breeze that rustled through the courtyard. Lorena! With sighs of relief and a quick sign of the cross over their breasts, they went back to work.

"*Dios mío*," sighed a heavyset Mexican woman. "I was certain our time had come. I forgot that Lorena was back."

"*Yo también*," said an equally heavyset man. "Just like our Lorena to cause a stir."

"You would have thought that fancy English school would have taught her to act like a lady," the woman said with an indignant sniff. "I knew Diego should have sent her to Spain . . . if she had to go at all. At least in Spain she would have learned the proper things a lady needs to know."

"Ah, Dalia, you know no more about what they teach in Spain than I do, and after five long years, I know you have missed Lorena as much as I."

A smile softened the lines of age that creased Dalia's face as she thought of the young girl whom she had cared for since birth. Yes, she was glad Lorena had finally come home. She only wished it was under better circumstances. It seemed so terribly unfair that tragedy could harshly strike one so young, taking first her mother when Lorena was no more than thirteen, then a year ago, her father, leaving Lorena alone in the world at nineteen. Nineteen years old! Dalia sighed to herself. Lorena should have been married before now. As in the past, Dalia wondered how Lorena's father could have been so remiss in his responsibilities to his only child. Diego Cervantes should have brought Lorena home long ago and found her a husband. But now Diego was dead and could do nothing for his child. Enough, she scolded herself. She and Pedro would do everything they could for the young girl whom they loved as their own.

Dalia glanced toward Lorena's room, then picked up her long skirt just as Pedro leaned over and nuzzled her cheek. "You should go see what our lively one is up to."

Dalia blushed a crimson shade, reminding Pedro of the sweet girl he had married forty years before. "Pedro," she admonished while playfully slapping her husband's hands, "you are too old to be pawing at me that way." Before Pedro could catch hold of her wrist, Dalia darted out of reach and fled in the direction of the noise that had startled everyone.

Pedro watched as she hurried away, ample hips swaying, before he turned toward the stables, a wide smile clearly outlining his face. "Old! I will show that woman old!"

Dalia bustled through the greenery-filled courtyard, then down a long narrow hallway, all the while following the off-key tune that led to Lorena's bedroom. Her knock on the heavy wooden door went unnoticed while the boisterous tune rang on. When finally she pushed open the door, Dalia caught her breath.

Lorena was dancing around the room, singing at the top of her lungs, a feather pillow clutched to her breast. Though Lorena would not have been included in the ranks of classically beautiful women in Spain or even Mexico, no one would have denied she was striking, but to Dalia, Lorena was the most beautiful of all.

The nightgown-clad figure swept about the small room as if she were in the grandest of ballrooms amid the most gallant of men. Red tresses flew in the air while green eyes danced with laughter as she twirled and swayed about the room. Such a beautiful child, Dalia thought. What was to become of her with her papa now dead?

As Dalia stood in the doorway unnoticed, she thought of the year that had passed since Diego Cervantes's untimely death. It seemed only yesterday that the towering Americano, Clay Wakefield, had come to the hacienda with the terrible news. He had been to the Cielo el Dorado before, and Dalia knew he was a friend of Diego's. But she had

been surprised and a bit suspicious when he had shown
Pedro the letter Diego had written that left not only the
hacienda but Lorena in his care. Diego had written the letter
on the trail before he died, and the man of whom it spoke
had brought it to the hacienda.

Emotion clouded Dalia's thoughts. She had wanted the
letter to be a fraud. Even now, with Pedro's apparent
unquestioning acceptance of the situation, she wished it to
be untrue. However, much to her chagrin, she had recognized Diego's flowery but shaky script as being authentic
enough. Dalia closed her eyes as if in pain. Was some man
who did not even know Lorena supposed to find her a
husband? Would he even try? Would he care? Would he
marry her off to some old, uncaring man who wanted a
young bride? Did not that exact thing happen to young
Maria Elena Comal not two years ago? Or, worse yet,
would he try to take for himself what rightfully should be
Lorena's? Dalia's mind had whirled with questions, but
when she voiced her opinions to her husband, Pedro only
said that Clay would do what was best.

Clay would do what was best! Dalia mimicked silently,
her eyes narrowed to angry slits. She did not like it one bit!
How could Pedro be so certain?

When the Americano learned that Lorena was still away
at school in England, he had sent word of her father's death
and asked her to return to Cielo el Dorado immediately.
Dalia remembered having been relieved when Wakefield
had sent one of his men and a chaperon to bring Lorena
home safely. She grudgingly admitted that Clay was not a
complete barbarian, like most Americanos, since he had not
left Lorena to her own devices to get home.

After determining the amount of time it would take to
deal with necessary business in his home state, and calculating how long it would take Lorena to travel from
England, Clay Wakefield had announced he would be back
in a year's time. With instructions left with Pablo as well as
several of his best men, the bold Americano had mounted

his black devil stallion and joined the well-armed caravan as it lumbered ahead toward Santa Fe and then, finally, Missouri.

"Dalia? Dalia!" Lorena repeated when she got no response. "What are you daydreaming about? You look as if you are going to strangle some unfortunate soul." Lorena laughed as she took her duenna's plump hands to twirl her about the room.

"*Tenga cuidado, chica.* I am too old to be treated like this," Dalia said with a smile that belied her stern voice, consciously banishing all thoughts of Clay Wakefield.

"Oh, Dalia, I *am* being careful—and if you are too old, I am the Blessed Virgin."

"Lorena, you should not say such things!"

Lorena had the good sense to look chastised under Dalia's reprimand, but as soon as the older woman turned to the armoire, Lorena twirled once again with laughter in her eyes.

Dalia gasped when she opened the heavy Spanish armoire that had belonged to generations of Cervantes women. Inside, a myriad of gowns, so different from the loose-fitting, free-flowing, Mexican garments the duenna was used to, hung side by side in a rainbow of colors. On further inspection, Dalia found ruffled parasols and tiny kid slippers that went with the assorted dresses.

"They are beautiful, *chica.* Just look!" Dalia pulled out an ice-blue gown, then after a few moments of searching, found a coordinating parasol and slippers.

"And there are matching gloves and ribbons for each," Lorena said. "They are the latest European fashions and the most uncomfortable garments you have ever put on. I told Luz not to bother unpacking them. I have no need for them here. But as you can see, she insisted." Lorena cocked her head in thought, a mischievous grin spreading across her full lips. "Maybe I could give them away, one for each woman here. We'd have the best-dressed, or at least the most colorful, servants for miles." Lorena giggled as she

imagined the elaborately gowned women around a courtyard well instead of an ornate ballroom, pulling up buckets
of water rather than twirling and swaying with a handsome
beau.

Dalia only shook her head.

Apparently bored with the subject of clothes, Lorena
continued. "Today I am going to ride through the vineyards
and down to the river, and maybe I will even go up to the
hills." Lorena plopped down onto the bed and looked up at
the ceiling, green eyes sparkling with excitement. "I can
hardly believe I am really here!"

"Well, you are here and you have been riding for
weeks . . . for months," Dalia said. "And before that you
were sailing across the ocean. You should stay inside.
Surely you need to rest."

"Riding in a caravan from Veracruz to Paso del Norte,
restrained by a slow, monotonous pace, is not the same as
riding unrestrained with the wind in your face. The ocean
journey was not nearly as bad as the land part. At least on
the ship I was able to move around." Lorena sat up and
hugged her knees to her chest. "I have dreamed of little else
but coming home, where I belong, to see my friends and the
land, the mission and my home." Lorena looked out the
window, her eyes misted with longing, but it was gone
before it settled and she turned back to Dalia. "Besides, I
would go crazy inside on such a glorious day. I could hardly
wait to get home and ride through the fields under the warm
sun. In London they have the dreariest of weather. The sun
would hide for months without having the good grace to
show itself. The cold, wet air seeped to my very bones. It
will be years, if ever, before I dry out."

Dalia turned back to the armoire, carefully putting the
dress and accessories back inside. "I think you exaggerate,
chica. You forget how merciless our sun can be. I suspect
that by the middle of the summer you will long for a cloudy
sky. And I will not allow you to darken your lovely skin like
a vaquero."

Rummaging through an old leather trunk, Dalia came up with a wide-brimmed straw hat that could be tied under the chin. It was similar to the sombreros the men wore, but since it was made of straw, it was not nearly as heavy. "I may not be able to stop you from going out in the sun, but I will insist that you wear a hat," Dalia said in a voice that brooked no argument.

Throughout Dalia's impassioned display, Lorena was going through the trunk as well. By the time the duenna had finished, Lorena had pulled on boys' pants that clung to slender hips and a white cambric shirt that revealed young rounded breasts.

"Lorena!" Dalia exclaimed, crushing the straw hat to her ample breast. "What are you wearing? I think you forget that you are no longer a child. You are a lady now! Is that not what your father sent you away to learn? It is time you put such childish things behind you. And as long as we are on the subject, I think you should be riding in a wagon instead of on a horse."

"A wagon!" Lorena cried. "The very idea! Really, Dalia! It is far more dangerous to ride in a rickety old wagon than on the back of a horse." Lorena grimaced as she imagined the rough-hewn *carretas* that bumped and swayed along the rutted roads of the area.

"What do the ladies do in England? Surely they do not ride around on horses." Dalia felt sure she was right, knowing nothing but life at the hacienda.

"They ride in beautiful horse-drawn carriages, or as you like to say, on the back of a horse, in a sidesaddle."

"What is this sidesaddle?" Dalia asked suspiciously.

"A crazy thing that allows a woman to ride with both legs on the same side of the horse."

"*Caramba*! You are avoiding my question," Dalia said, not liking to be proven wrong. "You must be concerned about what people think around here, not in England. What will your future husband do with a girl who appears to have so few womanly sensibilities?" Dalia added as she watched

Lorena finish dressing. Even as she said the words, Dalia knew that Lorena could be the perfect lady when she put her mind to it; however, in the past, and seemingly now, she rarely did. How opposite this child was from her mother.

"Ah, *Dios*," Dalia said with a loud sigh, "what am I to do with you?"

"I suspect you will come with me while I get something to eat and continue to scold me for my unladylike behavior for the rest of my days. Besides, you do not have to worry, I am not going to get married." Lorena ignored Dalia's raised eyebrow. "I know as much as anyone about making wine and harvesting fields. The Cervantes family has been doing it since the seventeenth century. Now it is my turn. So don't worry about my lack of womanly sensibilities, Dalia. I won't need them. I will carry on the Cervantes line and run the hacienda, myself."

"I hate to disappoint you, *chica*," Dalia stated, sure now of what she was talking about, "but if you want to carry on the Cervantes line, you have no choice but to marry and have many babies."

That gave Lorena pause, but then she laughed good-naturedly. "We will worry about that later," she said as she took Dalia's arm and pulled her out of the bedroom, leaving the duenna with an uneasy feeling about the Americano who was now in charge. Lorena did not seem to be aware of the man's existence. Had he not sent the letter to England to tell Lorena of her father's death? Possibly he had mentioned nothing of himself. Dalia did not want to be the one to tell her about the man but tell her she would—and soon, Dalia thought, for the Americano should be back anytime. But not yet, she sighed. She would let Lorena enjoy her homecoming. There would be time enough to tell her later on.

Signs of the burgeoning spring filled Lorena's senses when she stepped outside onto a walkway underneath the overhanging roof. Thick grass butted up against the smooth stones on which she stood. The grass carpeted the courtyard in tender green, fresh after lying dormant throughout the winter, while giant cottonwood trees sprouted an abundance of silver-green leaves.

Dalia came out behind her, and together they stepped from the porch into the courtyard to walk under the huge trees and pass the main courtyard well where several women were pulling up water to use for their daily chores.

"Señorita Cervantes, *buenos días.*"

"*Buenos días*, Concha. *Cómo estás*?"

"*Muy bien, gracias.*"

"Welcome home, señorita," said another.

"*Gracias*," Lorena replied, thrilled at being home after so long, comforted that some of the faces were still the same.

"Quiet, you should be working, not talking," Dalia reprimanded the women.

"We're working, Dalia, we're working," they grumbled as they went back to their labor.

"Still a demanding taskmaster, I see," Lorena said with a smile, "Miss Tidesdale from school would have loved you."

"Hmmp! I can see already that your Miss Tidesdale was not strict enough, as she failed to teach you how to dress properly. And I did not need to go to a fancy school to learn that!"

"Oh, Dalia," Lorena exclaimed with a laugh, "you haven't changed a bit, and how I missed you!"

After a few steps Lorena could smell a tantalizing aroma wafting through the air.

"Mmmm. Is that Dalia's very own world-famous bread I smell? Yes, I am sure it is!" Lorena exclaimed. "I'm ravenous, I cannot wait to eat!"

"*Dios mío*! No manners at all," Dalia said as Lorena pulled her toward the kitchen. "I think you need to be turned over my knee!"

Lorena only laughed. "But I know you will hug me and then feed me instead!"

Directly from the courtyard Lorena stepped into a large kitchen that was filled with reminders of her father and home. The thick adobe walls were painted a stark white, brightening a room that, with few windows, would otherwise have been dreary. Shiny copper pots and pans hung from the ceiling, and the floor was covered with blue and white tiles, which could also be found throughout the living quarters of the hacienda. The tiles had been brought in from Mexico City when Lorena was a child. Her father had seen them in the city's grand homes and decided his hard-packed dirt floors were no longer acceptable. It was a luxury this part of the country had never seen, but one the Cervantes family had come to love.

A well-worn wooden table stood to one side of the room. Lorena took a deep breath as she remembered how her father used to sit at the head of the table whenever he was home, with elbows firmly planted on the cottonwood planks, telling tales of all the places he had been. O, Papa, she cried to herself, why did you leave me? Her father who had been so handsome and so full of life; her father who had taught her to run the hacienda and to be proud of her heritage; her father who had spent most of his time away and caused her mother so much misery. Lorena had forsworn marriage years ago because she refused to live a miserable life like her mama. Men treated women like mere possessions, if and when they were ever around, and she for one would not have it!

Instantly she felt remorse for such unkind thoughts. How could a daughter feel such mingled love and anger for her father? With a sigh, she resolved that she would carry on his work, consciously putting from her mind Dalia's statement that she would have to marry.

Lorena turned to the stove and was greeted by a smiling young serving girl.

"Señorita Cervantes, Pedro came by on his way to the

stables and told me you would be ready to eat, so I have your meal ready. Is there anything else you need?"

"*Sí*, Luz. Please ask Jaime to saddle Rosinante, and as soon as I finish eating I will go to the stables."

Lorena had planned to grab a slice of bread and eat it on her way, but just as she reached for the bread, she heard shouts of greeting from outside.

Lorena turned to Dalia. "Who could be here?"

Dalia's nervous glance darted from the door to Lorena. Wiping her hands on her apron, the duenna started for the door, then whirled around and sat down. "*Madre mía*," she mumbled to herself.

Lorena looked at her curiously. "What is it, Dalia?"

Dalia took a deep breath, but before she could begin, the door burst open to reveal a man of average height and stocky build. He had blond hair, which was rarely seen in these parts, and brown eyes that glowed with laughter as he stood in the doorway looking Lorena over from head to toe. "I hear that if a man wants to eat the best breakfast this side of the river, this is the place." A smile curved his lips, and before he could step farther into the room, Lorena threw herself into his arms.

"Ramón!" she cried.

"For a moment I thought you had forgotten me," he said, his face turning red with pleasure.

"Never! I could never forget you . . . though for a second there I wasn't sure who you were." Lorena laughed as she pulled back to look at him. "You've changed quite a bit in the five years I have been gone."

"If anyone has changed, it is you, *querida*." Ramón smiled appreciatively as he looked at her. "Yes, you have changed quite a bit."

Dalia forced herself up from the table, relief washing over her in a great tide when she realized it was not the North American, Clay Wakefield, but sweet Ramón Valdéz from El Rancho Escondido, a hacienda across the river just outside of Paso del Norte. As Dalia watched the exchange, the beginnings of a plan began to form.

"Come, you two, sit down and have some breakfast." Dalia bustled around the kitchen as they sat down at the table.

"Dalia, let me help you," Lorena offered.

"No, no, no, sit, sit, sit. Talk to Ramón. You have much catching up to do, no?"

Lorena smiled at Dalia and shook her head before turning to Ramón. When she turned, Lorena caught him staring at her breasts. Red stained her cheeks as she quickly looked away, not knowing what to do. "Ramón," she started, this time sensing his shifting gaze before she turned her head back to him. "Tell me everything you have been doing these past years."

Ramón quickly looked up, having forgotten where he was, mesmerized by the changes in the girl he had grown up with. She had changed from a stick-legged little girl with red hair and freckles to a . . . a woman, he thought somewhat uncomfortably.

"Ramón?" Lorena looked at him curiously, wondering what could be wrong.

Ramón looked surprised by the sound of her voice. "Excuse me, Lorena, my head is filled with cobwebs. It has just been so long . . . and you have changed so much."

"In five years I guess I have." Lorena laughed, failing to notice the wonder in his voice. "No more pigtails and freckles. Miss Tidesdale saw to that."

Dalia set plates down on the table. "I must go and find Pedro. Take your time." She smiled at the two before she left the kitchen, leaving a gust of wind in her wake as she slammed the door behind her.

"She's certainly in a hurry," Ramón said.

"She, at least, has not changed a bit."

"This, I think, is the truth. So tell me, who is this Miss Clydesdale you speak of."

Lorena nearly choked on her cocoa and had to cover her

mouth to keep from spitting it out. Carefully she swallowed. "*Tidesdale*, Ramón! Though I must admit she did look a bit like a horse."

"So Tidesdale, who is this person?" he persisted impatiently, not understanding the joke.

"She is Miss Edwina Tidesdale, headmistress of Miss Tidesdale's Seminary for Young Ladies, of which I was one."

"One what?" he teased in return.

Lorena burst out laughing as Ramón merely smiled, all the while watching the girl who had blossomed into a striking young lady. But while her appearance had changed, her laughter and wit had not.

"Oh, how I have missed this place," Lorena said.

"You were gone a long time. You must have liked it there."

"Yes and no. I did like it, most of the time, but I wanted to come home many times . . . but Papa always said it wasn't time." Lorena looked into her cup as she swirled the liquid around.

"I'm sorry, Lorena, I did not mean to cause you pain. I'm sorry about your padre. We all loved him very much."

Lorena remembered the times she and her father had ridden into town to see Ramón and his family. Ramón's father and hers had grown up together, their ancestors having come up from New Spain in 1660 to settle the land. "*Gracias*, Ramón." With determination she looked up, her smile back in place. "Now dig into this food before it gets cold."

They feasted on fluffy eggs mixed with melted cheese, tender slices of ham, freshly baked bread dripping with butter, and steaming mugs of hot chocolate.

"So tell me what has been going on around here?" Lorena asked, forgetting the food in front of her.

"Unfortunately, I have no time to tell you, for now I must take care of the business I have come about."

"And I thought you had come to see me," Lorena said in a teasing pout.

Ramón stood to go and smiled. "Do not tell me England turned you into a flirt?"

Lorena made an unsuccessful attempt at batting her eyelashes.

"On second thought," he said, laughing out loud, "you still have much to learn! Maybe you can come back to El Rancho with me when I leave tomorrow. I am certain one of the many females in my family can teach you to flirt properly!"

With that, Ramón scooted out the door just as Dalia returned. Lorena had been so busy talking she had hardly eaten a thing. Impatient to be outdoors, but starved nonetheless, Lorena hurriedly finished the food on her plate.

Dalia picked up the empty plates and muttered, "After eating a meal like that, it will be a wonder if you can get on that horse of yours, much less stay on it."

"I couldn't agree more, I have definitely been a glutton. I just could not resist a home-cooked meal. Fortunately, Rosinante has a strong back to carry such a heavy load," Lorena said in a teasing voice as she kissed Dalia's cheek.

Ignoring the jest, Dalia added, "You be careful riding that horse of your, *chica*. Do not go far from the walls and make sure the guards can see you at all times. In fact, why do you not get Ramón to go with you?"

Anxious to be gone, Lorena merely nodded, adding that Ramón was busy, holding back the retort that she had been riding just about as long as she had been walking and could certainly handle her own horse.

Hurrying out the door, Lorena practically ran through the main courtyard and around a long thick adobe wall that led into the courtyard that housed the stables. The moment Lorena caught sight of Rosinante, she smiled. It had been five years since she had seen the mare, but neither seemed to have forgotten the other. Rosinante stood impatiently pawing the ground as if demanding Lorena's attention. With a chestnut coat and a glossy black mane and tail, Rosinante was truly a beauty.

A whinny brought Lorena out of her thoughts. With great pride she mounted the horse, pressed the mare's sides with booted feet, and sent Rosinante into a gallop through the outer gate that took them away from the hacienda.

Lorena lifted her face to the sun and savored its warmth. The dry desert heat penetrated flesh down to bones, banishing the chill that had clung to her during the long stay in England. It was so good to be home!

Lorena gave the mare free rein, taking in the sights of her home while paying no attention to the horse's direction. Lorena was surprised when she found that Rosinante had brought them to a cluster of cottonwoods, the giant trees bending and stretching to shade a pool of water.

"Oh, Rosinante," she said as she leaned over to run her hand over the horse's smooth neck, "you missed this spot as much as I."

Lorena felt the magic that had surrounded her whenever she came to the spot as a child. The huge trees with their rough, craggy bark made her think of the hundreds of years they had lined the river and of the many people who had passed that way to bring Christianity and civilization to the desolate region. Christianization of the Indian, the pride of her religion—or possibly, she sometimes thought, its shame.

The swimming hole would have been stagnant and unpleasant if it had not been for the tiny *acequia* that fed it on its north side, then emptied it on the south, taking the cool water back to the river from which it came. An old wooden bridge crossed the *acequia*, and as a child, Lorena had been convinced it was a place for elves to hide. With just a touch of fear, she had crept up many times without making a sound in hopes of catching sight of one of the little creatures. But luck had never been with her.

Today, however, she had no desire to sneak up on elves. Instead, she and Rosinante pranced around in a dance of their own making. Lorena's red hair bounced, and her hands barely held the reins as Rosinante half trotted, half cantered in a circle, the horse's huge head tossing up and down, as excited as its rider to be out.

Lorena's laughter rang in the air as she rode with a sense of release, freedom, and utter joy. No more confining clothes made from yards and yards of stiff fabric, and no more hanging precariously on the back of a horse in a life-threatening sidesaddle. She sat astride Rosinante, un-encumbered by the latest fashion. The feel of soft fabric against her skin, loose enough to allow her to move any way she pleased, sent a shiver of sinful pleasure through her body. Her unbound hair was caught in the wind, while her hat was cast off, hanging carelessly around her neck, flopping up and down with each jostling step the horse took. A devilish smile played on her lips as she thought of the expression that would be on Miss Tidesdale's face if she could see her now. Her fists would be planted firmly on narrow hips, her normally blotchy skin red all over, veins popping out on her forehead. How often had Lorena seen just that stance in all the years she had been at school?

"All that work for naught, Miss T.," she said primly to the trees before bursting into laughter at her own joke.

"And who, may I ask, is Miss T.?" A deep, resonant voice vibrated through the trees.

Startled, Lorena swung around in her saddle. She had to grab the saddle horn since just then Rosinante decided to take an exceedingly jolty step. After several seconds of confusion, hair flying in disarray, balance threatened, Lorena managed to stop the horse and regain her seat, only to find her breath taken away as she sat facing the largest man she had ever seen.

He sat comfortably astride a huge black stallion, one bulging forearm resting on the saddle horn, the other crossed carelessly on top. Sharp features and dark eyes that ordinarily would have been fierce were lightened by his amused grin. The man was covered with dust, while his horse glistened with sweat, telling Lorena they were just off the trail. She cursed herself for coming to the swimming hole where the guards could not see her. Why was it that she never listened to anybody, as if the darker side of life could never touch her? But here she sat, prey to this giant stranger, no one within seeing or hearing distance to help her. Her self-chastisement lasted only a second, for in the next, she reached for the small knife she had put in her boot. At the time, Lorena had thought of cutting flowers or carving a piece of wood. There were many possible uses for the small knife, though defending herself had not been one of them. But defend herself she would and with not a minute to spare as she saw his gaze pass over her body.

"You won't need the knife. I'm not here to hurt you," he said, trying hard to stifle his laughter. The thought of this little sprite defending herself with a knife so small, assuming she even knew how to use it, was absurd.

"And what, pray tell, are you laughing at, señor?" Lorena asked, green eyes flashing, her chin slightly raised, red hair cascading over thin shoulders.

"I'm not laughing at you. I'm merely amused by the picture you made while talking to yourself as you rode around in circles on your horse. Which I might add, looked as if it might soon rid itself of its careless rider . . . my sweet." The rugged stranger's smile and confidence aggravated Lorena.

"I am not your sweet, you overconfident . . . cow." She spit the words through clenched teeth.

"Cow!" He bellowed with laughter at her choice of words. "I've been called many things in my life but never a cow. You wound me, señorita." He put a large, tanned hand over his chest. "I don't know if I will ever recover."

Lorena could not help being amused by his dramatics. "Well, a cow you are and probably worse for coming here and scaring me. Besides, I don't even know who you are."

"Me scare you? Ha! I thought I was the one in danger. At any moment my heart could have been pierced. You might have knifed me to death, and no one would have known! I'd have been left to the vultures."

In one swift movement, the stranger swung down from his horse to bow gallantly before her. "Forgive me for not introducing myself. I am merely an ordinary man who wants nothing more than to see a lovely señorita smile." The words flowed easily after too many years of practice, meaning nothing other than a way to get what he wanted. But to Lorena they were kind words that were clear water to a thirsty heart. How long had it been since anyone had spoken kind words to her? Certainly not in the time she had spent at school. It seemed like forever.

When the stranger rose from his bow, Lorena was mesmerized by his incredible height. He was easily four inches over six feet. Much taller than any man she had ever met. And his eyes. They were a dark brown, almost black, darker and deeper than Lorena had ever seen. She felt as if he could look right into her and see the whirlwind of her thoughts, the pounding of her heart.

Thick waves of black hair tapered back from his face and down his neck. The stranger wore a shirt similar to Lorena's, but his stretched across broad shoulders that narrowed down into a slim waist. His shirt was opened at the neck revealing a V of dark curling hair. Lorena had never seen a man with his shirt opened and had the compelling urge to reach out and touch the dark hair. Powerful thighs strained soft buckskin pants as if the seams would burst at any moment. He had the rugged good looks of a man who had spent much of his time in the sun. Lorena was sure she had never seen a man who was so handsome.

Lorena forgot her fright altogether and gave herself up to naive dreams of knights in shining armor, the dreams of a girl who had not been taught the ways of flirting and game playing, of a girl who had spent little time around men. "Señor, you are too beautiful to be just an ordinary man, and I suspect you are a god sent down from the heavens to play havoc with my heart."

As soon as the words were out, Lorena blushed to the roots of her hair as she realized what she had said. Ahhgg, her mind screamed, this is not some silly dream, you ninny. This is a real man, and you should know perfectly well how horrible men are. This one is probably dangerous, too, and you just made a fool of yourself!

The stranger was as surprised as Lorena by the words, but when he noticed her embarrassment, instead of making her feel better, he mischievously added to her discomfort.

"A god, am I?" His eyes gleamed with amusement, somehow covering the unease she had made him feel by her words. "I'm afraid, señorita, that many would beg to disagree and find comfort in calling me a . . ." He searched for a word, finding none suitable to utter in front of a señorita, and finally, coming up with a lame "wretch."

Lorena's defenses rose at the taunt. Embarrassed and hurt she blurted, "You're laughing at me again, you . . . you cow! And I suspect the many others have better judgment than I, as you have made it quite clear that you are indeed a wretch! In fact, you're a wretched cow!"

Without waiting for a response, Lorena pressed Rosinante's sides, sending the mare into rapid flight as she tried to escape the sound of the stranger's booming laughter.

2

CLAY WAKEFIELD WATCHED IN AMUSEMENT AS THE redheaded spitfire galloped away, leaving a cloud of dust in her wake. She had been like an open book with her feelings, obviously not learned in the ways of coquetry that most women he knew seemed to specialize in. He remembered her words—a god, she had called him. Clay shook his head. No, she certainly was not a practiced flirt. He ran a large hand through his dark hair, leaving ridges where his fingers had passed. He was unaccustomed to the feeling. What was it? Regret? Surely not! Nonetheless, Clay was not comfortable as he thought that maybe he should have been nicer to someone so naive. But then, he decided cynically, she was probably a better flirt than most, since she had convinced him otherwise.

His train of thought shifted back to her waves of fiery hair. He longed to run his hands through it, caress her lily-white skin, and taste the sweetness of her lips. He remembered the all too brief glance at her body before he had noticed the small knife she held. Breasts straining against soft fabric, a slim waist, and the sensuous swell of curved hips. Clay felt the tightening of his loins. He was amazed at the intensity of his desire. He had reached a point where he was bored with the games and demands of

women. He satisfied his needs with their soft flesh but no
longer filled his mind with thoughts of them. He apparently
needed a woman's body more than he realized, to be so
aroused by this one.

A smile curved his full mouth. He looked forward to
finding her again, as he would enjoy the diversion her body
offered in this desolate country.

Feeling confident that he would find her, Clay turned his
attention to matters at hand—Cielo el Dorado and Diego
Cervantes's daughter, Lorena.

His mood turned black.

"Damn!" he muttered. Every time he thought about it his
blood boiled. But then he would remember Diego and that
last fateful trip up the Camino Real that had led to the
situation he was in now. Once again, Clay's mind drifted
back to that time a year ago . . .

The Camino Real was the portion of the Royal Road of
trade that ran from Mexico City to Santa Fe. The long
caravan of wagons had been between Chihuahua and Paso
del Norte, traveling up the sandy trail, slowly but steadily.
They had stopped for the night, the clear sky plunged into
blackness before the stars and moon rose in the heavens.

"Clay," Diego had called from one of the wagons that
normally would have been used for supplies. His weakened
voice was unable to carry over the sounds of the camp, but
fortunately Clay had been on his way to check on Diego.
When he heard the strained voice, Clay knew that Diego
would have to get back to Paso del Norte soon, if he was
going to make it at all. An impotent rage surged through
him with the knowledge there was nothing he could do
except try to get the man to his home. When it became
apparent to Clay that Diego was truly in a bad way, they had
been no closer to Chihuahua than Paso del Norte, there was
no reason to turn back, and they could only forge ahead and
hope to make it in time. When Clay pressed Diego as to
why he'd been so insistent about leaving Chihuahua, it only

upset him, making his condition worse. So Clay had stopped asking. It seemed pointless.

Clay reached the wagon and looked in. "Diego?" he asked, concern etched on his face.

"Sit down, *por favor*. I must speak with you," the older man said through gasps of pain, the exertion visibly draining him.

"We'll talk later. You need to rest."

"No!" Diego said, his trembling hand curling into a fist. "We must talk now."

In hopes of placating the man who was like a father to him, Clay tied the canvas flap back and hooked his massive arms over the side of the wagon.

"Clay, my time is near."

"No! We'll get you home soon, then you'll be fine," Clay said with more conviction than he felt.

With a limp wave, the rasping man silenced him. "You must listen, Clay, for I have not much time." Diego closed his eyes; whether in pain or sadness Clay was not sure. "We have been through a lot together these past four years. And now it is my time to ride the chariot of death." Diego swallowed with effort. "I am not unhappy about this. It is amazing how things that are so muddled in life become crystal clear as one draws close to the end." As Diego spoke, he stared at the rough canvas cover of the wagon, seeing not the dirt-filled creases but rather something only he could see. "I was not a good father, nor was I a good husband. I have lived selfishly, Clay, and only now I come to realize it. It pains me to know this, especially when it is too late to make it up to my Lorena. Maybe that is the price. Knowledge. But enough of an old man's meandering thoughts. It distresses me to think I am leaving her all alone with no one to look after her."

Clay shifted uneasily.

"But that is one thing I can do something about." Taking his eyes away from the canvas, Diego paused to look at Clay, a look so deep and knowing it was as if he were

looking into Clay's soul. "I am asking you as a friend, and
because of all we have been through together, to marry *mi
hija* and take care of her and Cielo el Dorado."

"Marry your daughter?" Clay stood back sharply as if to
avoid the words. Dark brows furrowed, his eyes darkened
with anger. A muscle tightened in his jaw. "I don't even
know her, Diego. Besides, this is my last trip to Mexico. I
have finished with the trail. As soon as I get you settled at
the hacienda, I'm on my way back to Missouri. It's been a
long trip, but as soon as you get home you'll be fine." Even
as he spoke the words, Clay knew they were untrue.
Diego's condition was worsening; short rapid breaths came
between spurts of racking pain that gripped his chest. Clay
felt cornered by honor and obligation as he tried to think of
some way out.

"Diego, calm down, you're making yourself worse."
Clay found a bottle of brown liquid in the wagon and held
it to Diego's lips. "Drink this, it will help."

Diego pushed the bottle away with a limp hand. "Nothing
is going to help but for you to promise to marry my
daughter. Clay, you must marry Lorena, *por favor*." Diego
paused, trying to catch his breath as he looked at the
stubborn set of Clay's jaw. Diego knew that it would not be
easy to get a man like Clay Wakefield to marry someone not
of his own choosing. But Diego could not afford to lose.
With no alternative, Diego Cervantes played his last card.
"Remember your father, Clay."

The few words, harmless in themselves, hit Clay unmer-
cifully hard, dredging up painful memories that surged over
him, leaving Clay raw and vulnerable. Clay's dark eyes
narrowed to slits of obsidian as he stared at the dying man,
knowing that what he wanted did not matter; honor and
obligation held him secure. He had no choice but to marry
Lorena Cervantes.

After what seemed like an eternity, Clay focused on
Diego. "Looks like you win." Without another word, Clay

Wakefield turned stiffly and walked away, losing himself in the cacophony of sound.

Later Diego had written a letter that had explained only that Clay would take over his affairs in case he did not make it back. A separate document, signed and witnessed, betrothed Lorena to Clay. Upon his arrival at the hacienda, Diego having died four days earlier, Clay had shown Pedro Gonzalez only the letter, hoping that by the time he had traveled to Missouri and back, he would have come up with a way to get out of the marriage. But in that time, nothing had come. The obligation still lingered over his head, forcing him to marry a girl he did not want.

Clay's grim mood darkened at the thought of his bride-to-be. He had never met Lorena but had heard Diego speak of her often. She had just been sent away to school when he first visited Cielo el Dorado. Clay cringed as he remembered the many conversations he and Diego had had about Lorena's schooling. She went to a private girls' school that scandalously taught mathematics, philosophy, and languages, along with the more accepted subjects: riding, etiquette, and ballroom dancing. Clay had always laughed outrageously, telling Diego how sorry he felt for the poor man who ended up with her. Fortunately, Diego had always taken the gibe in good humor and said that whoever ended up with his Lorena would be a lucky man indeed. Clay doubted it, for he had had the dubious pleasure of meeting a few graduates of that type of school. It was probably a good thing they had the skills they learned, he thought. They would surely need them, since it was highly unlikely that they would be able to catch a husband, regardless of the size of their dowry.

He sighed at the certainty of being strapped to a pinch-faced shrew for the rest of his life. In his ultimate plan he had always thought he would marry a sweet girl from Missouri to bear his children, to serve as the wife of the successful man he had become. And now his plans and dreams had all come to naught. All because of Lorena

Cervantes. But at least, he tried to console himself, there were sweet maids like the one he had just seen to spend a few mindless hours with. He would give Diego's daughter his name and the security that name provided. He owed Diego that, but it was too much for Diego, or anyone, to expect him to give up everything he had been working toward for the last decade. That he would not do. After the marriage, he would leave someone at the hacienda to run the place. He would not be able to marry in Missouri, but that didn't mean he couldn't live there and attain the success he had always dreamed about. He thought of Diego. Guilt pricked his conscience. Angrily he pushed the thoughts from his mind. He was marrying the girl, after all.

Clay had been to the swimming hole many times before to cool off after riding through the desert. Never before had he found another person there, male or female. Who was that girl? She obviously worked at the hacienda, as there was nothing else around. Common sense told him that she had not ridden across the river from town. A frown marred his face as the thought of the obvious lack of security if the girl was to be found riding outside the walls at will, clearly no escort in sight.

Clay had ridden ahead of his men to come to the *acequia*. He did not like to think about what could have happened had someone else found her. That was a situation he would remedy immediately. Clay Wakefield took care of what was his.

He looked at the water, then back to the sound of the approaching caravan. After quickly making up his mind, he got what he needed out of his saddlebag and stripped off his clothes, then plunged into the water.

The cool water soothed his parched skin, offering a welcome respite from the long days on the trail. Floating in the water, he let his mind drift to the little hellion he had met earlier. Desire flooded his body as he imagined her firm breast in his hand, his lips on his neck, as he plunged into the silky recesses of her body. When he realized where his thoughts had gone and felt the pounding desire in his loins, Clay grabbed the soap and began to scrub the grime vigorously from his body. He scrubbed his scalp until it stung, before submerging, leaving a circle of white suds on the surface. As the rumbling of the caravan drew near, Clay reluctantly pulled himself out of the water, not sure if his hesitation was due to the heat or the prospect of meeting his future wife. Neither thought was appealing.

He pulled on a clean shirt and tight pants, then rolled his dirty shirt and buckskins up and put them in his saddlebags. Dressed and ready, Clay mounted his horse and went to meet his men before the caravan arrived at the hacienda.

It could not be put off any longer.

Lorena rode through the gates in a flurry of dust and jumped off her horse with murder in her eyes. "There is a stranger on my property, and I want him removed," she ordered through clenched teeth to a surprised guard.

When he made no show of moving, she looked directly into the guard's eyes and added, "Now!"

"Yes, señorita," he said to pacify the frantic girl, but immediately headed to his superior for instructions. The guard knew who was on the property; he had spotted the cloud of dust the caravan caused when it was still miles away and had seen Mr. Wakefield riding ahead of it.

Thinking the guard was going off to do her bidding, Lorena relaxed. It would serve the arrogant wretch right to get escorted off her property after the way he'd treated her. With a small smile, she made her way to the bathhouse to clean up.

Lorena leaned over the pump and splashed water on her face. She did not hear the noise at first, as she was lost in her thoughts of the rude American who had been at the swimming hole. Her anger turned, without her knowing, to visions of the tall man as he dismounted to bow before her, and the flash of dark eyes and straight white teeth as he rose to greet her. It was then that the sounds of wagon wheels and loud voices filtered through her reverie. When the commotion finally roused her, she mentally kicked herself. "You silly goose, he was a wretch, like all men, not some knight in shining armor," she said emphatically to no one, stomping off in the direction of the noise.

"*Los Americanos!*"

"*Los carros!*"

"*La entrada de caravana!*"

Just as Lorena came around the corner, the main gate was being opened to let in a large contingent of dust-covered men who appeared to have just gotten off the trail. The women and children came out of the rooms and the men came from their work to greet the visitors. Lorena wondered who had given the order to open the gate. It occurred to her that she didn't know who had been running the hacienda since her father's death. She made a mental note to let the inhabitants of Cielo el Dorado know she was going to be in charge from now on. Because of all Miss Tidesdale had taught her, all the things thought unsuitable for a woman, Lorena felt confident she would be able to run the hacienda. And what she had not learned at school or from her father while growing up, she would simply learn. With barely concealed excitement and the rugged stranger forgotten, Lorena went to see who the travelers were.

The men were grimy from the long ride, but their eyes sparkled with excitement. Drawing closer to the gate Lorena could see the wagons lined up outside the big wall. Many of the wagons still had men in them and were obviously going on to Paso del Norte.

Dalia and Pedro were standing in the shaded courtyard waiting to greet the travelers when they saw Lorena approaching.

"*Madre mía*, Pedro. What are we going to do? With Lorena back only yesterday, I have not had a chance to tell her of Señor Wakefield, and now he is back," Dalia said worriedly to her husband.

Taking his wife's hand in a gesture of comfort, he said,

"Actually, Dalia, I think this way might be best. I have no doubt that Clay can handle everything."

"Pedro! Why is it that you favor this situation?" the plump woman said in outrage.

Pedro smiled at his wife with tenderness, his wizened face lined from years of hard work in a relentless world. "Because I think it is a good thing that he is here to take care of the hacienda. I am getting old—no, no, let me finish," he said when his wife began to protest. "Dalia, we are not going to be around forever, and then who is going to take care of Lorena? Without protection, she would be a target for anyone. There are many men out there who would not think twice about hurting our sweet Lorena."

"Like this Clay Wakefield!" Dalia sighed, knowing the words her husband spoke were true.

Pedro only shook his head.

"Do you think, then, that Señor Wakefield will find a suitable husband for Lorena?" she asked uncertainly, once again wishing Lorena's father had taken care of the matter instead of leaving it to a man none of them really knew. "What about Ramón?" Dalia asked hopefully.

Pedro smiled. "We will see," he said, having other ideas in regard to the Americano and Lorena. But neither of them knew of the plans that had already been made as they watched Lorena approach.

"Pedro, who are all these people?" Lorena asked, sweeping her arm in the direction of the men.

As if seeing Lorena for the first time, Dalia clasped her hands to her face. "Lorena, you must change. Look at you! You are indecent in those clothes. How did you get wet? Quickly, quickly—"

But Pedro stepped forward and interrupted her. "Clay, you are back," he said as he extended his hand to the tall American.

Not knowing anyone had come up behind her, Lorena turned to see who it was. She could not have been more shocked, thinking the handsome stranger long gone. She was struck once again at how handsome he was, more handsome than she remembered, if that was possible. He had obviously gone for a swim, as his hair was damp, curling in slick, shiny locks. At the thought of the swimming hole, Lorena was reminded of his arrogance, of the way he had treated her. Her face set fiercely. "You!"

Clay was as surprised as she, though pleasantly so. He was glad to have found the little waif so soon. She was apparently a servant of some sort, he reasoned as his eyes traveled down the length of her indecently clad body, the damp shirt clinging to the swells of her breasts. Possibly she would become his personal maid. He smiled at the thought. When his eyes found hers, he saw the surprise turn to shimmering anger. Obviously she had not gotten over their encounter at the swimming hole. He looked forward to taming the little spitfire.

"We meet again, señorita, and it's a pleasure as always."

Pedro and Dalia glanced uncertainly at each other. But there was not one speck of indecision about Lorena when she grabbed a gun that was leaning up against the wall. "A pleasure, my foot," Lorena said indignantly, pointing the gun at the towering stranger.

Dalia gasped in surprise. "*Madre mía!* Put that thing down."

"Stand back, Dalia. No one will get hurt. I am just going to escort this no-good trespasser to the gate and see that he is led from the property."

Clay said politely, "I believe the form of welcome has changed since the last time I was here."

Just as Lorena was about to respond, Pedro said, "Excuse her. Lorena does not know what she is doing." Pedro turned sternly to Lorena. "Put that gun down. This is your father's amigo, Señor Wakefield."

The phrase "father's amigo" slowly sank in. Warily she looked at the stranger as she slightly lowered the gun only to have it swiftly taken from her by the tall, dark man.

"Señor Clay Wakefield, may I introduce Señorita Lorena

Cervantes? Lorena, this is Clay Wakefield, as I said, a friend of your father."

Clay did not hear the last of the introduction, so stunned was he that this was not some maid but his betrothed, the woman he was to marry. Instantly his blood boiled at the thought of finding her out beyond the walls unprotected. He didn't stop to think that only a short time before he had longed for this same girl and should have been ecstatic that his future wife was not the shrew he had anticipated. All he could think about was her clothes, revealing every luscious curve to any lustful eye. The thought sent him into an inexplicable rage. Forgotten was the gun he now held in his hands, the desolate surroundings, and the dreams of Missouri. He focused on Lorena, seeing nothing but her defiance, as if she were the one who had been wronged!

"I've already met Miss Cervantes." His anger was almost tangible.

"Oh, I did not know." Pedro could not remember them ever meeting. Surely he would have known.

"It was only recently," Clay added as if to clarify, his eyes never leaving Lorena's. "We met earlier today by the old swimming hole."

Pedro looked sternly at Lorena, sensing now why the man was so angry. Lorena could have been found by anyone.

"Do you always ride about unattended . . . so indecently clad?" Clay demanded, his eyes traveling maddeningly over her body.

Only Lorena and Dalia were surprised at Clay's obvious anger and his blatant perusal of her body. Lorena's surprise turned back to rage—rage not only at him for such disrespect but at herself as well, for the tingling she felt as his eyes traveled over her body.

"Don't you speak to me in that tone. It is none of your business what I wear or where I ride, no matter if you are a friend of my father or not."

"I beg to differ, Miss Cervantes," he said in a tone that

sent shivers of foreboding through her slim body. "Everything you do is my business, since your father left the
running of the hacienda to me." Clay realized from the look
on Lorena's face that she knew nothing of the arrangements
her father had made. He saw total surprise, almost shock,
and for a split second, Clay could have sworn he saw a
flicker of pain, intense hurt. He chose not to mention their
betrothal just yet. One thing at a time.

"To you!" Lorena turned to Pedro in hopes of having the
stranger called for his lie. But instead, she saw only
confirmation of the unbelievable claim.

Men began to approach to ask for instructions. Clay saw
that they looked on with all too much interest at Lorena's
tightly clad figure. "Go change," he snapped, furious at the
whole situation, not understanding what he had seen in her
eyes or why he had not spoken of their betrothal.

"Change?" Lorena looked from the dark eyes down to
herself. "What are you talking about?"

"I will not have you traipsing about in next to nothing for
all the world to see."

The approaching men stopped, not wanting to intrude but
not wanting to miss out on what looked to be an interesting
confrontation.

"Traipsing about," she yelled in disbelief. "This is my
home, and I'll dress as I please."

Clay took a step closer and through clenched teeth said,
"I am in charge now, and you will go change."

Before Lorena could respond with all her mounting fury,
Pedro shook his head. "For now, go, *chiquita*."

Feeling outnumbered and helpless, Lorena swung around
sending her mane of red hair flying. "I will do as I please,
you arrogant cad," she said as she stomped off.

As Clay watched Lorena make her way through the
courtyard, he felt a great urge to catch her and turn her over
his knee. Of all the attributes he had mentally given his
future wife—ugly he had been sure of, shrewish without a
doubt—he had never dreamed she would be a willful,

spoiled hellion. He wouldn't let himself think about her unusual beauty, or of her father passing away and leaving her home in the care of a virtual stranger. It was as if Clay wanted an excuse to continue to dislike her. His new charge, his betrothed—he grimaced as he mentally corrected himself—needed to be taught some manners.

Pedro flinched when Clay's dark eyes turned on him.

"We will discuss Miss Cervantes's behavior as soon as I settle my men," Clay said, letting Pedro know he was displeased. Turning away, he found a dust-covered man gazing indolently at him, a half smile on his lips.

"And what is so funny, Bill?" Clay asked dryly.

Bill Hawkins was a life-long friend who had been riding with Clay since he started on the trail. On the long journey back to the hacienda from Missouri, Clay had told Bill about his unwanted betrothal to Diego's daughter who he was sure, he had said, would turn out to be a ferret-faced shrew.

"Well, friend, I was just thinking of a story you told me about a certain shrew not too long ago." Bill watched Clay's anger rise but continued to tease his friend anyway. "And I was just thinking that, since you aren't interested in that particular ferret, maybe I'd take her off your hands."

Clay's temper was frayed. The ride in general, dealing with Lorena, and now dealing with his friend strained his patience to the limit. Even though Clay knew Bill was joking, something in his words struck a nerve. Clay did not want anyone to get ideas about Lorena. She might be a spoiled, willful little hellion, but she was his responsibility. Clay did not want to study the apparent change in his feelings, not certain what he would find. Instead, he moved slowly toward Hawkins and said, "You would be wise to watch what you say, friend. Lorena Cervantes is none of your concern." Then he turned abruptly, shouting orders to get settled in after the long trip.

Lorena paced furiously back and forth across the hand-woven rug that covered most of the precious blue and white tile floor of her bedroom. She was furious at being treated like a child, and even more so at finding out that by some miserable quirk of fate the horrid stranger was in charge of the hacienda. With each step, Lorena became more aggravated, sure that this Clay person was lying, using her father's death as an excuse to get control of the hacienda. She didn't want to recall that his name was vaguely familiar, mentioned in the few letters she had received from her father while she was away at school. She refused to think about how confident he seemed, not to mention Pedro's and Dalia's confirmation of his ludicrous claims. She remembered the letter she had received in London. She had been too upset to notice much about it. Had it been sent by this man? Then the long trip home. The only thing that had kept her together was the thought of the hacienda, her home. Lorena looked around her room and remembered her papa. Why should it be such a surprise that this could have happened after all her father had done? But she wouldn't let it happen, she couldn't. With renewed hope and determination, she turned her thoughts to how she could get rid of the scheming man.

Despite her anger Lorena had changed out of the damp cotton shirt and pants and into a blue day dress with matching kid slippers. After pacing for a good deal of time, her mind whirling with thoughts, Lorena sat down on her bed, and before she knew it, she was sound asleep, the long trip and her overwrought emotions finally catching up with her.

After all was settled with his caravan—some men having been sent on to Paso del Norte, and his temper being held in check—Clay sought out Pedro. He found him sitting in the kitchen with Dalia.

"Clay," Pedro and Dalia acknowledged.

"Pedro, Dalia." Clay nodded to each in turn.

Dalia got up as if to leave the two men alone.

"No," Clay responded, "I'd like to talk with you as well."

Clay sat down, and Dalia poured him a mug of mulled apple cider mixed with cinnamon.

"About Lorena," Pedro began.

"No, Pedro, let me. I acted hastily earlier and I apologize for my conduct. I'm not accustomed to being met by the barrel of a gun. However, from now on there will be no more behavior like that which I witnessed today. I think you both realize what could have happened had anyone else found Lorena at the swimming hole." Clay didn't add that she had almost not been safe with him. "I'm certain you don't want that. Therefore, I expect your full cooperation in this matter." Looking into Dalia's and then Pedro's eyes, he asked, "Is that understood?"

Both Dalia and Pedro nodded their understanding, Pedro looking pleased while Dalia scowled into her cup.

"This evening I plan to begin getting acquainted with Diego's affairs as well as the running of Cielo el Dorado. Pedro, first thing tomorrow morning I want you to take me around and show me the day-to-day workings of the hacienda. You can introduce me to everyone here and give me a brief description of what they do." Clay began to rise.

"What of Lorena, señor?" an outraged Dalia asked.

"Ah, yes. Miss Cervantes. I will speak to her and explain to her what her behavior should entail. It would seem to me that Diego wasted his money on her schooling, as she certainly has not learned the essentials of being a lady."

Dalia fumed at his arrogant assumption that Lorena did not know how to be a lady. It didn't matter that just that morning she had said the very same thing.

"At seven o'clock," Clay continued, "I would appreciate a good hot meal for my men. Two of my men and I will eat in the *sala*. I expect Lorena to join us. Now if you will excuse me, I will find Miss Cervantes," Clay said with such arrogant assurance that Pedro quickly jumped up to head off his wife's anger. But Dalia was not about to be put off.

"Sit down!" Dalia fumed. "No one but me is going to go get Lorena, who is in her bedroom. You may be running this place, but you have no right to walk into her room," Dalia said, her large bosom heaving with indignation.

Clay was momentarily nonplussed at the woman's outburst, reminding him of an enraged female bear guarding her cub. With great effort, he swallowed the smile that quivered on his lips. "Then by all means, Dalia, go get your charge."

Clay and Pedro watched in silence as Dalia left the kitchen.

"Your wife is not too happy with me at the moment."

Pedro gave a small laugh. "I think you are right, but she will get over it. Soon she will see that you mean only good."

Clay looked at the older man. "And how is it that you are so sure of my good intentions?" Clay asked, a twinge of guilt pricking his conscience.

"Because, despite his faults, Diego loved Lorena and Cielo el Dorado as much as any Cervantes. He would not leave either of them in the hands of someone who would not do the same."

The men sat quietly for a few moments, lost in their own thoughts. They did not know each other well, but had known of each other for many years.

Pedro broke the silence. "I must admit that I have wondered for this year now why Diego was traveling back to the hacienda if he was so sick. Would he not stay in Chihuahua until he became well?" Pedro looked away from Clay. "Why did you allow a sick man to travel?"

Pedro voiced Clay's own doubts and questions, renewing the impotent rage he had felt when he realized he could do nothing for Diego other than hurry the journey as best he could. "I have thought of that often, but Diego was insistent on leaving. We did not know he was ill until we were several days out of Chihuahua and didn't realize how serious his condition was until we were no closer to

Chihuahua than to El Paso. He was in a hurry to leave, Pedro, almost frantic to get home."

Pedro looked at Clay, sensing the truth of the man's words, relieved that Clay was in no way responsible for Diego's death. "Maybe he knew he was sick and was hoping to get home to Cielo el Dorado before he died."

"I thought of that, but I don't think so. I'm not sure why, but it seemed to me that he was trying to get away from something, as opposed to going to something. I believe Diego wanted out of Chihuahua, and I don't know why. That is one of the things I'm hoping to find out while I'm here."

Pedro looked at the man whose father he had met first many years before. "You have become quite a man over the years. I am sure you will do what is best. Your father would be proud."

Clay's eyes clouded. "I didn't realize you had met my father."

"Yes, I met your father." Pedro got up from the table. "I have work to do, amigo. We will talk later." He left Clay beset by unanswered questions.

Dalia returned while Clay sat with the cup in his hand, the apple cider untouched. She was alone. His relaxed features transformed themselves into an unreadable mask.

"Where is Lorena?" he asked.

"She is sound asleep in her room. You will just have to speak to her later."

As Dalia watched the anger rise in Clay's face, she thought better of her words. "I mean, *por favor*, señor. Lorena is quite tired and I thought you would not want me to wake her."

Clay's voice was deceptively soft. "You seem not to remember who is in charge here, Dalia. Let me remind you that it is I, and I asked you to get Lorena. I will tolerate no further disobedience from you or anyone else." He slammed the cup down, the golden brown liquid sloshing over the side, leaving a puddle that was quickly absorbed

into the dry wood. After slamming out of the kitchen, Clay
headed in the direction he knew would lead him to Lorena's
bedroom.

Stepping out of the kitchen into the sunshine, Clay
crossed the courtyard with long determined strides and
entered another door. He stepped into a long, narrow
hallway formed by thick adobe walls on either side. He did
not bother to look into Diego's room or the small child's
room next to it that had been turned into a study. He went
straight to the end of the hall and stopped in front of a closed
door. Without hesitation, Clay opened the door, ready to
catch an errant Lorena more than likely not there, but
certainly not asleep. He was taken by surprise when he
found her sound asleep on the large bed. He noticed that she
had changed into a blue gown. Matching kid slippers
peeked out from underneath the dress, and Clay caught a
glimpse of ruffled petticoats and slim ankles. Red hair
framed an oval face with high cheekbones, milk-white skin,
and a pert nose. Lush lips burned red, tempting Clay to taste
their softness. He felt again the urge he had felt at the
swimming hole, an urge to press her lithe form up to his,
feel the dips and curves of her body against the angles and
planes of his. His anger began to fade like the dying embers
of a spent fire, to be replaced by the intense heat of rising
desire. In his mind, he saw the young girl at the swimming
hole, green eyes, one minute laughing, the next flashing
with anger. She certainly didn't know how to conceal her
feelings. For some reason, the thought pleased him immensely.

Lorena drifted down from sleep, a curious warmth filling
her as she slowly became aware that something was
different. It was a few seconds before she realized that the
stranger was standing in her room, staring at her, or perhaps
it would have been more accurate to say he was looking at
her without seeing her. When his eyes did focus on her they
showed first surprise, then amusement. Lorena felt they

should have shown embarrassment at having been caught in her room.

"And what, pray tell, are you doing in my bedroom?" Her anger of earlier found her again.

Reminded of her hot temper, Clay clenched his jaw as he bit out, "I need to speak to you, Miss Cervantes. I'll expect you in your father's study immediately."

Clay turned to leave, but Lorena said, "I'm busy right now, maybe later."

Without turning back to her, Clay said with a studious calm, "I don't care how busy you are, we are going to talk."

"Oh, all right," she said nonchalantly. "I'll be there in a while."

The boom of Clay's voice startled Lorena, sending her back against the headboard. "We will talk *now*! If you do not follow me immediately, I will fling you over my shoulder like a sack of cow feed and carry you to the study myself."

Clay stalked from the room. How had he gotten himself into this mess? He was strapped to a spoiled rotten womanchild, who was supposed to be a lady, not to mention his future wife, a pack of servants who were used to ruling the roost, while stuck out in the middle of the godforsaken desert a thousand miles from where he wanted to be. The thought of home fueled his anger. If it wasn't for her, he would be there. He ran a large, tanned hand through thick black hair and went into Diego's study.

Lorena followed a few seconds behind, furious for giving in, but not quite sure she wanted to brave the storm that threatened in the stranger's brooding eyes. How had all this happened? She wasn't sure if she knew what had happened. Everything was changing too fast. She had barely arrived home when this tall dark stranger came bursting into her life claiming to be in charge of the hacienda and everything in it, including her. How could her father do this to her? she fumed, unconsciously smoothing the wrinkles from her dress and quickly running a brush through her hair. But she was more sad than angry at the thought, not really surprised that her father had done something so inconsiderate of his only child. Oh, Papá, she cried to herself, how could you?

Lorena walked into the study without knocking, her head held high, refusing to show her uncertainty.

"Sit down," Clay said without preamble.

She wavered, not wanting to respond to the autocratic command.

"I said *sit*!" Clay slammed his fist down on the hardwood desk.

Clenching her hands, Lorena yelled back. "I'm not an animal to be ordered around!"

Clay closed his eyes, willing himself to be patient. "Please . . . sit . . . down," he said, trying to be calm.

Lorena sat down hard as if to emphasize her anger.

With much control, Clay also sat down. "I am here because your father asked me to be and for no other reason. I do not want to be at Cielo el Dorado any more than you seem to want me here, but here I am and in charge as well. Therefore, it is in everyone's best interest to attempt to behave rationally with one another. We must make the best of a bad situation. In the future you will heed what I tell you and do as I say, ensuring that things flow as smoothly as possible." He paused before continuing. "You will dress like the lady your father sent you away to learn how to be. You will not run around in boys' shirts and pants. Since you are now the lady of this house, you are expected to dress like one. In addition, you are not to ride out alone. Make sure you have a groom with you at all times."

Clay hesitated for a moment, thinking that now was the time to tell her of their imminent marriage, but something in her eyes warned him to wait. He finished by saying instead, "Do you have any questions?"

Lorena sat through his speech, every word he spoke adding fuel to the fire that was building within her until she sat immobile, not knowing if she could contain her anger any longer without going crazy. "Do you mean I get to ask questions?" Her voice dripped with sarcasm and hatred.

Clay sat back in the sturdy chair looking at Lorena with a hard stare. "You try my patience sorely, Miss Cervantes."

Seeing the handsome stranger sitting in her father's chair, reminding her of how her life had so drastically changed, Lorena felt tears sting her eyes. Why was this happening to her? Why couldn't things be the way they used to be? Once again Lorena longed for her father and at the same time berated him for getting her into this mess. Refusing to let the stranger see her despair, Lorena hid her tears behind more sharp words.

"I try *your* patience? Ha! You try *my* patience! You come waltzing into my life—a life, mind you, that was in no need of changing. You mock me, then start bossing me around, telling me how to dress and how to act, where I can go and what I can do. And now you have the audacity to sit there and tell me how I am lacking." The last words were shrill as she began to lose control. "And furthermore, I am not a child, and I will do as I please. Do you understand me?"

Intense dark eyes narrowed, bringing dark brows together as Clay leaned forward, planting his elbows on the desk in front of him. "If you are going to act like a child, you will be treated like a child. And children should be seen but not heard! Am I understood, Miss Cervantes?" Before Lorena could answer, Clay continued, leaving no doubt that he felt there was no need for an answer. "We will eat at seven o'clock. Don't be late." Clay got up from the chair and, without so much as a glance at Lorena, strode from the room with more grace than one would expect in a man of his height and build, leaving Lorena to stare at his receding back.

In a flurry of skirts and petticoats, Lorena raced back to her room, slammed the door, and threw herself onto her bed to take her frustrations out on her pillow.

3

❦

LORENA SAT IN HER ROOM, HER LIPS SET IN A FIRM line. She thought of the stranger. Her mouth turned down in a scowl. The cad! She remembered his broad shoulders and his wavy dark hair, and a tingling sensation raced through her body. It confused her, and then the confusion turned to anger. Damn him and his American hide for ruining my life, she raged to herself. No, she added, he's not ruining your life. Just disrupting it for a while. You are a Cervantes. You will persevere and overcome.

Lorena leaped up from the bed. Everything was going to be all right, she told herself optimistically. She held a small wooden cross to her chest. Yes, things were going to be just fine. She decided she must have a plan. Lost in thought, she walked around the room, touching reminders of a childhood that now seemed long past. Retablos depicting the saints hung on the walls, and small toys carved from wood sat on a small table. But hard as she tried to forget him, the stranger loomed in her thoughts, causing the curious sensation to flood her again, leaving her with images of laughing dark eyes and booming laughter.

Lorena swayed, her eyes closed in memory. "Damn!" she cursed out loud, green eyes flying open in disgust. This would not do! I must get away from him to make plans, she

reasoned. She thought of Ramón. She would leave with
Ramón in the morning and go to El Rancho Escondido with
him. Who better to help her than the Valdéz family? If
Ramón did not know what to do, surely his father would.
Hadn't Señor Valdéz been her father's very best friend?

Lorena went to the old trunk and took out a valise,
change of riding clothes, a hairbrush and comb, and then,
reluctantly, a dress with matching shoes. If she needed
anything else she was certain she could borrow it from
Señora Valdéz or one of Ramón's sisters.

Lorena knew it would be best to hide the bag and not tell
a soul about her plan. Nothing was going to get in the way
of her leaving. Somehow, after dinner, she would catch
Ramón alone and ask for his help. She did not consider the
possibility that he would not help her. She would leave
Dalia a note to explain, but let the arrogant American find
out after she was gone that she had foiled his plans.

Clay left the study furious at himself as well as Lorena.
Why was it that every time he was around her he lost his
temper? In the hour or so that he had known who she was,
he had spent more time angry than ever before. It seemed all
she had to do was look at him and his temper flared. What
was it about the girl that made him lose all control? With
determined strides, he made his way through the hacienda.

The life of Cielo el Dorado faced inward, protected from
the dangers of the outside world by the three-foot-thick wall
that surrounded the entire rectangular complex. The rooms
of the hacienda were built with the massive wall as their
backside. There was a shared wall between each pair of
rooms, every outside door opened directly into the courtyard. Because the rooms were built side by side, guards
were able to use the rooftops as a walkway to stand sentinel
over the surrounding land.

The walls of the hacienda had two entryways. The main
entrance, which passed under the *torreón*, or watchtower,
was large enough for wagons to pass through and was

secured by a cottonwood plank gate and an iron lock. The rarely used back entrance was also sealed by a wooden gate and secured with an iron lock, but was much smaller, allowing only foot traffic.

Cielo el Dorado consisted of two connecting courtyards, one surrounded by the main living area, and another surrounded by the work areas, where Clay headed now. The working side of the hacienda held a large storage area and wine-making room, the blacksmith shop, and another kitchen that was used by all the servants and guards who lived there. There was a tannery, a carpentry shop, a butcher block, and soap-making room. Cielo el Dorado was like a town in itself, providing everyone who lived there with most necessities; anything else could be had from the traders who passed through regularly. The hacienda also provided the fine Cervantes wines and brandies that were praised all the way from Santa Fe to Mexico City, one of the main reasons traders loved to stop at Cielo el Dorado.

However, neither wine nor brandy was on Clay's mind. He thought only of Lorena Cervantes and the fine mess she had gotten him into.

He sought out Tom Percy, the man he had left in charge. The sooner he got affairs in order, the sooner he would be on his way back to Missouri.

But visions of flowing red hair and laughing green eyes loomed in his mind.

In a rage, he bellowed for Tom.

Once Lorena had devised a preliminary plan, she decided to go for a ride. Damn Clay Wakefield and his orders.

She changed out of the dress back into a shirt and pants. Quietly she made her way to the stables, certain that the men would be busy settling in and cleaning up after their arrival. She needed to ride out, get away from the four walls that had always been comforting and now seemed confining. With all the commotion and the main gate still open, no one noticed as Lorena and her horse slipped out.

As soon as she was outside the huge gate, Lorena
overlooked the Río Bravo del Norte valley, known as the
Río Grande valley to some, with its furrowed soil that held
newly sprouting vegetation. The rows of green traversed the
land until the last row butted up against the swollen river.
She imagined the stalks of corn that would soon grow to
towering heights and the rows of wheat that would become
so thick that from above, the field would look like a waving
ocean of grain. But most of all, Lorena loved the rows of
grapevines that had been cultivated from the original vines
that Fray Garcia had brought to the valley in 1659.

Looking off to the left, Lorena could see the herds of
cows and sheep that the Cervantes family had raised for
years. To her right, she could see the lower ford of the Río
Bravo del Norte. It was at this ford that people crossed from
the north bank of the river to the south bank on which the
villa of Paso del Norte and the mission stood, the same
crossing she had made the day before with her father's men.

Lorena looked south toward Paso del Norte with the
gleam of anticipation in her eye as she remembered the
fiestas they had always had. Fiestas brought images of
dancing and laughing, of handsome young men lavishing
undivided attention on the ladies. Scenes of love and
romance always left Lorena with thoughts of knights in
shining armor who would die to guard a lady's honor. She
imagined their kisses and soft words until images of her
parents loomed in her mind, causing Lorena to chide herself
for such foolishness. She had no desire to be possessed by
a man as if she were an object, to be told to sit at home
crocheting doilies and altar cloths. Reality was not kisses
and soft words, she told herself; it was heartache and pain.
She had no intention of being like the many lackluster girls
she had known at Miss Tidesdale's Seminary for Young
Ladies who did nothing more than think and talk of men.

Tired of her wandering thoughts, Lorena pressed Rosinante into a smooth canter.

She rode for hours, experiencing the sense of release she

had sought earlier that morning. Instead of riding in circles, however, she galloped through the fields, up and down the dirt paths that divided the different sections.

After her ride, Lorena barely had time to bathe and dress before dinner. The ride had done wonders for her spirits, and Lorena began to dress as befit a lady of the house. Suddenly she was glad that Luz had unpacked her dresses. She would show that no-good American that her father's money had not been wasted. She would appear at the dinner table and make him eat every unkind and unfair word he had ever said to her—and that would be just the appetizer.

She labored over her hair, but without the girls from school to help, the mass of red strands was impossible to tame into one of the elaborate coiffures that were so popular. Instead, she finally settled on merely pulling it loosely back, leaving soft tendrils to curl about her face.

She chose a gown of golden brown glazed taffeta with a low, square neckline that just covered her breasts. She had bought it on a whim when her school roommate told her she wasn't brave enough to wear a neckline so daring. Puffed sleeves hugged the very edges of her shoulders leaving a wide expanse of milky white skin plain to see. After adding a matching ribbon to her hair and slippers for her feet, she stood in front of the old mirror. Suddenly losing her nerve, Lorena decided she could not quite bring herself to wear such a revealing dress. Quickly she added a fichu of embroidered silk tulle around her shoulders to pacify her modesty. Satisfied that she looked every bit the lady, she went straight to the kitchen, her head held high as if she dressed for dinner every night. She was surprised to find no one there but Luz.

"Am I early?" she asked.

Luz turned around from the work counter, and her harried look was transformed to one of pleasure. She clasped a small bag of dried corn to her chest and said, "You look beautiful, Lorena. Did I not say you would use those

gorgeous dresses? I would love to see the look on those
hombres' faces." Luz giggled at the thought.

"*Gracias*, Luz, and speaking of those men, where are
they?"

Luz turned back to the counter, a scowl marring her
features. "They are in the *sala*. The Americano wants to eat
fancy. So I must carry the food in there."

The Cervantes family had always eaten in the kitchen,
regardless of who was there, unless it was a grand celebration. Lorena's heart began to hammer, her small fists
clenching. But before her anger could swell much further,
she controlled herself. She had something to prove this
night; she would deal with the eating arrangements later.

Lorena walked with measured steps to the *sala*. Outside
the door, she took a deep breath and forced herself to smile
before she entered. The stranger and two other men stood
close to the table, quietly talking among themselves while
Dalia set out dishes of food. Lorena noticed again how
handsome the stranger was, his power and strength clearly
visible through his elegant but simple attire. He was much
taller than the other two men, and while all three had been
weathered by the sun, only Clay wore it well, the others
merely looking older than they were.

Angered by her reaction to the man, Lorena said over-
sweetly, "I would have been here sooner, but no one told
me we were eating in the *sala*. My family never dined here
unless there was a celebration. What is it we are celebrating? The loss of my home, perhaps?"

One dark eyebrow rose slightly as Clay looked at her.
Dalia set the last dish down hard, its contents spilling over
onto the brilliant white tablecloth.

"*Dios!*" Dalia exclaimed, not knowing what to deal with
first, the spill or Lorena.

Tom Percy and Bill Hawkins stood back and watched,
but when Bill saw the anger boiling in the girl's eyes and the
tightening of Clay's jaw, he decided he was too hungry to

let this feast be ruined. It had been a long time since he had eaten a good home-cooked meal.

"You're not late at all. We just got here ourselves." Bill sidestepped Clay and walked toward Lorena, ignoring most of what she had said. "I'm Bill Hawkins of Missouri." Bill extended his hand politely with a wide smile that made his ordinary face look friendly and sincere.

Lorena managed to regain her composure and resolve. Miss Tidesdale would have been proud as Lorena took his hand and replied, "How very nice to meet you, sir. I am Lorena Cervantes. Welcome to my home."

"Thank you, Miss Cervantes. I'm sorry about your father. He was a good man."

"Thank you. Now please, you must call me Lorena," she said with a smile, truly liking the kind man.

"All right, Lorena, but only if you'll call me Bill."

"Agreed." She nodded, wondering why Clay Wakefield could not be as nice.

Clay watched the interaction with growing annoyance, noting with ill humor how nice she was to his friend.

Bill Hawkins took Lorena's arm and led her to the table. "Lorena, this is Tom Percy, another of Clay's men."

Tom Percy was the shortest of the three men, with the reddest hair Lorena had ever seen. He had the type of white skin that burned easily, then peeled without ever tanning. His weathered face was lined and burned from both wind and sun, and Lorena assumed he had just come off the trail with the rest of them. She did not know he had been at the hacienda for the last year while she had been making the long trip home.

"It is nice to meet you." Lorena smiled.

Tom gave a slight nod of his head and Lorena immediately realized he was a man of few words.

Clay's controlled, deep voice broke in before Lorena had a chance to say anything else. "I believe our dinner is getting cold," he said with little humor.

Lorena glared at Clay before she looked around the room, then asked, "Dalia, where is Ramón?"

Just then, as if the words had summoned him, Ramón walked through the door. "I'm right here!" he announced jovially, causing all heads to turn in his direction. "I went to the kitchen. I didn't think to look here until Luz told me. What is the occasion?"

"I was just asking the same question." Lorena sent Clay another glare before turning her head away, her chin held high. "Come, sit down, Ramón. We are ready to eat."

Clay watched the affectionate care Lorena took with the stranger. The sight only increased his ill humor. After everyone was seated and Dalia had begun to serve, Clay turned his caustic glare on Ramón. "And who are you?"

Dalia's stopped, the ladle still in her hand, while everyone else turned from Clay to Ramón. Lorena was the first to react.

"Do you have no manners at all?" she asked furiously.

Ramón looked from Lorena to Clay, knowing that Clay was the man Diego had left in charge, but not knowing what had caused the obvious animosity between Lorena and Clay. Wanting to test the waters before he jumped in, he said, "Forgive me for not introducing myself. I am Ramón Valdéz of El Rancho Escondido. I believe you know my father."

Clay instantly placed him, remembering him only as the pudgy eldest child of Diego's good friend, Raymundo Valdéz. "How is your father, Ramón?" he asked, feeling no need to apologize to the boy.

"He is fine. You will have to come and visit."

"Ramón, tell me what everyone is doing now," Lorena asked. "You did not finish telling me this morning."

Clay lifted an eyebrow in question.

Ramón sat back. "Let me see."

Before he had a chance to answer, Lorena leaned forward, her green eyes wide and eager, filled with all the questions and excitement of being home after many years.

"How is your family? Your father and mother, grandfather and grandmother, Paco, Fernie, Consuelo, and Kika?"

Ramón held his hands up to the barrage of names. "I'm surprised you can remember everyone. Even my mother has a difficult time remembering all our names. Most of the time she reverts to just calling for a son or daughter, depending on what she wants done."

"Ramón! How disrespectful." Lorena laughed, then grew thoughtful. "I remember how much she loves you all, regardless of what she calls you."

Ramón looked at Lorena as he recalled a time that now seemed long ago. "I remember her calling you 'daughter' as well. You were always around."

"Under her feet, always in her way."

"I suspect having five children, one more did not matter too much, eh?" Ramón smiled.

"So tell me, how are they?"

"Well, Grandmother died," Ramón started.

"Ramón, I'm so sorry! No one wrote me."

"It happened soon after you left. Grandfather still grieves for her. Sometimes I think it is a way to get attention more than anything."

"Ramón!"

"Anyway," Ramón continued, dismissing the uncomfortable topic. "Papá and Mamá are still the same. They look forward to seeing you and send you their love. Paco is now nineteen and chasing anything in a skirt."

"Still?" Lorena laughed.

"Yes, still. Fernie is seventeen and prefers to be called Fernando. He is the serious one of the bunch."

"Little Fernie—serious, I can hardly imagine." Lorena tried to remember the little boy who now wanted to be called Fernando.

"Consuelo is sixteen and no better than Paco, though instead of chasing, she flirts outrageously. The house is never short of Consuelo's admirers. And Kika. She is thirteen and the best of them all." Ramón's expression softened. "She is a sweetheart. You will love her."

"I know I will. Soon I will come over to El Rancho and see everyone." Much sooner than anyone suspects, Lorena thought, smiling to herself.

Ramón carefully wiped his mouth before he went on. "Anyway, aside from my family, Rolégio Dominguez went to Mexico City to become a doctor."

"Really? I should have known he would do something like that; he was always so smart. How about Anna Maria Escobar?"

"She joined an order of nuns."

"No! Not Anna Maria!"

"Yes!" Ramón laughed.

Lorena shook her head. "A nun, just imagine!"

"Why can't you imagine?" Bill asked between bites of buttered tortillas, not one to be left out of any conversation for long.

"Oh, my word, because . . . because . . ." Lorena struggled.

"Because she was well acquainted with the hombres before she decided to become a nun," Ramón supplied, helping Lorena, who proceeded to turn bright red when she realized what she had been about to say.

"So, a loose nun, I'll be damned." Bill smiled at the thought, not having spent much time in anything resembling a place of religion. "What made her want to become a nun?"

"It was a calling, I believe," Ramón said. "It came a couple of years after Lorena left for school. Swore the Virgin Mary came to her while she slept."

"Did anyone believe her?" Lorena leaned forward in disbelief.

"Actually, no, but her parents got tired of hearing her go on about it, so they let her go," Ramón answered. "They seemed somewhat relieved, if I might say so."

Lorena shook her head and smiled. "How about Rosa?" she then asked.

"She married a rich Americano trader off the Camino Real. He retired, and they moved to Sante Fe, where I hear they run a thriving business."

"A rich trader. I cannot imagine. Why would she do such a thing? Marrying an American," she said in distaste, then quickly looked apologetically at Bill and Tom. "I did not mean . . ."

"Don't worry about us Americans," Bill said, a huge grin spreading across his face as he glanced across the table at Clay. "We have tough hides. Don't we, Clay?"

Clay looked at his friend dryly before taking another bite of his meal.

"Anyway," Lorena said, wanting to change the subject. "Ramón, tell me about Carmen Vega."

Ramón shifted uncomfortably in his seat, a slight blush tingeing his cheeks. "Well, I, uh . . ."

Clay's booming voice interrupted. "I believe, Miss Cervantes, you have touched on a subject that no man feels comfortable talking about with a lady." Clay sat back and watched Lorena's cheeks fill with red, as she realized that Ramón must have a relationship with Carmen which was not altogether proper. But Clay wondered more about her reaction to having to marry an American than about her embarrassment. He was certain, however, that once she found out she was to marry, she would be quite happy about the arrangement. After all, isn't that what all women wanted, to snag a rich husband? And what prospects did she have out in the godforsaken desert? Ramón? Clay laughed to himself, sure that the young pup was no option.

Lorena recovered from her embarrassment quickly, channeling the emotion into anger at Clay for his typically inconsiderate remark. "Well, Senōr Wakefield, you have proved once again what a . . . a . . ."

"It was 'wretched cow,' if I recall correctly," he said, teasing her, only aggravating her more.

Everyone else at the table sensed trouble brewing, and in an attempt to head it off, both Bill and Ramón began to speak at once while Tom merely squirmed in his seat. Lorena and Clay looked at the others, then reluctantly turned away, each determined not to be the one to create a scene.

As dinner continued, Lorena and Clay did a good job of outwardly ignoring each other, though each was constantly aware of the other's every word and movement. Lorena and Ramón talked and laughed—Ramón obviously smitten, Lorena unknowingly flirting. Clay's anger rose with each word that passed between the two.

"Lorena," Ramón said, "I saw you from the *torreón* this afternoon. I see that England has not taken away your ability to ride."

Lorena froze before swiftly carrying on. "Thank you, Ramón. You know how much I have always loved to ride."

Clay's fork stopped midway to his mouth. He was caught somewhere between total disbelief that she would ignore his orders and consuming rage, fully aware, even after knowing her such a short time, that she would.

His anger found its release as Clay pushed back his chair, the wooden legs scraping harshly, catching on the rug, almost turning over. Throwing his napkin on the table, Clay looked down at Lorena and Ramón. "When did you say you were leaving, Mr. Valdéz?"

Ramón looked from Lorena to Clay. "Tomorrow morning."

"Good" was all Clay said before turning to leave the room. But he stopped at the door. "Miss Cervantes, we will talk in the morning." And then he was gone, followed soon after by Bill Hawkins and Tom Percy.

When Lorena and Ramón were alone, Lorena sat back, relieved that she had escaped Clay's wrath, for the moment. And if things went as planned, she would miss it altogether, since she would be well on her way to El Rancho Escondido with Ramón before Clay had a chance to yell at her.

"What was that all about?" Ramón asked.

"Don't bother about him, he's just a coldhearted, mean-spirited American who has no manners at all." The last thing Lorena wanted to do right then was tell Ramón that Clay was mad because he had forbidden her to ride out alone. When Ramón looked as if he would question her, she continued, "I've decided to take you up on your offer."

Ramón looked at her curiously. "What offer is that?"

"Ramón! You asked me to go home with you tomorrow morning, remember?"

"Really?" he asked, forgetting about Clay's anger, excited that Lorena was going home with him. "This is wonderful. Mamá will be so pleased."

"Good. But Ramón we must leave early . . . very early."

"Why?"

"Because. Now, don't ask questions, silly," Lorena said, using her sweetest voice.

"All right, we will leave at first light."

"First light! We must leave before that, before anyone wakes up."

"Why do I get the feeling that you are not telling me something?" Ramón asked.

"Because you have a suspicious mind. Now, are we leaving early or not?"

Ramón thought of the American. He wavered. But then he looked at Lorena. "Be ready when I come to your door. I will take care of everything else this night."

Lorena leaped from her chair and threw her arms around Ramón. "Oh, thank you, thank you, thank you." Then she raced out of the *sala*.

In her room, Lorena wrote a quick note to Dalia, telling her where she was going and not to worry. Undressing, she found, was more difficult than dressing had been, all the tiny buttons stubbornly refusing to be undone, her fingers fumbling over them in her haste. When she finally got the

dress off, Lorena hung it back up in the armoire before
pulling on riding pants and a loose shirt. She planned to
sleep fully dressed. Then, having dressed and packed her
bag, she had nothing more to do than to sit and wait.

A short time later, Lorena heard footsteps coming down
the hall. Making sure nothing in the room would give her
away, Lorena slipped under the covers, clothes and all, just
as someone knocked lightly on the door.

"Lorena?" Dalia called.

"Come in, Dalia."

Lorena pulled the bed-covers up to her chin, partially
closing her eyes as if she were almost asleep.

"You are in bed so early, *chica*," Dalia said, looking
closely at Lorena, concern written on her face. "Are you
sick?"

"No, just tired, Dalia. It has been a long day." Lorena's
words were muffled by a yawn punctuating the end.

"Yes, it has," Dalia replied as she smoothed imaginary
wrinkles out of the bedclothes and looked around to see if
anything needed straightening. "You sleep now, and tomorrow you will get up and feel revived." The older woman
paused. "Everything will work out fine, Lorena. I am
sure." Dalia planted a motherly kiss on Lorena's brow, then
left the room.

Lorena tried to sleep, hoping to make the time pass more
swiftly. After tossing and turning for what seemed like
forever, she got up and found a book. She read without
paying attention, getting to the end of a page and having no
idea what she had read. Impatiently, Lorena slammed the
book shut and began to pace back and forth.

After an exceedingly long wait, the sounds of life in the
hacienda began to die down, and still Lorena was wide
awake. She sneaked quietly into the kitchen to get a glass of
milk, then back to her room, where finally she fell into a
fitful sleep.

Hours later a soft knock on the door woke her. Instantly
she was alert. She didn't light a candle or open her shutters.

Feeling around in the dark, she found the bag she had hidden the night before, then silently opened the door to find Ramón.

"Come," he whispered.

Carefully, they walked down the hallway, its length stretching out forever, every footstep sounding loud in her ears. She held her breath as they passed her father's room, knowing that Clay was sleeping inside. When they came to the end of the hallway, Lorena motioned for Ramón to stop. She listened. No sound came from her father's room. She was sure the American was still asleep. Hope filled her. They just might make it.

In the stables, Rosinante was saddled and ready to go, but Ramón's horse was still in its stall.

"Ramón!" Lorena whispered. "Why is your horse not ready? It will be light soon."

Ramón shrugged his shoulders. "I overslept and once I finished Rosinante I thought I should come get you. Come help and we will hurry."

Together they quickly saddled the horse, the blackened night sky rapidly turning shades of purple.

Finally, leading the horses behind them, Lorena and Ramón left the stable, walking out into the early morning, every crunch of gravel sending Lorena's heart into a faster beat. Step by step. Almost to the gate.

"Ramón, how are you going to get them to open the gate?"

"Last night I told the guards that I would be leaving early. They will be expecting me," Ramón said confidently.

"You told someone you planned to leave early!" Lorena cried.

"Do not worry, Lorena. Everything will work out fine."

No sooner had the words been uttered than the deep baritone voice Lorena had come to hate sounded across the courtyard. "I see you are leaving, Ramón."

Lorena wanted to scream in vexation but stopped herself

by reasoning that this man did not matter: he could not stop her.

Clay had heard movement as he sat in the kitchen drinking thick black coffee, discussing the day's projects with Bill and Tom. All three had been certain the movement signified the beginning of the workday. Clay would not have given it a thought had he not walked out of the kitchen in time to see two silhouettes coming out of the stables, leading horses silently behind. As Clay strode forward he was able to make out the shape of Ramón Valdéz and felt that the young man was surely trying to get away before he had to see him again. Clay felt a prick of conscience that he had been so rude to the boy the night before. It wasn't Ramón's fault that Lorena disobeyed at every turn. With that in mind, he had called out in an attempt to send Ramón off on good terms.

Preparing to stand up to the man, Lorena straightened, unaware of the effect the stance had on the shirt, the thin material molding itself to her breasts. With shoulders held back, chin out and proud, Lorena said, "*We* are leaving, señor."

Clay recognized Ramón's companion at the same moment that she began to speak. He stopped just in front of the two, Ramón coming only to his shoulder and Lorena just below that. Clay's goodwill toward Ramón vanished as he looked the young pup up and down before he turned his scathing glare on Lorena. His gaze perused her from head to toe, lingering over jutting breasts that heaved slightly from her rapid breath. Slowly his gaze met hers.

"*We* are leaving?" Clay asked sarcastically. "Where are *we* going? And with whose permission do *we* go?" He spoke the words softly and menacingly.

Lorena's heart beat faster, but her fear spurred her on. She was a Cervantes; this was her home. She would not be intimidated by this arrogant wretch no matter who he thought he was. "Yes, *we* are leaving," she stated as arrogantly as he had. "And *we* are going to Ramón's home,

where I have friends who are concerned about me, unlike
here. And with no one's permission but my own, am I
going." Not knowing how much longer she could stand the
dark stare, Lorena tried to pass by Clay, motioning for
Ramón to follow.

Just as Lorena got in front of Clay, he snatched the reins
from her hands, jerking the mare's mouth. Lorena looked
on in disbelief.

"You oaf!" she cried. Lorena went to her horse, forgetting her own predicament, and carefully looked over Rosinante's mouth. Finding no harm done, she turned back to
Clay. "You could have hurt that animal. Have you no
feelings?"

Clay took a deep breath, then said to Ramón, "I suggest
you be on your way, Valdéz. And just so you know, I don't
appreciate what you are trying to do here. Do you understand?"

Ramón's anger boiled, furious and impotent, his Spanish
pride having been trodden upon. He knew he did not stand
a chance against a man like Clay Wakefield—at least, he
reasoned, not in the man's own territory, with his men all
around. Knowing he could do nothing else, no balm for his
pride at hand, Ramón started to leave, flinging threats that
no one heard but him.

"How dare you!" Lorena screamed once Ramón disappeared through the gate.

"I believe you have already said that."

"Ahggh!" Lorena cried in frustration. "You have no
right, do you hear me?"

"Yes, along with everyone else in the vicinity," he
replied calmly, turning away from her as he led Rosinante
back toward the stables.

Lorena followed at his heels. "How can you do this to
me?"

Clay didn't answer, only continued toward the stable,
Rosinante resisting the rapid pace.

"Why won't you answer me?"

Still he didn't respond.

"It's because you know I'm right. You know you have no right, so you have no response."

Clay stopped, sending Lorena straight into him just as he turned back to her. "For your information, as I have already told you, *I* am in charge of this hacienda. Therefore I am in charge of you as well. So I do have the right! Every right to tell people what to do! Especially those people who have as little sense as you!"

"You hateful, scheming . . . thief!"

Her words were almost hysterical, but her rage went unnoticed as Clay's look of impatience was replaced with one of deadly rage. "What do you mean by that, Miss Cervantes?" He spit out her name as if it were a curse.

Lorena, aware only of her own distress, had no idea what he was talking about.

"I will only ask you one more time," Clay went on. "This time you had better answer. What did you mean by calling me a thief?"

Lorena began to laugh hysterically. "You have suddenly gained a conscience, is that it?" Tears streamed down her cheeks. "You don't like to hear the truth, is that it?" Her laughter stopped and she turned cold green eyes on him. "You don't like being called a thief because you know you are one. You are stealing everything that is rightly mine. Everything! And let me tell you, señor, you will not get away with it!"

Before Clay could respond, Lorena turned and ran through the courtyard, then down the hall until he heard the muffled thud of a slamming door.

Clay watched her go, furious and enraged. The ungrateful, spoiled rotten child. *He* was a thief! Ha! She had stolen his freedom, and he'd be damned if she was going to get away with this routine any longer. With that he went from place to place, giving orders that Miss Lorena Cervantes would not be going anywhere outside of the walls without special permission from him.

No one argued with his orders. The men merely looked at him and nodded. But when he told Dalia and Pedro, Pedro shook his head. "I think you make a very big mistake, my friend."

"I don't care what you think," Clay roared, his own twinge of guilt adding to the volume.

But where Pedro was quiet, Dalia was incensed. "You have no right to do this."

Clay looked at the older woman and pushed away his own doubt. "There you are wrong, señora. I have every right!"

After leaving the kitchen, Clay strode across the courtyard heading toward the stable, eager to throw himself into his work. He couldn't wait to get this place in order so he could go back to Missouri. He cursed as he kicked a bulging tree root that lay in his path.

4

❦

To most everyone at Cielo el Dorado, the days passed in peaceful routine, a routine that was slightly changed by the arrival of Clay Wakefield, but a routine nonetheless. Gradually the servants and others came to accept Clay as the head of the hacienda. He guided them with a firm but fair hand, and though nothing was said aloud, most everyone felt a security they had missed with Diego gone much of the time. It was probably the sense of security Clay provided that balanced the potential hostility that could have been caused by a stranger coming in and taking over.

Pedro, too, was pleased with Clay's handling of the hacienda, but his comfort with that was overshadowed by his growing concern over Lorena. When she had first come home, she was sad over the death of her father but resigned to it and ready to carry on. But since the first harsh confrontations with Clay, Lorena appeared to have lost her strength. A mixture of emotions seemed to tear at her—depression, anger, resentment, and sadness—none of which were helped by Clay's autocratic domination of her world. Both Pedro and Dalia had tried in vain to talk to Lorena, but she had locked them both out, not listening to their arguments that Clay was not as bad as she was making him out to be, that he had her best interests at heart.

"My interests. Ha!" she had shouted. "His only interests are his own."

Pedro contemplated talking to Clay about his concerns, but he was afraid that would do more harm than good, since he was sure Clay must see the problem, and surely he would do something about it. Clay saw Lorena at dinner every evening, since he still insisted they eat together. Pedro knew the meal was always a strained and uncomfortable affair, leaving empty stomachs and full plates, but he had been certain things would get better. But now time had passed and nothing had changed. Both Clay and Lorena were stubbornly set in their ways, not willing to meet each other halfway, and Pedro felt something must be done.

Lost in his thoughts, Pedro absentmindedly made his way toward the kitchen. When he pushed open the door he was hit by a wall of searing heat that stopped him in his tracks. Pedro frantically looked for the source of the heat, expecting to find a raging fire. Instead he found Lorena standing in the middle of the kitchen looking wild and disheveled, fires stoked high in the stoves behind her. The blue ribbon, which was intended to keep her hair tied demurely at the nape of her neck, had failed miserably. Loose tendrils escaped wildly, some askew about her head, others trapped on her face by the glistening sweat that she seemed not to notice. Lorena had the look of a madwoman as she stood scowling at a lump of dough that she was kneading over and over again. *Pound, squish, pound, squish.* She manipulated the dough mercilessly with unrelenting hands. With both stove fires stoked to full capacity, the kitchen was empty of all except Lorena, the servants having quietly disappeared in search of cooler temperatures and saner company. Flour covered the floor, and every step Lorena took sent small puffs of the white powder flying in the air.

Pedro went unnoticed as Lorena pounded the dough, imagining that every blow was somehow connecting with Clay Wakefield. Clay Wakefield—that scoundrel, that wretch, that, that . . . cow, she fumed. How dare he come into her home and take over as if he owned the place? And those treacherous servants, she thought to herself, how dare they take to him as if he were a godsend? They were traitors, and she was of a mind to send the whole lot of them packing. Even Pedro had turned against her to sing the praises of the scoundrel. She did not want to think about how the mere sight of Clay Wakefield made her heart beat faster, while he appeared not to know she even existed except to make some snide remark about her behavior, or call her a willful child. Why did he insist on eating dinner with her every evening when he made it quite clear he thought of her as a nuisance? He was probably trying at that very moment to find some way to get her out of his hair so he could have the hacienda all to himself. She threw a savage punch into the dough, bringing her knuckles into contact with hard wood. "Ouch!" she cried, cradling the dough-covered hand against her body. Lorena sat down heavily at the old oak table and put her sweat-soaked head in folded arms. Her mind raced with thoughts—of the sun shining on rows of crops and on the cool water of the *acequia*. How she would love to be out riding Rosinante, galloping through the fields, soaking up the sun, and cooling off in the chilly water. But instead, in order to avoid Clay, she was stuck in the kitchen trying unsuccessfully to fill her days by making tortillas. With Clay Wakefield claiming to be in charge, she had become a virtual prisoner in her own home. She was filled with uncertainty about what was going to happen to her life. But pride had kept her from asking the questions that had plagued her; she felt that if things were the way they should be, she would not have to ask at all.

For a second Lorena felt a surge of hope, thinking that she would drop everything and go out to ride, Clay and his scowls be damned. But the thought of his dark eyes and mocking smile instantly changed her mind. "Why does he do this to me?" she cried into her arms. She had never been one to cower and she did not understand herself for not

standing up to the man now. Why couldn't she bring herself
to walk right past him, jump on her horse, and ride out?
Whenever she felt she had to come up with a plan, and
whenever he was near, her thoughts turned into a jumbled
mess. As a result, Lorena avoided Clay entirely.

Pedro stood in the doorway watching Lorena with a sense
of helplessness. He didn't know how to help the young girl
other than to be there and provide comfort, but change
things he could not. "Lorena, I think you have baked
enough for one day."

A startled Lorena looked up to find Pedro standing near.
She recognized the look of concern in his old eyes and was
stung by guilt for causing Pedro worry. Slowly she looked
from his eyes to the room about her. She noticed for the first
time the overwhelming heat that enfolded her and the white
flour that covered the floor like a dusting of light snow-
flakes, and noticed that she, too, was covered with the
white powder. Dark, wet patches of sweat had soaked
through her light blue dress. Miss Tidesdale loomed in her
mind, pounding into her head that "Ladies do not sweat, nor
do they perspire." Lorena burst out laughing, thinking of
how outraged the old schoolmistress would have been could
she have seen Lorena now.

"Well, Miss T., if this isn't sweat, I don't know what is,"
Lorena cried aloud through bursts of hysterical laughter.

Pedro wasn't quite sure what was so funny and worried
that Lorena was going a bit crazy. He called a maid and sent
her to get Dalia.

Dalia bustled in followed by a knot of curious servants.
Breathing heavily from the exertion and the heat, she
immediately took control.

"Luz, prepare a bath for Señorita Cervantes in her room.
Maria, Alicia, clean up this mess." Dalia then firmly
grasped a still laughing Lorena by the wrist and pulled her
toward her room.

Dalia's concern grew with each step as Lorena's laughter
took on a haunted quality. Every servant in the courtyard

stood staring at the spectacle, jobs forgotten. They remembered the sweet child who had left years before. Never had any of them seen Lorena as anything except confident, happy, and loving. Dalia was glad that Clay had ridden out earlier that morning. She was not sure how he would have reacted to Lorena's behavior, though she knew he would hear about it eventually; every servant would be eager to give him the news. Dalia suspected that this outburst had something to do with the Americano, and that was one more reason not to like him, as far as she was concerned. Somehow she needed to get Ramón back to the hacienda to court Lorena. But since the last time he was here, he had stayed away. It was probably due somehow to Clay, she reasoned. She could not understand why every person in the hacienda, including Pedro, was ensnared by the rugged man. She, for one, was not taken in by his good looks and deceptive smile.

When they reached Lorena's room, the girl's laughter was subsiding, and by the time Dalia had Lorena in a sweetly scented bath, the laughter had completely stopped, replaced by silent tears. Sitting on a small stool, the old woman gently sponged the flour and sweat from Lorena's body. "Now, now, *mi chiquita*. It is going to be all right."

"No, it's not going to be all right," Lorena wailed. "It will never be right again, with Papa gone and that wretched Clay here. It's not fair," she cried into her hands.

Knowing better than to disagree with Lorena, Dalia sat patiently, murmuring soft endearments while her young charge tried to cry away the pain and hurt. Eventually the tears began to subside, fading away to a quiet hiccuping.

Dalia hated to see Lorena this way. Anger was preferable to this depression. And truthfully, Dalia admitted to herself, she did not totally understand it. If Lorena were a bit more malleable, things would not be so bad. Many of the restrictions that had been placed on her were due to her own sharp tongue and careless actions. Surely there must be more to this, she thought.

Lorena washed slowly, the warm water easing the tension away. She remembered her mother, her beautiful young mother, who had lamented her life; and her father, who came and went with such lively energy. She thought of the stories she had read, where people found true love; then she cursed all men for making that impossible. Barring love, Lorena had set her hopes on Cielo el Dorado—the land, the fields, the animals, the people. She was a part of the hacienda as she was a part of nothing else; it was her life.

Lorena suddenly sat up in the tub. Clay Wakefield had temporarily taken over, but things would change. She couldn't stand her simpering self. No more, she promised herself. Things would change. They had to.

By the time she was finished and standing up in the copper tub, the confident, happy Lorena Cervantes was back.

"Can you believe how silly I've been?" she asked, noticing relieved smiles of Dalia and Luz, who stood by holding a towel. "From the way I have been behaving, one would think I was just another simpleminded female. Well, I'm not, and that black-eyed, bullheaded Clay Wakefield is not going to turn me into one."

Lorena stepped out of the tub, leaving behind all remnants of depression and flour. "First thing tomorrow morning, whether Clay Wakefield is around or not, I will be astride Rosinante, riding through the fields. In fact, I think I will go over to Paso del Norte and visit with Fray Cristóbal."

Luz quickly glanced at Dalia, knowing that Clay had left strict orders that Lorena was not to ride without permission. Lorena would not even be allowed to go with an escort without Clay's permission.

Thinking the same thing, but not wanting to take the risk of upsetting Lorena again, Dalia motioned Luz to be silent, they would deal with that problem later. Hastily changing the subject, Dalia took the towel from Luz and said in a stern voice to cover her unease, "Lorena, I doubt you are simpleminded or ever will be, but I think you could stand a bit more modesty. Now, put this towel around you and get dressed. Luz will comb out that mess of tangles while I go see to the kitchen." After wrapping the towel around the wet girl, the duenna gave Lorena a quick hug and said, "This is the girl I know. Everything will work out just fine, you wait and see."

Without giving anyone a chance to reply, Dalia bustled out of the room. A surge of love welled up inside Lorena as she stared after the woman who was like a mother to her. The feeling of love reassured and comforted Lorena, leaving her with renewed confidence and excited anticipation of the next day. Things were going to be all right.

That evening Lorena made her way to the *sala* where the massive formal dining table stood. The *sala* was an austere room with dark-stained wood furniture as opposed to the natural, unstained, light wood in the other rooms. Red velvet covered the cushions on the seats, another import of some Cervantes ancestor. The backs and legs of the chairs were ornately carved to match the legs of the table. It was not a room to put one at ease, but Lorena ignored the formality as she came into the room and sat down, with a grace that even Miss Tidesdale could not have faulted, in the chair Clay held out for her. She took the linen napkin from the table and laid it delicately in her lap, all the while thinking of her ride and of the new clothes she would buy the next day.

Clay noticed a difference in Lorena immediately, the way she walked—no, glided—into the room. The way a slight smile curved the corners of her delicate mouth, as if she held some secret that no one else knew. The way she accepted the chair he offered without the scowl he had come to expect. Clay wondered if the change had anything to do with the episode he had been told about earlier. He had expected her to refuse to come to dinner at all after what Luz had told him. But there she sat, as regal as a queen, making him wonder if indeed there had been any such episode.

Bill Hawkins came in and sat down across from Lorena.

"Sorry I'm late. I'm still not used to this fancy sittin'-down dinner," he said with a half smile at Clay.

"Where is Tom?" Lorena inquired politely.

"He went into town for the night." Bill glanced at Clay before he leaned toward Lorena conspiratorially. "I think he's got himself a girl."

"Really?" Lorena said in surprise. "He seems too shy to have a girlfriend."

"It's those shy ones that get 'em every time. Isn't that right, Clay?" Bill laughed.

Clay lifted one dark eyebrow. "I believe your dinner is getting cold."

They ate in silence, an occasional voice drifting in on the cool night breeze to interrupt the click and chink of silverware against china. Finally Bill said, "We got the main *acequia* widened. Now we just need to keep it clear."

Each night the two men sat over dinner discussing the goings-on at the hacienda as they learned the skills of running it. Lorena was thankful for this, for it saved her from having to participate in any conversation with Clay. Tonight, however, she took notice of the talk and found herself interested and amazed at all that had been going on around her. "What was wrong with the *acequia*?" she asked, surprising both men with her question.

Clay looked at Lorena and wondered once again at the change in her. Inexplicably pleased that she was not her usual hostile self, he began to explain. "The stream that brings water from the river to the hacienda was partially blocked. It appeared that it had not been cleared in some time. As a result, the flour mill was not grinding at full capacity, and the machinery was breaking down frequently, since it was grinding so slowly."

Lorena thought about the mill where the wheat was ground into flour and the corn ground into masa. The mill was on the working side of the hacienda in a large room that was used to make the wine as well as to grind the grain. The *acequia* flowed under the hacienda wall to turn a water wheel connected to the mill equipment inside the room.

"Now that the water is running faster, it is cleaner as well, so it will help more than just the mill," Bill added enthusiastically.

Lorena smiled at Bill. "How do you know so much about the hacienda?" she asked, ignoring the fact that Clay appeared to know as much or more.

"I have a farm back in Missouri, and like Cielo el Dorado, it's self sufficient. The countryside, of course, is different, but the rudiments of survival are not that dissimilar between here and there." Bill went on about his favorite topic with relish. When Lorena happened to glance at Clay she noticed a look of barely held patience. She covered a laugh with a cough, not wanting to offend the enthusiastic farmer.

Clay looked at Lorena and saw that she was trying to stifle a laugh. Their eyes met, each sensing what the other was feeling about Bill's long explanation, and for the first time, they smiled at each other, having shared a conspiratorial moment.

Bill looked sheepishly from Lorena to Clay, realizing that he had gotten carried away. "Well, I guess you know everything and more about the workings of a farm in Missouri."

"Oh, Bill, I thought it was all very interesting. In fact, I would like to learn all about running a hacienda like this. Papa taught me about the fields and the animals and even how the grain is made. He also taught me about the wine, and our history, but not the day-to-day workings of Cielo el Dorado."

"Well, I would be more than happy to teach you all I know, Lorena," Bill offered.

Clay lifted one dark eyebrow at Bill's words. "I'm sure you would."

All three laughed, aware of the turn their dinner had taken.

"So tell me, Señor Wakefield, where are you from and what is it that you do?" Lorena asked, a teasing smile lighting up her green eyes, suddenly succumbing to the unspoken truce they had reached.

Clay realized for the first time that she truly did not know anything about him. He was surprised that her father had never spoken of him to her, especially since Diego had told Clay so much about Lorena. "Let's see," he said, leaning back in the high-back chair with a long-stemmed glass of deep red wine grasped in his hand. "I have been a trader on the Santa Fe Trail for ten years and have worked the Camino Real for the last five. That's how I met your father."

"How? Did you stay here or something?"

"Actually, my father knew Diego and told me about him," Clay explained. "I decided to work on the trail. Once I had established myself, and Mexico had won its independence from Spain, I extended my route from Santa Fe to Mexico City."

"Why did you wait for Mexico to win its independence? Why didn't you start on the Camino Real before that?" Lorena asked.

"Because the Spanish didn't allow Americans to come into New Mexico. Anyone who did, and was caught, was arrested as a spy."

Lorena was surprised by this, as she had spent much time in England where people came and went as they pleased. "How can that be?"

"I don't know, but I do know that a group of men, led by a man named Robert McKnight, thought that Hidalgo's revolution of 1810 had been successful, and so they traveled to Santa Fe in 1812 to trade. They were arrested as spies and transported to the interior, where they were held for nine years."

"No! That is terrible. How could the government do that to innocent men? What happened to them?"

"One of them managed to escape before he ever made it

to prison, and the rest were released in 1821 when Mexico finally won its independence from Spain." Clay looked down into the deep red wine. "The confinement must not have been too rigorous, as many of the men who had been captured came back to Mexico to live. They were better off than the one who managed to escape." The last words were barely audible.

"What do you mean?" Lorena asked quietly, sensing that the few simple words held a great deal of meaning.

Clay looked up then, his uneasiness gone. "Nothing, nothing at all. Anyway, I came down to the hacienda just to meet Diego. It was Diego who really got me started on the Camino Real."

"Where is your father now?"

"He's dead."

Lorena flinched at the pained look that passed over Clay's features as he spoke of his father. She understood the pain of losing a parent. "I'm sorry about your father. I know what it is like to lose someone you love."

Clay looked at the young woman who was to be his wife and saw the sincere hurt she felt, not only for herself but for him as well; a side of her he would have never guessed existed. He remembered the first time he had seen her, at the swimming hole, and thought of the spirit she had instead of the danger she was in.

His eyes dropped to her lips, which glistened red. This was to be his wife, the woman who would bear his children. Clay saw the situation in new light. He thought of holding her in his arms, of tasting her sweet lips. For the first time since his unwanted betrothal, Clay was not so displeased.

"Uh-hum." Bill cleared his throat, all too aware of where his friend's thoughts had probably drifted and aware as well of the blush that had crept up Lorena's cheeks. "It's getting late, and I have about had my fill of this great meal. I think I'll just mosey on out to the rooms and see what the men are up to."

"Bill is right. It is getting late, and I have had a tiring
day. So I'll excuse myself and say good night." Lorena
stood to leave, both men rising to assist her. When she
glanced at Clay, she thought she detected a flash of regret,
but quickly it was gone, making her believe she had only
imagined it.

Bill left shortly after Lorena, leaving Clay at the head of
the massive table. He had wanted Lorena tonight. The
thought surprised him, though he knew it shouldn't have.
Hadn't he wanted her badly when he thought she was only
an uncomplicated maid? Hadn't the sight of her rounded
breasts outlined by her thin shirt sent a jolt of desire through
his body?

But for a long time he had thought of Lorena, Diego's
Lorena, as an old maid of shrewish temperament, a shackle
to his freedom. Then, after meeting her, he had considered
her a willful, stubborn hellion who had to be brought to
heel. Now, after one meal of relative civility, he wanted her,
badly. But the cost was his freedom. A sneer twisted his
features. Whether he wanted her or not, his freedom was
lost. Or at least his freedom to marry one of his own
choosing. The familiar resentment was quickly extin-
guished as he wondered what it would be like to kiss her
lush lips, to let his hands travel over the smooth curves
of her body. As Clay Wakefield sipped the remains of the
heavy red wine, one candle flickering on the table, he found
himself reluctantly intrigued by the woman-child who was
to be his wife.

5

❧

LORENA PRACTICALLY FLEW OUT OF BED EARLY THE next morning, so eager was she to ride. Come hell or high water she was going to get out. She told herself that Clay Wakefield and what he thought did not matter one whit, but she got up early enough to leave before he woke. That was just because she was not a fool, she consoled herself. Knowing him, he would make up some reason why she couldn't ride, just to be disagreeable.

After a quick wash, Lorena threw on some old riding clothes that she found in the trunk. She chose a split riding skirt her father had bought her right before she left for school, reluctantly passing over a pair of boys' pants and a shirt. Though the skirt was a little tight and a bit too short, Lorena didn't care. Who would notice anyway? But when she thought of the possibility of running into Clay she paused, her heart hammering for one split second until she told herself he was probably still in bed, white linen sheets half covering his bronzed body, dark hair tousled from sleep, full sensuous lips . . . *Stop!* she admonished herself, feeling like a hundred kinds of a fool.

Quietly she opened her bedroom door. Peering down the hall, she noted the master bedroom door was still shut. Silently, chiding herself with each step for being a coward,

Lorena passed the closed door. As soon as she got out into the courtyard she breathed a sigh of relief.

The sky was colored in shades of purple as the sun tried to make its entry into the new day. Excited as she was, Lorena had to stifle a squeal of delight for fear of waking the rest of the household.

Crossing the dewy grass, leaving dark green footprints as she went, Lorena stepped into the kitchen, the warmth of the fire banishing the slight chill from the early morning air. Lorena was only a bit surprised to find people up and about. Apprehension gripped her until she reasoned that, although Luz and Dalia were up, in all likelihood, Clay would still be abed. Americans were so lazy, she mused with a toss of her fiery tresses, her confidence easily restored.

"*Buenos días*, Luz. *Buenos días*, Dalia," Lorena half sang as she came up to the stove, where a pot of steaming chocolate simmered. "Uhmmm, this smells delicious."

"Lorena, you are up so early. But I am glad to see it," Dalia looked fondly at her. "Come, *chica*, sit down and have something to eat."

"*Gracias*, but only chocolate and some bread. I am eager to get out. Today I'm going to ride to town to order some clothes. After that, I am going to the mission to see Fray Cristóbal."

Dalia was flustered as she served the chocolate and bread, trying to decide what to do. She knew as soon as Lorena got to the stables she would find out about Clay's orders and be furious. But, Dalia thought, just maybe Lorena would get there before anyone else did and be able to saddle up and ride out. She had not seen Señor Wakefield yet, and besides, Lorena needed to get out and see her friends. Nothing would happen to her between the hacienda and Paso del Norte. Dalia would gladly suffer the Americano's wrath if it would help her baby.

Having made her decision, the duenna wrapped some bread and fruit in a cloth and gave it to Lorena. "Here is something to eat later on. Now hurry up with your breakfast and get on that mare of yours."

Lorena stuffed the last bite of bread into her mouth and gave the older woman a quick hug. "*Adiós*," she called as she raced out the door.

Clay woke up early, eager to be out in the fields. He had spent so many hours inside that he looked forward to getting out. The hacienda demanded much of his time, more than he had expected. Several problems had needed his immediate attention, and he had wondered more than once how the place had functioned with Diego gone so much. Many repairs had to be done—widening the *acequia*, fixing equipment, and the like—with a few domestic squabbles in between. There had been enough to keep Clay occupied, and he had not had a chance to look over Diego's books. He told himself that after he checked the fields and irrigation ditches he would sit down and go over the journals. He had to do it before he left—and he planned to leave soon. Clay looked forward to getting back to Missouri. He had his eye on a piece of property, and his solicitor was negotiating with the owner. It should be taken care of by the time he returned home. *Home.* The thought reminded him he had to get the marriage over with so that he could get back. He needed to tell Lorena soon. His thoughts drifted to her sweet body and tempting lips. Clay smiled, a slow smile that revealed all too clearly his errant thoughts. He looked forward to the marriage bed, if not the marriage. If his heirs had to be gotten from her, he would make sure the getting was pleasurable.

He bypassed the kitchen, deciding he would eat later. As he made his way to the stables, his thoughts were filled with the young woman who was to be his wife. Much to his chagrin, Clay remembered that he had thought about her into the late hours of the night before—and if that had not been enough to drive a man crazy, she had relentlessly plagued his dreams as well. He kept remembering how she had looked by the swimming hole, one minute filled with laughter, the next, fire-hot fury, and then later, with the thin

cotton shirt clinging to her breasts, the long-barreled gun
clasped firmly in her hands, making her look like a
red-haired warrior ready to do battle. He would have
laughed had he not been so angry and so very uncomfortable about the way she made him feel. That thought had led
to an extremely miserable sleep that made him silently curse
her and then, in turn, long to pull her beneath him and
subdue the spirited warrior into submission. Damn, she was
making him crazy!

Dinner had turned out to be a pleasant surprise. Every
dinner they had shared before had been marred by her
hostility and anger, with only Bill and himself talking at all.
During the daytime he had seen very little of Lorena and
had noticed that she was making a great effort to avoid him.
So diligently was she avoiding him, in fact, that she had not
even gone to the stables. He had seen her on several
occasions heading in that direction, but as soon as she
caught sight of him, she had turned and slipped away. Since
she had not been to the stables, he reasoned, she had not yet
found out about the restrictions he had placed on her riding
or other activities. They were for her own good, he
reassured himself. He knew he had given the orders in a
rage, but while he might have gotten a bit carried away,
ultimately he was concerned for her welfare. At any rate,
Clay knew for certain he would hear about it as soon as she
did find out.

As Clay entered the stables, his thoughts were interrupted
by Jaime. "Good morning, Señor Wakefield. I have put
some food in your saddlebag. Dante is ready to go and
anxious to get out."

Clay laughed as he approached the massive beast. "So,
Dante," he said as he ran a hand down the horse's heavily
muscled hind leg. "You're tired of being cooped up, are
you?"

The stallion shook his stately head, then nuzzled Clay's
shoulder, only to have his attention diverted when the stable
door swung open and cool morning air filled the small outer
room.

Lorena stood in the open doorway, still holding the wooden handle, her red hair tied loosely back from her face. Her eyes turned from vibrant green to deep aqua as she realized who stood in front of her.

Clay was silent, her unexpected entrance leaving him momentarily entranced by the continual surprise of her beauty. Only hours before he had dreamed of pulling her beneath him. Now her lips turned into a pout, as if a kiss had been stolen from them. Had it been a dream? As they stood yards apart, their eyes locked in uncertainty, it seemed to Clay that it had not been a dream, that the feel of her flesh still burned his hand.

Her heart sank, her breath forced out of her as if she had been struck, until finally, air surged back in, each gasping breath searing her lungs. Her next thought was to flee. But then she remembered the long, lonely days and her determination to ride out. She stepped boldly through the doorway, her chin raised in defiance, daring anyone to question her presence.

"Jaime," she began with chin held high and a confidence she did not feel, "I am going to ride today. Could you saddle Rosinante, *por favor*?"

Lorena turned to wait outside, not wanting to stand so near Clay's dark handsomeness. Somehow, the morning after the dinner and conversation they had shared, his piercing dark eyes and dark waving hair seemed more threatening than ever before, but why, she didn't know.

As she turned, she missed Jaime's questioning look, though Clay did not. Lorena was there to ride. The inevitable confrontation had arrived. For some reason Clay did not want to examine too closely, he hated for Lorena to hear of his instructions, at least, not right then. Without thinking, he said, "Lorena, I'll ride with you today."

Lorena stopped at the door. He hadn't asked if he could; he'd stated it as fact. Without turning around she said, "I'll be quite all right. I don't need an escort."

He was unaware of what had caused the sudden anger

that laced her stilted words, but he chose to ignore it. "Actually, I'd like you to show me the area, as I haven't had a chance to look around," he replied. Not waiting for an answer, Clay turned to Jaime and nodded. Within minutes Clay was helping Lorena into the saddle before he mounted his own stallion.

Passing through the main gate, Lorena wondered how she had ended up riding with Clay, the very person she had so painstakingly avoided. She certainly hadn't wanted to, but he seemed not to have left her any choice. She did not want to think about it now; she was out of the gates, and she planned to enjoy herself thoroughly, with or without Clay Wakefield. Besides, with any luck, she would leave him choking on her dust.

They rode along, neither speaking, each all too aware of the other. But finally the sight of the land and crops filled Lorena with the usual sense of well-being, helping her to forget the disturbing man who rode beside her. She was home after all. Determined to lose herself in the ride, Lorena took off in a wild gallop, leaving a startled Clay behind.

Clay wasn't sure if he was more worried or angry at her flagrant recklessness, but when he heard her laughter filter back to him, he was caught up in her mood and went charging after her. Steadily Dante's strength and speed closed the gap until the black stallion and the chestnut mare were side by side, galloping on the hard-packed dirt road that trailed through the land.

After a short span of comfortable silence Clay called across the short distance between the two racing horses. "Do you think we might slow down? I'm not sure if this animal can stand the pace."

Lorena looked from horse to rider and then, with mischief in her eyes, remarked, "Are you referring to the horse or yourself?"

Clay threw his head back and filled the air with his bold laugh as both riders slowed to a trot. The sound of his laughter flowed over her body, filling her with warmth and inexplicable high spirits.

They trotted through the fields, stopping periodically to check a fence or crop. Under lowered lashes, Lorena studied the man who had come into her life so suddenly. She found him very hard to understand. One minute he was teasing; the next he would tempt her. Usually he was humiliating her, but now he made her heart beat faster and her body grow warm with unfamiliar feelings. How was she to deal with such a man?

When she realized the path her thoughts had taken and felt the tremors of her traitorous body, her anger returned, bringing a scowl to her face.

"Well, little one, whom are you scowling at? Surely I haven't done something this soon to upset you?" Clay said, trying to conceal the smile that lurked just below the surface.

Lorena realized that she was no longer looking at him demurely through lowered lashes, but outwardly glaring at him, sending silent daggers of hate. She felt the blood rush to her cheeks, embarrassed at being caught in her thoughts. Quickly, she averted her eyes and said, "Why, of course not, señor. I was only thinking about how sour grapes can be."

Without warning, Clay reined in his horse and jerked Lorena's mare to a halt. He seemed to tower over her as he looked down at her slender form. Strong fingers gently caressed her soft cheek, moving slowing down her neck to grasp one small shoulder, forcing Lorena to look up into angry black eyes. In a voice that was both calm and threatening he said, "Never lie to me again."

Looking down at her, Clay could see the fear in her eyes. The look he saw told him that he had made his point, and not wanting to ruin the day, he leaned down and gently kissed her lips. The contact shattered them both—the sudden and unexpected heat, the fire that burned, the desire that threatened to overtake them. Slowly Clay pulled back, amazed that such an innocent kiss could fill him with such longing. In a voice that was both strained and demanding, he said, "There will be no lies or secrets between us, little one." Then as abruptly as he had grabbed her, he let her go. "Let's see if that mare of yours can make it to the fence."

' Clay watched the string of emotions race across her perfect features—confusion, understanding, indecision. He fully expected her to give him a piece of her mind and was surprised by the relief he felt when, in a flurry of dust and flying mane, she took off toward the fence. He sat watching her for a few seconds, relishing the stark contrasts of the woman-child he was going to marry, before he realized he was in a race and without a second more delay, the powerful stallion was once again pursuing the lovely mare.

As the day progressed, Lorena and Clay went from field to field and fence to fence, chatting amiably all the way. Clay was amazed to see this new side of Lorena. Her humor was contagious, and for the first time, he began to catch a glimpse of the Lorena Diego had spoken of so often.

"Tell me about school," Clay said as their pace slowed.

"What would you like to know?" she said, her eyes twinkling mischievously. "About my grades, or are you interested in my deportment?"

Clay groaned. "I can just imagine your deportment."

Lorena tossed her mane of hair over one shoulder. "You most certainly cannot! I was thought of as an exemplary student."

Clay looked at her skeptically. "I find that somewhat hard to believe. Unless, of course, the mode of dress and the style of riding have changed in England."

Sheepishly she looked back before she burst out laughing. "Well, maybe I was the perfect model of how to get into trouble."

"Why do I find that easy to believe?" he asked with a half smile, his bold, sensuous lips curving into a smile.

Lorena tore her eyes away from his lips, trying to bring her thoughts back into order.

"Your mind seems to be elsewhere," he said softly.

Lorena's face turned tomato red. To cover her embarrassment she rushed into a monologue about her days at school. "No, my thoughts are right here," she improvised quickly, "I was just thinking about school and how relieved Miss Tidesdale must have been when I was called home."

"Ah, the famous Miss T."

"Don't you start, Clay Wakefield."

"Go on, finish telling me. Were you terrible at needle-point?"

"Terrible? Worse! I don't get along well with needles. I'm surprised that I didn't die from loss of blood before I ever came home. And dancing—I probably got in the most trouble during dance class."

Clay raised one dark eyebrow in question.

"They made us dance with one another! It made no sense at all!" she exclaimed, her fine features molded into a look of disbelief.

"Why?"

"Well, because! Someone had to be the boy," Lorena said indignantly.

"Of course," he chuckled, "and you were he."

"Yes," she said, pulling her shoulders back proudly. "And a damn . . . I mean, a darn good one, too." Lorena caught the look of disapproval on Clay's face, and before he could chastise her for her language, she hurried on. "So now I won't ever be able to dance unless I can lead."

Clay laughed, forgetting her language, imagining Lorena leading some poor man around the dance floor. "Well, don't worry, little one, when you dance with me, we will work you slowly into following." His eyes seared her with a bold promise.

Lorena's heart skipped a beat. How handsome this man was! She pictured herself dancing with him, his strong arms around her, a slight smile on his face as he looked down into her eyes.

Clay's deep voice interrupted her thoughts. "Woolgathering again?"

Lorena blinked twice, the images in her mind having been so real.

"How was it that, being the recalcitrant student you were, you managed to avoid getting kicked out altogether?"

Lorena cocked her head and sent him a shameless glare. "I may have received more reprimands in ballroom dancing and etiquette than any other girl in the history of Miss T.'s, but I earned the highest marks in mathematics and philosophy. Had it not been for that, I'm sure I would have been kicked out long ago."

Clay groaned. "I forgot. Miss Tidesdale's Seminary for Young Ladies is one of those scandalous schools that teach men's subjects to girls!" Despite his words, Clay felt a grudging respect for this young woman and all she had learned.

"Most girls my age are already married and have children— all because they were not smart enough to go to school and learn better."

"And what has all your learning gotten you?"

"I have learned better than to get married!"

"All women want to get married, Lorena." He looked at her with certainty and enough superiority for a roomful of men.

Lorena shook her head. "I should have figured as much coming from you! You sound just like my father." Lorena's gaze clouded, and she looked off toward the hills.

Clay was struck again, as he was the day he first met her, by the flicker of pain that passed through her eyes. But before he had a chance to question her, Lorena began to fill his ears with tales of her exploits as a child at the hacienda. Clay found himself holding his sides with mirth over stories of Lorena's days growing up in the river valley. And as they rode, he felt certain that underneath the laughter and the tales of unseemly exploits, Lorena had been a lonely child whose mother had had little time for her and whose father was rarely around. Clay felt anger well up inside him at Diego, who had left a wife and child in a house filled with servants while he spent much of his time away from home. Clay knew he owed much of his success to Lorena's father, but now he found it hard to forgive the man. The crack in his resentment at being forced to marry Lorena, that fissure that had opened the night before, now widened a bit more as he looked at her.

They rode until well after noon, when Clay remembered the package of food Lorena had stuffed in her saddlebag. He had brought some as well, and since they were near the swimming hole, he decided they should stop to eat. Lorena reluctantly agreed, not certain she trusted this new side of the man.

Clay dismounted by the water, then turned just in time to see Lorena jump down out of her saddle. An ominous scowl marred his face. "In the future, you will wait for me to help you down. It is dangerous to leap out of your saddle like a young boy."

"Really!" Lorena turned away unconcerned. "I have gotten in and out of my saddle by myself for years, and I don't intend to stop now just because I happen to be a girl."

Clay was amazed to realize that she was laughing at him.

"Besides, what would I do when I'm out by myself and need to get down? You certainly won't be going everywhere with me," she added with a teasing smile upon her lips.

Clay was enchanted. He couldn't tell her now that she was not allowed out without his permission and certainly not alone. He let it go and replied in a teasing voice that matched hers, "I sympathize with poor Miss Tidesdale. You must surely have left the woman with gray hair."

Lorena plopped unceremoniously down on the ground. "She had gray hair when I got there."

Clay laughed loudly and tossed a blanket in her direction. "Spread this out so we can eat, you scamp."

Life was wonderful. Blue skies contrasted with the dry brownness of the land, and birds serenaded from the trees. Was it possible that only yesterday she had been upset and depressed? And then there was Clay Wakefield, with his

rich laughter, his intense eyes, broad shoulders, and rippling muscles. She didn't understand the way he made her
feel—the rapid heartbeat, the heat she felt whenever he
looked at her. To cover her unease, she said stiffly, "Señor
Wakefield, shall I unpack our lunch?"

"Lorena, I'm tired of you calling me señor. My name is
Clay; I want you to use it. Now, just sit and relax."

Lorena sat back and watched as Clay set a bag of food
down on the blanket. What an arrogant, autocratic man! she
fumed. Did he ever think to ask her to do things instead of
ordering her? Had the man no common courtesy? But her
thoughts changed when he stretched his long body, his
rippling muscles straining the seams of his clothes. He
brought to mind a black panther, taut even in repose, ready
to strike at any moment, never defenseless, always alert.

When Clay looked over at Lorena, she quickly turned her
head. He leaned back to support his weight on one elbow
and drew a leg up to rest his other arm on. He watched
lazily as Lorena busied herself spreading the food out in the
narrow space between them.

After a few moments of going through their meager
provisions, Lorena forgot about the man and his muscles.
She was hungry, so with relish, she doled out their fare.

They ate hard bread with lots of cheese and dried grapes
from Cielo el Dorado vines, and they drank wine from
the one cup they found in the bag. Lorena was calm as she
looked around at the familiar sights. It had seemed as if she
would never get back home, but now, as she sat in the midst
of the land and its unique features, the long absence seemed
insignificant. And if she closed her eyes and inhaled the
pungent fragrance of wildflowers, the multitude of grasses
mixed with wet dirt and sand from the river, she could
almost believe she had never left. It was as if at any time her
father might cross the river and come home after a long
absence. If only her father would ride across the river now
and they could laugh at the joke played on them all. But no,
he would not come, ever again.

Lorena sighed and turned back to find Clay with a mound of raisins in his hand. He had been watching her, she was sure. But to prevent his questioning her, she said, "Did you know that in ancient times, the pharaohs of Egypt had girls who did nothing but feed them grapes?" She announced this with an exaggerated sniff of indignation.

Clay wavered, then smiled, replying in a husky voice, "I don't think that's all they did, little one."

Not understanding his deepened voice and not seeing his hungry perusal of her body, Lorena innocently continued. "I would like to think that is true. How worthless those girls must have felt! Feeding grapes to some man, whether he was a king or not, would be worse than sitting around knitting or doing needlepoint or planning menus or—"

Clay interrupted, though he spoke not a word, as he offered a raisin to her lips. He looked deep into her eyes, captivating her with his intensity. Slowly, finding no will to resist, she took the dried fruit into her mouth. His fingers lingered. "I don't think I would mind having their job." His voice was deep, but as soft as a caress. He watched as she chewed the raisin, her lips moving slowly, seductively, filling him with the burning heat of desire. She watched as he became taut as a coil, ready to spring. And Lorena was filled with a burning as well, though she couldn't have explained it.

Lorena swallowed, the lump in her throat making it hard for her to breathe. "Those are raisins, not grapes." It was barely a whisper.

"But aren't raisins nothing more than dried grapes?" His voice was like sandpaper, and while he said the words, he watched in something close to agony as she carefully slid her tongue over her lips. His loins ached for her, and without thinking, he touched her moistened mouth, then let his fingers trail back to her hair, pulling the ribbon from it to let the mass tumble down her back. Carefully, almost reverently, Clay pulled her to him, claiming her lips cautiously. "Lorena," he groaned. He kissed her again and

again, slowly, so as not to scare her, until he could feel the
tension leave her body, until her eyelids fluttered closed.
His tongue caressed her lips, gently parting them to taste the
sweetness within.

Feeling Clay's lips meet her own, Lorena momentarily
tensed, overwhelmed with feelings she did not understand.
She tried to pull back, but he only pulled her closer. Then,
succumbing to the warmth that beckoned her, a warmth that
made her feel safe and loved, she forgot all reason and
molded her body to his. Hesitantly, she flicked his tongue
with her own, relishing the feel, reveling in the new and
wondrous emotions that flooded her body.

Clay moaned deeply at her inexperienced attempt, surprised that such a small gesture could fill his body with
unbridled passion. Never had he desired a woman more. A
soft, barely audible moan sounded from within Lorena as
his strong hands gently caressed her back, moving slowing
downward. His tongue became more insistent, moving with
a rhythm as old as time. His hands moved from her lower
back to her midriff and slowly ascended to claim one young,
rounded breast.

With the brazen touch, reality flooded Lorena's senses,
breaking through the barrier of passion. Outraged, as much
at herself as at him, Lorena forcefully drew back, rolling
over to sit on her heels. How could she have done such a
thing? her mind screamed. She was acting like a common
trollop! So angry was she that she dealt him a resounding
slap across the face. "How dare you, you beast!"

Clay looked at Lorena, still not having moved, and
slowly a satisfied grin curled his lips. "Yes, how dare I.
But, Lorena"—he paused, one large hand touching his
face—"don't ever do that again." He was up in one smooth
motion, uncommonly pleased with her reaction. "It's time
to head back."

6

THE NEXT MORNING CLAY WAKEFIELD SAT BEHIND the massive desk that had been used by generations of Cervantes ancestors in their running of Cielo el Dorado. He had stayed up late into the night delving into Diego's books and records, and he had found many things that disturbed him—nothing he could put his finger on, but things that made no sense. Something had to be missing, some important facts that would be the key to the puzzle.

Clay had dragged himself to bed in the wee hours of the morning only to have his mind whirl with thoughts until he fell into a fitful sleep that was filled with images of Lorena, Diego, and Missouri. He woke exhausted after only a few hours, and with no more than a strong cup of coffee, he went straight back to the study. Unfortunately, the books were no clearer in the morning light. Something was very wrong, but he had no idea what it was.

A very tired Clay was sitting motionless in the chair, his head back against the soft leather, contemplating the situation when the door crashed open. Lorena burst into the room, fury written in her eyes, and came to stand before him with hands planted firmly on her hips.

"Please come in," he said sarcastically. "Has anyone ever taught you to knock?"

"Who do you think you are, giving orders to my servants?" Lorena shrieked, though she tried hard to maintain control of her voice. The last thing she wanted to do was act like a hysterical female in front of this arrogant man. "You have no right to come here and take over. I don't care how close you were to my father. He is gone now, and I am his heir, not you. I will run Cielo el Dorado!"

Clay looked at her, exhaustion leading to impatience as he wondered what could have provoked this new outburst.

Lorena had gone out to the stables first thing that morning, wanting to get an early start toward Paso del Norte. The day before when she had ridden with Clay, she had never made it to town to order her clothes. She had planned to do it first thing in the morning. When Lorena had asked for Rosinante, Jaime had stammered and stuttered until she finally dragged the truth from him: She was no longer allowed to ride without Clay's permission. Fury had filled her, and it was only with great restraint that she held her temper. She knew it wasn't Jaime's fault. That inconsiderate beast, Clay Wakefield, was to blame. She had turned on her heel and went to find the wretched man, her temper growing with every step. By the time she thought to look for him in the study her anger had almost taken hold of her, but instinctively Lorena knew she had to maintain some measure of control.

Before he had begun to work on Diego's books the night before, Clay had been thinking that he should rescind his order. He knew he had been unreasonable and angry when he gave the instruction that she needed his permission to do anything. Safety was his only true concern, and so as long as she had an escort there was no reason why she couldn't ride whenever she wanted to. But now his own fatigue and Lorena's manner did nothing but make him angrier. Clay ran a tired hand over the dark stubble that had yet to be shaved off. He had no time or desire to deal with a willful child.

Exhaustion spoke. "You are an insipid, willful child, not

to mention spoiled. Whenever something goes awry, you turn into a raving idiot. And *you* want to run Cielo el Dorado?" His words were not only harsh but unfair, but Clay was too tired to deal rationally with her.

"Insipid," she spat, all semblance of control lost. "Raving idiot! You, señor, are the raving idiot. An idiot who thinks he can come here and take over, order everyone around, and keep me, the true heir, virtually a prisoner in my own home! You, Clay Wakefield, will not get away with it. I will see you tossed out on your ear if it is the last thing I do." With a toss of her hair she turned to leave, unaware of the rage that burned just on the other side of the massive desk.

"You will do as *I* say, Lorena Cervantes, with no questions asked, or I will lock you in your room, where undisciplined children belong." His voice bellowed across the short space that divided them. "Then you will know the true meaning of being a prisoner in your own home."

"Oh, really! There's not a servant here who would keep me locked in my room."

"I wouldn't count on it."

Lorena turned back to tell him what she thought of his words, forcing herself not to be intimidated, but stopped when she confronted his glaring rage. Sensing it would be futile to cross him now, and afraid to find herself actually locked in her room, she turned with a harrumph and slammed out of the room. She might have lost the battle, she told herself, but not the war. She would find a way to get back what was rightfully hers.

Trapped within the thick adobe walls once again, Lorena found herself with few choices. Cooking was out, while sewing was not even a consideration. She had read until her eyes felt as though they would cross. She walked through the courtyard and, looking around, noticed for the first time how run-down the hacienda was. It wasn't noticeable unless you looked. The walls needed a coat of paint; some needed to be repaired. The flower beds were choked with weeds, and the walkways had holes in them.

Forgetting about Clay altogether, Lorena toured the entire hacienda, mentally making note of all that needed to be done. The disrepair confused her. How could her father have let things go like this? she wondered. Cielo el Dorado had always been a showplace, as the imported tiles and glass windows could attest. Her father had always been so proud of his ancestral home. How could he have let this happen? Lorena began to feel uneasy. She remembered the new clothes her father had always insisted she buy and the expensive school to which he had sent her. Surely he hadn't had money problems. If he had, wouldn't he have brought her home? Lorena's apprehension swelled, filling her with a sick feeling. Was it possible that he simply didn't want her around? In order to achieve that end, would he have spent money he did not have? Lorena's mind reeled, for while such an observation seemed absurd, she remembered all the times she had practically begged to come home. He had rarely been around while her mother was alive. Was it possible that after she died, he wanted to spend more time at home and didn't want his only child, a daughter, around? The hurt was almost unbearable. But when most would have succumbed to the overwhelming pain, Lorena remembered who she was, a Cervantes—whether a loved one or not—and she refused to wallow in self-pity over something that might or might not be true. Consciously pushing her thoughts aside, Lorena continued through the hacienda.

By the end of the day, all trace of her earlier torment gone, Lorena knew exactly what she was going to do. First thing in the morning, her home was going to get a much needed overhaul. She would use a few servants to help her. She couldn't, in her own mind, justify taking them away from their work just so she could ride, even if she could get the wretch's permission, but to clean and repair her home, she had no qualms at all. Feeling revitalized by her new sense of purpose, Lorena went to the bathhouse to wash away the day's grime.

Clay looked everywhere for Lorena but could not find her. He even went to the stables, expecting to find that she had disobeyed him and had managed to take her horse. He was only slightly pacified when he found Rosinante in her stall, quietly nibbling a few strands of hay. Giving up, assuming that she was probably hiding from him, he made his way to the bathhouse in hopes of soaking out the knots in his sore muscles. Hard manual labor never left him as exhausted and aching as desk work. And still he had not figured out Diego's affairs. Clay felt sure there were more papers; he just had not yet been able to find them. Not wanting to alarm anyone, Clay had not asked any questions outright.

Clay pushed through the door of the bathhouse just as Lorena was coming out. "There you are," Clay said, noticing the wet strands of hair that fell down her back leaving darkened imprints on the blue of her robe.

"Were you looking for me? Possibly you would like to tell me of some further limitations you would like to put on my freedom." Green eyes narrowed, daring him.

Oblivious to her anger, intent only on soaking in the warm water, Clay began to shut the door, leaving Lorena standing outside, as he said, "No, but I would like you to dress up this evening. My brother is on his way in, and I want you to meet him at dinner." He started to shut the door when a tiny hand slammed against it causing Clay to stop, not from the strength of it, but rather from the surprise.

"I'm afraid, señor," she said through clenched teeth, "that I am otherwise engaged and will not be at dinner this evening."

Clay pulled the door back open, and with one step, his formidable height towered over her. "So we are back to 'señor,' are we? I thought I made it clear that you are to call me Clay. Furthermore, you will join my brother and me for

dinner. And why is it," he fumed, "that you defy me at
every turn? Is it not possible, for once, just once, to
accommodate someone besides yourself?" he finished, his
full lips pressing into a hard line as he stared into her
upturned face.

His words pricked at her conscience, but she let the
unease fuel her anger. Suddenly Lorena was beyond caring
if he locked her away forever. "I will not take orders from
you!" Forgetting the robe she held closed she raised her
hand to slap his handsome cheek.

A long tan arm snaked out to catch hers. Momentarily
stunned at the sight of the sensual curves revealed by the
gaping robe, he let his dark eyes travel from her face. His
surprised expression was quickly replaced by an appreciative smile. "I suggest that you dress more appropriately
before you join us, little one." Without another word Clay
was gone, the solid wood door shut in her face, leaving a
mortified Lorena standing outside alone.

Later, just as Clay was coming out of the bathhouse, the
front gate was pulled open to welcome a lone horse and
rider. The horse was gray and seemed to match the
gleaming gray eyes of its rider. In one smooth motion the
man was down on the ground and tossing the reins to Jaime.
In the next second, he saw Clay. "Big brother," he shouted
across the complex as he took giant strides in Clay's
direction. His grip was as firm as Clay's when they shook
hands, and he almost matched his brother's six-foot-four-
inch frame as well. But while Clay was dark and serious,
the younger man's appearance was as light as his attitude.

"So, Ben, you appear to have made it without a scratch."

"Nary a one. In fact, I'm not altogether convinced that
the ride is as dangerous as you say," he said, teasing his
older brother in a way that seemed natural to him.

"I'd like to think you're right," Clay said, disregarding
his brother's disrespectful remark. "Where is the rest of the
caravan?" Clay asked when he saw the gate being closed.

"They went on into town 'cause they want to head out first thing in the morning. Nice guy, that Chapman fellow."

"Chapman is a good man. I was hoping to see him. Maybe I'll ride over to Paso del Norte."

Ben looked around at his surroundings. "So this is Cielo el Dorado. It's certainly different from Missouri, but I can't say it doesn't have a charm all its own." Mischievous gray eyes looked back at Clay. "When do I get to meet the future Mrs. Wakefield?"

"Tonight. However, the future Mrs. Wakefield does not know what the future holds for her yet. And I expect you to keep that little tidbit of information to yourself."

Ben laughed, ignoring his brother's autocratic demand. "And why doesn't she know, big brother? Is she such a shrew that you are still trying to get out of the mess you find yourself in?" Knowing Clay's past success with women and the slew of them in Missouri alone who would have loved to get their claws into him, Ben never considered the problem could be anything else except a shrewish bride-to-be.

"I'll let you judge for yourself tonight at dinner. Come on, let's get you settled in."

That evening the men waited in the *sala*, talking about the trail and home while they waited for Lorena to arrive. Every noise caused Clay to look toward the door, hoping it would be his future wife, and each time it wasn't, his agitation grew. The chances that she would disobey him and not come were high, he realized, but he continued to hope that she would arrive. He wanted her to be there.

All conversation stopped when Lorena finally entered the *sala*. In an ice-blue satin gown, she appeared to glide across the room, the most charming of smiles on her lips. As she was getting dressed that evening, Lorena had decided to prove Clay wrong in his assessment of her as a spoiled, willful child. She would carry herself with every bit of charm and grace her body had and take the breath away

from every man in the room. Like the sense of purpose her
new tasks at the hacienda provided her, the thought of
making Clay Wakefield eat his words proved immensely
satisfying as well.

Lorena came to stand before the men. "I hope I have not
kept you too long. I am afraid I was not given much
notice." She finished with a mocking glance at Clay.

Despite himself, Clay smiled. He had been afraid that if
she came, Lorena would descend upon them in a heated
wrath, lashing all of them with her sharp tongue. For some
reason, he wanted his younger brother to like this woman-
child who was to be his bride, even if he wasn't going to
spend much time with her, he added. But obviously he had
worried for naught, for there she stood, the picture of grace
and loveliness. She was more beautiful than he had thought
possible. Red hair curled down her slim back, the ice-blue
gown turned her green eyes aqua, and her luscious red lips
curled up in a tempting smile. A sense of pride surged
through him as he looked upon her.

Ben stepped forward and took Lorena's hand. "Ma'am,
I'm sure the other gentlemen would agree when I say we
would have waited an eternity to dine with one as beautiful
as you. May I introduce myself? I'm afraid my big brother
has neglected his duties. I'm Ben Wakefield," he finished
and pressed a light kiss on the back of her hand.

"I'm Lorena Cervantes and it is a pleasure to meet you,
Ben Wakefield." She offered a brilliant smile, the flash of
her white teeth and the sparkle of her green eyes mesmerizing all who stood about. She was surprised that this man
was related to Clay, and even more so to find that he was a
brother, for they were as different as night and day. He was
tall, nearly as tall as Clay, but had golden hair that curled
about his head like a Roman soldier's. Brilliant gray eyes
bespoke friendliness and caring, openness and giving.
Lorena knew instantly that they would be friends.

Clay glowered at Ben, not liking the looks that passed
between Lorena and his brother. Ben had just met her, and

already she smiled and cooed as if they knew each other well. In all the time he had known her, she had turned her charm on him only twice, once when she didn't know who he was and again when they had ridden together, both instances only lasting a short time. With more force than necessary, Clay turned to Lorena and said, "If you have finished flirting, I believe dinner is ready."

Lorena burned at his words. How could any one person be so mean and hateful? She turned a haughty glare in Clay's direction. "It wouldn't hurt if you took note of your brother's manners. It's good to know that at least one member of your family has some." Though she inwardly seethed, her outward appearance was serene as she took Ben's proffered arm.

As it turned out, the company was excellent as was the meal. Lorena had promised herself that she would be happy and gay, despite Clay Wakefield. But much to her chagrin, she hadn't had to try at all, for Clay proved to be a grand host. Ben filled the evening with tales of childish exploits, while Bill provided exciting stories of their days on the trail. Even shy Tom contributed to the conversation with a story of his own.

Clay laughed with them all and graciously made sure that everyone was included. Lorena found herself trying to control her laughter until, finally, giving up, she burst out in shouts of gaiety.

"I don't believe you," she said in response to one of Ben's stories, sending a teasing smile toward Clay. "I can't imagine Clay doing anything he's not supposed to do."

"It sounds to me as if my brother has pulled the wool over your eyes. Don't let him fool you. Clay has been as wild and crazy as the next." He winked at Lorena and added, "Probably wilder than the next. What has he done to make you think he's such a paragon of virtue?"

"I didn't say he was a paragon, just that from the way he talks, a person would get the impression that he has never

done anything wrong." Lorena turned a superior smile on
Clay.

"Sounds to me as if my big brother has been on the
warpath."

Clay interrupted. "You might ask her what she has
done," he said with an amused smile over his glass of wine.

Ben looked back at Lorena who sat somewhat sheepishly
in her chair.

"I haven't done a thing!" She laughed indignantly.

Bill and Clay, and even Tom, laughed all at once.

"Nothing?" Ben persisted.

"Well, I may have pulled a tiny little knife on him, and
then maybe a rifle after that, but how was I supposed to
know who he was? For all I knew, he was some desperado
come to steal my hacienda." Lorena looked through lowered lashes at Clay to find her words had hit home.

"Not to mention your virtue," an amused Ben added.

"Not to mention," Clay agreed caustically.

Ben watched the exchange between Lorena and Clay and
was amazed to realize that Lorena was not all that crazy
about his older brother. But underneath the facade of
dislike, Ben sensed an attraction that Lorena Cervantes was
not able, or maybe not ready, to admit. Maybe, he conceded, she didn't even realize what she felt for Clay. Ben
could almost feel sparks flying between the two and
wondered how long it would take before they succumbed to
the attraction. As it stood, it appeared that Lorena, the
woman Clay wanted nothing to do with, was giving his big
brother a run for his money. What a treat, he mused, his big
brother in a hot spot he didn't seem to know how to handle.
His threats and demands had gotten him nowhere, and he
probably had never had to cajole a person into doing
something in his life. Ben looked forward to the battle of
this courtship. And he wasn't sure who would win. Suddenly he wasn't in such a big hurry to get back to Missouri.
Things seemed to be a lot more interesting down in the
Southwest.

"Was it my imagination or did I see a vineyard when I rode in?" Ben asked.

"Yes," Lorena glowed, turning her attention away from Clay. "Cielo el Dorado boasts the finest wines between Santa Fe and Mexico City."

"You make wine in the middle of the desert?" Ben asked incredulously. "I thought wine came from Europe."

Lorena laughed. "Well, it does, but we make it here, too. In fact, the Cervantes family has been growing the wine grape since 1660 when the first Cervantes, Diego Lorenzo Cervantes, came to this land."

"No kidding." Ben was truly amazed. "How did he end up here?"

"Well, as my father told it, Diego Lorenzo came with Fray Garcia de San Francisco when the padre came to establish the mission. It was believed that the Manso Indians were friendly and wanted to be converted to Christianity. Diego Lorenzo was asked to settle at the Pass to the North."

"Hence the name Paso del Norte?" Bill asked, his interest piqued.

"Yes, Paso del Norte, Pass of the North. For coming, Diego Lorenzo was awarded the status of hidalgo and given servants, Indian slaves, and a wealthy Spanish bride. Every Cervantes male thereafter wed a bride brought over from Spain."

"What about the daughters?" Ben asked with a sly glance at Clay.

"They were sent to Spain to marry Spaniards." Lorena looked away. "It seems so unfair that the women had to leave their home." Then, looking back to Ben, she added, "That is another reason I am not getting married. I refuse to leave my home."

Ben smiled. "I take it there are other reasons as well?"

Clay's scowl deepened.

Lorena fidgeted, not wanting to answer.

Bill Hawkins saw her discomfort and Clay's rising anger

and decided to head off a scene. "Finish telling us about the grapes."

Lorena sent Bill a grateful smile. "Well, the padre brought the grapevines so he could make communion wine for the Indians he came to convert. The Cervantes family started planting the vines along with Fray Garcia, but we kept them thriving long after the mission let theirs go. I think wine gets into your blood."

All four of the men started to laugh. "Yes, Lorena," Ben offered, "wine definitely gets into your blood."

Realizing her unintentional joke, Lorena joined the laughter. "You are all terrible."

"So what do you all do after dinner around here?" Ben asked as he placed his napkin on the table and pushed back his chair.

When no one replied, Tom offered, "There's usually a good card game going over in the men's quarters."

Lorena's eyes lit up. "I would love to play a game. Let's go over."

She pushed back her chair, only to have Clay place a restraining hand on her arm. The touch sent her heart into a mad pace and kicked her defenses into action.

"The men's bunkhouse is no place for a lady," Clay's deep voice penetrated, sending shivers of feeling down her spine. Lorena looked at her tormentor. Feeling as though she would soon be lost to her senses, she started to protest.

When Ben saw the look on her face, as well as the look on Clay's face, he said, "Actually, I'd love to have a good cigar and another glass of that great wine of yours and I'd be just as happy as a possum. Maybe even sit out under the stars. How about it?" Lorena grudgingly agreed, not wanting to cause a stir in front of this nice man. Why couldn't her father have sent Ben to take care of the hacienda instead of the monster Clay? But even as the thought crossed her mind, Lorena was becoming aware of the strong attraction to the very man she assured herself she hated.

After a short stay out in the courtyard, Ben, Bill, and Tom excused themselves, pleading fatigue, leaving Clay alone with Lorena. Once the three receding backs had disappeared around the corner, Lorena said, "Tired, my foot. Those men are going to play cards."

Clay laughed. "I suspect you're right."

They sat quietly together for a moment, neither knowing what to say, but not wanting the moment to end. Clay's presence, combined with the moon and stars overhead, proved overwhelming for Lorena. As much as she tried to concentrate on the nicer brother or other things, her mind kept drifting to the tall, dark, and handsome man who sat next to her.

"It's getting late. I'd best be getting in."

Lorena started to get up, but Clay's large hand gently grasped her arm.

"Don't go," he said almost harshly, but when he realized that it had come out like an order, he added, "please."

Lorena wavered. Seeing her indecision, Clay didn't give her another second to think. Carefully he set down his empty glass and, with the arm he still held in his grasp, pulled her close. Slowly he leaned over and placed a gentle kiss on her lips. Moving back no more than an inch, Clay whispered, "I've wanted to do that all evening."

Lorena felt the pressure of his lips, then his whispered breath, which sent shivers through her body. Without thinking, she closed her eyes as overwhelming sensations flooded her. "Why did you want to do that all night?"

Not bothering to answer, Clay kissed her again, this time longer, coaxing, teasing, until his lips trailed down her cheek onto her neck. "You were lovely at dinner."

A tiny moan escaped Lorena's lips. The unmanageable combination of wine, kind words, and his searing kiss made her feel wonderful, and she wanted nothing more than to explore the heady feeling.

The moan sent Clay into a whirl of mounting passion. He

pulled her closer, his hand moving slowly toward her breast when a shout came from the distance.

"Hey, Clay, how 'bout a little poker?" It was Ben's voice that drew nearer to the couple on the bench.

"Damn," Clay cursed into Lorena's neck as she furtively pushed away.

Just as Ben came up to them, Lorena jumped up guiltily. "It's late. If you'll excuse me, I think I'll go to my room." Without waiting for a response, she hurried off, leaving the two men to stare after her.

Once Lorena was gone, Clay slowly turned his hard gaze on his younger brother. "Well, baby brother," he said in an unrelenting tone, "you better have a good excuse for interrupting."

The tone appeared to have been wasted on Ben, who only laughed as he sat down next to Clay. "I thought I'd save Lorena's virtue."

"It wasn't in any danger."

"You could have fooled me," Ben said with a knowing smile.

Then Clay relaxed, knowing that if the truth were told, he had wanted nothing more than to sweep Lorena up into his arms and take her to his bed. To have done so would have been disastrous, disrespectful not only of Diego but of Lorena as well. The thought unsettled him. When had he become so chivalrous?

The two brothers sat in companionable silence for a time before either of them spoke. All that could be heard was the sound of crickets calling their mates and every once in a while a loud hoot from the other side of the hacienda where the men were playing poker.

Ben broke the silence. "She's certainly no shrew."

Clay chuckled. "No, not in looks."

"Are you implying that that sweet little thing I ate dinner with this evening has a shrewish disposition?" Ben asked in disbelief.

"Something like that." Clay gazed in the direction Lorena had disappeared.

"If I was a bettin' man, I'd say that you expected to have some willing female fall into your lap, and instead you found someone who isn't quite crazy about you being here. Maybe, big brother, the shrewish temperament is divided around here."

Ignoring the insult, Clay said with an amused grin, "If you're not a betting man, then why did you look so anxious to play poker?"

Ben laughed. "I guess you don't want to talk about it anymore, so I'll leave it alone . . . for now. I might as well turn to a life of vice. You want to join me?"

"No, you go on ahead. I have some paperwork to do." Clay picked up his empty glass and made his way to the kitchen. A single candle burned in the empty room. All the dishes had been washed, dried, and put away, leaving the servants free for the remainder of the night. Clay set his glass on the wooden counter, thinking how very different this was from his home in Missouri, but where it had seemed so foreign and rustic before, it now felt more and more like home. The dry, clean air, the surroundings that had once been harsh and barren, now seemed beautiful in their starkness. The jagged peaks of rocky mountains stood in sharp contrast to the lush folds of the river valley that lay at their base. And fiery hair blazed in contrast to creamy white skin and green eyes. Yes, Cielo el Dorado was growing less foreign all the time.

After licking his thumb and forefinger, Clay pinched out the yellow candle flame and left the room.

Safe in her bedroom, Lorena undressed slowly. Her mood vacillated between anger at Clay and a giddy feeling she was not comfortable with, which only led to anger once again. What was wrong with her? How could one man cause her so much trouble? How could one man cause so much confusion? He had to be doing it on purpose, she reasoned. He wanted Cielo el Dorado, and when he realized she was not a simpering fool, he thought he'd better start charming her. Lorena fumed. Forcing herself to forget Clay, she turned her attention to her projects for the next day. As she brushed her hair, the excitement began to build and she thought of the things she was going to do. She was going to turn the place upside down and give Cielo el Dorado a much needed cleaning.

Lately, Dalia had been helping Lorena get ready for bed, brushing her hair, turning down the covers, and fluffing her pillows. Lorena suspected that Dalia was unsure if she was all right. Lorena hated to have her loved ones worry about her. But tonight she had not called Dalia, wanting instead to be alone with her conflicting emotions, not wanting to hear Dalia's well-meaning but unwanted probing questions. Questions that Lorena asked herself, but had no idea how to answer.

How could she be drawn to a man who was trying to steal everything from her? A man who treated her like a child—most of the time. With determination, she thrust thoughts of him away again, but as she lay in bed, her mind drifted back to black hair and black eyes, large hands that caressed her, strong arms that held her, bold lips that seared a path across her neck . . .

7

❦

IT WAS STILL DARK WHEN LORENA WOKE THE
following morning. Throwing back the covers, she leaped
out of bed, certain of a glorious day.

After dressing, she stepped out into the hallway, and for
the first time since Clay Wakefield had arrived, she did not
hesitate as she made her way toward the kitchen. Excitement welled up inside her, leaving no room for any other
emotions.

"Good morning," she chimed as she entered the already
warm kitchen, where Dalia and Luz were busy at work.

Dalia turned from the counter where she was preparing
the day's bread and tortillas. "What are you doing?" she
asked in exasperation, looking up and down Lorena's
rag-clad body.

Lorena twirled around to show off her attire, green eyes
twinkling with mischief. "You thought all those dresses
hanging in the armoire were the latest fashions, but you
were wrong! This is the latest fashion!" Luz began to laugh,
and finally Dalia grudgingly smiled. "I knew there was a
smile lurking under there somewhere," Lorena teased.

"*Chica*, what do you have on?" Dalia demanded.

"Why, it's the latest Lorena Cervantes design, created for
her new project!"

"Project?" Dalia asked in surprise, fearful of another confrontation with the Americano who always seemed to lurk around every corner. Even if Señor Wakefield did not get upset about whatever her project was, he was sure to be furious about what Lorena was wearing. Dalia grimaced at the old piece of cloth Lorena had tied around her hair. Her blouse was even older, if possible, and she wore a riding skirt that was split to make a type of pants. The Americano was sure to get angry.

"Yes, Dalia, the hacienda is a mess." Lorena looked lovingly at Dalia. "I know how hard you work to keep this place up, and I appreciate that," she said, not wanting to offend the dear woman, "but over the years it appears that many things have been neglected. And that, Dalia Gonzalez, is my new project! Getting this place back in order."

"You are right, Lorena. It has been many years since your father put in the time or money necessary to make repairs. Both Pedro and I did what we could, but we could not seem to keep up with the work."

"Dalia, I know how hard you work." Lorena was distressed to think that she could have hurt the woman's feelings.

Dalia squeezed Lorena's hand. "You are such a kind child. Do not worry about my feelings; they are not hurt. This old place needs work and I know it." The older woman turned back to the bread, not wanting Lorena to see the tears that glistened in her eyes. Truly she was not hurt, but she felt sad because the wonderful child who stood there with excitement in her eyes had been left alone in the world, first by her mother and then by her father, who had left her in the care of a heartless stranger. Was Lorena destined to work like a servant for the rest of her life? Then Dalia thought of Ramón. Yes, it was becoming clearer that he was indeed the answer.

Sensing Dalia's distress, Lorena came up behind her and hugged her tight. "I love you, Dalia, and I'm going to be just fine, don't you worry. Now, you make lots of tortillas and a big pot of beans, because by the end of today I'll be starving." Lorena snatched up a slice of bread and raced out the door before she started crying, too.

Lorena stood in the courtyard surveying her surroundings. The night before, she had decided to do all the rooms in the main house first, one at a time. Next would come the courtyard, after which she would go around to the other side of the hacienda and work her wonders there. So intent was she on her thoughts that she did not notice Clay as he stood in the darkened recesses of the porch.

"What's she up to now?" he grumbled to himself, taking notice of her attire. Just as he was about to come out and confront her, Lorena called to some servants who were entering the main courtyard.

"Juan, I need your help," she called.

Clay's anger started to build just as Ben came out of the house to stand behind him.

"Well," Ben said, noticing his brother's clenched jaw, "I see you're off to a wonderful start this morning." Ben followed Clay's gaze. "Ah, so the little miss has stirred you up again." Ben shook his head. "What has she done now?"

"It would appear that she is trying once again to enlist the aid of servants so she can disobey me."

"Disobey?" Ben asked with a knowing smile as he looked from Clay to Lorena, then to the man who stood next to her, politely listening to what she was saying.

"*Sí*, señorita, what can I do for you?" Juan asked.

"Juan, today I am going to start to put the hacienda in order."

Juan and Lorena looked around them. The cracks and weeds were more prevalent when one looked for them.

"I'd like you to get two very strong men to help me move furniture around so the rooms can be cleaned and painted. Some of the furniture needs to be repaired, so you'll probably need tools. We'll also need to make up paint. Do we have any gypsum and dyes or do I need to send a man into town to get some?"

Both brothers overheard the conversation, and after a few moments Ben looked at Clay and in mock disgust said, "Can you believe the little baggage?" With that the younger brother left, shaking his head in wonder at a little slip of a girl who was going to fix the hacienda and at his dark, brooding brother who was being so irrational.

Clay's anger evaporated, though he tried his best to hold on to it, only to have it replaced with disbelief. The frivolous girl was taking charge in an attempt to fix up her home. But "attempt," he reasoned, was the key word. He had noticed the state of disrepair and knew eventually he would have to get to it. But for now he'd let her make a big mess of things; then he'd step in and set things right.

As Clay made his way to the other side of the courtyard without being noticed, a smile curled on his face. At least she wouldn't try to sneak off for a while.

Lorena started in the chapel and planned to work her way around the main courtyard. She was in the chapel with three other women, vigorously sweeping and scrubbing, when Juan arrived with two other men.

"We had everything you asked for, señorita. Much of it is old, but it will do," Juan said as he came through the door carrying the items needed to make paint.

"*Gracias*, Juan, if you'll just set everything down outside. We can get it as we need it. Now let us carry the furniture out into the courtyard so we can clean and repair the chapel."

The small group became a whirlwind of activity, some carrying furniture, some mixing paint, the rest left behind in the chapel, cleaning furiously. Soon the room was empty except for the large altar. Then the men scraped and smoothed the walls, using mud mixed with straw to fill in cracks and holes. Fortunately, in the hot desert clime, the air was dry, so the wall would be ready to paint before long.

The women scrubbed the tile floors, cleaned the windows, and beat the hand-woven rugs relentlessly, ridding them of years of accumulated sand and grime. Not a corner or crevice went unattended.

From the chapel they worked their way to the *sala*, with its massive furniture, and moved on to the kitchen, where they cleaned out every cabinet and storeroom. Then it was time for the bedrooms—first, the priest's room, right off the chapel, which was used by the padre when he came over from the mission; then Dalia and Pedro's room, followed by a guest room that had been Lorena's parents' when her mother was alive. The sight of that room brought a surge of emotion, but Lorena closed her mind to memories and thought only of the work at hand.

Next, they cleaned Lorena's room, the library, and, finally, the room Clay was using. Lorena worked frantically in his room, hurrying to get it over with, as every time she turned around, some item reminded her of the man.

It took them two days to empty and clean all the rooms in the main courtyard, rarely stopping to grab a bite to eat. Normally, after lunch the Mexican people used the time for a siesta, but Lorena's excitement persuaded the workers to forego their afternoon nap. On the third day, the small crew began repainting the walls.

Most adobe walls were left their original brown color, but after learning how to make colors from the Indians, the Cervantes family had painted their drab walls with paints made of natural elements from the earth—white in the kitchen and bedrooms, red on the lower half of the wall and white on the upper half in the chapel, and a deep, rich red in the sala and dining room. All workrooms and servants' quarters were left their original color.

They finished painting just as the sun went down. Everyone was exhausted. All Lorena wanted to do was soak in a hot tub before crawling into her soft bed and sleeping until morning. She had not realized how much work her project entailed, and how much more they still had to do. She groaned at the thought. But the sight of the rooms they had finished encouraged her. The gleaming walls and the

smell of fresh paint were tangible evidence that she was
doing something, accomplishing something—that she was
not a worthless, simpering female. But her excitement
was diluted by her total exhaustion, so when she said to the
others, "Tomorrow we will do the outside," they could
barely contain their groans. Knowing how tired she was,
Lorena could hardly blame them. "I know!" she exclaimed,
suddenly having an idea. "As soon as we finish, we will
have a fiesta to celebrate! How does that sound?" This time
her enthusiasm showed through the fatigue, as she was truly
excited about having a party.

Juan was the first to show his unqualified support. "*Sí*, it
has been a long time since Cielo el Dorado has seen a party.
Tomorrow, we start again. Come, men, let us go eat."

Lorena thanked everyone and bade them all good night.
She went to her room, which smelled of fresh gesso paint
and got clean clothes before making her way to the
bathhouse, having forgotten all about Clay Wakefield.

Once at the bathhouse, Lorena found that a small fire had
already been lit and warm water filled the tub. Slowly she
peeled off the old clothes, dust and cobwebs falling off as
they were disturbed. Carefully she stepped into the water,
the heat stinging her skin, which had been cut and scraped
during the days of work. But the slight sting was negligible
compared to the feeling of luxurious warmth that enfolded
her body. Sinking down until the water lapped at her chin,
Lorena closed her eyes and relaxed.

She must have fallen asleep, for when she became aware
of the water again, it was lukewarm, almost cool, sending
a chill up her spine. Quickly she grabbed the soap and
scrubbed vigorously, suddenly as hungry as she was cold. A
good hot meal and then bed. Ah, life's simple pleasures.

The four men sat at the massive table in the *sala*, one
glaringly empty chair among them. Clay sat silently, not
tasting anything he put in his mouth. How could he chastise
her for not being at dinner when she had been working so

hard? But it irked him nonetheless that she wasn't there. He had waited patiently for her to give up. He had waited in vain. When Clay analyzed his thoughts, he did not understand why he wanted her to fail or why he felt so uncomfortable with this new Lorena who had shown herself. It wasn't like him to be so childish.

Ben interrupted his thoughts. "Seems our little lady has worn herself out. I don't think I've ever seen anyone work so hard." There was sincere respect if not a little amazement in Ben's voice. "If she keeps going, she'll have this whole hacienda shipshape in no time. Yes, sir, no time at all."

"The key word is '*if*', Ben. *If* she can keep it up."

"Sounds to me as if you'd like it if she couldn't keep it up." Ben sent an amused smile at his brother. "It also sounds to me as if you're looking for reasons not to like her."

Clay's scowl quieted his younger brother. Ben recognized the clenched jaw as a sign that he was treading on thin ice. So he merely smiled and said, "Come on, Bill, let's go find us some fun. We certainly won't find it here." Bill and Ben laughed and joked as they left the *sala* while Tom followed quietly behind, leaving Clay alone.

He stared at the flickering flames of the tallow candles that lit the room. Ben's remark had indeed struck a nerve. He didn't understand why he wanted Lorena to fail at what she was doing. He knew he should be more than pleased with her work. He felt childish for his thoughts. He was acting like a schoolboy. In fact, since he had met Lorena Cervantes, he was acting as he had never acted before.

Thinking all the men had left, Luz and Dalia came into the dining room from the kitchen to clear the table, interrupting Clay's thoughts.

"Oh!" A startled Luz jumped back at the sight of the formidable-looking man, bumping into Dalia.

"What is wrong with you?" Dalia asked, impatient with the maid's clumsiness.

"I believe I startled the poor girl, Dalia."

"Oh, Señor Wakefield, I did not know you were still here. Come, Luz, we will return later."

"No, that's not necessary. I was just about to get up anyway."

Dalia had been avoiding Clay as best as she could all evening, afraid he would insist that she summon Lorena to dinner. She held her breath as he pushed his chair back and left the room. Dalia sighed with relief when he was gone.

Day four of the project came all too quickly for Lorena. It was pitch black outside. Lorena's body ached, and she yearned to roll over and go back to sleep. But with great determination she pulled herself out of bed so she could dress in the old rags once again. Muscles groaned as she picked her hairbrush up, so instead of brushing out her hair, she simply wrapped her thick sleeping braid around her head and covered it all with the old scarf she had worn the day before.

She picked up the empty bowl from her nightstand with a smile. She hardly remembered the caldillo she had eaten before falling asleep.

The kitchen was empty. With strained movements, Lorena found a loaf of bread in the pantry and cut a thick slice, which she ate plain while she made a pot of coffee. When it was ready, she poured a steaming mug, then cut another slice of bread and sat down at the oak table. Plain bread had never tasted so good.

Lorena savored every bite. It was so good to feel productive and alive. Thinking of the work they had accomplished, Lorena imagined each room that now sparkled with cleanliness, no longer shabby and in a state of disrepair. Today they would finish, she hoped, or at least get close. Before long, all of Cielo el Dorado would stand proud.

"Good morning."

Clay stood in the doorway. How could he be so handsome? she wondered. "Good morning," Lorena answered before returning to her meal.

"You're up early this morning." Clay walked to the stove and poured a cup of coffee, then sat across from her. He saw that even in rags she was beautiful—and that made him mad. So instead of praising her for the work she had done—as he had planned to do after lying awake for hours cursing himself for acting so childish—he said nothing.

"I guess," she said noncommittally, wishing he would remark on the improvements she had made. Surely he had noticed them; he had slept in a room smelling of fresh gesso paint. But he merely sipped on his coffee, looking at her in a way that made her feel uneasy. "Excuse me," she said as she got up to leave, her bread and coffee no longer tasting so good.

He wanted to say something to make her stay, but for some reason, all he could manage was "Have a good day."

If Lorena was disappointed, she did not show it. Instead, she concentrated on the man's ingratitude, holding tears of frustration at bay. He was infuriating, she fumed, slamming the kitchen door. "Have a good day!" The wretch! She would show him a good day.

As Lorena left the kitchen she saw Juan and the other men coming into the courtyard armed with picks and shovels and various tools.

"*Buenos días, señorita.*"

"Good morning."

A few minutes later the women joined them, and the work began. They weeded gardens and trimmed those bushes that did not need to be pulled out altogether. Grass that had grown tall in corners and along the walls was cut to form a perfect carpet of green over those parts of the courtyard that weren't paved with adobe brick or planted with trees and flowers. They smoothed paths and reset stones, making easily traversed walkways for everyone at Cielo el Dorado.

The blazing sun grew hotter overhead, sending each

worker deeper into thoughts of the fiesta that would follow
their labor. By the end of the day they had managed to do
the entire courtyard. Lorena was surprised to find that the
outside walls had already been repaired, and when she
asked Juan about it, he said that Señor Wakefield had had
them fixed earlier. Lorena bristled, though she wasn't sure
why, since that was one less thing she had to do.

Lorena found that Clay Wakefield had been busy on the
working side of the hacienda as well, at least in every area
that had some machinery or some significance in the
running of Cielo el Dorado. The mill had been cleaned and
was working perfectly, as were the blacksmith shop, the
wine-making equipment, and the stables. When Lorena
turned her gaze on Juan once again, he only shrugged.

The project was completed at the end of the fifth day.
Lorena was exhausted but pleased with the work they had
done. She forced herself not to think about the fact that Clay
had not said one word about the transformation.

Lorena made her way to the bathhouse, wanting nothing
more than a warm bath and a hearty meal. She soaked in the
tub until the water became tepid, then scrubbed until her
skin was pink and her scalp tingled. A pot of warm rinse
water waited by the fire.

She finished her bath, then went out into the night,
bundled in a big robe, and walked across the courtyard
relishing the feeling of cool grass between her toes, her
stomach grumbling in anticipation of the large meal that
would be immediately followed by her soft bed.

Dinner that night was much the same as it had been the
last few nights. The four men didn't speak much, all aware
of the empty chair that sat among them, and aware of Clay's
anger.

To break the uneasy silence, Bill began to relay the news
of the day. "We've got just about everything fixed that
needed fixin'. I suspect we'll be able to head on out of here

in the next couple of days." Bill was eager to get back to Missouri. "That fiesta that everyone is talking about will be a great way to tie things up before we leave. The men will love it."

Clay's countenance darkened, and the fork in his hand stilled. "What fiesta is that, Bill?"

Bill looked from Clay to Ben, then back to Clay. "Uh, nothing, probably just been hearing things." Bill was surprised to realize Clay didn't know about the party, and he sure didn't want to be the one to tell him about it.

"Bill," Clay said impatiently, "what have you heard?"

Knowing he had no choice, Bill told him. "Well, there's going to be a grand party to celebrate all the hard work."

"And who is planning this affair?" Clay asked, though he was sure he already knew the answer.

"I think Lorena is."

Ben interjected, "You have to admit, Clay, that it's a great idea. It'll raise the morale after everyone has been working so hard."

Clay sent his younger brother a scowl as he pushed back his chair and left the room in search of the instigator.

Lorena sat in front of the mirror in her bedroom, tiredly brushing out long strands of red hair. As soon as it was dry, she was going to fall straight into bed. Dalia had brought her a steaming bowl of beans mixed with tomatoes and onions, which she had scooped up with soft corn tortillas. She could barely keep her eyes open when the door burst open to reveal the formidable height of Clay Wakefield.

The brush dropped from her hand, but her surprise quickly turned to anger, an intense anger that she no longer felt compelled to control. The anger had grown a little for every day he had not said a word about the work they had accomplished—and for that matter, she added, every day since the arrogant, self-assured man had come into her life at the swimming hole, leaving her without a single moment's peace of mind. This man had ruined her life, coming to her home, taking over, bossing her around without a thought for her wishes or feelings, calling her a nuisance and a helpless child. And then when she had worked so hard to put the place in order, proving as much to herself as to him that she wasn't helpless and that she could indeed make a valuable contribution to her home, the monster hadn't even noticed. Lorena wondered why she cared. Why had she worked for five days, hoping for a kind word from the wretched man, when it should have been enough to have done it for herself and for the Cervantes tradition? Why had he come here and disrupted her life?

"You haven't been coming to dinner," he said with one shoulder resting against the door frame.

"Get out," she yelled, not even trying to appear calm.

For a moment Clay was put off. He had expected calm indifference or even a childish tantrum, but he had not expected the wild look that filled her eyes. He felt a moment's regret wondering if he had been wrong to take out his anger on the poor girl, who was innocent. Was he blaming Diego's daughter for her father's actions? The idea amazed him and left him more than a little uncomfortable.

Lost in his thoughts, he didn't see her pick up the brush from the floor, and he jumped when it flew in his direction, barely missing his left temple.

"You spoiled little brat," he said through clenched teeth, forgetting his earlier doubts. "You could have hit me."

Clay managed to sidestep a glass bottle before it shattered against the wall behind him.

"I was trying to hit you, you beast." She was on the verge of tears but held them back with anger.

"Lorena! Put that down." This time he ducked then charged at her, only to come up empty-handed. Lorena had leaped to the other side of the bed.

"You defy me at every turn." His voice was a growl. "You will learn to obey!"

"Never! Never will I obey you or anyone. I'm not an animal who learns tricks and obeys its master's every command."

"You don't obey any command." Clay pulled the door shut and moved steadily closer to the bed, never taking his eyes off his prey. "I tell you to wear skirts—you wear some hideous thing split up the middle. I tell you to come to dinner—you eat in your room. I tell you I want to talk—you tell me to get out."

"Talk! All you ever do is criticize me, berate me, and call me names. You are an inconsiderate boor, and I loathe the day you came into my life." Lorena looked toward the door, hoping she could get there before he did.

Anticipating her move, he intercepted her easily, grabbing her delicate wrist, pulling her into his hard body. The impact knocked the breath out of her. Finally, great gasps of air came flooding back into her lungs, wrenching a sob from her anger-racked body.

Her slender form slumped against him as she cried into his shirt. Gently he cradled her in his arms as he sat down on the edge of her bed. He stroked her hair and whispered gentle endearments while she cried out her anger. He rocked and cooed in a manner he didn't know he possessed. As her tears began to subside, Clay could almost see her thoughts begin to churn again.

"You're a beast, you know," she said into his neck. Lorena could feel his neck muscles tighten, and she sensed that he smiled.

"Yes, I know, little one," he said into her hair.

"A horrible monster," she added.

"Yes, a horrible monster."

"How could you?" she asked plaintively.

"How could I what?" he asked, puzzled.

"How could you be such a beast?"

Clay laughed at her. "It couldn't be that I was provoked at times, could it?"

Red-brimmed eyes looked up at him, accompanied by a teasing smile that nearly took his breath away.

"You are so beautiful, little one." Without thinking, Clay bent his head to taste the sweet redness of her lips. He drew

back slightly to look at her, and instead of setting her down
and leaving, as he knew he should, he succumbed to the
beckoning pleasure and captured her lush lips in a sweet
kiss.

Anger and reason were forgotten as Lorena's fingers
found their way into the thick waves of his dark hair,
savoring the texture and feel of the silken mass. Her senses
reeled when his tongue demanded entry to the hidden
recesses of her mouth to explore and taste, leaving her
shaken with desire.

"You are so sweet, my Lorena."

He could not get enough of her, could not get her close
enough. He turned to lay her on the bed and mold his hard,
lean body to hers.

Lorena was flush with desire, awash in waves of a new
and overwhelming need. With trembling limbs, she clung to
him, lost in the swirl of mounting desire.

Feeling her tremble, Clay groaned as his lips left hers to
trail down her neck, his hands expertly pulling off her robe.
The only thing that separated Lorena's body from his
probing hand was the thin cotton of her nightgown. He
could feel each curve and knew if he did not relieve her of
the gown he would go mad with wanting. Carefully, using
every ounce of restraint he possessed, he undid the tiny
buttons down the front of her nightgown, his warm lips
never leaving her, constantly kissing, teasing.

Cool air hit Lorena as he pushed her nightgown aside, but
when she tried to protest, her senses turned to fire as Clay
gently pressed his lips to one firm breast, sending a jolt of
wild sensation coursing through her.

He licked one nipple and then the other until Lorena was
awash with a pulsating sensation, leaving her clinging
desperately to his strong form. She could feel the hardness
of his body as he pressed into her, slowly, again and again,
but firmly, causing her to want, but for what she was
unsure. When his hand began a slow, hypnotic path lower,
leaving her breast, Lorena feebly protested.

"Clay, no."

But he only drew her closer, wrapping her in his arms, devouring her with a mindless kiss, probing with his tongue until he found hers. He pulled her lithe body toward him, and then his hand continued its slow downward path along her body with his mouth soon to follow. He wanted her more than he had ever wanted a woman before. He wanted her with every inch of his body. And he felt a flicker of something else. Yes, he wanted her body, but there was more, something he was not quite sure of, and not quite sure he wanted to look at too closely. In that moment, that moment of partial recognition, he knew that he wanted her but not this way, a stolen moment that both would later regret. So in that instant Clay pulled back and looked down into Lorena's questioning eyes and felt a moment of regret.

Reality slowly crept in, and she was amazed at where she was—in bed with a man! A man she detested! Cool air wafted over her skin. Embarrassment and outrage engulfed her. "Get off me," she demanded through clenched teeth.

He gave no response other than to continue to caress her body with his black eyes. Lorena, not knowing what to do, lay perfectly still, commanding her body not to respond to the flames of heat that threatened to consume her, his mere look sending shivers of desire coursing through her.

"I will say it one more time. Get off me." She spit each word at him.

It was a few seconds before his mind cleared enough for him to understand what she was saying. "You're right. If I don't stop now I'll have to finish what I started. And as much as I want you, sweet Lorena, this is not the time." Clay looked deep into her eyes conveying a message she did not understand; then he bent down and placed a kiss on her forehead. "Sleep well, little one." He got up and left the room, leaving Lorena to stare after him, confused and afraid of what he meant when he said it was not the time. Was this something new she would have to contend with in addition to his cruel and mocking words? Not having the energy to

think clearly, Lorena rolled over, vowing to think about it
the next day.

Clay walked out into the night. The black sky was
scattered with flickering white lights, the moon shining
silver in its crescent shape. The servants had gone to the
other side of the hacienda, and he knew Bill and Tom were
there as well. He could see silhouettes of the guards as they
walked back and forth over the rooftops. Clay climbed the
wooden ladder to the roof.

"*Buenas noches,* señor," a guard greeted.

"*Buenas noches,* Miguel." Clay had learned Spanish
over the years he had spent on the trail and loved the
romantic sound of the language.

He found a seat on the highest level that looked out over
the great expanse of land. Looking to the south he could see
a sprinkling of light from the fires of other settlements on
the north bank. A black ribbon of darkness divided those
lights from the larger glow of Paso del Norte on the south
bank. When the breeze was just right he could hear a few
bars of mariachi music or the hooting and hollering of
boisterous men as the sounds floated on the wind to the
hacienda. Again Clay thought how different this land was
from his home in Missouri—different terrain, different
people, a different language, a different country. Some
people said that one day the river would be a dividing line.
He smiled. If that was true, Cielo el Dorado would be in the
United States or in the Republic of Texas.

To his right, the black ribbon that was the river curved
northward and separated him from the large expanse of
mountains known as the Sierra Madre. They were old
mountains, and Clay imagined the layers of rock that were
visible in the daylight, reminding anyone who looked of the
great power of the earth. To his left and slightly behind him
were the towering heights of the Franklin Mountains. He
had heard them called the Organ Mountains and a few other
names he couldn't remember, but he knew they were the
southernmost tip of the majestic Rocky Mountains that

divided the continent in two. The first time he had seen the mountains he was struck by the harsh, rugged terrain, but he had come to be in awe of them, thinking their jagged peaks and craggy arroyos were beautiful in their own right. They were colorful mountains with red rhyolite showing through the younger layers of gray granite. At sunset, they glowed with a startling purple hue that could take a man's breath away.

Clay was coming to love this land more and more each day. The more sweat and labor he put into it, the more he understood the proud heritage of which Diego had often spoken. Yes, he mused, the place grew on you.

He thought of Lorena then, having saved it for last, not yet ready to take out the emotions he was feeling and try to make sense of them.

When had he started to want her? He had wanted her at the swimming hole, but that desire had been strictly physical. Now he wanted her for his wife. It wasn't love, he was sure. Love didn't play a part in his life. He was simply intrigued by her. One minute she was a ball of fire, and the next, she was melting into his arms, consuming them both in passion. She was innocent, he was sure, but passionate as well. Not a timid ice maiden like most marriageable women. He was certain that, with Lorena, he would never be bored. How strange that things had worked out as they had. Had Diego known?

Clay had always believed he'd have a hard time finding a woman he could marry. It surprised him that he had known about the one he was going to marry for so many years. The only problem was that she disliked him—but not completely, he amended, when he thought of what had transpired between them earlier. He couldn't forget what had happened. Clay laughed, the sound echoing into the night sky. Lorena Cervantes was going to be his wife, and the shrewish brat he had resented so before he met her had turned out to be worth having. And have her he would—and soon. The mere thought made his loins ache with unfulfilled desire. Clay knew he could marry her tomorrow, but he didn't want an unwilling bride. No, he would give her time, time to realize how much she wanted him, which he had no doubt she would.

With relief born of decision, Clay began to plan how he was going to win Miss Lorena Cervantes.

8

❧

DALIA WAS SURPRISED TO FIND LORENA STILL IN bed, as she had been up and about hours earlier for the past five days. Knowing the girl must be exhausted after all her work, Dalia quietly turned to leave.

"I'm awake," Lorena said, her voice sounding like gravel.

"Are you sure I did not wake you?"

"No, I have been lying here trying to convince my muscles they should work."

Dalia laughed. "*Sí*, I suspect your muscles are a bit tired. I forgot that you had finished your work, and I expected you to be up and gone by now. Why don't you lie there for a while? I'll bring you a cup of coffee with cream and sugar."

"Hmmm, that sounds delicious, and yes, I'll have some coffee, but not in bed. There is still a lot to do and if I don't get up now, I think I'll sleep the day away."

"More to do?"

"*Sí*. I promised we would have a fiesta when all was done, so now I must plan a party."

Excitement danced in Dalia'a eyes. "A fiesta! It has been so long, *chica*. It will be so much fun," she said, her plump hands clasped to her breast. "I will help you. Come, up with you and we will make plans."

A few minutes later the two women sat at the kitchen table sipping hot coffee and eating rolled tortillas with butter. Lorena wrote out a list of all the things she and Dalia came up with.

Mariachis, piñatas, all kinds of food, and invitations that had to go out as soon as possible. Luz joined in the excitement with ideas of her own while the word made it to Pedro, who eagerly came in to contribute to the preparations. Lorena had not thought to tell Clay of her plans, and no one else thought she would be making such plans if she had not asked him.

"I hear we're having a party." Clay stood in the open doorway, his dark countenance unreadable.

All eyes turned from Clay to Lorena. The workers had become used to the constant tension that existed between the two; they just didn't want to be a part of it.

"A fiesta," Lorena corrected in a tone that dared him to question her.

Clay stood absolutely still in the doorway, one muscular shoulder casually propped against its frame. His fathomless dark eyes never left Lorena's as they seemed to penetrate to her very soul. The kitchen was completely silent, only the distant hammering of the blacksmith could be heard when his metal music occasionally carried on the breeze.

"Good. I think everyone could use a reward for all the hard work that has gone on around here."

Lorena released her breath in relief, and the kitchen once again became loud with plans.

A broad smile lit Clay's face, and at that moment Lorena could not imagine ever being mad at him. In a way, a very small way, she conceded, he was recognizing the work she had done.

The group of people became merrier if possible, all relishing the good feelings that had been absent for so many weeks.

Clay walked over to the stove, poured himself a cup

of coffee, and leaned his hips against the counter. "Tell me about this party."

"Fiesta," the others chimed in unison.

Clay laughed, "Excuse me. Tell me about this fiesta."

They all spoke at once, telling of their own ideas. Only Clay and Lorena said nothing, each smiling in amusement. As if in silent communication Lorena got up from the table and walked out into the courtyard. Clay followed.

Lorena sat on a bench beneath a huge cottonwood tree. Clay sat down beside her, extending his long legs in front of him. For a moment, neither spoke, each remembering the intimate moment they had shared the night before.

"Thank you for not saying anything in front of everyone," Lorena began.

Clay noticed for the first time how deep her voice was. It surprised and pleased him, the sound seeming to caress his every sense. "You're welcome, but I think you know you should have told me first."

Anger flared, sending Lorena to her feet, but Clay quickly caught her wrist.

"Sit down, I don't want you to get mad." And truly he didn't.

"Why should I have to tell you anything?" She pouted, mad at what he had said but also that the perfect moment was ruined.

"If your father were here, wouldn't you have asked him first?" he asked, though he already knew the answer.

"Yes," she conceded, then added with vehemence, "but you are not my father."

Her eyes were sad, and he could see the effort she made to hold back the tears. He realized he had never spoken to her about her father, except to say he was sorry. Clay had been so concerned with the hacienda and so angry at being stuck with so many responsibilities that he had forgotten about the girl who had lost a parent. And for the first time he truly considered the pain she must have suffered.

Clay looked away from Lorena but did not see the well at

which he stared. He saw instead his own father as he lay
dying, leaving a wife and two young sons. How sad he had
been at the death of his father, but angry and confused as
well. Turning his gaze back to Lorena, he wondered if she,
too, was angry and confused. A surge of pride welled up in
him as he thought of how she had come back to Cielo el
Dorado and never shown her pain, not crying and simpering
or feeling sorry for herself, as most women would have
done. Instead she had fought against him, then thrown
herself into work. Clay wondered if maybe the work she
had done was her way of relieving the pain.

"I know I'm not your father, and I'll never try to fill his
shoes. However, he did leave me in charge, and I'm doing
what I think best . . . for everyone concerned," he added
after a brief pause as if to emphasize his point.

Lorena knew his words were sincere, and for a second
she was embarrassed at the way she had been acting. But it
was so unfair—her father gone, and now some stranger,
who disturbed her more than she would like to admit, was
here to take over. What about her! Guilt began to creep in
at her selfishness. She had always been one to give, rarely
thinking of herself. Lately, however, she had been thinking
only of herself, no one else—not Dalia or Pedro or any of
the others whose lives were dependent on the hacienda. And
she especially had not given any thought to Clay Wakefield.

She had said she could run the hacienda and she was sure
she could, but maybe it was best for this man to help her
make the transition. For now she didn't want to think about
it anymore. She would delve into these new thoughts later,
when he wasn't sitting next to her, making it difficult to
think.

Not wanting to concede anything, but wanting to reclaim
the happiness they had shared, Lorena hesitantly offered,
"Truce?"

Clay looked down into her green eyes, eyes that cried out
in innocence. "Truce." Clay's smile lit his face, making
him look less formidable.

Half teasing, half serious, Lorena added, "For now."

Clay's laugh resounded through the courtyard. "Yes, sweet Lorena, for now." Clay admired her determination. "I'm going into town today. Why don't you come with me?"

Lorena looked longingly toward the massive oak gate that held her within the walls, then looked back toward the kitchen where the preparations were being made. "I'd love to, but I really need to help prepare for the fiesta. It *was* my idea," she added with a teasing half smile.

Once again Clay was amazed. Of all the different sides he had seen in her these last weeks, he hadn't seen her tease. What a treasure she was! Clay was more certain than ever that the red-haired, green-eyed temptress who sat before him could do a lot of things to him, but she would never bore him.

Neither of them noticed that Dalia had come up and had overheard the last part of their conversation. "We have everything under control," she said. "You go to town with Senōr Wakefield and order those clothes you have been wanting." The woman spoke with such authority that Lorena and Clay glanced at each other with a conspiratorial grin.

"Did you hear that?" Clay said. "You have no choice but to go now."

Lorena jumped up and hugged the older woman. "*Gracias*, Dalia. I'll be back soon to help."

Dalia left and went back to the kitchen, her heart lifting at the sight of her happy Lorena. Maybe Lorena would see Ramón while she was in town, she thought excitedly.

When Dalia was out of hearing distance, Clay asked, "When I order you around, why don't I get a reaction like that?"

Saucily she replied, "Because you don't order me to do things I want to do. Now I must hurry and change. I'll meet you at the stables." Before Clay could respond, Lorena was running into the house.

Clay went down to the stables to get the horses.

"*Hola!* Senōr Wakefield," Jaime said as he stepped out of a stall with a wheelbarrow and rake.

"Hello, Jaime. Miss Cervantes and I are going into town today. I'll get Dante while you get Rosinante."

"*Sí*, señor," Jaime responded enthusiastically. "She will be most happy to get out."

"Who will be?" Clay asked not sure if the stable hand meant the mare or Lorena.

Jaime laughed. "Actually, I think they both will enjoy getting out. I will hurry."

Turning back to get Dante, Clay added, "I doubt you will have to hurry. Miss Cervantes has gone to change, and if I know women, it will be some time before she arrives."

But before he had completed the sentence, Lorena raced through the doorway, grabbed the door frame, and swung to a stop. In her free hand she carried a bundle wrapped in a towel. Clay stood staring at her, nonplussed. She had entered like a hoyden, but instead of being angry Clay only wanted to laugh. And if her entrance was tomboyish, her appearance was anything but. Leather ties held a wide-brimmed hat to dangle on her back. A blouse of flowing white cotton with long billowing sleeves and a delicately embroidered front flowed provocatively over her skin, but it was partly covered by a leather vest, forcing him use his imagination. The skirt came decorously to her ankles revealing newly polished riding boots, and though it was split down the middle so that she could ride astride, it was ladylike and practical at the same time. How could he argue with that?

Lorena held her breath as she saw him make a slow perusal of her attire, hoping he wouldn't ruin the day by telling her to change. But he only smiled when his eyes reached hers and said, "I believe your horse is ready."

"Oh, good!" she exclaimed, flashing a smile that took Clay's breath away. "I brought some food in case we stop for lunch." When she reached Rosinante, Lorena deftly tied the bundle to the back of her saddle. "There, that should hold."

The day was already growing hot, though it was still fairly early. Although Clay had been traveling through this part of the country for years, he still was amazed that it could get so hot during the day, only to cool off so much at night. They cantered down the main road that led away from the hacienda to the west. If they had ridden south they would have gone directly toward Paso del Norte through the small settlement on the north bank. But the only ford there was a haphazard affair that was good only as a boat crossing. It consisted of a rope that stretched from the north bank of the river to the south, with which people could pull themselves across in small boats. So Lorena and Clay rode west to the small ford that the caravans used.

Clay watched Lorena as she rode at his side. She was unaware of anything but the ground below her and the wind in her face. He had never seen a woman ride as well as she, and certainly never one who abandoned herself so completely to the ride. He thought of the night before. She had abandoned herself to passion as she was now abandoning herself to the ride. Ah, sweet Lorena, such a treasure!

"You ride well," he said when they had slowed to a walk. He consciously pushed thoughts of last night out of his mind, for they made it difficult for him to ride.

Lorena looked at him, not sure if he was teasing. "Thank you," she finally said.

"Did you ride much in England?"

"Yes, though not my own horse. Papá did not want to buy one there and have to bring it back when I came home."

Clay didn't think the explanation made much sense. Diego could easily have sold the horse in England when she was through. But since he had come to the hacienda, he had begun to question a lot of things Diego had done, so he didn't say anything. Instead he stayed on safer grounds.

"Didn't they teach you to ride sidesaddle while you were there?"

Lorena's laugh floated to his ears. "They tried, and I did it whenever I had to, but it seems the most absurd way to ride a horse."

"Absurd!" he seemed incredulous.

"Yes, absurd. And you sound just like Miss Tidesdale."

"The same Miss Tidesdale you spoke of the first time we met?" he asked mischievously.

Lorena blushed as she remembered the scene by the swimming hole. "Yes, one and the same."

"And how is it that I sound just like her?"

Forgetting her embarrassment, thinking only of her former schoolmarm, Lorena laughed. "You are like her, because you think of propriety instead of safety. Have you ever tried to ride a horse while clinging precariously to its side, more off than on."

Clay laughed. "No, I haven't."

"Well, let me tell you, it's a dangerous affair, not to mention extremely uncomfortable and no fun at all."

"But ladylike."

"Until you land face first in the mud."

Clay threw his head back and laughed, bringing a smile to Lorena's lips. He looked at her then and said, "You are so beautiful when you smile."

Not sure what to say, uncomfortable with his words, she covered up by teasing, "And I'm not when I don't?"

"You really are a minx aren't you, little one?" he said, his black eyes bright with merriment.

"Why do you keep calling me 'little one'?" she said, desperately trying to resist the magnetic attraction she felt.

"Does it bother you?" His voice was deep and husky, reminding Lorena all too readily of the night before.

"Yes." She did not admit that what bothered her was the tingling sensation that passed through her body every time he said it.

"Why?" he persisted.

"Why not?" she challenged. "How would you like it if I called you 'big one' all the time?"

"You are priceless, you know." He reached over and, as the horses walked, gently stroked the line of her jaw with one strong finger.

More uncomfortable than ever, wanting nothing more than to succumb to the traitorous feelings, to savor his touch, Lorena took the only refuge she could think of. "Race you to town."

Before Clay could respond, she left him in a cloud of dust, his horse eager to follow. "Follow the ladies, Dante," he commanded, a satisfied grin on his face.

Paso del Norte had changed in the five years Lorena had been gone, not drastically, but enough so that Lorena felt she was in a town she no longer knew. The dirt roads were the same, as were the adobe buildings, only now there were more of them. New people had moved in, and old ones had moved on.

"You look as though you don't recognize the place," Clay said.

"Yes and no. It's the same, only bigger and with a lot more people, a lot more Americans."

"When they opened the Santa Fe Trail and let foreigners trade on the Camino Real, the towns on the trails got a lot more traffic."

Lorena looked at the man who rode beside her, telling her about the town she had practically grown up in. Who was this man? she asked herself. She had spent so much time berating him and avoiding him that she really knew very little about him.

Lorena's thoughts were brought up short when they came to the mercantile. Clay quickly dismounted and sent Lorena a forbidding glare when she started to dismount on her own. Impatiently she waited for him to come around to her, not willing to make a scene on her first day back in town.

Solicitously, Clay held her elbow as he guided her into the store.

"Morning, Harold." Clay addressed a short burly man with wiry red hair. Lorena had never seen the man before.

The man turned to Lorena then and said, "This pretty thing must be Miss Cervantes."

"Yes, I am," Lorena answered politely. "And who are you?"

"Lorena, this is Harold Selig. He owns this store," Clay said.

"It's nice to meet you, Mr. Selig."

"The pleasure's all mine."

"You must have come to town while I was away at school."

"Yes'm, I came down the trail about three years ago. Knew your father well. Good man. We were all sorry to hear about his death."

Lorena lowered her eyes then looked back up. "*Gracias*, señor," she said, reverting to her childhood language.

The burly man turned his attention to Clay, uncomfortable with the emotions that were clear on the girl's face. "What can I do for you?"

"I have a list of supplies I need sent over to Cielo el Dorado. Miss Cervantes and I have some things to do around town, and I'd like you to put the order together and send it to the hacienda this afternoon."

"Well, sure, Clay." The man glanced uncomfortably at Lorena.

Clay noticed his reluctance to speak. "Is there a problem?"

"Well, I'm sure it's not a problem, but there are some back bills of Diego's that need to get cleared up."

Clay's face darkened, and the burly man hurried to explain. "I know you haven't been around to take care of this stuff, and that's why I thought I'd just let ya know." He quickly looked over the list Clay had given him. "I'll have this order out in no time at all."

"I'll stop by on our way back to the hacienda to pick up the past bills," Clay said, "and I'll pay for this order in cash."

Clay took Lorena's elbow to lead her out.

"Now, Clay, I hope there are no hard feelings," Harold Selig said, not wanting anyone as powerful as Clay Wakefield mad at him.

"Of course not, Harold. We'll see you this afternoon."

Clay and Lorena left the store. A young boy stood by the horses, which waited outside.

"*Hola*, Senōr Wakefield. I take care of your horses, *sí*?"

"*Sí*, Pepe," Clay tossed the boy a shiny coin. "I expect you to take good care of them."

"*Sí, sí, sí*, señor," Pepe said excitedly. "For you and the pretty señorita I take care of the horses," he said with dimples appearing in a huge grin.

Clay rumpled the boy's hair, and Lorena smiled. "I see you're already quite a ladies' man, Pepe," Clay teased as the boy led the two horses off.

As they walked down the road, Clay was silent, thinking about the unpaid bills. It seemed that every day something new sprang up, and Clay still had not pegged the problem. He had been on the trail with Diego a long time, and he knew Diego had made a great deal of money. Where had it all gone?

"You seem lost in your thoughts. Is it my company or are you concerned about the bills at the mercantile?" Lorena asked.

Clay looked down into her concerned green eyes. "Neither," he said, shaking off his worry, not wanting to alarm Lorena. "My business is done," he said, quickly changing the subject. "Where do you want to go?"

Lorena looked closely at Clay and decided she must have imagined his concern. "To the dressmaker!"

"Uhh," he groaned, "this could take the rest of the day."

Lorena laughed. She was excited to be out, enjoying the old town. "I doubt it. There are too many other places I want to go." Forgetting how recently she had thought of this man as her enemy, she grabbed his hand and pulled him into a small building filled with bolts of material and chattering women.

When they entered, every woman in the tiny store stopped talking to stare at the handsome man and beautiful young lady. It was a few moments before they realized who the two were. In that instant, the talking started again, all of the women speaking at once.

"*Madre mía*, it is Lorena Cervantes!" cried one.

"Come in, come in." An older woman bustled over to Clay and Lorena. "It is good to have you back!"

The women cooed and clucked over Lorena. In their eyes, she was one of their own, and if their children had the misfortune to be orphaned, they knew that the people of their town would take care of them as well.

Clay stood back and watched, and when he saw that he was not needed—or wanted, for that matter—he caught Lorena's eye to signal that he would be back later. Lorena watched him leave and felt an emotion so powerful it took her breath away. Writing it off as excitement over seeing so many friends, Lorena turned her attention back to the women. Before too long they had her swathed in material, every woman there having her own ideas as to what would look best with Lorena's distinctive features.

"And I need something special," Lorena chimed in.

"Special?" several women asked in unison.

"For your handsome *novio*, Senõr Wakefield!" The women all giggled together as they teased Lorena, though any one of them would have died to have the Americano as her love.

Lorena's cheeks turned a rosy red. "Senõr Wakefield is not my *novio*!" she said indignantly.

"No? We see the way he looks at you. You cannot fool us, Lorena Cervantes."

Lorena stamped her foot. "He is not! He is here simply to

help me get things in order. He will be leaving soon to go back to wherever he came from."

As soon as the words were out, Lorena's heart stopped. It was the truth, and she had never even thought about it before. Of course he would be leaving soon. Wasn't he a man of the trail, just like her father? Lorena was torn, and she hated herself for it. She should have felt thankful that he would be leaving. Then she could run the hacienda by herself with no interference from him. Then why did she feel so empty at the thought of him going? But he would go, she reminded herself. He would leave, just as every man did. They were all the same!

"So, Lorena, if this special dress is not for Senõr Wakefield, then what is it for?"

Turning her attention back to the women, Lorena had to force herself to appear cheerful. "A fiesta. We are having a fiesta at Cielo el Dorado."

"When?" they all asked excitedly.

"Soon," Lorena promised then shifted the women's attention to the task of ordering her dress. After the details were discussed, she gathered her things and said, "We will send invitations to everyone as soon as we have a firm date."

Before the women could ask any more questions, Lorena waved good-bye and fled.

She ran into Clay as she charged through the door. His strong arms reached out to steady her before she tumbled back. Their eyes caught and held until Clay's slowly lowered to her lips, forgetting where they stood. Before he could act, Lorena pulled away. "I would like to go to the mission," she said, her eyes never leaving his.

"Yes," he said, "to the mission."

They walked side by side along the dusty roads on their way to the mission, neither knowing what to say.

Lorena loved the old mission. The church had always provided her with a sense of love and security. She knew

what the church expected of her and in turn, it provided her
with love. Lorena merely had to pass through the wooden
doors into the high-ceilinged building to be enfolded by the
loving arms of God. The trappings of religion, Miss
Tidesdale had always warned her, were not what one was
supposed to long for, but rather God himself. But Lorena
found her God in the wooden beams that crossed the
towering ceilings and in the cross that hung at the front of
the nave. The altar with its cloth, the priest in his vestments,
the statues of the saints, all filled her with God. Was it so
wrong that the trappings, with all their beauty, filled her
with the presence of the Lord? She thought not. For Lorena
knew she did not covet the material objects; rather, they had
the ability to evoke in her a sense of peace, a sense of
oneness with God, that nothing else could.

She walked up the aisle, momentarily forgetting Clay,
and knelt before the altar. She bowed her head to pray, but
she wasn't sure what she was praying for. When her mind
wouldn't settle on anything, she asked God to bless all her
loved ones, and as she brought her prayer to an end, she
silently asked God to bless Clay Wakefield. Quickly, when
she remembered Clay was with her, she crossed herself,
then got up. Clay stood behind her, gazing down on her
with a look that she did not understand.

"Where to now, little one?" he asked in a whisper that
could only have been called a caress.

"To find Fray Cristóbal," she answered uncertainly
before she turned and went in search of the priest.

They looked all over but found no one. "He must be
out," Lorena said unnecessarily.

Clay smiled. "Yes, I believe you're right. Come on, you
will have a chance to see him later."

Before she could ask him when, Clay caught her elbow
and led her from the church.

9

❦

WHEN THE SUN HAD TRAVELED HALFWAY DOWN THE western sky, Clay and Lorena prepared to make their way back to the hacienda. First, they stopped at the general store, Clay insisting that Lorena wait outside. He returned with his strong jaw set and his dark eyes emotionless. Normally, Lorena would have questioned him, but she was wrapped up in her own thoughts—thoughts that Clay Wakefield was a man of the trail.

Flowering cacti and dry desert sand gave way to flowing green grass and cottonwood trees when they crossed some invisible barrier that distinguished the river valley from the desert plain. At the ford they crossed back to the north side of the river, neither saying a word as the horses traveled along the well-marked road.

They made it back to the hacienda in record time, and by dinnertime Lorena was renewed after a long soak in the bath. When she entered the dining room only Clay and Ben were waiting for her, both men looking elegant in their dinner clothes.

"My, don't we look handsome this evening," Lorena said. "Is there a special occasion that I'm not aware of?"

Ben stepped forward to take Lorena's small hand in his and press a chaste kiss to her knuckles. "Every night is a special occasion when you are joining us."

137

Clay scowled as he looked on.

"Such flattery, Ben." Lorena smiled. "Somehow it just doesn't ring true, as I dine with you almost every evening."

All heads turned toward the door when an unfamiliar voice said, "I would not like to think that the dressing up for the evening meal had anything to do with me."

"Padre!" Lorena said in surprise at finding the priest from the mission standing in the doorway. "When did you arrive? You should have ridden over with us. Clay and I went to the mission today but could not find you anywhere."

"That is considerate of you child, but I had some business to attend to away from the mission. I have some matters to discuss with Señor Wakefield as well. Had I known you were coming into town, I could have taken care of it then. But," the priest said with a guilty shrug, "since my evening and tomorrow were free, I thought I would take advantage of Cielo el Dorado's fine hospitality."

Lorena wondered what possible matters the priest could possibly have to discuss with Clay Wakefield but couldn't bring herself to ask. Instead, she said, "You know you are always welcome, Padre. Please sit down and have some wine before dinner while I see to your room."

"*Gracias*, child," the priest said as he sat in one of the carved dining room chairs.

Lorena went to the room next to the chapel, wondering what could have brought the man there. The small guest room had been used by priests for years, first by the one who had lived at the hacienda in earlier days, then by the priests who came periodically to stay. The room had not been used very often in recent times, as the inhabitants of the hacienda led their own prayers except on Sundays when most everyone traveled the short distance to the mission for the service. Before Lorena's housecleaning project, the room had been covered in cobwebs and dust. Now as she entered the newly cleaned room she found Dalia arranging roses in a clay vase.

"Dalia, have you prepared the room already?"

"*Sí*, I just brought some flowers to freshen it up."

"I'm glad we cleaned before he arrived. It would have been awful had he arrived to a roomful of cobwebs."

"This is true," Dalia said as she stood back to admire her handiwork.

"Dalia?"

"*Sí*, Lorena?"

"Why has the priest not been here in so long, and what possible business could he have with Clay Wakefield?"

Dalia gathered up stems and unused roses. "I do not know. But your father was not here much during the time you were gone."

"But he was never here much, even before I left," she said, not understanding. "The priest came then."

"Lorena, your father rarely came back at all once you left, and with no one here except servants, the priest had no one to visit with."

Still feeling unsure, but sensing Dalia knew no more, she went back to join the men.

"Lorena," the priest said as she walked into the room. "I was just telling the men what a lovely young woman you have grown up to be."

Lorena's cheeks tinged pink at his words. "*Gracias*, Padre."

Clay stood at the massive fireplace, one arm resting on the adobe mantel, an amused grin stretched across his face. "He also told us about a few of your escapades in the river valley."

Both Ben and the priest laughed when Lorena's cheeks changed from pink to bright red.

"From the looks of the most becoming blush that has crept into your cheeks," Ben teased, "I'd say that our lovely young lady was indeed something of a hoyden."

"Never," she replied while taking the wine that Clay offered her.

"Never?" the priest asked, his eyes twinkling with mirth.

"It seems to me I recall specifically a little girl with long red braids sitting high up in a tree bombarding passersby with dirt clods from a slingshot. And then there was the time . . ."

Just then Dalia walked in to announce dinner. Lorena gave a sigh of relief.

Clay sat at the head of the table, as had become his habit, while the priest and Lorena sat on either side of him with Ben next to Lorena. The priest said the blessing, after which they all began to eat the luscious meal.

"Now, where were you, Father?" Ben asked, as if not remembering. "Oh, yes, I remember. Lorena up in a tree sending dirt clods down on unsuspecting souls . . ."

"Sí, I remember," the priest said, smiling affectionately at Lorena. "I was just going to mention the time that Lorena said she was starting a carnival. Unfortunately, there was some doubt that she could," the priest said mildly. "So Lorena got on her horse backwards, with no saddle, and started riding in circles. She did quite well, I must admit, for a time."

"For a time?" Ben pressed.

"Well," the priest said, clearing his throat to hide his smile, "the next thing we knew, Lorena was lying on the ground in a cloud of dust."

Lorena went from embarrassment to mortification that quickly turned to defensiveness, remembering the episode all too clearly. "I would have stayed on had it not been for Ramón! He distracted Rosinante to make her swerve." Lorena seemed indignant. "I was good at riding backwards, I had practiced for hours."

All three men laughed outrageously. "So its true. Underneath the facade of frills and long hair is a tomboy at heart!" Ben roared.

Caught up in the fun, and realizing these men were not laughing at her, she chimed in, "Had Ramón not thwarted my plans, I would have stood on Rosinante's back."

Clay sat back and watched the bantering at the table. It

was a pleasure to see Lorena totally at ease, not watching everything she said. She seemed so much more natural tonight. She was able to laugh at herself instead of taking offense at being teased. And she seemed completely unaware of the alluring picture she made, sitting there teasing as much as she was teased.

"What is this I hear about a fiesta?" the priest asked, changing the subject.

Lorena leaned forward, excitement dancing in her eyes. "Padre, we are having a grand fiesta for everyone around. We are only just planning it now but it will be soon."

Clay was suddenly glad that the party was to be given. It would be the perfect time for Lorena to see all her old friends and for the town to see that the little tomboy, Lorena Cervantes, had come home a lady. Pride surged through him. She was a lady, and much, much more.

When dinner was over Ben went to the working side of the hacienda while Clay and Fray Cristóbal went to the study to discuss business, leaving Lorena excited and at loose ends. She walked out into the courtyard and felt the cool night breeze on her cheeks. The moon was overhead, gigantic and round. Stars glistened in the heavens, surrounding the huge moon. As she strolled about the courtyard, she would see the silent shapes of the guards pacing back and forth on the rooftops. When she glimpsed Pedro, she climbed the ladder to join him.

"Hello, Pedro," she said when she reached the old man, who gazed out over the land.

Pedro turned to face Lorena and smiled. "I thought you were eating dinner with the padre."

"We finished and now he is speaking to Clay about business. I could not resist the gorgeous night. And you? What are you doing up here? Are we short of guards?" she looked around to see how many other guards were on patrol. There was a guard on each wall, Pedro being one of them.

"No, there are plenty of guards, especially now that Clay has come, but I like to come up here sometimes at night. When I do, I let the guard go down for a while."

"Before I left for England I used to love to come up here and dream. There is something peaceful about sitting up here looking out for miles. It is as if you and God are sitting alone together under the stars."

"Your father used to sit up here as well, and his father before him and his father before that."

"You have been here that long?" Lorena's voice was filled with amazement.

"*Sí, chica.* I am an old man."

"You're not that old, Pedro."

The old man laughed softly, the lines of age more pronounced. "I was born during the time of your great-grandfather. My father came to work for him and I have lived here ever since."

"Dalia was born here, so you must have grown up together if you came here as a child."

"*Sí,* this is true," he said, looking off into the distance, seeing not the darkened landscape but the vision of memories long past. "Those were good times in many ways, but frightening as well."

"Why?" Lorena asked, interested.

"The savage Indians were very active and unhappy then, and we had much need of these walls. It was not like these times when we have had many years of much peace."

"But I thought the Manso Indians had always been peaceful."

"For the most part this is true. It was primarily the Apaches who roamed these parts, who did not accept the white man and raided and killed."

Lorena looked out around her as if seeing the land for the first time. A worried expression crossed her face. "It seems so strange."

"What, *chica*?"

"That people can think and believe the world is one way

and then find out they were wrong all along." Her voice was barely audible. Pedro might not have heard at all if her soft voice had not carried on the cool breeze.

"What has changed, Lorena?"

"Oh, I don't know. Everything. It is as if I lived in a dream world all my life and suddenly I woke up to find everything I believed in gone."

Pedro knew that his story of the Indian raids and killings only added to her sense of upheaval at her father's sudden death. Even though her father was seldom around, he had loved his only child dearly, and had spent time with her whenever he could.

"Things will get better, Lorena." He patted her hand reassuringly.

"How can you be sure?" Despair tinged her voice.

"It will. Have faith."

Approaching footsteps caught their attention, and they looked up to find the tall figure of Clay standing behind them.

"There you are," Clay said to Lorena, his dark handsomeness sending shivers of pleasure racing down her spine.

Pedro stood up. "Dalia is sure to be wondering where I am," he said, wanting to leave the two alone. "Good night."

Clay and Lorena watched Pedro disappear down the ladder. Lorena stood then. "I really should be going in."

Clay put a hand out and touched her arm. "Stay." He sensed her sudden anger and added "Please."

Lorena looked up at him, then sat down again.

Clay joined her, automatically searching the countryside for signs of danger before he turned his attention to the young woman who was to be his wife. The moonlight cast its golden glow on her face, and as he looked at her he thought he had never seen anyone so lovely.

Lorena sense his gaze and felt uneasy under his scrutiny. To distract him she said, "It's so beautiful up here."

Clay looked out over the land. "Yes, it is. Diego and I often came up here at night to talk."

"Papá did not like it much here at Cielo el Dorado." Lorena's voice was so soft that Clay almost did not hear the words she spoke. He saw the hurt in her eyes and sensed again the pain her father must have caused her. He knew that Diego had rarely been at the hacienda, preferring the faster life in Chihuahua to the serenity of the desert. Looking out across the land, Clay wondered at the man who could prefer anything over what he saw before him. The anger he had felt toward Diego earlier returned, anger that he could have hurt Lorena. Wanting in some way to help her, he offered, "Your father loved you very much."

Lorena's sad laugh surprised him. "Yes, I know he did. But not enough to be here with me or even to want me here when he came home."

"In his own way he loved you very much. He spoke of you often." He wanted badly to cheer her. "In fact, he spoke so much of you I felt as if I knew you before I actually met you."

Lorena looked at him speculatively. "Then why were you so hateful to me?"

Clay looked at her with one raised eyebrow.

"Most of the time," she added.

Clay reached out and, with one strong finger, gently traced the line of her jaw. "I could never be hateful to you, little one." His voice was deep, low, and husky, mesmerizing her.

"But you were," she contradicted, staring at him all the while, hardly conscious of her words.

Long fingers trailed back to the nape of her neck, slowly pulling her close. His lips hovered over hers. "Never, Lorena. I could never be hateful to you." Without giving her a chance to reply, he hungrily covered her mouth with his. The intensity scared her, and she tried to pull back. When he sensed her fear, he gentled his kiss to a slow seductive journey. He pressed his lips to her forehead and her cheek, then claimed her lips once again. This time the kiss softened in its demand, coercing her to respond.

Lorena's senses were on fire. Her heart beat wildly, though not in fear. Tentatively, she opened her mouth to taste him. The innocent gesture brought a groan from his chest as he pulled her to him, plunging his tongue into the sweetened recesses within.

Lorena's senses reeled. She wrapped her arms around his shoulders for support, forgetting her father and her uncertainty of what the world had in store for her. The only reality was the passion this man made her feel.

"Lorena, you are so beautiful," he said, his voice filled with passion.

Strong hands spiraled down her back as his lips returned to hers to delve within, pulsating in and out as he gently pressed her to him.

Sensations flooded her body, centering in the core of her being, that place she had been unaware of until this man filled her with emotions she did not understand. She pressed herself closer, wanting more. His lips seared their way down her neck as his hand found one breast. Lorena gasped at the intimate contact. Expertly, he teased the bud of her breast with long fingers through the thin cotton of her dress. His lips grazed her neck down to where it met her shoulder; then slowly he began to push her dress away to reveal the soft silkiness of creamy white shoulders. His lips followed the dress in its downward descent, revealing the top of one perfectly formed breast. He kissed her, and Lorena quivered at the unexpected pleasure of his warm, smooth lips on her skin.

Lost in the world of consuming passion, they did not hear the approaching footsteps.

"Uh-hum." The guard cleared his throat uncomfortably.

Reality crashed down upon Lorena. She was mortified beyond words at her behavior—and to have it discovered as well! Clay released her slowly to gaze steadily at the man.

"There had better be a good reason for this," he said in a deadly calm voice as he shielded Lorena with his body.

The guard flinched as if hit. "Pedro sent me up to take over the duty."

Lorena blushed a furious red. How could she have acted this way, again, like a common hussy? She leaped up, then swiftly made her way down the ladder and out of Clay's sight, leaving him to glare at the unfortunate guard.

"In the future, you would be wise to remember who is in charge here," Clay said with clenched jaw.

"*Sí*, señor."

Clay climbed down the ladder to find Pedro just going in. He started to call to the old man and chastise him for his meddling ways. But then he thought better of it—Pedro was probably right. Lorena was not ready for the intensity that they experienced together, and she probably already felt guilty about what little they had done. Clay smiled. He probably should have chastised Pedro for leaving them alone in the first place. Still smiling, Clay went to play cards with his younger brother.

Lorena lay in bed that night, having left the shutters open. She gazed out into the starry night wondering what was happening to her. How could she have acted so wanton with the man who had come to ruin her life? She did not like him, she told herself firmly. She could not let herself like him. He was a man like her father, someone who worked on the trail, someone who was never home. She would never be like her mother, left to sit alone without the man she loved, wondering where he was or if he was alive. Never, she vowed, would she marry a man like her father. If she was forced to marry at all, she would choose a simple man who farmed or ranched and had no desire to go off on the trail. She thought then of Ramón Valdéz, her dear child-hood friend. He would stay at home. He was the type of man she should marry. Inwardly she recoiled, feeling a sense of loss at the thought. With determination, she reaffirmed her resolve never to marry. Lorena Cervantes would take over the hacienda. That was all there was to it! She would not be a servant to any man. The idea of having no children left her bereft. But everyone had to make sacrifices. She, however, would not make the kind of sacrifices her mother made.

Isabelle Cervantes had died in 1824, leaving behind a husband and daughter. Officially she died from a fever. More likely, she died from loneliness and despair.

In 1660, when the first Cervantes came to this desolate region, he had brought with him a beautiful young wife from Spain. Each Cervantes son thereafter had acquired a bride from one of the finest families in Spain. Those women had sailed across the Atlantic Ocean to an unknown land. Some of them adapted, but others did not, for it was a far different world out in the desert than they had known in their native Spain. Gone was the pleasant climate, gone were the elegant balls and gowns, gone were the visits and social gatherings where they could while away the hours over gossip and embroidery.

Isabelle Basesteros, who became the wife of Diego Cervantes, was one of those unfortunate souls who did not take to the relentless heat and desolate life that the frontier hacienda provided. It had not been so bad at first, with the excitement of being the young bride of a rich man. But somewhere along the line the excitement had run dry. Miraculously, the frail woman, not much more than a child, had survived the harsh journey across the ocean, confined to her cabin by choice rather than by the weather. The six-month trip across land from the port of Veracruz to Cielo el Dorado, was made bearable only by thoughts of her impending marriage and children. Though the daughter she bore drained her of what strength she had, it was that same daughter, Lorena, who provided her with the little joy she knew.

After Lorena's birth Isabelle was told she could have no more children. Diego, devoted at first, slowly lost interest

in both his wife and the hacienda. He loved Lorena, but she
was not the son he wanted and needed to carry on the
Cervantes line, and she was not enough to keep him at his
ancestral home. Isabelle turned from an excited bride to a
lonely and unhappy wife who constantly complained to her
daughter of Diego's betrayal. At first she spoke only to a
baby who had no idea what she said, but as Lorena grew the
words became clearer, each year that passed bringing more
meaning to the age-old lament.

When Diego was home, he indulged his daughter and
endured his nagging wife. Lorena loved both her father and
her mother, and felt a sense of betrayal every time her father
came home, for he took her with him everywhere he went,
leaving her mother behind to sit alone.

With her mind racing, Lorena could not sleep. Finally,
for some inexplicable reason, she got up from her bed and
crept quietly to her mother's suite. She stood outside the
heavy door that led to the sitting room. Even now, six years
after her death, it had not changed. Not for the first time
since she had been home, Lorena wondered why Isabelle's
things had not been packed up or given away, instead of
staying out as if her mother might walk in and sit down at
any minute. She had first noticed the rooms when she was
cleaning the hacienda. Shocked, she had asked Dalia about
it, but the duenna had said her father insisted that the rooms
be left alone. Had he cared more than he let on? Lorena
dismissed the thought as soon as it came. What did it
matter, since he had never shown his feeling to Isabelle?
Again she was pierced with the hatred of men, all men. And
then her thoughts drifted to Clay.

"Clay," she said out loud. She felt confused by the
emotions that warred inside her. The desire to run the
hacienda herself, the desire not to marry, the desire not to
end up like her mother, all standing in stark contrast to the
new desires that the man kindled within her. Why did her
heart beat faster when he was near? Why did she forget her
resolve when he looked into her eyes? And why did his kiss

turn her into a mass of quivering emotions that made her yearn for something she could not explain? What was he doing to her? He didn't even like her; he had made that clear from the beginning. But it seemed that now something had changed, but what, and why?

Lorena walked into the sitting room, its bright white walls broken only by the blue stencil bordering the ceiling. Lorena had added the border, thinking she would use the room, as her mother had.

A work table stood by the window that looked out into the courtyard. This was one of the few rooms in the house that had a window into the courtyard, so the matriarch of the family could watch over the kitchen, the well, and the rest of her domain as she sat in her room. Lorena realized that if she took over the hacienda she would be dealing with not only the books and ledgers she had learned about at school but also with the cooking, cleaning, and mending that she had always tried her hardest to avoid. Fortunately, Dalia could deal with that, as she had for years.

A mother-of-pearl needle case sat on the table, next to a tortoiseshell, ivory, and teakwood box that held silver scissors, a little penknife, several spools of thread, a gold thimble, and a magnifying glass with a silver-gilt handle. It was at that table that Lorena's mother had tried fruitlessly to teach her daughter the gentle art of embroidery. Isabelle had put her daughter to work on altar cloths, bedspreads, tablecloths, and linens, only to patiently take them back to lessen the damage. But they had both persevered, never giving up, as Isabelle wanted someone to lament to, and Lorena felt obligated to fill the empty spot her father left.

Beside the table in the corner was a fireplace that warmed the room in the winter months. While most rooms were lit by iron candelabra, this room had candelabra carved from wood and painted with gesso and gold leaf. Lorena went to a leather chest studded with brass nails to remove her mother's clothes, but when she opened the old trunk she found them gone, replaced with tablecloths and linen. It

dawned on her then that this was not a museum for her dead
mother, but rather a place for the Cervantes matriarchs who
would continue to use the room for generations.

After closing the chest, Lorena stood up and walked
through an archway into a spacious room dominated by a
large bed. Similar to the rest of the furniture in the house,
it was heavy, dark, and formal, like the Spaniards who had
made it. It was the bed she was born in, along with the
generations of Cervantes babies who had come before her,
and who would not come again unless she chose to bear
them. The thought of a child to love filled her with joy, but
that joy was soon replaced by heartache at the realization
that she would never have any, for she would not marry. For
the first time it seemed to Lorena that she was faced with a
double-edged sword, unfulfilled either way. But Lorena's
love of life rebelled against such a thought. She had faith
that all would work out as it was meant to.

In the corner of the room was a long narrow spot, empty
now, once lined with her father's boots—boots for every
occasion from sloshing through mud to dancing in the *sala*.
On one wall was a velvet hanging embroidered with an
image of Our Lady of Remedies, the patroness of the River
Kingdom in which they lived. Not a day had passed through
the ages that the Lady was not sent a thought or a prayer for
her kingdom and all its possessions.

An armchair cushioned with the same material and design
as the bedcover stood next to another window. Lorena sat
down and rested her head against its high back. What was
happening to her? Why, when she knew how important it
was not to marry, was she thinking more and more of Clay
Wakefield, a man who was everything her father was, a
man of the trail? She looked across the room at the bed and
wondered what it would be like to have Clay's children.
What would it be like to wake up next to him, to feel his lips
on hers? Angry with herself, she leaped up from the chair as
if to run away from her feelings. She would not marry! All
men were the same, and she would not die alone, a mere

possession of some uncaring man. But a sliver of doubt wound its way into her thoughts. Clay loomed in her mind. She remembered the time and energy he had put into the hacienda, the care he took with the people of Cielo el Dorado. Was it possible that he was not like her father? Was it possible he would not leave?

A tiny flicker of hope kindled in her heart . . .

10

❧

MESSENGERS WERE SENT FAR AND WIDE TO INVITE friends and neighbors to the grand fiesta. Every capable hand that remained busily readied the hacienda for the big event.

The women baked all different kinds of bread in the huge ovens. They sifted the flour once for the heavy whole wheat bread and twice to make the cookies, cakes, and pastries that everyone loved. Then they stored the baked goods in the cool, dark storeroom off the kitchen.

While the women were cooking, some of the men readied rooms for the many guests who would stay overnight, though some would bring gear and set up small camps. Lorena expected them to arrive on Friday for the fiesta on Saturday, which would be followed by mass on Sunday before the guests set out toward their homes.

The day before everyone was due to arrive, Cielo el Dorado stood transformed. Boughs of pine, brought down from the mountains, were carefully woven together to form a long rope, which the men strung from post to post around the courtyard. From the roof beams they hung tin lanterns pierced with holes to admit the light of slowly burning candles. They filled the courtyard with rough wood tables covered with multicolored table cloths that had been passed down from generation to generation for just that purpose.

The Cervantes family, after living in the river valley for close to two hundred years, had accumulated a wealth of goods from the region. And in keeping with Spanish tradition, they brought out their goods and shared them, with gracious hospitality, whenever they entertained.

Wooden benches provided seating and a spot was cleared on the porch to accommodate the musicians who would come to play. Though many fiestas had the dancing in the *sala* with all the furniture moved aside, Lorena preferred to dance under the stars, the cool night air brushing against dampened skin.

An empty expanse of hard-packed dirt would serve as a dance floor, and Lorena chose a young boy to sprinkle water on it whenever it turned dusty.

Much to Lorena's surprise, Clay had let her remain in charge. He helped as much as anyone and only smiled a devilish grin whenever Lorena asked him to do something. She smiled to herself, wondering what retaliation would come later.

The clothes that she had ordered arrived well before the gathering. And though Clay said nothing about them, she sensed that he approved.

Saturday arrived to find the hacienda filled with old friends and neighbors from near and far. Everything looked wonderful, and Lorena was filled with pride. This was her home, and these were her friends.

When finally she was no longer needed, she went to get ready for the party. She washed her hair before sinking down into fresh scented water to soak her slim body. Since she had been home, Lorena had gained a tan, not swarthy and rugged, but soft and golden bringing blond highlights to her hair and making her eyes seem even greener. She felt healthy and alive as she soaked in the warm water, filled with anticipation of the night to come. Good food, friends, dancing—and as much as she hated to admit it, Lorena looked forward to seeing Clay. What would he wear? she wondered. Would he dress the part of an American gentlemen? Maybe he would simply wear the more traditional attire of the area. Whichever, she knew he would look wonderful.

She pulled on a flowing dress of white silk lace that hung off her shoulders to accentuate her golden skin and riotous mass of red curls. The dress was belted at the waist with a thin sash of matching lace, then fell to her ankles, where white slippers encased her small feet. Standing before an old beveled mirror, Lorena did not quite recognize the woman who stood before her. This surely was not the same girl who had left England only months before to confront challenge and uncertainty in the land of her birth. She knew she had done only a marginal job of dealing with it all, but she was getting better, of that she was sure. As she made the last adjustments to her attire, Lorena felt a mixture of trepidation and exhilaration.

Just as she was ready to leave, the door opened.

"Ah!" Dalia clasped her hands to her cheeks, tears welling up in their dark depths. "If only your mother and father could see you now."

"Do I look all right?" Lorena questioned hesitantly.

"Do you look all right!" Dalia exclaimed. "You look beautiful. You are a vision, *chica*, and every man here this night will lose his heart when he sees you."

Some might, she thought, but never Clay.

"*Gracias*," she said, surprised at her feelings. Then she gave the plump woman a hug before she ventured out to greet the guests.

Lorena found Clay waiting outside for her, and despite her resolve, one look made her heart skip and flutter. He was not dressed in the traditional garb as the other men were, nor as an American gentleman, as she had imagined, but Lorena was sure she had never seen a man so devastatingly handsome. He wore a stark white shirt, open at the neck, tucked into crisp black trousers that hugged muscular thighs. And his black boots shone from a recent polishing.

"You look lovely," she offered without thinking.

Clay was momentarily at a loss, but before she had a chance to regret her words, he looked into her eyes and smiled. "Thank you, Lorena, but I think it is you who are lovely." He raised her hand to his lips, but instead of kissing the knuckles lightly, as was acceptable, he turned her palm to his lips, sending a tingling sensation through her body.

Self-consciously, she snatched her hand away but not before Clay saw the passion surge in her eyes. A small chuckle left his lips as he took her hand once again, putting it on his arm as he led her out to join their guests.

She spoke easily to everyone, introducing Clay to those he did not know. He smiled noncommittally whenever Lorena introduced him as her father's amigo who was helping with the transition of the hacienda. Clay watched with growing pride as she made her way through the crowd, her loveliness catching the attention of men and women alike.

After making all the introductions, Lorena excused herself to see if Dalia needed help.

She sighed with relief when she left Clay's side, having been uncomfortably aware of his presence as she spoke to all the people she had known as a child. Clay had been at ease with everyone, unaware of the turmoil he caused in her. She made her way toward the kitchen where she found Dalia busily instructing the other servants.

"Dalia," Lorena said firmly, "go find Pedro. I'll finish in here. This fiesta is for all of us to enjoy."

Reluctantly Dalia left, excited to find her husband and meet with old friends.

Food of all kinds covered the massive tables. Roasted chickens basted with spiced wine were stuffed with piñones nuts and raisins. There was baked ham and ribs of beef covered with seasoning, and baskets filled to overflowing with bread and tortillas. Bowls of hot chilies and bowls of beans sat next to kegs of wine and flagons of brandy made from Cielo el Dorado grapes. The libations flowed freely as friends and neighbors forgot about hardship and toil and simply enjoyed themselves.

After everyone had a chance to talk and say hello, adults followed the children's lead and made their way to the tables of food. They sat in groups, usually women separate from the men, talking and renewing the friendships that were seldom attended to as most lived so far apart. The ladies gossiped, before turning to fashions, but since there was so little of it in northern Mexico, they quickly moved on to everyday chores of running a household. Anyone who had a new item that had made its way up or down the trail would tell of her new treasure. But all in all, it didn't matter what they spoke of; it was purely a pleasure to have someone to talk and share with.

Clay was standing with a group of men when a black-eyed beauty sauntered up to them.

"*Hola*, hombres," she almost purred as she slipped her hand through one young man's arm.

"Hello, Carmen."

The men stood up straighter and vied for the beauty's attention—all the men, that is, except Clay. Leaning back against the wall, he seemed not to notice the new arrival. But he did not go unnoticed by Carmen Vega.

"Are you not going to introduce me to your amigo?" Carmen pouted.

"Oh, *sí*. Carmen, this is Señor Clay Wakefield. Señor, this is Carmen Vega from Paso del Norte."

Carmen had heard of Clay Wakefield and knew why he was here, so she was surprised that she had not guessed who he was right away. But in all that she had heard about the man, never once was it mentioned that he was so utterly handsome. Most men who worked the trail were a rough-looking lot that seldom did more than cuss and spit. Not that she minded—it was just a surprise to find one who was apparently a different sort of man. With that, she experienced a flash of jealousy that was not uncommon when it came to anything related to Lorena Cervantes. Lorena had always had everything, while Carmen had had to beg, borrow, or steal what little she had. And now, based on what she had heard, she was sure Lorena had this man as well. She could tell by the way he continued to glance in Lorena's direction, making sure that she was never out of his sight.

Lorena stood a bit away from the crowd, catching a cool breeze that stroked her warm body. She caught sight of Clay and noticed how well he moved among the people as if he belonged. But why shouldn't he? she reasoned. He had spent more time in this part of the world in the last five years than she had and apparently had been quite close to her father. It was as if the people here knew him better than they knew her. Especially, she noted irritably, Carmen Vega, who was shamelessly flirting with him. Just then Ramón, with his Spanish good looks, walked into the courtyard, and though she liked him only as a friend, suddenly she found herself walking up to greet him.

"Ramón!" Lorena called, smiling as he drew near.

Ramón turned to her voice and was taken aback by her beauty.

"Lorena," he said with the utmost propriety, "how good it is to see you."

She was surprised by his formality. Was he still mad at her for getting him involved in her plans to escape from Cielo el Dorado? "To think that the person responsible for my falling off a horse in the middle of town stands before me now as if we've just been introduced." Her teasing smile caught Ramón by surprise, but gradually a warm smile spread across his face.

"I am certain now that England did not change you."

"Much to everyone's chagrin." Lorena laughed and then looked at him seriously. "Are you mad at me for getting you involved in my attempted escape?"

Ramón had to force himself not to flinch, for the memory still filled him with anger—anger that had festered and grown. He was always thinking of a way to get back at the arrogant American. "No, Lorena," he lied, "I had forgotten all about it."

"Good," she said, relieved. "What do you say we get something to eat?"

"*Sí*, I think that is a fine idea."

Ramón took Lorena's arm, pulled it through his, and led her to the tables laden with food.

Clay's eyes were never far from Lorena and he had been aware of the moment the young pup, Valdéz, came in. He did not like the appreciative look the Spaniard had given Lorena, and he liked it even less when the boy took her arm. Clay stood with one shoulder propped against a thick cottonwood post, his anger boiling as he watched Lorena stroll across the courtyard on the arm of the young man. He was further infuriated when he overheard two matrons exclaim about what a handsome couple they made. But when Clay started toward the wayward couple, he was stopped by Ben.

"Clay," Ben cajoled, "this is a fiesta, a time for merry-making. From the looks of you, there is going to be murder tonight." Ben's teasing remarks only darkened his older brother's countenance. Wondering what could be wrong, Ben followed Clay's gaze. "So she is at it again." Ben laughed at his brother's discomfort. "You have a rival now, do you?" Slapping him on the shoulder Ben said, "The competition will be good for you," then turned to leave.

Clay started once again in Lorena's direction when he was stopped by Fray Cristóbal. "This is a wonderful fiesta," the priest said.

Knowing that to leave would be rude, Clay reluctantly stopped. "You'll need to tell Lorena. She has put together this whole affair."

At the mention of Lorena, as if reminded of something else, the priest looked seriously at Clay. "Have you told Lorena of the betrothal?"

Clay sighed. "No, Padre, I haven't."

The priest grumbled his disapproval. "She needs to

know, if for no other reason than that," he said while
gesturing to where Lorena sat next to Ramón eating a
plateful of food.

"I was just on my way to take care of that, so if you'll
excuse me . . ." Clay began to walk off when the priest
laid his hand on his arm.

"Tell her soon, Clay. It is best." The priest's eyes
implored him.

"Enjoy yourself, Padre," he said, avoiding any further
comment.

As Clay made his way through the crowd, Lorena's
tinkling laughter floated on the breeze. A frown furrowed
his brow as he came up behind the two.

"Tell me you didn't," Lorena said, laughing.

"Yes, but all turned out well," Ramón said confidently.

Clay felt a sudden urge to pull the young pup up by his
leather vest and flatten his aquiline nose.

As if sensing his presence, Lorena turned and found Clay
standing by them. "Clay!" she exclaimed, startled at
finding him there, but somehow relieved that he was no
longer talking to Carmen.

Ramón set his plate down on the bench next to him and
reluctantly stood up to greet the man he had come to hate.
It was not just the humiliating encounter while trying to
leave with Lorena; the entire town had been talking about
the man who was turning Cielo el Dorado around. People
spoke of Clay Wakefield as if he were a saint, a man who
could do no wrong, and that more than anything did not sit
well with the eldest Valdéz son. Standing in front of the
man now, his dislike was only intensified.

Clay looked down at the man who had claimed Lorena's
attention for longer than he liked and saw the man as the
self-indulgent, pampered son of a rich landowner. How
anyone could be pampered in this country was beyond him,
but pampered he seemed. He also saw right away from the
way Ramón stood possessively next to Lorena that the
young man planned to continue his pursuit, and that was

unacceptable. It was one thing for Lorena to get used to Clay in the confines of the hacienda but quite another for her to be courted by someone else.

Lorena could feel the tension that flowed between the men. Wanting to ease the awkward situation, she said, "Everyone seems to be enjoying—"

Not waiting for her to finish, Clay clasped Lorena's elbow firmly. "I would like a word with you, *querida*," he said meaningfully.

When Lorena tried to resist, she felt a firm pressure that brooked no refusal. "Excuse me, Ramón," she said almost over her shoulder as Clay led her away.

"You lout! How dare you! Not only do you come over and command my presence, but you call me *querida* as well, giving the impression that we are more than . . . than . . ."

"Than what?" he asked dryly.

"Than we are," she practically shouted, then lowered her voice when she saw that eyes had turned in their direction.

"And what are we, *querida*?" he repeated suggestively.

Lorena stopped abruptly. "I am not your darling! And *we*, Señor Wakefield, are nothing!" Earlier hopes were banished, crushed by his infuriating habit of domination.

"So, we are back to 'señor,' are we?" Clay wondered wryly why she disliked him so, and more important, why he cared. Certainly he would have preferred a willing bride, but for all the trouble she was causing him, why not just marry her and be done with it? The idea was instantly distasteful. He disliked the thought of an unwilling bride. Angry with the situation, he unfairly lashed out at Lorena. "In the future, you will not display yourself in such a wanton fashion."

"Wanton fashion!" she shrieked, outraged. "What was I doing?"

"Come now, Lorena. Sitting there with that young pup, gushing over him shamelessly." Jealousy he would not admit, so he blamed his emotions on his responsibility to watch over Lorena.

"Gushing over Ramón!" Lorena became more outraged by the second. "If anyone was acting shamelessly it was you, making a cake of yourself over Carmen Vega!"

Clay looked at Lorena in surprise, not immediately knowing who Carmen Vega was. Then, when he remembered, an amused grin found his lips, his ill temper swiftly gone. "Jealous, little one?"

Wanting nothing more than to wipe the arrogant grin off his face, Lorena replied in as haughty a voice as she could muster, "You think too highly of yourself, señor," after which she turned on her dainty heel and left him to stare at the smooth skin of her retreating back.

Ben Wakefield came up to his brother and, following the older man's gaze, caught sight of Lorena. "You certainly look pleased with yourself. Could it possibly have anything to do with a particular redheaded female we all know and love?"

Ignoring the comment, Clay turned to Ben and smiled. "Are you enjoying yourself, little brother?"

"Yes, enough to make it harder to leave in the morning."

Clay couldn't have been more surprised. "Leave in the morning? What are you talking about? We were going to go back to Missouri together."

"That was when you said you'd only be here for a month, two at the most. It's been almost three months now, and it doesn't look as if you're any closer to having your affairs in order than when you first got here. I have my own business to run, and I've already been away too long."

Clay knew he was right and as much as he wanted his brother to stay, he said, "Well then, I guess that makes this a going-away party as well. Have you told Lorena you are leaving?"

"No, I was going to do that as soon as I told you. I think I'll find her now."

Just as Ben walked off in the direction he had seen Lorena

go, the musicians began to tune up their instruments. There were two violins, a guitar, and a *guitarrón*, or bass guitar. The little boy whom Lorena had employed to keep the dance floor in order importantly sprinkled the area one more time with water, then went to stand to one side like a sentry ready to sprinkle the floor again at the slightest sign of dust.

The sun had plunged their world into darkness. Only the glow of candlelight shimmered about the courtyard, casting the group in a cocoon of light surrounded by darkness. The wine and brandy continued to flow, relaxing yet intensifying the emotions that stirred between the people. Older women sat stiffly in the straight-backed chairs, casting their protective eyes over the many young people who maneuvered toward the dancing partners of their choice. The old matrons' heavily powdered faces, fashionable in their youth, took on a purplish tint with the cast of the candlelight. Old men whose women no longer desired to take part in the rich Spanish dancing sat under the trees, smoking home-grown tobacco, drinking the fine brandy, and telling fantastic stories of their past, recounting tales of bravery, by the end of which, almost every man there began to believe his own words.

The music started in earnest then, usually a faster version of the songs that were played in church. They started with La Raspa, with its thundering parade of paired dancers.

Lorena danced with Ben, forgetting her worries, finding her release in the music she loved. When the song ended, Ben pulled her to the table of wine.

"I'm leaving tomorrow, first thing."

"So soon?" Lorena was surprised. She had genuinely come to like the carefree man and had enjoyed his playful banter. "Why have you not told me before?"

"I only just decided myself. Your hospitality has been wonderful, and I hope to see you again soon. Maybe in Missouri."

Lorena looked at him with a laugh. "I doubt I will ever go to Missouri."

"Oh, I don't know about that," Ben said cryptically, but before Lorena could question him a familiar voice joined them.

"I see my younger brother is informing you of his imminent departure." Clay's voice caressed her.

"Yes, but before I leave, it is back to the dance floor."

Ben offered his arm to Lorena, but before he could lead her away, Clay said, "I believe this is my dance with Lorena." He looked into Lorena's eyes, making her heart flutter out of control. Taking her hand he led her out just as a song was starting up.

The dance was fast and wild. Lorena abandoned herself to the strains of music, Clay moving with the controlled proficiency of a man who had danced it many times before. Watching Lorena, he felt a surge of desire sweep through his loins. He wondered how much longer he could wait for her as he watched her green eyes dance with excitement and her full lower lip curve up in a sensuous smile. His eyes traveled down the swanlike length of her neck and lingered over the mounds of flesh that stood tantalizingly concealed under the white lace of her dress. Just a small movement of his hand would reveal her breasts.

The music slowed down, giving the dancers a brief chance of intimacy before abruptly ending. Side by side, Lorena and Clay looked into each other's eyes, and instead of keeping his extended arm decorously away from her, Clay touched the smooth skin of her cheek, then let his hand trail down the neck he longed to kiss, stopping possessively on one bare shoulder.

Lorena's heart stopped as the exquisite sensations traveled through her body, leaving her weak in the knees. Afraid she could no longer stand, she leaned into his extended arm for support, her eyes never leaving his. The guests ceased to exist as the two stood on the dance floor oblivious to all except each other. It was the most perfect moment, time suspended, as they looked into each other's eyes. Was it possible? Could it be?

"I believe the music has stopped," Clay said, suddenly aware that all eyes were turned on them. He didn't care himself, but he didn't want to hurt Lorena.

Lorena jerked back as if burned. "Get your hands off me, you licentious libertine."

Clay's gaze darkened. The little shrew! "If I'm a licentious libertine, I hate to think what that makes you." As soon as the words were out of his mouth, Clay could have kicked himself, seeing the pain that struck her face. "I didn't mean that."

But his words went unheard, for Lorena was already storming away in a swish of white silk skirts. Clay ran his hand through thick black hair, leaving ridges from his fingers. His mouth was set in a grim line of frustration as he made his way toward the brandy, wondering how it was possible for a relationship to go so wrong so easily. He thought of how easy it had been with other women, so easy in fact that all he had to do was be available, as he had always been pursued. Suddenly that way of life looked awfully appealing. But then he smiled, knowing that it didn't appeal to him at all. What did appeal to him was a green-eyed spitfire who was going to be his wife . . . and soon, he added to himself, knowing he could not wait much longer.

His thoughts were interrupted. "Señor Wakefield, you must dance with me." Clay turned to find the dark beauty of Carmen Vega. Her black hair, which hung straight to her hips, framed black eyes and creamy olive skin so unlike Lorena's. Carmen was a traditional Spanish beauty, much sought after by both reputable and disreputable males in this faraway land that offered so few females. With nothing better to do, feeling it best to leave Lorena to cool her heels a bit, Clay accepted.

Lorena fumed as she sat next to Dalia, not listening to the chatter of the women around her. She was furious at that

no-good scoundrel, Clay, and even more so now as she
watched him dance with Carmen. The sight of the two made
Lorena boil. When Ramón sought her out, she agreed to
dance with him.

, The dance floor was crowded, but Clay was distinguish-
able by his incredible height—not to mention his incredible
good looks, she thought wryly. In an irrational attempt to
anger Clay, Lorena danced as if she were a part of the
music, causing the crowds on the floor to move back and
circle around to clap and cheer her on. Ramón, relishing the
attention, stood tall while Lorena danced the traditional
steps around him, his sleek, small movements standing in
stark contrast to the abandoned movements of her partner.
The music came to an end, and the crowd roared its
appreciation. A smile of pleasure curved Lorena's lips as
people once again began to dance. She turned to leave the
dance floor, only to meet Clay's dark scowl. Abruptly he
turned on his heel, Carmen Vega following.

Lorena had purposely set out to make Clay angry, but
now it seemed childish, and it hurt even more to see him
stalk off. She was certain Carmen had not made him mad.

At midnight the dancing was well under way, the older
women no longer so carefully watching. Lorena watched
for Clay, her hopes sinking as the time passed and there was
no sign of him. She decided to go to bed, sure that he was
off with Carmen. Her festive mood long gone, she left the
party unnoticed.

She lay in bed unable to sleep, listening to the pounding
of booted feet and the music, now an unpleasant reminder
of Clay and Carmen. When sleep finally came it was filled
with dreams that made her toss and turn.

The sounds of night nestled around Clay as his thoughts
drifted to Lorena. How furious he had been at seeing her
dance with Ramón! That had been bad enough, but to see
the lust in his eyes and in those of almost every man
there had made him want to pull her off the dance floor. But

he had restrained his anger, knowing that to make a scene would ruin the fiesta. Instead, he had left, thinking he would bury his anger in the eager flesh of Carmen Vega. The girl had been more than willing. Her hands had known all the right places, and it had been a long time since he had enjoyed a woman.

But now Clay sat on the roof looking out over the land, having rejected the attentions of the overbearing Carmen. Her ripe curves had been there for the taking, and after having gone so long without he had been tempted to take her up on the offer. But the picture of rich red hair and teasing green eyes made the offer seem pallid and uninteresting. When he pushed Carmen away, her eyes had flashed with anger. "She is no better than me," she had said cryptically before she stomped off. But Clay's mind was not on Carmen and what her remark could possibly mean. His thoughts were with Lorena.

Why was it that all his good intentions of winning her flew away the minute he was near her, making him act like an insecure schoolboy? Not for one minute did he think he was in love, but Lorena was his and nobody's else's. With that thought in mind, Clay climbed down the ladder, leaving the guards to themselves, and went in search of her.

In the courtyard he looked at the dance floor, expecting to find the errant girl dancing with the spoiled Spaniard. Not finding her there, he looked to the wine table. His hands clenched at his sides as he looked around and saw neither Lorena nor Ramón. She had done it now. It was one thing for her to dance with another man, but he'd be damned if he would put up with anything else. He strode over to Dalia.

"Where is Lorena?" he asked, obviously displeased.

Dalia looked around the courtyard and turned back to Clay. "I do not know. The last time I saw her she was dancing with Ramón." The duenna unconsciously drew back at the threatening look that crossed the man's face. The sooner she got Lorena married to Ramón and out of Clay Wakefield's hair, the better, she thought.

Clay went to the kitchen, then the *sala*, and when he found nothing, he went around to the other side of the hacienda. Drunken men shouted at him to join them before turning back to their bottles and card games when they were ignored. The men who had worked for him for years didn't give his behavior a thought, and the men from the hacienda were becoming used to him. Only the men from the surrounding areas, who did not know Clay, thought him rude.

It was in the cool, darkened recesses of the mill that he heard sounds that turned his anger into a maddening rage.

"Oh, Ramón," a soft voice moaned.

Ramón had not a second to respond to the seductive moan before he was pulled up from his passion to find a fist in his jaw. The vest was gone, and his shirt gaped open revealing a smooth hairless chest as Ramón stumbled back against the mud wall from the force of the blow.

Clay didn't waste any more time on the vermin he had just hit. He went instead for his betrothed, having no idea what he would do when he found her. When he had heard the telltale noises of lust, his rage knew no boundaries, but at the same time he felt sickened to think that his Lorena would be lost to him.

He reached into the darkness, caught a small wrist, and pulled with all his might, only to have the voluptuous curves of Carmen Vega crash into his body. For a moment her identity did not register on him. Who was this person? Where was he? What was he doing here? But then the reality of the situation came down on him like a downpour of cold rain, relief washing over him at not finding Lorena. Before he had a chance to explain, he felt a pain in his shoulder as Ramón wildly struck out in anger. Not having had much opportunity for fighting, the younger man was not very good, but what he lacked in skill he almost made up for in anger.

Clay turned with the blow, only to be caught unaware by a left hook to his jaw. He was too elated to be angry about a punch he knew he deserved, so instead of pummeling the man to the floor, Clay pinned him to the wall.

Ramón flailed wildly for a few seconds until exhaustion set in, after which he stood listlessly, panting from the exertion.

"Clay," Carmen said suggestively, "had I known, I would have waited for you."

Her offer repulsed him. He wondered how he ever could have thought she was even remotely pretty. Brushing her aside, he said to Ramón, "My apologies. I thought you were with someone else." His tone was apologetic yet brooked no argument.

Ramón was filled with impotent anger. He could think of nothing but that he had to teach the arrogant man a lesson. Yes, he would show him. He might not be as strong as the Norteamericano, but he would use his cunning to think of a way. Ramón had seen the possessive way the man looked at Lorena, and he was sure that was who Clay suspected he had been with. The thought brought a sinister smile to his lips as he watched the tall man walk out of the mill. Ramón promised himself that the next time Clay Wakefield found him, it *would* be Lorena underneath him. He would make sure of that.

Ramón turned back to Carmen, once again confident. "Where were we?"

Sounds of the party were dying as Clay made his way into the main courtyard. He had searched everywhere but found no sign of the missing Lorena. He'd checked the servants' quarters, the stables, the workrooms, and even the storerooms, the bathhouse, and the roof, none of which held Lorena. Guests were making their way to their rooms in the house or to their bedrolls outside. Some of the larger groups had set up camp outside the thick walls under the protection of the guards who patrolled through the night. Walking underneath the overhang of the porch, Clay passed the chapel and several guest rooms. When he passed Lorena's

room he noticed for the first time that her door was closed
and the windows shuttered. Why had he not thought of her
room in the first place? Clay didn't want to think that maybe
he had tried and convicted Lorena before she had done
anything wrong.

Relief flowed through his body, and without hesitating,
needing to reassure himself that Lorena indeed was there
and safe, he pushed the door open and stepped inside. If
anyone had seen him enter, Lorena's reputation would have
been ruined, but he was thinking only of his intense need to
see her.

A single candle glowed on the bedside table, casting its
yellow light on Lorena's sleeping form. Clay quietly closed
the door behind him, walked over to the bed, and sat down
on its edge. Her red hair shimmered as it lay spread out on
her pillow. His tanned fingers touched the locks that curled
about her face, then trailed gently through the long tresses,
luxuriating in its silky texture. She was so beautiful. Clay
felt his heart constrict with protectiveness. He let his fingers
caress her face, following the line of high cheekbones to
press seductively against her rosy lips. Lorena moaned in
her sleep, instinctively turning toward the warmth of his
body. Desire surged through him, his manhood swelling to
life. Leaning down, he let his lips follow the path of his
fingers, not stopping at her lips but continuing down her jaw
to find the silky softness of her neck.

Lorena dreamed of the tall dark stranger, of his tantalizing kisses, of his lips searing a path along her face to her
lips, only to be taken away as the journey continued down
her neck. One finger teased her nipple through the thin
material of her nightdress, her breast rising at his touch,
straining for more. Lorena arched toward the burning touch
only to have it disappear, leaving her bereft, filled with
desire, yearning for more. She sighed in disappointment,
sinking back down into the depths of sleep.

The unrestrained passion that she showed was almost his
undoing. When her delicate body arched up to his touch, it

was only with great restraint that Clay refrained from succumbing to the overpowering desire to bury himself deep in her welcoming flesh. Knowing that if he stayed there much longer he would not be able to stop what he never should have started, he pulled up the sheet that had fallen away from her shoulders, then stood up to look down into her sleeping face. Clay smiled when he envisioned Lorena's reaction had she been awake during his visit. She would not have been so acquiescent, he knew, and she'd have been furious after he stopped. It pleased him immensely to know she was as passionate as she was beautiful, but that she was not like Carmen Vega, who would share her gift with anyone. Only he, yes only he. He would be Lorena's only lover, and he looked forward to awakening her to the joys of his love.

11

THE FOLLOWING MORNING THE FRIENDS AND NEIGH-bors of the Cervantes family awakened after a night of feasting and dancing and prepared to pack up their things, then give thanks to their Lord and reaffirm their faith.

They stretched and yawned. The men began to pack their belongings as the women prepared a meal to break their fast. Later they would all gather for Mass. Usually Sundays were days of visiting and relaxing after the religious ceremony, but as the night before had held a fiesta and many people had to travel a long way to reach their homes, the guests would leave promptly after Mass.

Lorena woke feeling gloriously alive. She had no idea why she felt so good, especially when she thought about the hurtful words Clay had said. But for some unknown reason, her body tingled with excitement. She didn't care to contemplate the matter as she slipped into a Mexican dress made of a soft blue cotton that caressed her smooth skin as she pulled it over her head. A sash of the same blue mixed with white accentuated her small waist. Lorena used a small piece of the same material to tie her hair back, leaving a few soft tendrils to frame her face. Looking herself over in the old mirror, Lorena decided it was good enough, though anyone else would have said she was lovely.

"Good morning," she said to no one in particular as she walked onto the patio where people were beginning to move about. While the patio and courtyard held only the first glimmers of activity, the kitchen was alive and buzzing when she walked in.

Dalia turned her head, not turning her body away from her task at the counter. "*Buenos días, chica.* How are you this morning?"

"Fine, thank you. What is going on?" she asked, already having seen the outside table covered with food for the guests who wanted to partake. "It looks as if you already have the food prepared."

"For the guests, yes, but Señor Ben is leaving this morning and we are preparing food for him to take."

"Before mass? Why?" Lorena asked, knowing well enough that the caravan would leave by first light, which was rapidly approaching.

"*Sí,* he is leaving before mass. Go out and look for yourself if you do not believe me. And as for why, I do not know. You ask me questions I have no answers for. You must ask Señor Ben or Señor Clay. Now out of the kitchen with you; we have much to do in a short time." Dalia shooed Lorena out of the kitchen, a dried piece of meat in one hand and a knife in another.

Out in the courtyard Lorena noticed what she had missed earlier—general activity in the vicinity of the front gate, which gaped open as men walked freely in and out.

"Who are all these people?" Lorena asked Pedro, who stood to one side surveying the activity. "I don't recognize many of them."

"They are the men of the caravan that Ben Wakefield is to travel with. They are loading up his things and fixing wheels, axles, harnesses, and the like before they set out toward Chihuahua."

"Chihuahua! I thought he was going back to Missouri," Lorena said in confusion.

"I think he did not even know himself until late last night

when a rider came and told us of the caravan that had arrived in Paso del Norte."

"Well, regardless of where he is going, I must find Ben and say good-bye."

Lorena rounded the thick wall that separated the two courtyards and found Clay talking to Ben. They were standing close together, intent on whatever they were saying, neither noticing Lorena as she approached.

"Good morning," Lorena said as she came up to the two men, the mere sight of Clay filling her with an uncomfortable but undeniable sense of joy. She told herself to remember Carmen Vega, though to no avail as her heart continued to race.

Clay and Ben turned to Lorena at the same time, both with an inviting smile.

"Good morning," Ben said.

Clay merely smiled as his eyes perused her body.

Lorena felt heat creep into her face.

"Really, big brother, it's not nice to embarrass a lady," Ben teased.

"I'm not embarrassed," Lorena stated emphatically, pride asserting itself, mad at herself for acting like a flighty fool. And before they could say anything else, she continued. "Anyway, I came to say good-bye, Ben. If you were not going away, and I knew when I would see you again, I would chastise you for not letting me know sooner that you were leaving. If I hadn't gotten up early I probably would have been shouting my good-byes to the tail end of a cloud of dust!"

Ben picked Lorena up and swung her around, then crushed her to his chest. "You are something, you know that? And thank you for not chastising me," he added in mock thankfulness. "It seems to me, however, that I told you last night."

"Well, yes," she conceded, "but not that I was not going to have a chance to say good-bye unless I got up at the crack of dawn."

"I apologize profusely, lazybones," he teased.

"You're a scoundrel, Ben Wakefield. Now put me down." Her smiling eyes belied her stern words.

But Clay's eyes were no longer smiling. "Yes," he said dryly, "put her down."

Setting her down, Ben threw his head back and laughed. "I may not be leaving after all, Lorena. It looks as if I may be fighting a duel."

"You two are impossible!" she said shaking her head, long tresses brushing her back. "Before you go, is there anything you need?"

"No, Lorena, but thank you for offering." Ben's face lost its smile as he looked seriously into her eyes and took her hand decorously. "And thank you for the hospitality in your lovely home. Since my plans have changed," he said, momentarily turning a meaningful gaze on Clay, "I will be back soon to impose once again on that very kindness."

"What is this about you going to Chihuahua instead of back to Missouri?" Lorena's features turned serious.

Ben looked at Clay, who gave a barely perceptible shake of his head, then turned to Lorena. "Ben has some business to take care of in Chihuahua."

Lorena looked doubtfully from Clay to Ben and then back to Clay. "Why did he not know about this business before last night?" she asked, sensing that Clay was not truly answering her question.

It was Ben who answered. "I just found out about it last night when a messenger came," he replied truthfully. "And don't you worry about me," he continued. "There's nothing for you to be concerned about. Now I've got to go. I'll see you soon."

"Adios" was all she had a chance to say as he walked to the gate to mount his horse. As she watched him walk his horse through the gate, she could feel Clay next to her, his shirt brushing against her bare arm. "You are worried about him, yes?" she asked without looking at him.

Clay watched the gate close behind his brother, then

turned to Lorena. "No, I'm not worried about him. It is strictly business he has to take care of." When Lorena looked at him skeptically, he added, "Really." And it was true—only he failed to tell her that it was his business, or rather, their business—business that Diego had left behind for them to take care of. He cursed Diego. How could he have left such a mess for his only child? Though Clay still did not know the extent of what Diego's affairs entailed, he had a fairly good idea that his good friend had been in deep trouble before he died.

Lorena looked at Clay and decided it would be futile to question him further. "I think I'll go to mass."

The chapel was already filling when Lorena and Clay walked in. Soon people would have to pull up benches in the courtyard to listen to the ritual from outside. Dalia and Pedro were sitting near the front when Lorena and Clay joined them.

The mass began. The musicians who had played the night before now played tunes that filled Lorena with a sense of peace. Lorena looked at the altar, above which hung a crucifix, while the priest spoke to the crowd.

When the sermon ended, communion was offered, and soon the group was making its way toward breakfast.

Eggs, ham, beans, fruit, and bread crowded Lorena's plate when she passed the kitchen table, where a group of guests sat partaking of the feast.

"The fiesta was wonderful, Lorena." It was Harold Selig from the general store and while she did not remember seeing him the night before, she knew he had been invited.

"Yes, very nice," another chimed in.

Lorena was pleased. "Thank you, I'm glad you enjoyed it."

"Sit down here," a woman scooted over to make room for Lorena at the crowded table.

"Thank you, but no. I am going to go sit outside on the patio."

Lorena sat down in a secluded corner under a huge tree, relishing the quiet. As much as she liked her friends and neighbors, she looked forward to the peace that would follow their departure. With eyes closed, savoring the taste, Lorena slowly chewed a slice of succulent fruit.

"You eat more than anyone I know."

Lorena opened her eyes to find Clay standing over her. A shiver of excitement swelled in her breast as she looked at him. A smile broke out on her face. "Surely someone you know eats more than I do?" she asked with a teasing smile.

"You would think so, but I have yet to see it." Clay looked appreciatively at her smile. "It's a wonder you don't weigh two-hundred pounds."

"Don't worry, I'll probably be there soon."

Clay sat down beside her on the bench, leaning back against the adobe wall, looking out over the activity in the courtyard. "I'd say the party went well."

"Fiesta," Lorena corrected with a giggle.

Clay looked at her sardonically with one raised eyebrow as he drawled, "Yes, fiesta."

They sat in comfortable silence, Lorena eating her breakfast, Clay gazing out into the courtyard. When he looked back at Lorena, she was taking another bite of fruit, and a tiny rivulet of juice was running down her chin. Before she could wipe it away, Clay reached out with one long, tanned finger to catch it. His touch was a soft caress, starting at the base of her chin and slowly burning a path up to her lips. He pressed a juice-covered finger to her lips as his eyes burned into hers. Instinctively Lorena parted her lips, then timidly touched her tongue to his finger. Clay leaned forward as if to capture the tantalizing tongue with his own when the sound of wagons broke the spell.

Lorena jerked back at the sound and, with a fluttering stomach, hastily stood up. "The guests are leaving." As Lorena tried to walk off, Clay stood, gently grasping her elbow. Taking the plate of food from her, he set it down on the bench, never letting go of her arm. Then he propelled her toward the gates to bid their friends farewell.

Ramón and Carmen had been among the first to leave, neither having waited to attend mass. They made their way through the heavy wooden gate, having met by chance while readying their horses. They rode together in silence, lost in their own troubling thoughts.

Ramón had been looking forward to spending a great deal of time with Lorena, but Clay Wakefield had interfered at every turn. And the man had come upon him and Carmen, then simply turned and left, as if he was in no way out of line. Ramón burned with rage. "He is an arrogant piece of scum!"

His words startled Carmen out of her thoughts. "Who is?"

Ramón looked at Carmen and rolled his eyes heavenward. "Need you ask? Clay Wakefield, that is who." Ramón looked out across the land. "How I despise the man."

Carmen's eyes narrowed. "You despise him, do you?"

She did not listen to his answer as her mind churned with thoughts. Finally she said, "You are right, Ramón. Clay Wakefield is a horrible man." When she saw that Ramón lapped up the words like a thirsty dog drinking water, she continued, "It is a shame such a man will have Lorena."

"He will not!" he shouted, his face growing red, his eyes wild with anger. "She is mine, not his!"

Carmen hid her smile. She did not ask him why, if he was so taken with Lorena, he spent so much intimate time with her. Instead she went about adding fuel to his fire. "She will not be yours if you do not do something about it."

Ramón looked at her suspiciously. "What do you mean?"

"I mean, Ramón," she stressed the words, impatient with his slow-mindedness, "that if you do not do something to prevent it, Lorena will indeed belong to Clay Wakefield."

Blood surged to his face; his eyes bulged in his head. "What would I have to do?"

Carmen hesitated. "Let me think about it."

"I must know—now!"

"Patience, Ramón, patience."

Carmen left Ramón once they arrived in Paso del Norte. She rode west into the foothills of the Sierra Madre where she approached a small camp nestled in a tight canyon. Had she not known where it was, she never would have found it. She heard rhythmic sounds volleyed through the ravine, and she knew she had been spotted and announced. She rode into the camp, and though outwardly no one appeared to notice her arrival, she could feel their hard stares from beneath lowered lashes and downturned hat brims.

There were no more than a dozen or so people roaming about the area, and Carmen paid them little heed. She went directly to a makeshift lean-to and dismounted.

"Calderón," she called.

A man of no great height but substantial girth stepped out into the light. He squinted his beady eyes a few times before focusing on the young woman before him.

"Ah," he said at last while running a gnarled hand over his unshaven face. "Señorita Vega. What brings you to our humble abode?"

"I have a proposition for you. A way to make some money."

The man laughed. "You have come out here to tell me how to make money? We don't need your money right now." Calderón hated working for this woman. "We already have a few things going. Maybe another time, eh?"

Carmen clenched her fist at her side but held her temper. "I am not talking about a little money. I am talking about a great deal of money. Enough so you and your friends would not have to take on . . . odd jobs anymore."

Calderón eyed her speculatively. "Come, sit down. Tell me about this job."

Carmen looked about the camp before following the man. She took an old tin cup filled with coffee once they sat before a smoldering fire, then got right down to business. "There is a girl—many say she is a great, exotic beauty— who will bring you much money in Mexico City."

Calderón eyed her. "Who is this girl?"

"A servant," Carmen answered immediately. "A servant who will not be missed. In fact, with her beauty, it will be suspected that she ran off with some man."

"Why do you tell me about this girl?"

Carmen moved uncomfortably.

Calderón smiled. "What, pretty señorita, is in it for you?"

Her black eyes flashed with anger. "Never mind what is in it for me. There is money in it for you. She will bring you a fortune. Many will want her."

They looked at each other across the small space.

"Will you do it?" Carmen asked.

Calderón laughed. "*Sí*, I will do it."

When the heavy wooden gate was finally pulled shut after the last departing guest, Lorena sighed and would have leaned back against Clay had she not caught herself first.

"That takes care of that," Clay said.

"Yes, I suppose it does. Now for the cleanup."

Everyone pitched in to tidy up the hacienda. They put away tables and benches and cleaned stacks of dishes. Tablecloths, linens, towels, and the like they put in a heap for the big washing that would take place the next week.

By the time everything was done Lorena was dripping with sweat from the burning sun.

"How about a swim?" Clay asked.

Lorena wavered in indecision, wanting badly to go, but thoughts of Carmen Vega loomed darkly in her mind. Just as Lorena was about to ask Clay about the time he spent with her, Pedro interrupted. "That is a very good idea. Luz, Jaime, you go for a swim with Lorena and Señor Clay."

Clay looked at the old man in disbelief, ready to make a sharp retort, putting him in his place, when all three eager swimmers cried in unison, "That is a great idea."

With a scowl, Clay started toward the stables. "If we're going, hurry up."

Lorena, Luz, and Jaime quickly scurried after him, and when they got to the stables Lorena said, "We really don't need to take horses."

Clay raised one thick, dark eyebrow in question, knowing that the times he had been there he had ridden.

Lorena went on to explain. "If we go out the back gate it is only a short distance to a swimming hole."

The other two chimed in their agreement, and Jaime added, "*Sí*, Señor, we swim there often."

Clay wondered if they were talking about the same swimming hole that he knew of, the one where he had found Lorena when he first arrived, the one he had always thought was distant and secluded.

The small group of four strolled down the sandy path that led toward the river. Sure enough it was not the same swimming hole. This one was larger, surrounded by old cottonwood trees. Silver poplars intermingled with the craggy cottonwoods, and tall grasses hid the area from unsuspecting eyes.

Jaime swam in trousers cut off above the knee while the girls wore heavy muslin chemises and pantalettes. While technically the women were in their underclothes, the thick garments showed no more curves than the dresses they normally wore during the day.

With Luz and Jaime around, swimming no longer held much appeal for Clay, so he lay back on the grass under a tree and closed his eyes. He heard the splash of water as they dived and played, and he wondered if possibly he had been fooled about their ages. They all acted like young children.

After some time, the splashes calmed down, causing Clay to open one eye to see what was going on. Luz and

Jaime were treading water as they looked up into the towering heights of a tree. The sight that Clay found when he followed their gaze stole his breath away. Fear surged through his limbs, pulling him up from his grass bed in one pantherlike leap. "What are you doing up there!" he raged.

Lorena sent down a tinkling laugh, "Silly, what do you think I'm doing up here? I'm going to jump."

"Like hell you are!" he bellowed, causing the two in the water to scurry to the bank and clamber out of the cool depths. "Get down here . . . *now*!" he commanded, hands on hips, feet spread wide, debating if he should go up and get her.

Defiance and anger swept through her. Why did he always order her around? She had been jumping off this tree branch for as long as she remembered, and just to show how little influence he held over her, she stepped off the bough and plunged gracefully into the water.

Clay's stomach plummeted at the sight of Lorena falling through the air. He felt a panic that he had never felt before. What if she missed? What if she hit the bottom? A number of other possible mishaps raced through his mind, leaving him shockingly afraid that he would lose her. Before he had a chance to examine his thoughts, the wet head of Lorena popped out of the water as she took a deep breath of fresh air. The smile that lit her face only served to turn Clay's fear into an all-consuming rage. He knew she could have killed herself, and yet she had popped up like a circus clown, ready for praise and laughter! A few swift strokes brought Lorena to the riverbank, where Clay caught one small wrist and pulled her unceremoniously out of the water.

Fury etched his face. Lorena tried to step away, but his iron grip held her, not letting her escape his impending rage.

Without turning his head, Clay spoke to the two spectators who stood uncertainly on the bank. "Go back to the hacienda," he said through clenched teeth.

"Come, Lorena," Luz braved.

"Not Lorena. Now go!" Clay's dark eyes burned like coals, never wavering from Lorena's face. His chest heaved with the superhuman effort it took to remain calm. Her disobedience could have led to injury. She could even have killed herself. His orders were only for her own good.

Luz and Jaime quickly gathered up their discarded clothing and shoes, tripping over themselves in their haste to escape.

When Clay knew they were gone, he spoke in a voice that Lorena could barely hear. "You could have hurt yourself."

"I've jumped from that tree a million times," she said defiantly.

He jerked her closer so that she had to tilt her head back to see his face. "You haven't done it in at least five years, since we both know you were in England."

"What does that matter?" Her eyes snapped.

"For your information"—it was almost a snarl—"the water level could have changed, and there's no telling what type of debris could have found its way into the pool— wood, rocks, any number of equally dangerous objects. And for another—"

Lorena looked away rebelliously, though without much conviction. "You don't need to tell me another." She felt embarrassment squelch her defiance altogether, as she thought of how truly reckless she had been.

When Clay saw the understanding look in her eyes, his rage slowly began to die. "Don't ever do that again, little one." His voice was a hoarse whisper.

Lorena began to protest, but Clay added, "Please." Then as if to reassure himself that Lorena was indeed alive and well, he clutched her to him and captured her lips in a punishing kiss.

Lorena mumbled a protest. Clay lessened his pressure but did not let her go. He molded her lips to his, then trailed fiery kisses across to her ear, where he took the small lobe between his teeth, gently nipping, sending a shiver of pleasure down her spine as his warm breath caressed her skin. After kissing her ear, his lips made their way down her jaw to the rapid heartbeat in her neck. Biting and tasting her sweet skin, he continued his onslaught down to that juncture between neck and shoulders, all the while guiding her to the ground. He brushed the strap of her chemise to one side and kissed the skin beneath it.

Despite the sweet sensation, reality intruded, causing Lorena to pull back from the confusing emotions. She tried to turn away from his kiss, but a grip of iron held her fast. When she tried to push him away, he captured her wrists, holding them on either side of her head as he looked into her eyes, searching for answers, answers that he wanted, that she was unwilling to give.

Clay reclaimed her lips, reluctant to let her go, molding them to his once again, demanding entrance to the hidden depths. He tasted her gently at first until she tentatively flicked her tongue against his. The timid touch sent spirals of shock through his body. So sweet was it that his tongue grew bolder, more demanding, as it plunged, then pulled back, only to plunge again. He pushed her to the ground, never letting her go, to continue his plundering kisses.

Lorena tried to push him away, push away the emotions he was making her feel. Not able to fight his massive body, she turned her head away, only to feel Clay's lips move sensuously across her cheek to her ear where his hot tongue licked and his teeth gently bit, sending shivers of feeling through her body, making it difficult to breathe. "Clay, no," she whispered through panting breaths. But Clay was undaunted, moving his lips from her ear down the sensitive column of her neck, chasing all reason from her mind.

He was unaware of anything except her body, her passion. In that moment, lying on the hard ground, her body pressed against his, Clay lost his resolve to wait until they were married. The intensity was almost unbearable; he

wanted her as he had wanted nothing else in his life. He
wanted her with every fiber of his being; every inch of his
body was aflame, ready to explode. And he would have her,
now. They would just have to marry sooner. His decision
made, he pursued her relentlessly, turning her insides to
liquid, making it impossible for her to resist.

With one last gallant effort Lorena tried to push him off,
knowing that if she didn't, she would not be able to turn
back. But reason deserted her, leaving her body to arch
against his.

Lorena gave herself over to the fire that burned out of
control within her, savoring the sensations as they coursed
through her body. She sought his tongue to taste his
sweetness, and with a groan, Clay took hers into his mouth
to suck sensually. He let go of her arms to find them
wrapping around his neck. As he plundered her mouth, his
hand sought her skin, finding it at her midriff, underneath
the thick chemise that she wore. Slowly he pulled the
garment up to reveal the soft swells beneath. He looked
down in appreciation before his mouth took one sweet
breast.

Sensation exploded through her as she felt his lips on her
breast. A moan escaped her lips as she arched closer to the
pleasure. Clay pushed the garment up as far as he could,
then brought his hand down to cup the breast he had just
left. He pulled one rosy nipple into his mouth, biting gently.
He went from one to the other, biting and nipping, sending
shocks of pleasure through Lorena. His mouth trailed back
to her mouth as he shifted his weight, coming to lie on top
of her, careful not to put his full weight on her. His tongue
sought her mouth, and as he plunged inside, the hardness of
his manhood pressed against her belly. His breath sent
tingles of pleasure down her spine when he ordered thickly,
"Put your arms around me."

When she tried to protest his demands, he plundered her
mouth, kissing her into submission, as her arms slid around
his body to explore the contours of his back. The fire began

to build, starting in the depths of her being, building until it engulfed her entire body, filling her with a want, a need that she wanted to explore, to satisfy. Reaching out for that elusive something, Lorena began to return his kisses, exploring his eyes, his face, his lips, with her own.

His lips trailed once again down her neck, stopping only when he came to one full, rounded breast. Finally he released her from her few garments, leaving her splendid body open to his ministrations.

Lorena felt cool air hit her skin, followed immediately by hot searing kisses. He took one erect nipple in his mouth to lave it with his tongue again and again, sending a sweet pulsing sensation to the core of her womanhood. "Oh, Clay," she cried, arching up to meet the rhythm of his lips.

The simple movement sent Clay into a whirl of almost uncontrollable need. His mouth shifted to her other breast while he lowered his hand to her ribs, then down her abdomen, until it met the sweet triangle of curls that covered her womanhood.

Instinctively Lorena pulled back, frightened by the unfamiliar touch.

"Don't," he commanded thickly, his hand not relinquishing its sweet treasure. His lips reclaimed hers, one long finger gently circling the core of her being, never entering, only teasing until the tension left her. Her hands began to wander down his back until they reached his tightly muscled hips. Slowly, erotically, Lorena began to move her hips against his solitary finger, wanting, needing, mindlessly pushing away his shirt, wanting to touch him as he touched her, with nothing between them, nothing in the way. But her senses were doused with icy water when she heard her name, spoken not in passion, spoken not by Clay but by someone else, from a distance.

"Lorena!"

The sound barely pierced Clay's consciousness.

"Lorena!" This time the voice was closer, more demanding, forcing Clay to pull back and take account of his surroundings. He looked down into the passion-glazed eyes of Lorena, trailed a smoldering gaze down the sweetness of her body, and reached for her again, forgetting the interruption until her named sounded again.

"Damn," he cursed hoarsely. It was Pedro, and he was looking for them.

"Get up, little one. It seems Pedro is looking for you."

Just as Lorena pulled herself together, Pedro came around the corner. Her body still tingled with sensation, but her mind was rapidly filling with disbelief at what had just taken place. Not daring a glance at Pedro, she hurried back to the hacienda, leaving Clay and Pedro on the riverbank.

Once out of their sight, Lorena hastened her step. As her breathing slowed, her mind tumbled with thoughts, and ultimately she reaffirmed her resolve to stay away from Clay Wakefield, the unscrupulous cad. He had made it more than clear that he thought she was little more than a bother—a wanton bother at that. And he treated her like a possession, just as her father had treated her mother. Lorena painfully remembered the lonely days and nights her mother had spent, but instead of confronting her father when he did finally come home, her mother had fallen into his reluctant embrace, only to be left behind again and again. She would never be like her mother! *Never!*

Knowing that she could never marry, Lorena returned to the hacienda feeling lost and empty. Yet, the aching thrill she had felt with Clay near the swimming hole still echoed through her body, refusing to let her forget her desire . . .

Back at the swimming hole, Clay turned a dark scowl on Pedro. "Your timing is not good," Clay said, still thinking about the passion that raged in his body.

Pedro only chuckled. He felt sure that Clay was going to marry Lorena, and his suspicions had only been confirmed by the cryptic remarks of the padre. Yes, they would marry, and though Lorena fought against the Americano now, he knew that in the long run there was no better man for his headstrong girl. "No, Clay, I think I arrived not one second too soon."

Clay looked at the old man, and his dark countenance turned to an amused smile. "Pedro, I think you're acting like a protective father."

"If not me, who?" He shrugged his shoulders resignedly.

"Yes, who? I guess I am going to have to concede to you this time, Pedro. She was indeed in need of protecting." But all Clay could think of was Lorena's passionate body. For a second he had been ready to damn them all, strap her on a horse if she fought him, take her across the river to the priest, and have him marry them right then. The thought was extremely tempting, but his original reason for the delay came to him, though unwelcome at the moment. He wanted her now, this instant, willing or not. But his reason asked about the future. Didn't he want her to come willingly to his bed? He would have to wait. Damn! Clay wondered if Lorena would ever be willing. Sometimes he doubted it.

As if sensing his thoughts, Pedro said, "You know, Clay, it is said that the more you try to tame something, the wilder it becomes as it fights against what someone or something else inflicts upon it. Show her the way, Clay. Don't force her to follow it."

Clay looked at the man, his face a map of time. He looked doubtful.

"She will come around, Clay. I know it."

"You sound so sure; how is that?" Clay asked, truly curious.

"I have known Lorena since she was born. I have seen her grow, and the things that have caused her to be the way she is."

Clay looked at the man, trying to discern from his words the meaning that eluded him. "What do you mean?"

"You will know soon. Be patient. All will turn out well."

"You're a wise man, Pedro," Clay said sincerely.

"No, not wise. I've just been at it longer than you."

Pedro turned to leave, but stopped as he started to walk away. Without turning around he said, "The fruits of marriage are a privilege only to those who are married." And then he left, leaving Clay no doubt that Pedro had guessed his intentions.

12

THE SUMMER DAYS CRAWLED BY, AND THE HEAT that Lorena had cherished before now only added to her frazzled nerves. She was back to avoiding Clay, though it didn't take much effort, as he spent much of his time locked in her father's study. When he came out, he was in no mood to talk, often saddling a horse to ride out toward town.

"Blast him," she swore, then kicked a rock that lay in her path. "Ouch!" she cried as her toes throbbed with pain. She sat down on a bench and rubbed her foot, her gaze inadvertently finding the study where Clay Wakefield sat at that very moment. He made her so mad she could have screamed. He still treated her like a burden, a bother, as if she had no brain, like a possession! The thought made her fume, and to add salt to the wound, she would remember the look in his eyes as he, in essence, called her a wanton hussy. She ignored the fact that he had actually said she was dancing in a wanton fashion, and that indeed, she had been dancing with wild abandon, and that both Dalia and Pedro had chastised her for her behavior. No, she did not think of that. Indeed, she thought of nothing that redeemed the cad. But eventually she always forgot his ill behavior and recalled his dark eyes penetrating her soul, his hot kisses searing a path across her body. Whenever she happened to

catch sight of him, across the courtyard or talking to a
guard, her mind swirled with images of his lips caressing
her skin while his hands danced a forbidden dance in places
that pulsed with longing every time he was near. He was a
devil, she was convinced, to fill her with feelings she had
no desire to feel. Why couldn't she look at him with
indifference as she did other men, or as a friend as she did
Ramón? Yes, Ramón was only a friend. But wouldn't her
life be simpler if she could bring herself to marry him? That
would solve her problems. He, she knew, had no desire to
go on the trail and would probably be more than glad to
relinquish the duties of running a hacienda to her. But
though this was what she said she wanted, she could not
find any pleasure in the thought.

The days became monotonous. The only surprise was
when Jaime came to tell her proudly of his new responsibility: He was to be available to ride with her whenever she
wanted.

"Who told you that?" she had asked, though already she
knew.

"Señor Wakefield," he had responded, his chest puffed
up with pride.

So she had been riding daily, disgruntled that she could
not ride alone, but grudgingly thankful that she was able to
get out at all.

Lorena and Jaime had ridden into Paso del Norte on more
than one occasion to visit friends and make purchases from
the traders. She had seen Ramón once or twice and had even
gone to visit his family at El Rancho Escondido.

That day she had stayed at the Valdez hacienda too long,
forgetting the time, only remembering she should be getting
home when the lowering sun began to cast lengthening
shadows across the room. Hurriedly, so as not to worry
anyone, Ramón, Lorena, and Jaime quickly left, Jaime
cursing that he was surely going to lose his new responsibility, Ramón cursing that his father had insisted that he see
the two home. They raced through town, then across the

swollen river to arrive at Cielo el Dorado just as the sun went down.

"Where have you been?" Clay asked, anger lacing his voice, not bothering to look at Ramón or Jaime.

"At El Rancho Escondido," she responded, "the time just got—"

"*El Rancho Escondido!*" he exploded when he heard she had been at Ramón's home. He looked at the young pup with contempt.

The explosion of words and the anger in his eyes made Lorena step back, but when he grabbed her arm and said, "You will not go there again," fury almost choked her.

"Not go there again! You have no right!" she seethed, outraged. "I am not a possession. And I do as I please!" She tried to pull away to no avail. His grip was like a band of iron.

"You will not go there again," he repeated. "Ever!" His voice was deadly calm, his dark eyes black with fury. "Now go to your room before I punish you with more than words."

Lorena started to protest, to kick and scream as she longed to do, but the glint in his eyes bespoke something she was not sure of, something that sent a chill through her body, that scared her more than she admitted.

She pulled her arm away, and this time he let go. But as she walked toward her room, after she was well out of his reach, she hollered over her shoulder, "I will do as I please!"

When she heard a sound come from him that could only have been called a growl, Lorena ran to her room and began to breathe again only when her door was safely slammed behind her.

Lorena was as surprised as anyone when Ramón Valdez began showing up at the hacienda frequently, always bringing some small gift for her.

Clay was curt but polite at first, not being hospitable but not sending him on his way either. But as time wore on, and

Ramón's visits became even more frequent, Clay took
notice, coming out of the study more often, seeking Lorena
out.

One morning Clay stood at the study window gazing out
into the courtyard, one shoulder leaning against the wall. A
scowl marred his handsome features as he looked without
seeing. He had been working on the financial records, going
through every entry since Diego had begun doing the books,
then back even further. What he found did not please him,
and the resentment he had begun to feel toward Diego
Cervantes, first over Lorena, and now over his financial
condition, was growing day by day. It was not that he
wanted the money or a problem-free hacienda. It was that
Diego could have done these things to his daughter.
Lorena's father had betrothed her to a man she did not even
know, and now Clay was finding that he had left her with a
debt-ridden home. Clay wondered where it would all end.
The more he delved into the matter, the more he found.

Just then, movement from the kitchen caught his attention. He focused his gaze to find Lorena coming out, Dalia
close behind. A smile lit Lorena's face, causing a tightening
sensation to grip Clay's chest. She was so beautiful, he
thought to himself, and she would be his.

Lorena laughed at Dalia.

"You put that hat on, *chica*, right now," he heard Dalia
say, clenched hands planted firmly on ample hips. "Your
skin is already too brown. Soon you will look like the
vaquero I told you about when you first got back."

Lorena giggled as she put a large piece of bread firmly
between her teeth. Then she took the straw hat she had
smashed under her arm and tied it on her head. "There,"
she said, pulling the bread from her mouth, leaving one
large bite inside. She waved the bread in the air and started
quickly across the courtyard on her way to the stables.

Quickly making up his mind, Clay left the desk covered
with papers and followed her.

By the time he got there, only a few minutes after she, the

hat she had put on for Dalia was already hanging on her back. Clay smiled at the errant girl, forgetting all the problems he had been dealing with, intent on enjoying her company.

"Off to ride?" His voice was deep and smooth.

Lorena had not spoken to him since their run-in over her visit to El Rancho Escondido. Her pulse quickened. How she had missed the sound. Turning around, wondering what he could possibly want, she found a smile spread across his face. Her breath caught at his handsomeness. "Yes," she responded breathlessly, hoping she didn't have butter running down her chin.

Clay saw Jaime with a saddled horse. "Jaime, I will be riding out with Señorita Cervantes today."

Lorena turned quickly, afraid that Clay would see the excitement in her eyes. He was just like her father, she reminded herself, but at that moment nothing mattered but being with him.

A few minutes later the heavy gate was pulled open, releasing them to the land that spread out before them. The crops were heavy with their burden, and soon they would be harvested.

"I read in Diego's notes that the grapes are harvested in September," he said, his eyes scanning the rows of vines.

"Yes, the vineyard is just around the corner. People will come from miles around to help with the harvest. I remember it as a time of great fun." Lorena's eyes smiled at the memory.

Their horses walked down the hill toward the grapes that would be harvested to make raisins, wine, and brandy. Clay could almost feel the tension flow from Lorena's body as she neared the vineyard. He turned slightly to look at her and found that she was totally unaware of him, lost in thought, a slight smile playing across her face.

"You love this land, don't you?" he asked.

A sigh escaped her lips. "Yes, I do. It is my home, and I love it, but most of all I love the vineyard."

"Didn't you like England?" he asked, though he felt sure he knew the answer.

Lorena gave a small laugh. "I hated it at first."

"Really? Why? Because they made you dance with girls and embroider altar cloths?" he teased gently, remembering their earlier conversations about her school.

Lorena glanced at him in mock disgust. "Wouldn't that do it to anyone?"

The horses walked contentedly on while Lorena seemed lost in her thoughts. After a short time she said, "My world had been turned upside down. My mother had recently died, and then my father shipped me off to a foreign country. The people in England spoke a different language, they ate different foods, and their weather was very different." She paused before continuing. "I never got used to the weather. Papa said it was best for me to go away—I still wonder why."

Clay took her words in and saw a small, lonely little girl being sent away. How could a father do that to his child?

A scowl darkened Clay's face, and Lorena, not wanting his pity, instantly brightened. "Actually, it got much better," she offered, thinking of her best friend, Anna Montgomery. "Just think, if I had spent all of my life in the blazing sun, I would look like a road map by now." His countenance lightened, so Lorena continued, wanting to see him smile. "On top of that, if I hadn't been taught how to be a lady, to be sedate and biddable, I would be simply impossible to deal with."

Her comment brought a thunderous laugh booming from his chest. "Sedate! Biddable! There are many adjectives I would use to describe your many attributes"—he looked at her with a suggestive smile—"but 'sedate' and 'biddable' are not on the list."

She laughed, knowing he was right.

Clay thought of the young girl who had been thrust into his life. She was a mixture of excitement and passion, calmness and timidity. She drove him crazy with her stubbornness one minute, only to make him crazy with desire the next. She was a mixture of many things all wrapped up in one package—his package. The thought pleased him immensely. Suddenly he was in a hurry to make her his wife, and he wondered how long it was going to take to win her. For a second he thought he wouldn't wait, but as he thought it over, he squelched his impulse to rush her. He wanted her to want him as much as he wanted her.

They rode along until they noticed a cloud of dust announcing the approach of riders. Clay pulled the rifle from his saddle, resting it with deceptive calm against his other arm, ready if the need arose. Sitting, waiting, neither spoke, curious about who was coming. As two horses drew closer, Lorena said, "It's Ramón, but I cannot tell who he is with."

Clay looked from the riders to Lorena, apparently not happy with the news. "How do you know it's Ramón?"

Lorena smiled. "He always rides the same horse, a fine horse that I much admire."

Clay did not like it, did not like it one bit. He had allowed the young pup's visits only because of his encounter with him the night of the fiesta—and because he could think of no good reason not to let him visit.

Lorena's smile disappeared as the riders drew near. "It appears that your friend Carmen Vega is with him."

It was Clay's turn to smile. "Surely you're not jealous, are you?"

"Do not flatter yourself, señor."

Clay's answer was to laugh into the skies. Lorena scowled.

Ramón rode up and, eyeing the rifle, gave an uneasy grin. "I see the form of greeting at Cielo el Dorado has changed since I was last here."

Lorena couldn't help but laugh.

Both Clay and Ramón looked at her, Clay amused, Ramón indignant.

"And what, may I ask, is so amusing?" Ramón asked, sitting stiffly in his saddle. Carmen had not said a word.

"Oh, Ramón, I am sorry. I was just laughing because I have heard those very words spoken before."

Only Clay and Lorena understood, each remembering the day Clay had ridden into the hacienda, only to look down the barrel of the gun Lorena pointed at him. Ramón still was unsure if he was being laughed at.

Feeling guilty for being so rude, Lorena impulsively invited Ramón to come to the hacienda, then wanted to kick herself when she realized that she would have to invite Carmen as well.

"*Gracias*, Lorena," Carmen said with a smile. "We would love to."

Lorena looked away from Clay's dark stare and quickly spurred her horse on so as to avoid a confrontation with the man.

Ramón was as surprised as anyone by the invitation, but pleasantly so, as he still was angry at Clay Wakefield for his treatment of him the night of the fiesta. So he accepted graciously, noting with pleasure the anger that flashed through Clay's eyes.

Clay wanted to counter Lorena's invitation, but he knew he would look like an ogre if he did. He cursed under his breath and wondered at himself for trying to win Lorena over. At times like this, he wanted to have the ceremony performed and be done with it. He would be glad when she was his wife.

They rode back to Cielo el Dorado, Lorena and Ramón chatting about friends and relatives, Clay scowling ominously, Carmen riding slightly behind, a sly grin on her lips. Clay had reached the point where he didn't care what Lorena thought of him, and he was ready to send the pup packing when the front gate swung open to let them enter. Frustrated, Clay tossed his reins to Jaime, then without so much as a good day, he left.

Dalia and Pedro sat in the kitchen relaxing over a cup of

coffee. Their conversation came to an abrupt halt when they saw Clay stalk through the courtyard, a black scowl on his face. He made his way toward the study, Lorena nowhere in sight.

"He looks ready to do murder," Dalia observed.

"*Sí*, this is true," Pedro agreed.

"I wonder what Lorena has done now?" Dalia said, shaking her head.

Pedro laughed, "What makes you think Lorena did something to make him angry?"

Dalia gave Pedro a tired smile. "We both know Lorena. I just hope it is not so bad that everything goes back to the way it was before."

"*Sí*, it was hard on everyone. The tension was quite heavy."

"Pedro, what is to become of this situation? It cannot go on forever this way. People will begin to talk, if they are not talking already. It is not right for a single man to be here with Lorena."

"No one is talking, Dalia," Pedro reassured his wife, taking her plump hand in his, "and there is nothing wrong as long as you and I are here as chaperons."

"But where is this situation leading?" she asked heatedly, pulling her hand away. "Will Señor Clay leave the hacienda and let Lorena run it as she wants?" Before Pedro had a chance to answer, she went on. "No, I doubt it. If ever there was a man who is bullheaded and domineering, it is that Americano. In fact, he reminds me of the old señor, Diego's father."

The two old people sat for a moment remembering the man with fondness. "He was domineering, yes, but fair," Dalia said.

"Fair, yes, but so is Clay."

Dalia looked at her husband intently, studying the man who had been her husband for forty years, wanting to deny the truth of his words, knowing she could not. "You seem to like Clay very much. You don't want him to leave, do you?" It was more an accusation than a question.

Pedro did not have a chance to answer, for Lorena came walking into the courtyard with Carmen and Ramón. Dalia's eyes lit up; Pedro's darkened.

"Now I know why Clay is so annoyed," Pedro remarked.

"*Sí*, this is true. But I am glad Ramón has come, if not that hussy Carmen Vega," she added with annoyance. "Ramón would make a perfect husband for our Lorena, and that would solve all her problems."

"There you are wrong, wife. This is not good. Lorena deserves better than that coward who has had everything handed to him on a silver platter. That boy has known not one day's work. And in this country that is a sin," Pedro said in disgust.

Dalia was shocked by the vehemence in her husband's voice, never having heard him speak ill of Ramón before.

Ramón had begun to visit more frequently when he realized that the conceited Americano wanted Lorena for himself. While he was sure that Lorena was unaware of the stranger's feelings, the truth was written clearly across Clay Wakefield's face every time he looked at Lorena. But Ramón also knew that, while the American wanted Lorena, she wanted no part of the arrogant man. And that he planned to take advantage of. Clay Wakefield might be bigger and wealthier and have an army of men at his disposal, but he did not have Lorena. Ramón smiled. Lorena would be his. He did not bother to think about the fact that he had not wanted her until he knew Clay Wakefield did. He had been amazed at the change in the girl when she came home, so he conveniently told himself that he had always loved her, that they were meant to be together, somehow justifying what he was trying to do.

There was nothing more that Clay could do with Diego's mess until Ben got back from Chihuahua. He had thoroughly searched every cabinet and drawer, but nothing more had turned up. The answers had to be in Chihuahua, and Ben was seeking them now. Clay was grateful for his brother's assistance, as he was loath to leave the hacienda with things still up in the air. Or so he told himself. He did not want to think that his lengthy stay could possibly have anything to do with Lorena. No, he would go as soon as Ben had done the legwork.

After Clay's extensive work in each area, the hacienda ran smoothly, each and every individual knowing his or her job. As he toured the facility he spoke to people, remarked on how well they were doing, and answered any questions they had. But over the past months he had done his job well, and now he was no longer needed. He had done it on purpose, of course, as he planned to leave for Missouri as soon as he had Diego's affairs straightened out. The hacienda needed to run without his help. But somehow that plan no longer sat so well with him.

Clay would have ridden out, possibly gone into town, just to get away from his thoughts, but with Ramón there he didn't want to leave. So instead, he went up to the roof and took the place of one of the guards. There had not been an Indian raid in some time, but Clay felt it necessary to have at least a couple guards on duty at all times, increasing that number at night and when rumors of trouble came. The sentinels diminished the threat not only of Indians but also from the growing number of *bandidos*. Clay felt that at this time, the threat of the *bandidos* was far greater than that of the Indians.

The sun beat down on Clay as he scanned the distance. Only an occasional hare darted across the terrain to break the still horizon. Tingling laughter filtered up to him, and his jaw clenched tight. Since Carmen and Ramón had arrived, Clay had seen a Lorena that he had only caught occasional glimpses of in all the time he had been at Cielo el Dorado. The antagonism and bursts of anger were gone, replaced by a fun-loving, carefree young woman who, he

was sure, was totally entrancing Ramón. Clay looked down
into the courtyard. Carmen was nowhere in sight, but
Ramón and Lorena were sipping on something, laughing
and talking as if they were betrothed. Clay made a decision
then and there: If the insolent young pup did not leave by
tomorrow morning, then he would ask him to leave,
whether it angered Lorena or not. By allowing Ramón to
stay, Clay had hoped to show Lorena that he wasn't as bad
as she seemed to think. He also hoped that when Ramón
finally went home, perhaps Lorena's raised spirits would
linger. But if he had to send Ramón on his way and Lorena's
cold disposition returned, then so be it. With renewed
determination Clay called the guard back.

Carmen had to wait some time to get Ramón alone. She
had watched the glances and exchanges between Clay and
Lorena and knew that something had to be done soon. Clay
was not going to wait much longer to stake his claim. With
that in mind, Carmen found Ramón and led him to a
secluded corner where they would not be overheard.

"What is this about, Carmen?" Ramón asked.

"It is about your precious little Lorena. If you want to
keep her, you must get her away from here. You must marry
her, but we both know Clay Wakefield will not give his
consent. Therefore you must sneak her out at night, and
soon. Clay is getting ready to take her for himself."

"How can you be so sure?"

"Because I have eyes, *estúpido*!"

Ramón seethed with indignation. But before he could
vent his outrage, Carmen continued. "You must take her
away from here, Ramón, or she will be lost to you."

But Ramón remembered all too well the rage that had
burned in the American when he had tried to sneak Lorena
out once before. "I do not think this is a good idea. I will
not sneak her out." Then he calmed a bit. "I will win her for
myself. Just you wait and see."

* * *

"Dalia, this meal is wonderful, as usual," Clay said in his new good humor, certain that Ramón would be gone the next day.

The duenna smiled her pleasure, wondering what could possibly have caused Clay's mood. "*Gracias*, Señor Clay."

"May I have another serving of those delicious enchiladas?" he asked.

Lorena nearly choked on a laugh. He was almost flirting with her duenna.

Dalia importantly served up another helping of hot chili sauce, cheese, onions, and tortillas.

"*Gracias*," Clay said with a smile, pleasing Dalia even more by speaking in her language.

"Oh, my God!" Lorena mumbled into her napkin.

All eyes shifted to her. "Did you say something, Lorena?" Clay asked mischievously.

"No," she replied, her honeyed words only adding to the mischievous glint in Clay's eyes. "I was just clearing my throat."

When everyone but Clay turned away, Lorena childishly stuck her tongue out at him.

Clay's roar of laughter startled even Lorena, who blushed furiously when he leaned forward and asked, "Would you like to share that with me?"

Providing Lorena a reprieve, Clay turned to Pedro. "How is the mill running, Pedro?" Clay asked.

"Good. It has not broken down once since it was fixed. The water flow has been much better and the gears are smoothed."

Lorena watched the interaction with an amused grin. She wasn't sure what Clay was up to, but for some reason he appeared to be trying to win over Pedro and Dalia, though everyone knew Pedro had already been won.

The discussion continued, and Lorena noticed that when Clay was trying, the man was practically irresistible. She laughed when she thought of Dalia being helpless to resist

such a man. But then she sobered. She knew that Clay
Wakefield was impossible to resist.

With Ramón there, she had tried wholeheartedly to prove
to herself that she was not captivated by Clay, but simply at
an age where she was naturally attracted to men, naturally
curious.

Now seeing Clay in this fashion, he seemed more dangerous than ever. Here was a man she could easily lose her heart
to. *Never!* she said to herself. It was only desire that this man
made her feel. Once that was satisfied he would be off on his
journeys, rarely giving her a thought.

"Lorena," Ramón interrupted her thoughts. "Would you
care to walk about the hacienda? The night is cool and the
sky is clear."

Lorena thought of how she was falling prey to Clay's
charms, so when Ramón asked her to take a walk, instead
of saying no as she had the night before, she said yes to
escape Clay's disturbing company.

"Yes, Ramón, that would be nice," she answered without
looking at Clay.

"If you will excuse us," Ramón said with a smile of
superiority directed at Clay.

It was all Clay could do to stay in his seat as they
departed. He was furious that the young pup was obviously
trying to antagonize him, furious that Lorena would go, and
furious with himself because he felt he could do nothing to
stop them. Yes, he could, he corrected himself. After all,
why was it so damn important that she be willing? He
should have told her they were getting married in the first
place, gotten it over with, and then gone back to Missouri
where he belonged. He was not used to not being in control
and he didn't like it one bit. With that he threw his napkin
down on the table while pushing back his chair, almost
tipping it over with the force. "I've had just about enough
of this," he grumbled to no one in particular.

Walking out into the courtyard he noticed with increasing
anger that the two were nowhere to be seen.

* * *

Lorena let Ramón lead her toward the *acequia* that ran through the hacienda. She held back a bit when she noticed that he was leading her to a secluded spot that was hidden from the sight of others walking about. When she hesitated, Ramón smiled an endearing smile, and she felt silly that she would not trust him.

"I thought you might like to put your feet in the water as you used to when you were a child," Ramón said, making Lorena remember a better time.

"Yes, that would be nice."

Lorena did not notice the glint of amusement that flashed in his eye when she was not looking.

"You are no longer a child, Lorena."

Lorena looked at him, a bit embarrassed by his words.

"You are a woman," he clarified as he gazed at her lips.

Lorena sensed that he was going to kiss her. She started to pull back, then decided this would be the best way of all to show herself that it was not Clay who caused such emotions in her, but the kiss.

Ramón leaned closer, dipping his head to capture her lips. When she did not resist, he became bolder, pressing his thin lips into hers, pressing hard against her teeth until she thought she tasted blood. She was expecting a pleasant emotion to course through her, but she was sadly disappointed. Lorena felt only a sick revulsion. No tingling, no skin on fire, only disgust at Ramón's kiss and at herself for allowing it.

But she had no more time to think of it as Ramón abruptly backed away from her. For an instant, relief surged through her, but then a sickening "ugh" dispelled the relief.

Her head jerked around to see what was happening. Shock left her momentarily unable to move as she saw Clay's huge right fist smash into Ramón's midsection.

Ramón's eyes were wild. He flew at Clay, arms flailing, making a lucky connection with Clay's right eye. With that,

Clay proceeded to pummel the younger man until Lorena finally came to her senses.

"Stop! Stop! You are going to kill him," she screamed, frantically throwing herself between the two.

"That's better than he deserves," Clay said through panting breaths.

Ramón lay in a heap on the ground, blood spilling from his nose, moaning in pain.

"Look what you've done to him," Lorena shrieked as she bent down to the battered man. But before she could reach him she was pulled roughly back, a grip of iron clasped around her delicate arm. "What are you doing?" she screamed.

"I'm taking you inside where you belong."

"I cannot believe you! You nearly killed a man for no reason—"

Her sentence was cut off when he abruptly jerked her around to face his deadly scowl. "I had plenty of reason. Get this through your pretty little head. You are mine, no one else's, and no one else touches what is mine."

Clay stared down into the turbulent depths of Lorena's green eyes. Never having been in love before, Clay did not recognize the emotion that was beginning to grow inside him. He saw instead only what he wanted to see—that she was his, and he kept what was his. Had he suspected the love he probably would have crushed it under his boot like the new bud of a flowering plant.

"I . . . am . . . not . . . yours," she said, jerking her arm away from his grip, succeeding only due to his surprise. She turned quickly, her thoughts in turmoil, and started toward the house, Ramón forgotten. Her mind raced. She wondered what Clay could have meant. Was it somehow possible, with everything that had gone on since her father's death, that there was some truth to his words?

"You will be if you are my wife," he said.

Without turning around, for fear that the uncertainty would show on her face, Lorena stated, "That is irrelevant, Señor Wakefield, for I would never marry you."

Clay had not wanted it to be this way and he cursed himself for his careless words, but he also knew that he had to tell her now of their betrothal. "Lorena," he said gently, all traces of anger gone, "come here, little one, we must talk."

Wanting desperately to flee, but knowing she must find out the truth, Lorena walked quietly to the towering figure who stood waiting for her.

She didn't think about Ramón or about the servants who had gathered around to find out what the commotion was about. She was aware only of the man and the pounding of her heart.

Looking into Lorena's proud, slightly upturned face, Clay was at a loss for words. If he had ever imagined how he would propose to the woman he was to marry, which he hadn't, it would never have been like this. He could tell from the defiant glint in her eye that she was not going to be pleased with his news. Clay was surprised, though he shouldn't have been, that Lorena was not thrilled by the prospect of marriage. Deep inside, Clay had always assumed that once Lorena was told, she would be excited.

"We are to be married, Lorena," he stated. "It was your father's dying wish, and the papers were signed before he died. Father Cristóbal has made all of the necessary arrangements."

Lorena was stunned. How could her father have done this to her? She could not believe she was standing there listening to this! A man she could hardly stand was speaking of their marriage as if it were a business deal. What had happened to bending down on one knee and exchanging oaths of undying love? Not knowing what to say, Lorena turned and walked to the house, unaware of the crowd of people who had gathered.

Clay watched her straight back recede as she left. His emotions were mixed. He was angry at her for leaving and at himself for telling her at such an unfortunate time. He was angry as well that he wanted to take her in his arms and

kiss her resistance away, to make her want him as much as
he wanted her. But his anger was mixed painfully with pride
in her dignified retreat. Lorena was certainly a woman to
contend with, and the thought made him extremely happy.
He knew that his life with her would never be easy but, oh,
the rewards.

The murmuring of people brought him out of his thoughts
just in time to catch a glance that passed between Carmen
and Ramón, but he gave it no notice. Instead, he said to
Pedro, "See to this fool's cuts and then send him on his
way. He has worn out his welcome."

Dalia huffed over the turn of events while Pedro grinned
widely as he pulled up the tattered Ramón. Yes, Pedro
thought, this is good. Clay and Lorena would have a strong
relationship once they got beyond this stage, where Clay
felt the need to dominate, not letting himself lose his heart,
not wanting to need. Soon Lorena would relinquish her fear
that all marriages were like her parents'. He knew she
remembered her lonely mother, who did not like the hacienda
and who would not have been happy even if her husband had
stayed around. Lorena had also loved her father, who had the
wanderlust and was not able to stay in one place for long.
Lorena had only partial pictures of her parents, neither part
helping her to live the life she was meant to live. Pedro sensed
that she fought Clay because she was afraid he was like her
father. But there she was wrong. Clay and Diego were like
night and day. Clay understood obligation; Diego did not.
Clay Wakefield would make the perfect husband for Lorena,
and Pedro felt sure it would only be a matter of time before she
realized that. He thought about talking to Clay, but as soon as
the thought passed through his mind, he stifled it. The
powerful American was not the type to take advice, no matter
how well intended.

Pedro looked at his wife then. She would come around
and so would Lorena, of that he was sure.

13

❦

LORENA AWAKENED WITH A FEELING OF DREAD SO strong and terrible that she willed herself back to sleep. She was uncertain of the cause, sure only that she was not ready to face whatever it was.

It was still dark when her eyes opened again. Something had awakened her. She lay quietly and listened, but no sound came. Eventually she forgot about the noise as reality began to penetrate. She remembered Ramón lying on the ground, blood streaming from his face. Guilt assailed her when she remembered that she had left him, selfishly consumed with her own concerns. Was she so self-absorbed that she forgot all else when problems were at hand? If last night was any indication, Lorena conceded, indeed it must be true.

Her thoughts turned to Clay and the rage that had burned in his eyes when he had seen Ramón kissing her. Lorena wanted to laugh that such a scene had been caused by a disappointing kiss. But the laugh did not come, suppressed by the overwhelming heaviness she felt. Marriage. The dread she had been holding at bay broke through, though subconsciously she had known it was there, lingering on the edges of her consciousness, teasing her sanity. Yes, marriage. Marriage to a man who had no love for her. Lorena wondered if she hadn't known, or at least suspected all along. Didn't everything he had done since her return indicate that very thing? Thinking back, even the summons to come home from England had been from him. His men had brought her back to Cielo el Dorado. Had she purposely put the obvious truth out of her mind, not wanting to confront it? Lorena hated to think she had been a coward. She told herself that after the death of her father she had been unable to think straight, but that did little to allay her unease.

It hurt to think of how stupid she had been, but more so to think that her father could have done this to her. "Oh, Papá," she cried into her pillow, "wasn't it enough that you made us unhappy when you were alive?" Choking sobs raked her body, cries of sadness, frustration, and anger. "Did you dislike me enough to tie me to unhappiness for the rest of my days?" Her questions were unfair, for deep inside she knew her father had loved her, but when logic spoke, it was many times overridden by her heart and her feelings of betrayal. And it was hard to remember being loved, knowing her father had signed her away like the mere possession she had sworn she would never be.

Her thoughts had no opportunity to go further when Ramón appeared. He opened her door, stepped inside, and closed it with barely a sound, startling Lorena out of her dismal thoughts.

"Ramón! What are you doing here?"

"Shhhh!" he hissed as he moved closer. "I have come for you. We must be quiet."

Lorena looked unsure. "Where are we going?"

"To El Rancho Escondido. You wanted to go there when you first got back. I will take you there now, and this time I will not fail."

Lorena wavered with uncertainty. Ramón sounded angry, and while one part of her saw this as a chance to escape, another part of her wanted to stay. But then Ramón lifted the single candle closer to his face, and she caught sight of swollen lips and eyes. "Oh, Ramón!"

He brushed her sympathy off. "As a lifelong friend, I cannot, in good conscience, leave you in the hands of such a barbarian."

Lorena did not know what to think. Should she go with Ramón or stay and see what happened? The thought of sitting around waiting to see her fate decided spurred her into action. She would go with Ramón to El Rancho Escondido where his family could help her sort out her troubles.

Ramón waited outside while Lorena hastily dressed. Then, together, they made their way to the back of the hacienda. The small gate, which was rarely used, stood ajar. Two unfamiliar horses, saddled and waiting, pawed at the ground, eager to be off.

It was still dark, with no moon and very little starlight to guide their way. Lorena started off slowly, picking her way carefully so as not to guide her horse into uncertain territory.

But Ramón was not so patient. "Lorena, for God's sake, hurry up! Do you want that devil-man to catch us once again?"

"If you don't lower your voice, you are going to wake everyone, and then we will surely be found out. And I have no intention of endangering my horse or myself racing through the dark."

"You have traveled this road hundreds of times. You could ride it blindfolded. We must be quick before the guards awaken."

"Awaken! Why are they asleep?" she asked suspiciously.

"How did you expect to get away without a bit of help? Do not worry," he said with little patience when he saw she would protest further. "They will only have a headache."

Lorena was uneasy and still she took her time.

"*Caramba*," he swore under his breath. Ramón looked

from Lorena to the hacienda, which was still too close
behind for comfort, then back to Lorena. Before she could
see what he was about, he slapped the hindquarters of her
horse, sending the gelding into rapid flight, with Ramón
close behind.

Lorena held on, crouching low over the horse's mane.
With great skill, she controlled the horse, using her voice
and pressure to calm the frightened beast. But it was
Ramón's horse that needed controlling, the animal scaring
itself every time it slipped or tripped on a rock that it had not
seen in the dark. Passing Lorena like a flash, Ramón clung
to his horse until, with one sharp turn, he went flying into
the air before landing in a tangle on the road.

Lorena rode up and brought her horse to a stop. She could
hear Ramón's groans before she dismounted.

"Dear God! How badly are you hurt?" She leaned over
the tattered body of Ramón. She could not tell the difference
between the scrapes and bruises he had just received and the
ones Clay had dealt him earlier. But he moaned miserably,
and Lorena feared that the injuries might be internal.
"Ramón, can you hear me?"

"Yes," he groaned. "It is my leg. It hurts badly." He
tried to push himself up, but when he moved, his body
screamed with pain.

"Be still. I will go back to the hacienda and get help."

Despite his agony, Ramón reached out and grabbed her
arm. "No! You must not go back there."

"But you need help."

He thought for a moment, then said, "You must go to El
Rancho Escondido and get my father."

It was pitch dark, and thoughts of Indians and outlaws
passed through her mind. But then she remembered how
selfish she had been earlier, thinking only of herself, and
knew she must do as he said. "Lie still. I will go and get
your father. I will hurry."

She left Ramón stretched out in the road, his horse
nowhere in sight. The road, indeed, was as familiar to her

as her own house; she had traveled it hundreds of times. She told herself this over and over again as her horse made its way toward Paso del Norte.

She crossed the river with great difficulty, but somehow, with the grace of God, she made it through. But as she saw the first glowing light in the distance, her breath caught in her throat. She was no longer alone.

She heard horses approaching, though she could see not a soul. Quickening her horse's gait, Lorena tried to make it to El Paso before the riders caught up to her. But the faster she went, the faster the hoofbeats came until she was galloping toward the town, her pursuers close behind. She leaned over the horse's mane, her heart pounding in her chest. If only she could make it to the flickering light of a house up ahead. But her pleas went unanswered, for in the next second, she was surrounded by four dangerous-looking men who forced her to stop.

"Well, well, well," one man said. "Look what we have here, amigos."

He was interrupted by a harsh command from another. "Where is Valdéz?" he demanded of Lorena.

"Ramón?" she asked, her mind racing with possible explanations as to why this man would ask about Ramón. Perhaps they were friends of his who wanted to help.

All four men peered into the darkness, as if by doing so, they would find the man they sought.

"Where is he? Where is the bastard?" The man jerked back to Lorena, clearly upset, convincing her that their intent was anything but good.

Lorena remained silent, her fear growing by leaps and bounds in her chest. She did not understand what was going on, what the meaning of the situation was. The way the men spoke about Ramón, further convinced her that they knew him, but they had no good in mind for her. Was it possible that Ramón had set this up? He had been angry and insistent that she go with him. Her sudden memory of the look in his eye when she suggested she go back to the hacienda for help left her cold with fear. He had sent her off across unfriendly land to get help from his father. Ramón must have wanted her to be caught. What other conclusion could she draw? She closed her eyes in pain. She had been betrayed yet again. She sat still for a moment trying to will back tears. This was no time to wallow in self-pity, she chided herself. So she took a deep breath and said, "Who are you, and why have you halted my journey?"

Enrique Calderón was startled by her abrupt question. Had she been anyone else, he would have backhanded her without a second thought for speaking in such a tone. But with this one, it was different. He looked at her closely. It was still quite dark, and it was hard to tell what she looked like, but he sensed from her voice and the gleam of her eyes that indeed she was a fiery one. Carmen had been true to her word. This one could very easily bring them riches in Mexico City. But then he remembered Ramón Valdéz. He was supposed to be with the girl, and they needed to get rid of him so no one would know. But he was nowhere in sight. Enrique shrugged his shoulders. So who cared? Enrique thought. Ramón was Carmen's problem. He and his men would be well on their way to Mexico City before anyone realized the girl was gone—if anyone cared about her.

Clay woke with a start. He looked around the room, but nothing was out of place. Lying perfectly still, he listened for any sounds. None came, but still he could not shake the feeling that something was wrong.

Quietly, he got out of bed and pulled on some clothes. Gun in hand, he made his way out of his room. He was drawn first to Lorena's room, wanting to be certain she was all right. Not bothering to knock, Clay pushed open the door. The room was dark, and it was a few seconds before his eyes adjusted. The bedcovers were rumpled, giving the effect of someone underneath, but still he was not satisfied. He stepped up to the bed and carefully extended his hand, but the covers collapsed under the pressure, revealing the emptiness beneath. He spun around, instantly taking in every corner of the room. But Lorena was nowhere to be seen. With no more thought about keeping quiet, Clay raced from the room. If Rosinante was gone, he would know that she had tried to leave him once again. He cursed himself with every step he took for the callous way in which he had told her of their betrothal. The chiding didn't last long, however, and before he entered the stable, his anger was starting to rise. When was she going to learn?

He jerked open the stable door and stalked directly to Rosinante's stall. His heart leaped in his chest when he found the mare there. What did it mean?

After leaving the stable, Clay quickly searched the hacienda, to no avail, and when finally he was convinced that she was nowhere within the four massive walls, he alerted Pedro.

"What has happened?" Pedro asked, his hair still rumpled from sleep.

"Lorena is gone. I am going out to find her."

The gate was pulled open by a guard who looked suspiciously as if he had been asleep. Clay rode out swearing to himself that things were going to change.

Dante moved quickly but carefully, though at this point the sun was already beginning to rise. Clay checked the swimming hole first, then turned toward Paso del Norte. As he made his way over a small rise, he could see a horse grazing in a field, its rider sprawled against a boulder. Relief engulfed him, but it was only temporary when he realized it was not Lorena, but Ramón Valdéz.

"Where is Lorena?" Clay demanded, knowing without having to ask that Ramón was involved in Lorena's disappearance.

Ramón flinched from the words, the fight already gone. Sitting in the dark for so long now without any sign of

Lorena, Ramón was filled with dread. "She traveled to El Rancho Escondido to get help for me."

Clay looked down at the broken man and said, "You will pay dearly if anything has happened to her." And with that he was gone, riding like the devil to find Lorena.

14

AFTER THE INITIAL CONFUSION PASSED, LORENA WAS
bound and gagged posthaste. It didn't matter that she kicked
and screamed; her efforts were wasted. There were four
outlaws and only one of her. But she fought nonetheless,
managing a few well-targeted blows.

The small group rode for some time before they arrived at
a small camp. When they approached, the campers were
still asleep, their day not yet begun. The arrival of the riders
brought a few people from their tents, while others merely
raised their heads from the hard ground on which they slept
out in the open.

Lorena surveyed her surroundings and determined it
would not be all that difficult a place to escape from. In fact,
she planned to be home in time for breakfast. And then she
remembered what she would be going back to. A life
dominated by Clay Wakefield. Her head spun with the idea.
She couldn't let that happen. She recalled Ramón, battered
and torn by Clay, but then she remembered as well the
conversation of her captors when they had found Ramón
was not with her. Was it possible that Ramón had something
to do with her abduction? If so, why?

Her head spun all the more, thoughts cluttering her mind
until she could not think straight. But the thought that kept

surfacing through the muddle was Clay. And for a moment she was filled with the desire to see him, for him to come and make everything all right. The meaning of these thoughts scared her, then in turn infuriated her. Clay Wakefield was as much her enemy as the men who now held her prisoner. She had to find a way to escape Clay, just as she had to flee from these men.

She was led to a small fire where a woman worked. Lorena's leg was tied to the trunk of a bush with a rope. After a few tugs she knew she was held secure—at least for now, she amended. She sat down to think about just what she was going to do. It surprised her to realize she wasn't really afraid, but then, the men had shown little interest in her. In fact, when she thought about it, she realized that the men actually seemed almost annoyed with her capture. Lorena shook her head. None of it made any sense. She didn't take into consideration the fact that the men had not seen her in the light of day.

Trying to figure out her situation, Lorena watched as her abductors circled around another fire farther away. The sun began to rise, and the fire glowed orange on their faces. She could tell they were having a heated discussion. If only she were close enough to hear.

The sun shone brightly when finally the man who appeared to be in charge approached her. Before he had a chance to speak, the woman who had tended the fire called to him.

"Enrique," she called, "*qué pasa*? What am I to do with this girl?"

His hand shot out like lightning and knocked the woman to the ground. Lorena's eyes opened wide and she tried to yell at him through her gag. Enrique turned to Lorena. "Yes, you are a fiery one." But though his step had never faltered during the short altercation with the woman, he came to an abrupt halt when he caught sight of Lorena. He stared at her, his dark brown eyes traveling up and down her body. With a filthy hand he grabbed her chin and moved it from side to side before he spoke again. "Who are you?" he asked, forgetting her gag.

The question surprised Lorena. Her mind raced. He knew who Ramón was but not who she was? It didn't make any sense.

When she didn't answer, Enrique's hand shot out once again, slapping her face so hard she staggered and would have fallen had he not grabbed her arm. While the question had surprised her into speechlessness, the slap served to bring forth a flow of words. She started in so fast, mindless of the gag that muffled every word, that Enrique took a step back.

Then he smiled. "Yes, pretty one, you will bring us a great deal of money."

He pulled off the gag, and a torrent of words spewed from her mouth. "You vile vermin! Slapping poor helpless women around!"

He slapped her again in answer, but this time he did not catch her and she crumpled to the ground. When she looked up, his brown eyes had narrowed, and for the first time since her capture, she felt fear.

He stepped closer, his booted foot less than an inch away from her riding skirt. Squatting down, he looked at her closely. "My guess is that Carmen lied." He loosened her hands and held one up to see. "These are not the hands of a servant. You must be the daughter of a rich hidalgo." He dropped her hand. "Who are you?" he repeated as he yanked her to her feet.

Lorena's mind raced. He had said that Carmen lied. The only explanation could be that Carmen, along with Ramón, had planned this whole affair. Her eyelids wavered, but she willed herself to be strong. The idea of Carmen being involved didn't surprise her; Carmen had always been jealous of her. But Ramón—he had been her friend since childhood. He had acted as if he wanted to marry her. How could he have done this to her? And why?

Enrique's grip tightened, effectively disrupting Lorena's

jumbled thoughts. "I asked you who you are. Answer me!"

Lorena looked straight into his eye and spit. She hit the ground before she registered his expression. And then he was gone, stalking back to the group of men who had not moved since she arrived at the camp.

During the day, Lorena was forced to walk to the end of her rope to tend to her personal needs. Though the *bandidos* ignored her for the most part, every time she moved they looked in her direction to make sure she was not getting away. At one point, she found a sharp rock and thought to sever the bond that held her. But Enrique watched suspiciously until finally he walked over, forced her to stand, and found her makeshift tool.

"What are we going to do with her, Enrique?" a man asked.

Enrique sat down slowly. He took an old tin cup, filled it with coffee, and looked into it as he swirled the liquid around. "She is not a servant, that I am sure of."

"Who is she?"

"I do not know. That is what I want to find out. If my guess is right, she is the daughter of a wealthy man. If this is so, it will be easier to ransom her than to take her all the way to the interior and sell her."

"But she has seen us. We cannot let her go back." The man was clearly disturbed by the prospect of being identified as a criminal.

Enrique thought on this for a moment, then said, "We will deal with that when it happens." He turned to a man who had not yet said anything. "Pablo, go into town. There is sure to be much talk about this girl's disappearance. Find out who she is. Then we will make plans."

Pablo leaned back against a rock and inhaled smoke from his handmade cigarette. His gaze traveled from the group to the lone girl who was busy pacing back and forth over the small space allowed to her by the rope. Then he tossed the burning stub into the fire, pushed himself up, and strode to his horse.

* * *

Ramón was found shortly after Clay had galloped away. He was taken back to the hacienda where Dalia tended his wounds. Fear filled his mind and body. He had been angry when he persuaded Lorena to go with him, but now, in the aftermath of that anger, he realized what danger he had put her in. If anything happened to her, he would be blamed. His stomach churned and his head pounded. In his heart, he knew something was wrong, very wrong, for so many hours to go by without any sign of Lorena. By now, if Lorena had made her way to his home, someone from his family would be out looking for him. How could he have been so stupid as to let Carmen talk him into such a plan?

Clay arrived back at Cielo el Dorado dust-covered and weary. Pedro pulled him aside as soon as he dismounted.

"Where is Lorena? Ramón told us what happened."

Clay wiped his forehead, leaving streaks where his fingers had mopped away the grime. "So Ramón made it back."

His look was dangerous and Pedro took a step back. "What has happened? Did you not find her?" Pedro demanded.

Pain passed through Clay's dark eyes. "I have been all over Paso del Norte. She is nowhere."

Pedro moved about frantically. "No one has seen her?"

"I didn't tell anyone she is missing."

"What? If you have not asked, how can you be sure she is not there?" Pedro actually felt a moment's relief. "After the display last night, Ramón said she wanted to leave to get away from here."

Clay grimaced. "That's probably true. But once Ramón was hurt, she went to get help."

Pedro could see where Clay's thoughts were taking them. "Yès, I see now. Some of our men found Ramón. No one else had come to help him."

"That's right. Lorena is headstrong and willful, but we both know that she would never leave anyone helpless."

"*Sí*, and Lorena would have gotten help—"

"If she could," Clay finished the sentence.

"We must go after her—now, in case she has been taken away from here. We must ask people in town what they have seen."

"I've been everywhere. As rarely as Lorena goes into the small town, and as much as people concern themselves with everyone else's business, someone would have mentioned something if they had seen her. It's best if the person who took her relaxes. Let them think that no one has noticed. If everyone in town is frantic with worry over Lorena, then the person who took her will be on the alert, not as likely to make mistakes."

Pedro looked at Clay closely, doubt written clearly across his face. "Are you sure, Clay?"

The muscles in Clay's jaw tightened. "Yes, I am sure."

"What are you going to do?"

"I am going to send men in every direction. One group toward Santa Fe and another toward Mexico City. My guess, though, is that they are still around here. No one had seen anyone leaving town. I'm going to do some tracking."

But before Clay had a chance to organize the men, Carmen Vega galloped into the courtyard and threw herself into Clay's arms. "Oh, Clay! I have just heard. I came as quickly as I could."

Clay stiffened, his eyes went still and fathomless. "What have you heard, Carmen?"

Carmen hesitated for a moment. "About Lorena, of course."

Clay held her away from him, the muscles straining in his arms as if at any moment he would snap her in two. "What about Lorena?"

Carmen looked about the courtyard, her concerned eyes growing cautious. And then she saw Ramón, and caution turned instantly to disbelief. She tried to step back, her eyes growing wide with incredulity and anger, and when she did, Clay saw the emotions that raced through her eyes. In that second, Clay was sure that Carmen was in some way involved in Lorena's disappearance. He forced himself to relax, to ease the death grip he had on her arms. "Come, let's go to the kitchen and have something to drink." He took her arm and led the way.

Pedro fumed. He yanked his sombrero off and wiped the sweat from his brow. He started after the two, but something made him stop in his tracks.

Ramón was equally disturbed, but for different reasons. Unlike Pedro, he had a sense of what was going on. He, too, had seen the look of surprise on Carmen's face when she saw him. Was it possible that she had planned to let Lorena and him meet their demise? She had been awfully insistent that he escape with Lorena that night. It was Carmen who had provided the horses. And had his horse not sent him flying, he too would have been gone, with no one left to tell of Carmen's involvement. He knew he should tell Clay, but if he did, he would also be revealing the extent of his own involvement. It was one thing for Clay to think that Ramón had acted on Lorena's behalf, but quite another for the man to think he had persuaded her to leave. Fear and guilt warred within him. But in the end, he decided it was best to stay quiet, at least for now.

Once out of sight, Clay grabbed Carmen and pulled her around to face him.

"You are hurting me," she snapped before remembering her situation, then quickly tempered her voice. "Please, Clay, I do not understand what is wrong. I only came to help and you're acting as if I am a criminal." She forced her eyes to water.

Clay's grip tightened. "Don't play the innocent with me. Tell me what you know about Lorena."

"I have come to help. Of course I will tell you all I know."

"Stop your lies. You didn't come to help. You are involved."

"Clay, no." She leaned up against his broad chest. "The only thing I know is what I heard in town—that Lorena was taken by a group of *bandidos*."

He slowly pushed her back to arm's length. "You heard that in town, did you?"

"Of course," she said.

"No one in town knows about Lorena's disappearance."

"What do you mean? I saw you in town today." Her eyes grew wide and frantic.

"But I didn't tell anyone that Lorena was missing."

In that second, Carmen knew she had made a grievous error. And with that knowledge came an urge toward self-preservation. "I do not know what you are talking about," she said venomously. "And take your hands off me." She tried to pull free but failed as Clay held tight.

"Tell me what you know." The words were a demand.

"I know nothing," she answered emphatically.

His patience finally broke, the control he had maintained shattering before her very eyes. "You tell me what you know right now, or else."

"Or else what?" she challenged, though her bravado was clearly shaken.

He looked down into her eyes and raised a hand to strike her, but at the last moment he lowered it, unable to hit a woman. Instead he called to a guard. "Lock her up."

A burly man took Carmen. Clay could not strike a woman, but this man looked like a different sort.

"You cannot do this to me," she shrieked, as the man dragged her off kicking and screaming.

As Clay rounded the corner, he met Pedro and Ramón.

"What is going on?" Pedro asked.

"Carmen is involved in Lorena's disappearance."

"How?"

"I don't know. Once she realized I was on to her, she

reverted to her usual vindictive self. I've had her locked up for now. That should loosen her tongue."

"You cannot lock her up," Pedro stated, outraged. "She may have been helping Lorena with her own plans, just as Ramón was."

Pedro and Clay looked at the silent Ramón.

"Is that not what happened, Ramón?" Pedro asked.

Ramón stammered and stuttered, but when he looked up at the American's towering height, he said, "Yes, this is what happened."

Clay stepped closer to Ramón. "Why do I find that hard to believe?" He did not wait for an answer. Instead, he said to Pedro, "I am now forced to ask some questions. I'm going to Paso del Norte."

"Then I am coming with you," Pedro said.

"Stay here."

"I will not. I have known these people all my life. I can help."

Clay hesitated, but only for a moment. "Then come on, we must hurry."

It took the men only a short while to ready themselves for the ride to town. Within minutes they were galloping through the gate, leaving a cloud of dust in their trail. Once out of sight of the hacienda, Clay stopped the men and told them of another plan.

Ramón didn't waste time, either. He would have run if his body had been capable of it, but he settled instead on a slow limp that jarred his body with every step. The guard who had taken Carmen away was drinking water from the well. Ramón came up beside him. "Where did you put the woman?"

The guard looked pensive, then said, "That is none of your concern, señor."

The man was older, and Ramón knew he had been a guard here years before Clay Wakefield arrived. "You forget who you are speaking to. I am Ramón Valdéz, from

El Rancho Escondido. If you value your position, I suggest you tell me where you have put her."

The guard looked toward the gate through which Clay had passed only moments before, then back to Ramón. He wavered in indecision until finally he said, "She is in the storeroom."

Before he could say anything else, Ramón hobbled off.

The storeroom door was held secure by an iron lock. Ramón pulled it, trying to loosen it. He was virtually alone, the area being relatively empty, as most of the men were out working in the fields. After an aggressive pull, the door still held tight, and Ramón gave up.

"Carmen," he finally called softly through the door. He could hear someone moving about inside, but no one answered. "Carmen, it is me, Ramón."

"What do you want?" she growled, making no attempt to keep her voice down.

Ramón glanced furtively about the courtyard and did not speak again until he was sure no one had noticed him. "What have you done with Lorena? Why did you not tell me you had alternate arrangements when we made our plans? You know I would have kept her away from here. There was no need for any change."

"You," she sneered. "You can do nothing right. You cannot even stay on your own horse."

Ramón's head pounded. "Carmen, tell me what you have done with Lorena."

"Where is Clay?"

"He has gone."

Carmen laughed then. "Very well, I will tell you, but it is too late. She is gone."

"Where!" Ramón demanded, thick dread filling his body.

"She has been taken and is to be sold as a slave."

Ramón reeled with the import of her words, and thought he would pass out when he realized that he had played right into Carmen's hands. But before his thoughts could go any further, Clay leaped from the roof and grabbed Ramón by his shirt.

"Where did you come from?" Ramón sputtered.

"Did you really think I was going to leave you here without finding out what you know? And now that I do, let me say that you will regret this, mark my words." He tossed Ramón aside and ran toward the back where his horse waited just outside the rear gate.

It was late afternoon when Pablo returned. The sound of the horse galloping toward camp filled Lorena with hope until she realized it was one of the men who had abducted her. She would have given anything for the sight of Clay Wakefield at this point. The day had disabused her of any notion that Clay was more of a threat to her than these men. But as morning stretched into afternoon, which now began to stretch into night, Lorena's hopes began to flag.

Pablo didn't wait to be asked what he had learned in Paso del Norte. He merely stood in front of the others, looked down at Enrique, and said, "You were wrong."

Enrique jumped to his feet. "What do you mean?"

"She is a nobody."

"How do you know this?"

"Because I spent all day in town, and not one word was spoken about anyone being missing. Nothing was amiss. No talk, hombre, none at all."

Pablo looked over to where Lorena leaned back against a boulder, wisps of hair curling about her face. Her eyes were closed, but he knew they were green, rich green surrounded by dark lashes. Full curves were hidden by her skirt. He turned back to the men. "Let me take her to Mexico City. I will get a good price for this one."

"You! Why you? How do we know we can trust you?" asked one man.

"I give you my word." Pablo's broad smile showed several missing teeth.

Enrique grunted. "Your word!" He shook his head.

"Let him take her, Enrique. He will bring the money back. Besides, we do not have time to go to Mexico City. Since Pablo has offered, let him go. I did not think we should do it in the first place."

Eventually Enrique nodded his consent. "Take her, but be quick. We were supposed to have left hours ago."

Lorena watched the men and knew that something was going to happen. The man with the evil smile looked over at her all too often for her not to begin to panic. In the back of her mind, she realized, she had been convinced that Clay would find her, that her rescue was at hand. But now, after many hours had passed, Lorena's hope began to dwindle. To add to her concerns, the man she heard referred to as Pablo walked up to her and stared. He circled her and then with one finger lifted her chin as if to study her face.

"You will not get away with this," she stated with feigned certainty.

Pablo only laughed. "We already have. You are here, aren't you?"

His hand moved along her jaw, then up to her mouth, and before he knew what was happening, Lorena's teeth clamped down on his fingers. He shouted in pain, brutally knocking her down in his attempt to disengage his fingers. Pablo shook his hand as if to shake off the pain, then looked down at her.

"Get up," Pablo demanded. "We are leaving." He smiled a terrible smile. "I will teach you how to treat a man."

Her face was swollen from the earlier abuse, but now, after hours in the sun with no protection, no food or water, Lorena felt sure she could not get up. She didn't move, couldn't move, until she saw his booted foot coming toward her. Quickly she rolled out of the way, and his boot passed less than an inch from her head. When he came closer, Lorena pushed herself to her feet. She didn't bother to wipe the sand from her face and lips. She merely stood before him, proud and tall, and said, "A man would never hit a woman."

His smile disappeared, and he raised his hand, but when she merely stood before him as if daring him to strike, he lowered it, then leaned down to cut the rope that bound her to the bush. "We will see how long your pride will last."

They rode out of the tiny camp, Lorena with her hands tied and her mouth gagged, being led along on her horse behind Pablo. She held on to the saddle horn with her tied hands, but after several hours of complete exertion in the attempt to stay on, she was exhausted. Her captor rarely bothered to glance at her, much less check on her needs. Her body ached, and finally she could hold on no longer.

She landed with a grunt on the hard-packed dirt trail. Her head had barely missed the spikes of a cactus, but she didn't care. In fact she barely noticed.

Pablo circled back. He dismounted and forced her back on her horse, then led her to a small clearing off the road. "This is as good a time as any to stop for the night."

He untied Lorena so she could take care of private matters, but she had to plead for that privilege. Now he sat leaning back on one arm, watching her. She concentrated on the tough dried meat he had given her, and wouldn't have bothered with it at all if it hadn't been a full twenty-four hours since she had last eaten. So she worked hard at the food, doing her best to ignore the blatant stare from the man across from her.

After a while the sun grew dim on the horizon, and she could ignore her predicament no longer. She had to face the reality that no one was going to find her, and from the look on the man's face, he intended to use her well. That she could not let happen. She had to get away. So, under the guise of slowly chewing her meal, she began to formulate a plan. It didn't discourage her that every plan she had made previously had been foiled. This one would work, she told herself. It had to.

The sun was almost gone when she decided to make her move. Pablo came over to her and ran his callused hand down her arm.

"I must relieve myself," she said, trying her best not to show the revulsion and fear she felt inside.

"I think," he said, moving closer, "you try to play with me. You have already gone into the brush."

"Sir, please."

She sat up straight and looked ready to start arguing, so Pablo let her go. "Be quick." Then he reached out and grabbed her arm as she tried to stand. "If you do not return soon, I will come and get you." He thought for a moment, then added, "And if you try to get away, I will find you." His eyes glittered dangerously. "When I find you I will use you until I am tired of you. Then I will kill you."

Lorena's response was to get to her feet and stride purposefully into the brush.

Once she was out of sight, she began to run. She ran for her life, tripping and stumbling on the harsh terrain. She had only run a short distance when she realized her mistake in trying to escape. The barren terrain offered virtually no place to hide. But she had had no choice, she reminded herself. She had to find someplace to hide. Had she waited even one minute longer, no telling what the man would have done to her. So she continued to run, hoping for a miracle.

But no miracle was in sight. Behind her she could hear that Pablo had discovered her escape. She heard him leap on his horse. It was mere seconds before he was upon her, his horse effectively cutting her off. He leaped from his mount but just missed her, grabbing her skirt. She pulled free and screamed at the same time, and when he caught hold of her, she kicked and screamed like a wild animal caught in a trap.

Clay rode quickly but was alert at all times. He watched for tracks and signs of passage. Just outside of El Paso, he found fresh tracks made by two horses. It probably didn't mean anything, as he knew from Carmen that Lorena had been taken by four men. But he had found nothing else and, since he knew they were taking her to Mexico City and the tracks led in that direction, Clay kept them in sight.

He had gone several miles from town when he heard the scream. His heart leaped in his chest. The voice held terror, and he knew without a doubt that it belonged to Lorena. Not wasting a second he jumped from his horse and approached stealthily on foot. He crouched behind a small rise dotted with scrub brush and saw them just as the man threw Lorena to the ground. Her arms and legs flailed in the air, catching the man in the face.

"I will teach you a lesson that you will never forget," Pablo snarled into her face.

He raised his hand to wipe away the blood that dripped from a cut near his mouth. But when he was about to throw himself down on top of Lorena, his eyes opened wide, and his body stiffened. Then he fell forward without a sound.

Lorena stared in shocked disbelief as Pablo lay in the sand unmoving, a knife protruding from his back. The miracle she had wished for appeared to have arrived. But as soon as she thought that, her fear grew tenfold. Indians. They were being attacked by savage Indians. Hoping to get away, she scrambled to her feet, panic threatening to consume her. The sand was like chains on her legs, making it difficult to run, as she so desperately wanted to do. Before she advanced more than a few yards she was grabbed around the waist from behind. A despairing scream filled the air. No matter how hard she fought, the grip only tightened, pulling her frantic body up against a huge expanse of chest.

"Lorena! Stop this." Clay held on, though it took every bit of strength he possessed to keep his grip. He knew she thought she was fighting for her life and that his words were not penetrating her consciousness, but he feared setting her down as he wasn't sure what she would do. He knew she was a fighter and would try frantically to get away, not bothering to look where she was going, and a cliff stood perilously close to their present location. Not willing to take any risks, he fought to turn her in his arms.

"Lorena," he repeated once she was facing him. "Little one, you're okay now, you're safe."

The words, together with a glimpse of the man who held her, registered in a rush of clarity. The realization hit her like a blow, the knowledge that she had been saved filling her with relief so quickly and suddenly that her head spun. She didn't know if she wanted to laugh or cry, and it was a huge gust of both that burst from her chest as her taut body collapsed against Clay's chest.

"Oh, Clay," she cried.

"Yes, Lorena, it's over."

She looked up at him then, her eyes puffed and red from crying, her face swollen and bruised from her ordeal, and smiled. "What took you so long?"

Closing his eyes, Clay pulled her close and smiled into her hair.

15

LORENA CLIMBED THE WOODEN LADDER TO THE ROOF-top, trying to escape the confines of the hacienda. Some days her home was a prison, its thick mud walls holding her within. On those days she sought the heights of the roof to look out at the land, to catch a cool breeze, to dream of how her life might have been.

The weather had begun to change, providing a reprieve from the scorching heat. Fall was the nicest time of year as far as Lorena was concerned—cool weather, clear skies, and still the sun to brighten the land. Lorena turned her face to the sky. The huge yellow orb extended long rays of glowing heat to caress her smooth skin. A cool breeze drifted by, catching her hair, sending it in a dance about her face.

Several months had passed since that long silent ride home after Clay had rescued her from the *bandidos*, several months since Clay had announced they were to be married. She had managed to put it off, all the while waiting for him to leave. When would he leave? She was sure he would, eventually. The longer he stayed, however, the harder it became to resist him. The longer he stayed, the more persistent he became, the harder it was to maintain her resolve. How she wanted to succumb to his tall good looks

233

and the humor that glimmered in his eyes. There was much she liked about him, but that did not change the inevitable fact that he would leave, just as her father always had. Yes, just like her father, he would leave, coming back every now and again, enfolding those who loved him with a charm that only made it harder when he left again. And leave again he would. It would have been easier if Clay had remained mean and demanding, inundating her with directives, instead of this new and disturbing attention he was lavishing on her. But now he enticed her at every turn. Charming, laughing, causing her to want nothing more than to drown in his nearness, accept his offer of marriage, and live happily ever after.

A vision of her mother loomed, the look on her face every time her husband went away vivid in Lorena's mind. If Lorena had been older or had a clearer memory of those years, she would have recognized that it was not loving disappointment but rather burning hatred that had festered in her mother since the day she was told she had to leave her beloved Spain to come to the New World and marry a man she had never seen. Instead, Lorena believed her mother was lonely and miserable because the man she loved kept leaving her. Lorena Cervantes swore to herself she would have none of that.

She blamed Clay for ruining her life. If she had been honest with herself, she would have admitted that he had merely made her aware of something more, something that the life she had envisioned did not offer, something that at this point she was not sure she could live without. But she laughed in scorn, thinking that what he had shown her was only temporary, lasting until he left, leaving her worse off than before he came. Was it love? Was it feeling cherished? When she was in his arms she felt both. Damn Clay Wakefield and his infernal ways for ever showing her a glimpse of what she truly would miss out on in life.

Her thoughts drifted. Strong arms held her, comforted her, made her feel secure. His lips pressed against hers. Her heart beat wildly, every sense afire. His deep voice breathed words that made her body ache. Then the voice became louder, and she realized it was real.

"Why is it that you are never where I expect you to be?" Clay asked as he walked up behind her.

Lorena blushed furiously. Could he tell what she had been thinking?

"Have I grown a third eye?" he asked, his lips turning up slightly at the corners, giving him the look of a mischievous young boy.

Lorena couldn't help the smile that found her lips. "Yes, I believe you have," she teased, a flash of humor crossing her face, "but I'm not sure where it came from as it is a very strange color."

"Strange, is it?" His mouth twitched with amusement.

"Yes, strange, a bit of green I believe, contrasting sharply with what I guess could only be called the black of the other two."

Clay stood next to the retaining wall that traveled the perimeter of the roof. The sleeve of his shirt brushed her breast when he turned slightly. "If it is as green as your eyes, it must be beautiful. I have never seen more beautiful eyes than yours."

He was so close Lorena thought he would surely kiss her. Her heart beat faster. Desire engulfed her. His kind words and his nearness overwhelmed her, making her lose what little resolve she had left, causing her to forget that soon he would surely leave. She forgot that this was the man she had to persuade not to marry her, that she would make a horrible wife. At that moment all she wanted was to feel his lips on hers.

Clay looked down at Lorena and saw the openness, the giving. Forgetting all about the reason he had sought her out, he leaned forward, touching her lips with one finger. They yielded to his touch, pliant, soft, moist. He dipped his head to taste, and his senses reeled. How could one small, willful woman-child make him feel this way? But rather than examining this question, he pulled her to him, pressing her against the hard planes of his body.

"Lorena," he breathed in her ear sending shivers of pleasure down her spine, "the things I will show you when you are my wife . . . but not now." He reluctantly set her away.

She gazed up at him, and he wanted to laugh at the look he saw. Desire flooded her eyes, turning them a dark shade of jade. "Soon, little one, soon."

His words had the effect of dousing her with cold water. "You arrogant wretch!" she fumed through gasping breaths, embarrassed at his assumption, knowing all the while that he had assumed correctly.

"I think you forgot 'cow,' " he added, amused.

"You can't do this!" But when she struck out at him he caught her tiny wrist, easily pulling her to him, the humor swiftly gone from his gaze.

"I do what I please," he stated with unwelcome frankness.

Still furious at his arrogant assumption, Lorena tried to jerk away, but with fingers like steel, he held her tight. "I came up here to tell you I was riding into town. I knew you would want to see about material."

"For what?" she asked suspiciously, thrown off by his abrupt change of subject.

Clay raised one dark eyebrow, wondering if he was in for another battle. "For your wedding dress."

Lorena stamped a tiny foot in disgust, arms crossed as she turned away from him in a huff, escaping his grip by virtue of surprise. "No, thank you!"

"No, thank you, what?"

"No, thank you, I do not want to go."

"Lorena"—he barely held his patience—"we have been through this already."

"Yes, and I have already told you that I will not marry you," she responded caustically after which she turned away and left.

The fact of the matter was that Lorena had been much more agreeable since her abduction than when Clay Wakefield first arrived at the hacienda. She cursed herself for such behavior. If she had only kept up her ill-mannered behavior instead of feeling so happy that Clay had saved her, he would surely be close to giving up on her by now. What man wanted to marry a shrew? she thought with growing excitement. She had gotten soft with the man, and she would have to work hard to make up for lost time. She could hardly wait and see how long it would take for the arrogant American to call off their betrothal. Oh, she would make him squirm before she let him off the hook, but then in an enormously magnanimous gesture, she would grant him his wish. Then she would be free to run the hacienda just as she had planned all along.

Once in her room, Lorena clapped her hands, her bright green eyes dancing with excitement, as she ran over to the old chest and rummaged through it until she came up with what she was looking for. As fast as she could, she pulled on a white cambric shirt, almost ripping it in her haste. Then she donned the smooth-fitting boys' pants she had worn the first time she saw Clay Wakefield. She sat on the edge of the bed to pull on riding boots, then hastily braided her long hair into one thick plait that hung down her back. She didn't bother with a hat and, glancing at herself in the mirror, gave a nod of approval before leaving the room.

Staying in the shade of patio overhang in hopes of not being seen, she made her way to the stables. Jaime was busy cleaning stalls when she arrived.

"*Hola*, Jaime," she called cheerfully.

Jaime turned to the voice, surprised to see Lorena. "*Hola*, Lorena," he replied cautiously, wondering what she was about, fearful that he was about to get into deep trouble.

"Is there another shovel?" Lorena asked with a glint of mischief in her eye.

"A shovel?" Jaime asked as if he'd never heard of the word.

"Yes, silly, a shovel."

"Over there," he pointed to a row of tools against one wall.

Lorena chose a shovel that she could carry and immediately went to work cleaning the stalls.

Jaime stood back with mouth agape at the sight of Lorena bent over shoveling horse dung as if she did it every day.

"Quit staring, Jaime, and get to work," she said with a teasing smile.

Lorena shoveled and scooped, all the while wiping the sweat from her brow on the sleeve of her shirt. By the time she had finished the first stall, sweat was dripping down her back and arms, causing the thin material to cling to her skin. Stretching her back, she sighed when she looked down the row of dirty stalls, suddenly wondering if there wasn't a better way to go about discouraging one Clay Wakefield. But with no better ideas at hand, she groaned and started on the next stall.

Four stalls later her arm and back muscles were screaming in protest. Whose stupid idea was this anyway? she wondered miserably. Surely she just hadn't thought hard enough for a better way to dissuade the man. Maybe she should abandon her exhausting plot and take the time to come up with some other way. But then the image of Clay Wakefield loomed menacingly in her mind, sending her into a whirl of shoveling, the disturbing picture effectively strengthening her resolve, if not her back.

Clay spent the morning with Bill, checking fences, fields, and irrigation ditches. When the two men rode up to the stables, Jaime came running out.

"I'll take your mounts," he said so fast that Clay looked at the boy questioningly. But heat and hunger made him leave the horses, and the two men made their way to the kitchen to get something to eat.

In the kitchen, Bill spread out a large handmade map of the area. They had to move their meal out of the way. "If we put an irrigation ditch here," he said, pointing out a spot, "and a drainage ditch over here, I think we can get a better flow."

Clay studied the rough drawing, mentally picturing the land they had just covered. After a few minutes, having considered the suggestion, he said, "Why don't we close the ditches here and here"—he marked the ditches with one stroke for each—"then build one major ditch here with drainage over here. Then you could irrigate all of the upper fields with one main ditch."

Looking over what Clay had just drawn, Bill smiled. "I guess that's why you're the boss."

Clay laughed with the man. "No, it's just that I have seen it done before."

The two men were sitting quietly when they heard two maids approach, talking and giggling. "Can you believe it, Lorena mucking around in horse manure?" The girls snickered.

"No, I cannot. I was surprised . . ." Both girls stopped when they entered the kitchen to find the two men. "Senōr Wakefield!"

Neither maid knew what to do, neither wanting to be the one to inform him of Lorena's activities, so before Clay could get a word out, they disappeared through the door.

"What was that all about?" Bill asked.

"I have no idea, but I'm about to find out. Dalia," he shouted. But no one came. Clay stood up, shoving the chair roughly back, knowing Lorena was up to no good, certain that she was making some attempt to aggravate him.

Clay went straight to the stables. Jaime saw him come through the door and wished, not for the first time, that he had not let Lorena do this thing, but how could he stop her? A dark scowl from Clay let Jaime know that he was not off the hook, however.

Clay stalked down the corridor between the rows of

stalls. Toward the end of the left-hand side, one door stood open, a wheelbarrow wedged against it. As he approached, manure flew out of the stall and landed expertly in the wheelbarrow, making him doubt that Lorena was inside. Clay came to stand before the stall, hands planted firmly on his hips, feet spread wide. When his eyes became accustomed to the darkened stall, he saw Lorena's tightly clad, prettily rounded rump. He had almost forgotten over the last several months what an enticing body she had, since it had been covered up with loose gowns. Her rounded buttocks gave way to long slender legs that he longed to wrap around him.

He was so engrossed in his wayward thoughts that he didn't notice the heap of manure she sent flying in the direction of the wheelbarrow until it landed with a thud on his boots instead of its intended receptacle.

"Damn," she cursed, recognizing the sound of a missed shot. She turned to find an incredulous Clay in the doorway ready to do murder. Instinctively she drew back, but remembering her resolve, she ventured forth. "If you weren't standing where you shouldn't be standing, you wouldn't get hit with things you don't want to get hit with."

Clay could not imagine being any angrier than he already was, but when she sassed him, then turned back to her work, he thought he would explode.

"If I were you, I'd put that shovel down before I got myself into any more trouble." His voice was barely controlled.

Without turning around, Lorena said, "Well, you are not me, so just get out of the way."

"Lorena"—her name was a command—"put that shovel down and get out here . . . now!"

Lorena jumped at the explosion of words. "You do not have to shout, I'm not deaf," she replied, trying to remember all the reasons why she was there.

"If you are not deaf, do you mind telling me exactly why you are dressed in a fashion that I have strictly forbidden?"

"Yes, I do mind," she said, her heart beating so rapidly she could hardly breathe. "So if you'll excuse me, I'm going for a ride." It was a statement, not a question.

"Like hell you are!"

"Really, Clay," she said coyly, "you should not curse in front of ladies."

She was laughing at him. She stood there under the threatening gaze that made strong men cower, and she was laughing at him. "If there were any ladies around, I assure you I would not be cursing." Clay should have felt satisfaction that his barb had hit home, but he felt instead perverse for such childish behavior. But she did things to him he did not understand, making him continue all the same. "Ladies don't shovel out horse stalls wearing next to nothing, and you are no one to talk to me about cursing, you who stood in that stall cursing like a sailor."

"Me, curse like a sailor? When?"

"I distinctly heard a 'damn' come out of your mouth."

"If you think 'damn' is bad, just wait, you . . . you donkey!"

It took him a second to realize she had called him an ass. Anger boiled. Clay had had enough. Roughly he grabbed the soft flesh above her elbow and pulled her back toward the door of the stable. Jaime and Bill were standing at the entrance not sure just what to do.

Stubbornly she dug in her heels. "Let go of me, you damn blackguard!"

"You use the word 'damn' one more time and I won't care who is around. I will yank you over my knee and spank you until you can't sit down for a week."

"Damn . . . darn you," she quickly changed when his step faltered, not wanting to test his threat. She was sure he was enough of a beast to do just as he said.

"You try me sorely, Lorena Cervantes," he said as he continued to pull her out of the stables and toward the study. As he pulled her along, his mind turned. With a gallant effort, he told himself that she was young and needed time

to adjust. After that, she would be as agreeable as any
female to the upcoming nuptials. As much as he was
tempted to shake some sense into her he felt the best
approach would be to sit her down and calmly talk to her
about the situation. Clay was the first to admit that he
should have held his temper and told her about the betrothal
in a less antagonistic manner. But what was done was done.
Now all he could do was to lessen the damage, and that he
had no doubt he could do. He had let it simply hang in the
air, hoping that over time, things would work themselves
out. Apparently he had been wrong. It was time to take
matters into his own hands.

His tight grip on her arm lessened, though the rage that
built in Lorena did not. When they reached the door to the
study, Clay opened it then let go so Lorena could go inside.
Before he entered he turned back, holding on to the door
frame, thinking he had heard someone call his name. Seeing
no one, he turned just in time to see the heavy wooden door
closing, a smile of satisfaction on Lorena's face. Reflexes
long honed by the dangerous trail, Clay quickly removed
his fingers just as the door slammed shut with a deadly thud.
He stood frozen to the spot, not believing what he knew he
had seen. And with no other choice or any other thought,
Clay entered the room with a censurious stare.

Lorena had acted without thinking, a childish fit of
temper causing her to slam the door, hoping to hurt the man
who continued to hurt her. But as soon as the door left her
hand, remorse filled her, for she knew full well what a
childish and potentially dangerous thing she had done. The
heavy, solid wood door could have crippled the man's hand.
When Clay walked into the room she knew without a doubt
that whatever he did to her was well deserved. But that
knowledge did little to make it any easier to stand there and
not try to flee.

Walking past Lorena without even touching her, Clay
went to the overstuffed sofa that stood against the wall and
sat down. For a moment Lorena thought he was not going

to do anything, but when she looked again she knew she was wrong.

Black eyes bored into her. "Come here, Lorena," he commanded.

Reluctantly she drew near, though just out of reach.

"Closer." His voice was like steel, devoid of emotion, cold to the senses.

Lorena quickly sat down next to him on the sofa before she lost her courage, willing herself to remain silent no matter how sternly he lectured her. But her resolve turned to disbelief when he hauled her across his lap.

"What are you doing?" she screeched, all resolve instantly gone.

"Just what you deserve, something I should have done a long time ago."

"I am a nineteen-year-old woman, you wretch," she said indignantly. "I'm well past the age of being paddled."

"If you are not careful, I will wash your mouth out with soap. And as far as being too old to paddle, I will treat you as the child you are acting like."

Before she could respond, a firm hand came down on her backside, sending her into a rage, but Clay held her firmly, as his hand came down again and again. Lorena finally gave way to tears. She cried because she knew she deserved the punishment, and she cried because of the whole wretched situation. Without being aware that the spanking had stopped, Lorena was in Clay's strong arms, where she cried out her tears into his massive chest.

He held her as she sobbed, feeling an angry impotence at the situation. How had things come to this point, that he would strike the woman he was to marry? He had never struck a woman, and though he felt that Lorena needed to be disciplined, he did not feel the least bit better. He had wanted nothing more than to take care of this spitfire who lay huddled in his arms. He began to wonder if it would ever work out between them, if they would ever have the kind of relationship he wanted. He laughed to himself when he thought how exceedingly clear it was becoming that she wanted no relationship with him, good or bad. Holding her close, he kissed the top of her head.

"I don't want to marry you," she cried through broken sobs.

"I know, little one, I know," and he was surprised that he did. He remembered being so confident that she would want to marry him, to be grateful for the use of his name. What a fool he had been.

The room grew quiet. Clay held her close as her tears subsided, wanting only to see her smile again.

"I shouldn't have tried to slam the door on your fingers." Her soft voice startled Clay out of his thoughts.

He smiled into her hair, knowing that it was her way of apologizing.

Lorena could feel his smile against her hair, the feeling filling her with an inexplicable joy. Forgetting her tears, she leaned back to look up into his face. "You're not mad anymore?"

"No, Lorena, I think you have learned your lesson," he said as he wiped the tears from her cheeks.

Serenity pervaded her, and willing everything else from her mind, she put her head back on his chest. "I don't think I'm finished crying yet," she said as if to explain why she did not get up.

"Oh" was all he said, a half smile breaking across his face as he relaxed against the back of the sofa.

"You never finished telling me why you came to see my father," she said sometime later. "How did you know him?"

Silence filled the room as Clay went back to another time. He stopped the curt reply that had automatically come to his lips. He was not used to putting up with questions about his past, but he knew she deserved an answer. As he thought of that time, of his own father, with Lorena in his arms, Clay wondered how it could have ever plagued him. Now it did not seem so bad.

"I met Diego in 1825."

"That was the year I went away to school."

"Yes, I arrived at the hacienda not long after Diego returned from taking you to Veracruz."

Clay felt Lorena tense.

"He was probably extremely happy." Her voice was bitter.

"Happy? He was anything but happy. He missed you terribly, Lorena." Clay remembered the time well and how sad the older man had been to have sent his only daughter away to school.

"If he felt so terrible, why did he send me away?"

"He said he felt he must provide all that you would miss out on by not having your mother alive. He wanted you to be like every other Cervantes woman—a lady."

"But I could have learned that here."

"Maybe, maybe not. You will never know." Clay felt her resistance to his words. "He did what he thought was best, little one."

"Hmph," she said petulantly.

"He loved you very much." It was barely a whisper, but she heard, and she began to cry once again.

"I have never cried so much in my life." The words were muffled by his chest and her tears. With renewed resolve she pulled away from him and sat next to him on the sofa. Clay released her reluctantly.

"Enough of me. You never did finish telling me about how you met my father and how you came to Cielo el Dorado."

Clay walked over to the table and poured some brandy into a small glass. Twirling the liquor around, he walked back and sat down on the sofa and took one long sip as if to fortify himself. "I came to the hacienda because before my father's death, he told me of Diego."

Lorena had not thought much about Clay's family, or that he even had one besides Ben. It was hard to imagine this rugged man having a father much less a mother.

"How did your father know Papá?" The more he said, the more confused Lorena became.

"Well, I suspect I should start at the beginning." He took another sip, then leaned his head back. "In 1812, my father set out to make his fortune. He was always trying to make his fortune." He gave a low, sarcastic laugh. "But this time it was different, he was going to trade with Mexico. He and a number of other men bought up everything they could imagine, spending what little money we had, loaded up a caravan, and set off for Santa Fe when I was fourteen and Ben was twelve. They went because they had heard that the revolution had been successful and trade had opened up. But as we know now, the revolution was not successful until 1821. So when my father and his associates arrived in Santa Fe, their goods were confiscated, and they were imprisoned as spies."

"Imprisoned!" Lorena sat engrossed in his story, feeling sorry for two young boys and angry at a father who would leave them.

"Yes, imprisoned in Santa Fe. They were being transferred down to a prison in Chihuahua when they stopped in Paso del Norte. For some reason they stayed for a while."

"Is that when your father met my father?" she asked earnestly.

Clay smiled at her. "Yes, that is when our fathers met. Anyway, during their stay in Paso del Norte their confinement was not rigorous. For some reason unknown to me, Diego went to the jail, and there he met my father. I guess they started talking and found a common interest. Diego visited every day after that. They became friends, and when the officials were ready to transfer the prisoners the rest of the way to Chihuahua, Diego went with them. Somewhere along the way, he helped my father escape."

"No," Lorena gasped, amazed at this new side of her father.

"Yes," Clay said.

"But how?"

"I'm not really sure. All I know is that he did it in such a way that no one suspected him of doing it, or if they did they could not prove it."

"Didn't your father tell you?"

"No, he never got around to it." It was a bitter regret for Clay.

"Well, what about Papá? Didn't you ask him?"

"Yes, I asked him, but he would not tell me. I respected that and didn't ask him again."

Lorena thought about that before asking, "What about your father? Did he return home?"

"Yes, he did." Clay got up and refilled his glass. Looking out the window into the courtyard he saw the image of his father's beaten figure instead of the busy hacienda. "He made it home, a ghost of his former self. I suspect it's a miracle he made it at all."

Her questions were relentless, but she sensed that he had never spoken of this before, and she knew it would do him good. "How did he get there?" she asked quietly.

"He walked all the way to the Santa Fe Trail, then was able to travel to Missouri in a caravan."

"He walked! That's hundreds of miles! How could he possibly have survived?"

"As I said, it was a miracle that he made it." Clay moved to the desk, where he had spent so many hours recently, and sat down in the chair. Lorena hadn't moved. "When he got back home, we didn't even recognize him. He had changed so much. He was broken, but not beaten. He was ready to stay home; he was tired of trying to make his fortune." A bitter laugh left his lips. "I wonder how long that would have lasted."

"I suppose your mother was happy," Lorena asked tentatively.

"My mother had died within a year after he left."

"Oh, Clay," she said, wanting to comfort the fourteen-year-old boy whose father and mother, in their own way, had both left him. How she could empathize with that!

"When my father found out that my mother had died shortly after he left, he was beaten. He died within a month after his return."

They sat in silence, each lost in thought, neither knowing what would come once the precious moment was gone, both content simply to share it.

16

❦

THE IMPORTED CLOCK CHIMED THE HOUR. ABSENT-mindedly Lorena counted along: one, two, three . . . until finally the old clock wound its way to a stop at nine o'clock. Lorena sighed as she looked around for something to do. Dinner was over, and Clay, as usual, was busy in the study. She sat at the table, its long dark expanse now cleared of all dishes. Restlessly she pushed back her chair and walked to the kitchen. No one was there. She wondered when Clay would be finished with his work, then immediately chastised herself. She didn't care when he finished. She should have been glad he was busy working instead of forcing his company on her. But she did care; she had grown used to his company. The thought that she was truly succumbing to him scared her. She had to resist. But somehow resisting him no longer seemed so important. Lorena found herself extolling his good qualities, diminishing his bad, though she could not think of many bad ones. When had she come to think this way? She could not answer herself.

As she stood in the empty kitchen near the old oak table where she had shared meals with her father, the truth came to her with startling clarity: She did not want Clay to leave; she wanted him to stay. A huge burden was swept from her

shoulders when she realized that he had proved her wrong in
her assumption that he was just like her father. Suddenly she
wanted nothing more than to be with Clay, to stop fighting
the overpowering emotions that drew her to him, to yield.

Lorena practically flew out into the courtyard, under the
stars that pierced the black sky. A slight breeze caressed
her skin, and she thought of Clay. Relief surged through her
body, banishing the tension that had played havoc with her
for the last few months. Joy followed relief, and Lorena
skipped under the huge trees in the courtyard and found
herself at the door of the study. The light from a lantern
shone dimly, its golden glow shining through the glass
panes in the window. Peeking inside, Lorena saw Clay
leaning over her father's desk, reading intently. For a
moment the familiar wariness tried to claim her, but
resolutely she pushed it away, feeling all the stronger when
she succeeded.

His black hair appeared glossy in the glowing light,
shadows cast on his face underneath his cheekbones making
him look all the more severe. His strong jaw clenched,
causing Lorena to wonder what he was reading. He looked
up as if sensing someone near, but she quickly fell back out
of sight. Why had she done that? she wondered. But she
knew: She wanted another chance to look at the man, to
study his handsome features at her leisure, to relish her
delight in him and in her newfound joy.

Peeking into the room, she saw that he was reading
again. He looked up, but not toward the window. He stared
at the wall, and Lorena knew that he saw more than the
bricks of mud and straw that stood before him. The dark,
fathomless eyes that she remembered from the day at the
swimming hole, the first day she met him, looked without
seeing. The memory of their first encounter had always
made her angry, but tonight it only made her laugh.

He pushed the papers away and leaned back in the large
chair. Lorena left the window and walked to the door.

The tentative knock did not surprise Clay, though he felt

sure that it should have. He couldn't recall a time when, of her own volition, Lorena had sought him out without guns blazing or heated words flying.

"Come in," he called through the door, not getting up, not sure what to expect.

"*Buenas noches*," Lorena ventured uncertainly.

Clay smiled at her use of Spanish. Though she talked to Dalia and Pedro in Spanish, she rarely spoke to him in her native language. "*Buenas noches*," he replied, his deep, sensual voice filling the room.

Lorena stood staring at him, rooted to the spot, and when she said nothing else Clay filled the silence. "Is there something you need?"

All her bravery fled as she stood alone in front of this dark, powerful man. How could she have dared to come in here? What had she planned to say? For lack of courage Lorena pounced on the first excuse that came to her. "I . . . I thought you might like to play chess."

Clay was surprised; he wasn't expecting a game of chess. He was disappointed but reasoned to himself that it was amazing that she had come to him at all, for any purpose.

"Chess, is it? I didn't realize you played the game," he stated in his own very arrogant manner, pricking Lorena's all too easily aroused ire.

All her good intentions were lost. "Is that because I am female, señor, or because we are out in the desolate desert, hundreds of miles from any 'civilized' city? Precisely why are you surprised that I know how to play chess?" Her voice dripped with sarcasm.

Clay wanted to laugh. Would she ever change? "I guess it was too much to expect you to have lost your acerbic tongue, but then, I suspect I would miss our regular bouts of verbal fencing," he said dryly, bringing a flush of pink to her cheeks.

Lorena had not wanted to fight with him, but he made her so mad! Not wanting to leave but not knowing how to change her tone now, Lorena said, "Are we going to play or not?"

"By all means," he said as an infuriatingly gorgeous smile sliced across his face. "Set up the board. I'll put away these papers and we can play right here."

Lorena turned to a leather trunk, her long hair flying from the force of her sudden turn, and pulled out a hand-carved wooden chess board and a large leather pouch that held the pieces. Forgetting the man who sat across from her, Lorena took the figures out one by one and placed them almost reverently on their designated squares of black or white.

"Where did you get this set?" Clay asked, wondering if it had been Diego's, knowing it was special by the way she handled it.

"It was carved by the very first Cervantes who came to this land. Don Diego Lorenzo Cervantes. I was named after the man. He had sent for a set in Mexico but by the time it arrived he had already carved this whole set. The set from Mexico City is beautiful, but I prefer playing with this one. It is amazing to me to hold the pieces and wonder what he was thinking when he carved each one."

Clay had never considered the long Cervantes line, the two hundred years the family had lived on this site, unbroken until Lorena. Though the Cervantes name would cease, the line would not falter, it would be carried on through him. Clay had his brother and only fading memories of a mother and father. No line of history. He had no idea who his grandparents had been. The thought of his children being the continuation of history filled him with a surprising sense of pride.

"You first," Lorena said, breaking into his wandering thoughts.

Clay looked down at the board, then swiftly turned it around. "No, ladies first."

"Always the arrogant male," she sighed in mock disgust.

"And you'd do well not to forget it." He gave back as good as he got.

Lorena moved her knight up two and over one. Normally she would have moved a rook conservatively up two, but tonight she felt compelled to play aggressively. "I hope I beat the pants off you."

Clay didn't remark, only looked up from the board and gave her a penetrating look, which mixed teasing and desire in a combination that brought a blush to her cheeks.

"I mean . . ." she stammered, only to be cut off by Clay.

"Your move again, *querida*."

Lorena was flustered. Her innocent remark, his dark sensual eyes, topped off by him calling her '*querida*' . . .

She scolded herself silently for getting fanciful in her old age. And then she smiled and pulled her wayward attention back to the task at hand.

They played in companionable silence, the lantern flickering its golden light, casting shadows against the walls.

"Check" was the next word that was said. Lorena preened with pleasure at having bested him.

"You know, you're really quite good," he said.

"You sound surprised."

"Pleasantly so," he admitted. "Unfortunately, you're not as good as I am." Clay moved his bishop, effectively countering her check and putting Lorena in an inextricable checkmate of his own. "I believe that, my dear, is checkmate, and game."

"Ahhg! How did you do that? You must have cheated!" she accused.

Clay only sat back in the high-backed chair laughing at her outrage. "I have learned a lesson today."

Lorena looked at him and wondered what he meant.

"You are a poor loser." His smile was infectious, making her realize that indeed she was acting like a poor sport.

"Well, if the truth be known, I let you win."

One thick black eyebrow rose skeptically. "Oh?"

"I knew your ego could not take defeat at the hands of a

mere female, so I threw the game," she said haughtily,
though she had wanted badly to defeat the arrogant male.

Clay laughed louder. "You are priceless, Lorena Cervantes. And if you continue to tell stories, I just might have
to take you over my knee and teach you a lesson."

Simultaneously their thoughts went to a different time, a
time when he had done just that. Lorena's eyes clouded, and
Clay cursed himself for having reminded her of it. "I'm
sorry," he conceded.

Looking up into his dark eyes, she saw the regret. "Next
time I will not throw the game and I will beat you soundly."

Clay's billowing laugh rumbled through the room, filling
every crevice with its fullness. Lorena loved it when he
laughed, the sound filling her with pleasure.

Clay was still chuckling when he said, "Well, I suspect
tomorrow evening is as good a time as any for you to . . .
umm . . . beat me soundly. For now, however, I have
work to finish."

A streak of disappointment flashed across Lorena's face,
a streak that Clay did not fail to notice and had a difficult
time believing he really saw. He would have teased her
about it, but he stopped himself, not wanting to break the
fragile bond that had formed between them.

Lorena quelled her disappointment as quickly as it came,
not at all comfortable with it. It was one thing to enjoy his
company, as she was now ready to do, but to be disappointed when she had to leave him was absurd. As always,
the irritatingly frequent thought recurred: Clay was a man of
the trail. He would leave eventually. But the doubt that had
entered her mind that day when she had sat in her mother's
room, the doubt that he was like her father, surged, giving
her sudden hope.

A smile spread across her lips, lighting her face. "Yes, I
believe I will beat you soundly, after dinner tomorrow." She
turned to leave but stopped before she had turned all the
way around. "If for some reason you are not here, I will
accept that as a sign of your willingness to bow to my

superior ability at the game and of your realization that you could not possibly win." With a dramatic flip of her long, shiny hair, Lorena completed her turn. The only thing belying her haughty tone was the twinkling laughter in her dancing green eyes.

Clay sat back in his chair, an appreciative gleam in his eye as he watched the saucy swish of Lorena's skirt as she made her way to the door. What a jewel she was. And she was his. "Lorena." He stopped her before she was gone. "I'll be checking the fields tomorrow. I thought you would enjoy the ride."

"Sure," she said. "I was planning on going out tomorrow as well. We can go at two o'clock."

Clay looked at her, one dark eyebrow raised in question. Would she ever be soft-spoken and ladylike, "sedate and biddable," as she had once said? But his eyebrow lowered and his full lips slashed across his face in something resembling a smile when he realized with a start that he wanted her no other way. "At two" was all he said as he watched her disappear through the door.

The next day, as much as she didn't want to be, Lorena was excited about the two o'clock ride. Though she told herself she looked forward to riding and that was all, in her heart she knew it would not matter what they did. She was excited about the prospect of being with Clay.

Rosinante was saddled with Lorena perched impatiently on top when he leisurely entered the stables.

"You're late." Lorena smiled down at him, not knowing what else to say as her breath caught at the mere sight of him.

"At Miss Tidesdale's Seminary for Young Ladies, time-telling must have rated with needlepoint and ballroom dancing," he remarked dryly as he went to saddle Dante.

Jaime skidded around the corner just as Clay was finishing. "I am sorry, Señor Wakefield," he panted, clearly out of breath. Jaime was terrified that he would lose

his much loved job, afraid that one slip-up would condemn
him in the eyes of this formidable man. "Pedro asked me to
do something for him. Had I known you would be riding, I
would have told him I could not."

Clay stood up, absently testing the cinch, to tower over
the relatively small figure of Jaime. "If Pedro needs you,
you are to do what he asks, Jaime. As long as you are doing
your job, which you are, you have no fear of losing it." His
voice was low and reassuring.

Relief filled the boy, though Clay didn't notice. He had
already turned back to Dante, gently slipping the bit into the
horse's mouth. Clay had always dealt with people fairly,
even when he had just started on the trail, before he had
made his fortune. He only expected people to do their jobs,
and that Jaime had always done.

Though the incident did not faze Clay, it did not go past
Lorena. Her heart surged with pride and she recognized the
act of kindness as just one of many that he had rendered
since he had come to Cielo el Dorado. He was a fine man,
a fair man, as Pedro had once told her, a man who was not
like her father. Clay Wakefield had come to the hacienda,
taken on the responsibilities of another, and executed them
with a firm but fair hand. Cielo el Dorado had flourished
under that hand as it obviously had not for many years.
Lorena remembered the long line of Cervanteses who had
built everything that surrounded her, a line of hardworking
men and women who had turned the barren desert into a
home. According to the stories, all of them were strong
brave men, and Lorena realized with a stab of pain that her
own father, the last man to carry the Cervantes name, had
been a man of a different breed. It was in that moment that
she realized her father was not infallible, that she had a
glimpse of being an adult. She had seen things in him that
hurt her or made her angry, but she had never before seen
him as wrong. Emotion washed over her as she sat
immobile on Rosinante's back. She had experienced anger
and, moments before, a new and unfamiliar pain, but as she

sat there the anger and pain were replaced with understanding and, ultimately, forgiveness—forgiveness of her father as she realized that he had done the best he could, but more importantly, forgiveness of herself as she finally realized that no matter what she had done, she would never have been capable of changing her father. With a clarity that pierced her soul, Lorena realized that it wasn't her fault and it never had been. She felt her being soar as the weight of a lifetime was magically lifted from her shoulders, freeing her to believe in a man.

Lorena looked at Clay, the man who was to be her husband, and as she looked at him she realized that she loved him. She felt as if she couldn't breathe, the feelings and emotions swelling inside her, filling her until she thought she would burst. Ah, yes, she loved him, with every fiber of her being. She would have staggered with the import had she not been firmly seated on Rosinante's back.

How long had it been? she wondered. She remembered the day she met him. She had seen him as a knight in shining armor, a storybook character out of one of her dreams. And now she knew she had been right: He was the man of her dreams, the man to fill her with happiness and joy, the man with whom she would spend the rest of her life.

Lorena did not notice that Clay had mounted his horse and stood ready to go. "Lorena?"

Her eyes cleared, and she focused on the man before her. She noticed that he must have been hard at work somewhere besides the study, as his face down to his bronze neck glistened with sweat. A streak of dark blue staggered down his shirt where perspiration had soaked through. A breeze floated through the air, and she smelled leather and hard work. The rich smells of man filled her senses and she longed to be held by him, to tell him of her love. But she could not yet. Soon, though, she assured herself. Soon she would shower him with all the love she felt.

"Lorena, are you sick?" he asked bluntly, interrupting her excited thoughts.

"Sick?" she asked in confusion, wondering how he could possibly think her sick when she had never felt so marvelously alive. "No, why?"

Clay smiled as he shook his head. "It was nothing. It's just that you had a sick, moony expression." Before she could say anything else, Clay added, his smile growing ever wider, "Now come on. We want to get out before the sun goes down."

"Oh," she cried, but she knew he was teasing so she pressed Rosinante's sides and flew by the black stallion before they had even reached the gate.

As they had done before, Clay and Lorena rode past the fields, checking crops that had not yet been harvested, then lingering near the burgeoning vineyard.

"We'll harvest next week," Clay said as much to himself as anyone.

"How do you know about wine-making?" Lorena questioned.

Clay turned to her, shaking his head. "I know next to nothing about making wine. I am following what your father had written down in his notes. Between the notes and Pedro, I'm hoping this year won't be too bad."

"Really?" she said, surprised. "You seem to know what you are doing all the time."

Clay laughed. "I try."

They rode on, checking the land, making sure all of the laborers were doing their jobs. As they rode past the workers, several tipped their hats, offering greetings.

Lorena was contented as she had never been. Riding the land with the man she loved. Home and family. How silly she had been to think she would have been content without a family.

They came to the river and dismounted to let the horses cool off. Lorena and Clay stood side by side in silence, looking at all that was around them, each sharing in a peace neither had ever felt before. But their tranquil world was pierced by the high-pitched squeal of Rosinante.

Clay spun around, every muscle tense beneath his skin, shielding Lorena's body with his own, ready to protect her from any impending danger. Nothing was there except the two horses, but Clay was not willing to concede to false alarm. He scanned the hills but before he could get very far, Dante bit Rosinante, bringing forth another shrill squeal from the mare. Once they got over their surprise, Clay met Lorena's eyes, and they burst out in gales of laughter as Dante once again bit into Rosinante's flesh.

"That beast of a horse you have is as much a tormentor as you." Lorena laughed, a teasing twinkle lighting her eyes.

"Or maybe Dante has an eye for desirable flesh," Clay retorted with a sly grin.

"You beast!" she cried as a rosy blush crept into her cheeks.

Clay only laughed harder, then reached out to grab Lorena's wrist and pull her close, but he came up empty-handed when she turned out of his reach and quickly skipped away.

"Unlike my horse, Clay Wakefield, I have sense enough to get out of the way," she laughed over her shoulder.

With feet planted firmly apart and arms akimbo, Clay watched her with a mixture of amusement and desire. She skipped through a stretch of long grass mixed with yellow wildflowers as if she had not a care in the world. He thought of love, but instantly dismissed it. He did not love her. He was not some callow schoolboy who followed his sweetheart around like a puppy dog. But he would concede that he was intrigued by Lorena—her mind, her wit, her beauty. She was everything he could want in the mother of his children, in the woman who would share his bed. He thought about Missouri and knew that he would spend more time at the hacienda than he had originally intended. For a moment he was engulfed with unease, but then he reassured himself that the reason for his desire to spend more time at Cielo el Dorado was not need; it was simply a matter of pleasure.

Well out of reach of Clay's strong hands, Lorena stopped in a stretch of grass. She looked around her, then opened her arms wide to twirl about as if to embrace the entire world. Her hair was loose, billowing out behind her, her smiling face turned up to the sun. "Is this not the most wonderful spot in the world?" Her voice carried on the breeze like a song.

Her voice drifted back to Clay, and he knew her words were true. He had come to love the land as had every Cervantes through history, back to that time in 1660 when the first Cervantes had arrived.

Lorena stopped in mid-twirl to bend over and pick some of the yellow wildflowers that grew sporadically among the grass. Clay came to stand before her, and when she stood up, meeting his eyes, he felt his chest constrict with an emotion he could not place.

Lorena's eyes met the bottomless depths of his, and she knew with a feeling of intense joy that they would spend the rest of their lives together. A glimpse of children passed through her thoughts, and she hoped they would have their father's devastating good looks. And then, impulsively, with no thought to what she was doing, Lorena offered her bouquet of yellow wildflowers to the man who stood before her—the man she loved.

Clay looked at the flowers, then touched the tips of his fingers to her jaw and could see in her eyes that she was giving more than the bouquet she had gathered. Very gently he extracted one flower from the bunch. "Thank you, little one. You honor me. I will take this one. It will always remind me of you on this perfect sunny day."

"But what of the rest?" she asked, taking a step back, momentarily rebuffed.

He delicately caressed the side of her face with the flower and said, "They are for you. A bouquet of flowers is much more appropriate for a lady, especially one as lovely as you."

Lorena felt her insides turn to liquid, his soft words, the gentle stroke of her cheek, coming together to make her want to reach out to his strong body. Instead, not ready, and not comfortable enough to be bold, she made herself laugh, a small laugh that did not sound much like a laugh at all.

Clay only smiled. "Come on, we have been gone long enough. It's time we headed back."

They rode at a comfortable pace, talking pleasantly of the world around them. Jaime met them outside the stable, taking their horses to be curried and put up for the night. Later that evening Jaime told many of the love he saw shining in the eyes of Señorita Cervantes and Señor Wakefield.

When Clay and Lorena reached the hallway that led to their rooms, Lorena turned toward her door, only to be stopped by the weight of Clay's hand on her shoulder. He turned her around to him and gently cupped her chin. "I enjoyed our outing today," he said as he bent down and placed a tender kiss on her lips. He looked for a long moment into her eyes and started to pull her to him, then suddenly released her. "Go, Lorena, before I ravage you in the hallway. I'll see you at dinner." With that, Clay abruptly turned and entered his room, leaving Lorena to stare at the closing wood door.

Dinner that evening was filled with laughing conversation and much taunting as to who would win the chess game. After their meal, Lorena and Clay went to the study, but before she could set up the board, a bell sounded, warning of someone's approach. They looked at each other, wondering who it could be at such an hour. Within moments after the bell had sounded, Clay was out of the study, Lorena close at his heels.

"Señor Wakefield, someone has crossed the river and is heading this way." The guard on duty shouted down to him.

"Only one?"

"*Sí.*"

Clay climbed the ladder to look out. The sound of the rider could be discerned better than the shape. The men on the roof were armed, just in case. But it was Ben Wakefield who wheeled his horse up to the front gate of Cielo el Dorado.

"Ben?" Clay called.

"Hey, big brother," Ben called back, his ever cheerful self.

"Why in the world are you riding around in the dark? How did you get across the river?"

"If you let me in, I'll tell you all about it."

Slowly the gates, which had been locked for several hours, started to open. Ben trotted through the entrance, his blond hair barely discernible in the dim glow of lanterns, grime streaking his face and clothes.

Clay was just coming down the ladder and turned to Ben. "You young fool, you could have killed yourself riding here at night."

"Welcome home to you, too. And I'm not that much younger than you." Ignoring his brother, Ben turned to Lorena. "Lorena, you look as lovely as ever. I'm glad to see you have survived my brother's attentions."

Lorena giggled at his flirtatious ways, glad to see him back. "You should not ride over here in the dark."

Ben pointed to the sky. The huge golden orb of the moon shone brightly. "I had a light to guide my way. Besides, I couldn't stand the thought of camping out one more night when I knew the comforts of Cielo el Dorado were only a hop and a skip away."

"But the river?"

"Yes, that was a bit difficult, but nothing is too difficult for a man like me." Ben touched his chest proudly.

"You Wakefields are a conceited lot," Lorena teased.

"Yes, we are, aren't we?" Ben said good-naturedly. "Now how about a meal for this conceited fool?"

Ben put a casual arm around Lorena as they walked toward the kitchen, leaving a bemused Clay to stare after them.

After making sure the gate was securely locked, Clay followed the two into the kitchen, knowing Ben would not have come at night if he did not have important news to deliver. Clay was anxious to get Ben alone and see what he found out in Chihuahua.

Pedro and Dalia had gotten up when they heard all the commotion, and when Clay entered the kitchen Dalia stood at the stove. He could tell she had dressed hastily, not bothering to put up her long gray braid. Pedro appeared to have run a hasty hand through his hair, his clothes as hurriedly thrown on as his wife's.

Dalia placed a bowl of beef, potatoes, and beans in a thick brown sauce in front of Ben.

"Dalia, you are the best cook in the world."

"You only say that because you have been on the trail this long time, and anything looks good to you," she said, though she beamed with pleasure at his compliment.

Clay sat down and listened as Ben told tales of his adventures on the Camino Real. Ben appeared to be enthralled with his own stories, just as Pedro, Dalia, and Lorena were. Clay had been on the road for so long he had forgotten that such stories were exciting for people who did not travel and for those like Ben who were riding the trail for the first time. Patiently, Clay waited for Ben to finish so he could hear what he'd found out.

As Clay waited, he watched Lorena, excitement dancing across her face. She was lovely. And she was his. Soon . . . soon he would hold her in his arms and teach her of the intense passion within her just waiting to be released. Lorena looked up and, as if sensing his thoughts, blushed but held his gaze.

"Now really, you two, I'm telling great tales of adventure, and I'd be surprised if you've heard a single word," Ben teased.

Clay sent his brother a dry look as he pulled his eyes away from Lorena. "As you were saying, little brother?" he added for emphasis.

"Yes, as I was saying," Ben said, ignoring his brother's taunt, "I am going to go out to the stables to check on my horse, and I thought it might be nice if you joined me."

The two men walked to the stables, neither speaking until the horse had been checked and Clay had led his brother to a place where they could speak without being overheard.

Clay spoke first. "The news must be bad if you risked your neck to come here at night."

"Actually, I really didn't want to spend one more night sleeping under the stars on the hard ground. But you're right, the news is not good, but not insurmountable."

"So what is it?"

"Well, it seems Diego was something of a gambler."

"A gambler?" Clay showed his surprise. He had known Diego for years and never suspected he gambled.

"A poor gambler," Ben clarified.

"What is that supposed to mean?"

"He wasn't very good. In fact, usually he lost."

"So how does that affect Cielo el Dorado?"

"Diego signed notes to a man in Chihuahua, the amount of which is staggering. They are due in two months. If they are not paid off, the hacienda and everything in it will go to a Señor Medina."

Clay was stunned, though after all the time he had spent trying to figure out Diego's mess and continued to come up empty-handed, he shouldn't have been. He knew that something was very wrong, but had never imagined that Diego could be so stupid, so careless. Rage swept his body that Diego could do that to Lorena. His "precious Lorena," he had always said. The man had obviously cared for no one but himself. But it would do no good to berate a dead man. All he could do now was get Lorena out of this mess. He suddenly knew why Diego had been so insistent that he marry Lorena. Diego had left Clay to clean up the mess he had made.

"What are you going to do?" Ben asked, wondering how Clay could possibly settle the gambling debt in such a short period of time.

"I will go to Chihuahua and pay off the notes."

"How will you get there in time?"

"I will take a small contingent of men and ride like hell," Clay said, his mind already racing with plans.

"But where will you get the money?"

"What did you bring back with you from the last sale?"

Ben told him of the amount that he had received when he took the goods Clay had given him to sell. "That's not enough to cover the debt."

"I know, but it will do. I brought enough to make all necessary repairs on the hacienda."

"I don't understand."

"When I came through here after Diego died, I looked around and saw the state of disrepair. I felt obligated to remedy the situation by fixing it up myself."

"That makes no sense. Diego gave you the hacienda when he betrothed Lorena to you. You could have done all of the repairs with the profits of Cielo el Dorado."

"Yes, I could have, but I don't want something like this hacienda just handed to me."

Ben knew that it was a matter of pride so he dropped the subject. "We'd better leave tomorrow, first light if we are going to make it in time."

Clay looked pensively out into the night. Things were just beginning to go well with Lorena. He had hoped to have things squared away before he had to leave again. He sensed that in the last couple of days she had finally begun to come around. But it couldn't be helped; Lorena would have to wait.

"What will you tell Lorena?"

Clay thought for a moment before he answered. "Nothing of the problems. Only that I must go to Chihuahua on business and will be back soon. I don't want anyone to know about the notes. I don't want anyone to worry."

They went to work preparing for the journey that would take them south to the city of Chihuahua. They organized supplies, men, ammunition, and horses—the fastest and the best.

It was several hours later when the small contingent bedded down to get a few hours of sleep before the long ride ahead of them.

17

❧

CLAY STOOD IN HIS ROOM, A SINGLE CANDLE FLICK-ering in the dark. He wore only tight pants—his shirt lay discarded on the bed—and absentmindedly massaged the tired muscles in his neck. He knew Lorena would already be asleep but knew as well that he could not go without speaking to her before he left. Yes, he knew he should tell her he was leaving, but more than that, he wanted to see her.

Leaving his room, he walked quietly down the hallway to her door. No light shone through the crack underneath, so he didn't bother to knock. He lifted the latch, then pushed through and softly closed it behind him. Lorena was fast asleep, silver moonbeams caressing her as they fell silently through the unshuttered windows. She was so beautiful. What would it be like when she slept beside him every night?

He walked over to the bed and sat down, his weight pressing down, causing Lorena to shift toward him. She murmured something he could not make out, then was cast back down into the depths of sleep. As always, her beauty stirred him. It was not an ordinary beauty but rather a beauty of the wild prairies and the majestic heights of the Rocky Mountains, beauty that a man could not capture or hold, only delight in, taking it in and savoring it. Her beauty

was not just that of face and body, but of mind and soul as
well. "Lorena," he murmured, looking forward to a lifetime filled with her spirit. The thought of leaving her, even
for the short time he would be gone, left him bereft. He did
not want to leave her. He wanted her in his bed, and he
wanted her company as it always kept him amused. He
would take her to wife because he enjoyed her, and to pay
his debt, but he would never become dependent on her. He
would never let himself need her or love her. Love was
absurd; there was no such thing. Love was a nonexistent
emotion of which frivolous poets wrote. Lust, desire—
those were true emotions, and in marriage a man was lucky
to have those, and for that he would be grateful. He
chastised himself for his meandering thoughts, telling
himself that he was turning into a poet himself. No, he
knew the realities of life. Hard work with little time for
happiness. And especially no undying love. Hadn't Diego
spoken of his wife with love? Then why had he left her
alone? Because love didn't exist, Clay's cynical mind told
him. And his own parents? If his father loved his mother,
why did he leave? And look what loving got his mother. An
early grave. No, love was not a consideration, and every
man would be well off to remember that.

He looked down at Lorena, and all thoughts of parents,
hard work, and what he saw as reality fled. His breathing
was rapid, causing him to take long, deep breaths as he told
himself he needed to get up and leave. But he couldn't. He
wanted her, in his arms and by his side. He wanted her, and
he did not know how he could wait until he got back to
marry her. He wanted her with an ache so intense that he
thought he would burst, right there, right then, as he looked
at her exquisite beauty.

Lorena moved, still asleep, unaware of his presence.
Clay looked down into her face, at the lips so soft in sleep.
He bent his head to capture her lips in a barely perceptible
caress. Only to taste. But his body began to burn, slowly,
intensely. His mind reeled. He kissed her again, this time

harder. Unknowingly she sought the pressure. Desire surged through him, uncontrollably, turning his kiss into a demand.

Lorena moaned in her sleep as she sought the pressure and was left wanting more as Clay pulled away. She was in a swirl of sensation, caught up in a dream of passion. She yearned for it, strained toward it, trying desperately to capture the intensity that came, then went, then came again.

He nipped at the corner of her mouth, trying to pull back, telling himself he must get up, he must leave. But like a man out in the cold, he sought the warmth, unable to pull away, telling himself he would take only a taste.

His tongue sought entrance to her mouth, and unknowingly she gave way. And at the touch of tongue on tongue, Clay forgot everything, his only thought being Lorena, her feel, her warmth. *Lorena*, his mind repeated, over and over, matching the thrusting of his tongue, slowly, languidly.

"Lorena," he whispered, his voice thick with passion, gravelly and rough. Her only response was to turn toward him.

Unable to help himself he lowered his desire-filled body to the bed, stretching out beside her, cursing himself for a cad as he did it, but knowing all the while he could not stop.

Lorena nuzzled up to the warmth of his chest, caressing the dark hair with her cheek. Clay looked down at her lying in his arms, thinking perhaps she had awakened. But when he saw her eyes delicately closed, he knew she had no idea what she did. She lay there trusting, loving, so incredibly gorgeous, so very much his. With a groan, he pulled her body to his, pressing her to his hard length, to his burgeoning manhood, and traced the curve of her ear with his tongue.

Trusting. She lay there in innocence, trusting him. He could not take advantage of her. He had only come to say good-bye. "Lorena." It was a breath of air, warm and moist that caressed her skin. "Lorena, wake up, little one." She sighed, moving closer, her fingers intertwining with the thick curls on his chest. Damn! he wanted her, and she wanted him, deep inside she did. Of its own volition, his hand found the hem of her nightgown, and when he touched the satiny skin of her leg, he knew he was lost. His lips found hers and his hand made a slow, torturous journey up her thigh, barely grazing her womanhood, moving on, making slow circles over the slight curve of her belly, until he captured one firm breast, her nightgown pulled up revealing the beautiful length of her body. "Lorena," he growled, "you are so beautiful." He took one rosy nipple into his mouth, feeling it rise.

She moaned, arching her back, letting the gown fall farther away.

With his other hand he pulled her body once again to his, pulling her to his manhood, making him feel as if he would burst. "Lorena, love." This time it was a demand, he wanted her, he wanted to make love to her, to feel every inch of her body, but he wanted her awake, he wanted her to want him as much as he wanted her.

Her eyes fluttered open only to close again, still lost to sleep. He lifted her up and pulled her free from her restraining garment and parted her legs with his thigh, pressing against her, rubbing slowly back and forth. He watched her until her eyes opened again.

"Clay," she whispered huskily, her eyes glazed and wide.

"Yes, little one, I'm here." His voice was thick with wanting as his lips traveled down her neck to the other breast while his hand circled down, lower and lower, until his fingers found her nest of curls. His fingers entangled in the mass, and when he touched her intimately, she gasped. But he had no mercy as he continued his tender assault. His lips left her breast to trail down, one arm under her hips, his other hand seeking the moist folds of her being. Her arms reached out, but his lips only continued to torture, grazing her skin, nipping, licking, as his finger stroked her relentlessly.

"Clay," she moaned, the sensations in her body warring with some feeling, dulled by sleep, that told her he must stop. "Please, Clay."

He wasn't sure what she asked, but knew what she wanted, if not with her mind, then with her body. "Lorena," he demanded gently, "let me love you."

His hand continued to tease, to bring her to the brink of some unknown and just when she thought she would reach that something, he would stop. "Not yet, little one. You will know all the joys of love before this night is over." He got up from the bed and pulled his trousers away from his body.

Her eyes closed, her body alive and wanting, though her cheeks were stained with red.

"Lorena, look at me."

She opened her eyes and kept them fixed on his face.

"No. Look at all of me. All of me that is yours."

She looked, her eyes taking in every inch of his glorious body, so different from hers, and she longed to reach out and touch him—his chest, his arms, all the way down to his toes. When she held out her arms, he came to her, pulling her roughly to him, capturing her mouth in a wild kiss.

It was frantic and wild, and Clay knew he must be gentle, so with great effort, he eased himself back. When Lorena tried to follow, he carefully pushed her back to lie flat on the bed, propping himself up on one elbow. He just looked at her for one long moment before his fingers lightly touched a path along her curves. When she closed her eyes, he said, "Don't. I want to see your passion. Look at me, Lorena."

Her head arched back, and her eyes glazed, first with confusion, then with longing, as his fingers performed their magic. She arched to him, her fingers winding in his hair until she thought she might die. His lips burned a path across her body, giving her no mercy. "Reach, Lorena," his words were muffled as her breath came in short spurts as she

drew closer and closer until finally her body reached a
pinnacle of sensation causing her senses to explode.

"Clay," she gasped, her body still in the throes of
passion, as she lay on the bed dazed.

Slowly Clay began to kiss again, nipping, sucking. The
anticipation of their joining filled his mind and body with
yearning. He rose up above her, Lorena watching, her lips
slightly parted, her hair flowing over the pillow like rays of
sunlight. "Oh, God, I want you as I've never wanted
anything in my life." He pulled her underneath him, and he
looked down at her, loving the unveiled longing that filled
her eyes. "Lorena, look at me, at us, at the love that we are
making."

He could tell she tried to focus, and when she reached out
to him he could hold back no longer and plunged into her,
her earlier pleasure easing the way as he broke through her
maidenhead. He plunged into her first slowly, then fast,
deeper until he could hold back no longer, before his face
contorted as if in pain, though in reality it was the most
intense pleasure he had ever felt.

"Lorena," he groaned.

She looked up at him then, reaching one hand out to the
damp hair that clung to his forehead and gently pushing it
back. "Clay," she whispered in awe, "I love you."

Clay pulled up and looked down into the jade depths of
her eyes and felt his chest tighten. What was it? This feeling
inside him that made it hard to breathe? It wasn't the feeling
of earlier when his body was filled with desire, with lust.
But the answer did not come, possibly because he was not
ready to face it. "Forever, darling, and for always." And
then he rolled over, pulling her with him to rest against him,
held tight in his arms.

They lay there, lost in their own thoughts, not knowing
exactly what to make of what they had just experienced.
And Lorena wondered what she felt. She had told him she
loved him, but he had not told her he loved her, or had he?

What did "forever and for always" mean, if not love? Not wanting to ruin the precious moment, she put it out of her mind to bask in the glory of their love.

Some time later Clay remembered why he had come and knew that if he planned to ride hell-bent on leather the following day he had to get some sleep. The sooner he got the debt straightened out the sooner he would be back to Cielo el Dorado, the sooner he would have Lorena in his arms forever. The thought pleased him immensely, but he squelched it as soon as it came. He would not need!

Lorena's arms sought his skin, and Clay almost damned the trip and turned to her again, but he couldn't.

"Lorena," he said almost harshly as he pulled her arms away. His voice was angry; he was angry that he had to leave. He hated pushing Lorena away when she was so open, so giving.

Lorena did not understand what was happening. Why was he pushing her away?

"I have to leave tomorrow, little one." His voice was deep with regret, but Lorena did not hear it. She did not hear him say that he would come back as soon as he could or that he had urgent business in Chihuahua that could not wait. She only heard the voice inside her head screaming over and over again, *You fool, they are all the same, every last one of them. They never stay, they always leave.* She could hardly think for the pain. She had given him her heart and her body, leaving her open for the hurt. She had been a fool to think he could possibly love her. Oh, the pain, how it hurt! She should have known. And she knew she had only herself to blame. She had disregarded all the painful lessons she had learned over a lifetime. Shame and hurt consumed her as she thought of her stupidity, of actually believing he would stay.

"Lorena." He shook her. "Lorena, you're not listening to me. As soon as I get back we will be married. I expect you to have everything ready."

It was a command, no soft words of love, no words of missing her. At least he was honest. She wanted to laugh. Clay was not like her father, who had always said he could hardly stand the pain of being away from them. Ha! Men are liars, all liars! She did not know that he was hurting as badly as she and did not know that to ease his pain as well as hers, he should have opened up and told her so. Instead, he was harsh, not liking the idea that it would be impossible to live without her.

She lay there and swore she would not marry an arrogant brute who would do naught but fill her with child and then leave her for more interesting adventures.

"Lorena!" This time anger replaced the impatience his voice had held before. "I said I expect you to be ready to marry me when I return. Do you understand?"

Sparkling green eyes clashed with his, and the fury in hers sent sparks that singed Clay's being. "Yes, I understand." It was a sneer. "And you can rot in Hades before I will ever marry you."

Clay had been expecting a bit of anger when he came to tell her he was leaving. Then, after what they had just shared, he'd expected disappointment and sadness, but he was completely taken aback by the naked hatred that seethed in her words.

"Lorena—" he started.

"Don't you 'Lorena' me, you bastard. Get off my bed and out of my home. And never, *never come back!*" Her words ended in a high shrill scream.

"Lorena." He tried again, this time grasping her wrists and forcing her back. "You're angry now, but once you've had time to cool down, you will realize your words were said in anger. I'm going to leave now because I have to. But I will be back, and don't you ever doubt it."

Clay got up from the bed, barely missing being raked by her small tapered fingernails. "Lorena," he said at the door, "you are mine, and don't ever forget it."

As he shut the door behind him he thought he heard a

hastily muffled sob. But when he remembered the fury that had emanated from her he knew that his mind was playing tricks on him; he just wanted to think she would cry for him.

With heavy footsteps, Clay walked tiredly to his room and tried to get a few hours of sleep.

18

❦

LEAVES TUMBLED OVER STONE AS A LIGHT BREEZE
pushed them on. The early morning air held a slight chill,
but the still dark sky was clear of all except bright stars that
pierced the black.

Six men waited at the front gate, their horses eager to be
off. The night guard was still up in the *torreón*, but instead
of surveying the land, he leaned out the glassless window,
his gun cradled carelessly in the crook of his arm. He spoke
to the men below, disappointment etched across his brown
face, envious that he had not been chosen to travel with the
small band of men who were going to Chihuahua.

The news of the unexpected departure had spread
quickly, making the rounds until everyone at Cielo el
Dorado knew. Emotions were high as those who had never
been on the trail envisioned the excitement and adventure
the Camino Real promised. Many asked to go, having never
been farther away from the hacienda than brief trips to Paso
del Norte, if that could be considered a trip at all. But only
six had been chosen, all men who were experienced. It was
to be a quick trip. The contingent of men was meeting
another group that was already in Paso del Norte, left by
Ben Wakefield the night before.

Ben mounted his horse, weary after the long ride from

Chihuahua, but insistent that he accompany his brother back to deal with Señor Medina. He rubbed the sore muscles in his neck and wondered what the outcome of this trip would be. Was Medina as uninterested in the hacienda as he had appeared to be? Ben wasn't sure. The man had seemed nervous when questioned about the notes, but at the time Ben had put it down to his being questioned by an American. Now he didn't know. However, Ben shook off his uneasiness. Surely lack of sleep was causing his mind to make things out of nothing.

The men waited for Clay, wondering what could possibly be keeping him. The black sky was slowly lightening and soon would be streaked with rays of purple and red. The men continued to wait, saying nothing about the precious time that was passing, certain that Clay Wakefield knew what he was doing. All of them had ridden with him before, most since the beginning.

Clay sat in the kitchen going over instructions with Pedro, wasting much-needed time in hopes of seeing Lorena. After her heated words of the night before, he was leery of seeking her out, hoping against hope that she would find him. But he had lingered and tarried until he could see the dark sky changing colors and knew he could wait no longer.

Pedro sat listening to the instructions, knowing why Clay kept glancing at the door. He also knew that Lorena would not come. Having had such high hopes himself, Pedro was disappointed to hear that Clay was leaving. How could he have been so wrong about the American? How could Clay have turned out to be like Diego after all? Ironically, Dalia, who had been against the man for so long, had whispered to Pedro while they were still in bed that she felt this trip was different, that Clay was not like Diego. When Pedro snorted his disagreement, she only responded, "We will see," as she pulled herself out of bed to dress for the day. Pedro hoped, for everyone's sake, that she was right. But as he sat in front of the man in question, he hardly remembered his wife's words.

The sky grew brighter by the minute. Finally Pedro said, "I think you must leave or it will be even longer before you return."

Pedro spoke with barely held patience, underlined with a hint of betrayal. Though Clay normally would not have tolerated such blatant disrespect, he understood the man's reasoning and Clay felt the need to explain. But he couldn't. It would have served no purpose other than to worry him, and there was nothing the older man could do. So as Clay was leaving, instead of explaining the problem, he said, "I *will* be back."

Pedro looked at Clay and, before he could stop himself, said insolently, "For how long?"

Clay stopped cold and turned to the man who sat at the wooden table. "You are lucky I understand that you are concerned for Lorena. Otherwise you would be packing your bags and looking for work elsewhere. I will tell you only this: There are things that need to be taken care of, and I am going to do that; then I will be back, to marry Lorena and take care of her and the hacienda as I promised Diego I would." Clay walked to the door and, without turning around, added, "In the future, Pedro, I will not be so tolerant." And then he was gone, the heavy wooden door closing behind him with finality.

Lorena sat in her favorite spot on the roof, a place that usually filled her with comfort. Today, however, it provided none. She held a woolen shawl wrapped tightly around her, but still she couldn't banish the feeling of cold that had been with her since Clay had left her the night before. She had been sitting on the rooftop since the men started getting ready, occasionally catching a glimpse of Clay calling out instructions as he walked back and forth between the kitchen and the stable. After the last time he went to the kitchen, he had not come back out.

She watched the men ready their horses. Dante was already saddled and had been left to stand alone waiting for his rider. Biting back tears, Lorena wanted desperately to climb down the wooden ladder and be pulled into the strong arms of the man who was leaving. But disbelief still held her in its strong grip, swaddling her in hurt, keeping her rooted to the spot, not allowing her to go to the man she knew she loved. How could it have happened? How could she have let down her defenses to the man she knew would only cause her pain? The proof that she had been right all along was no reward, even to her pride. And while she had known that men like her father hurt the ones they loved, she had never imagined that the pain would be so unbearable.

Finally Clay appeared below, walking toward his horse. Lorena crept closer to the edge of the roof, trying to get a better look, to see his perfect face one last time. He wore a white shirt and buckskins; she was sure they were the ones he had worn the day he found her by the *acequia*. Her heart beat rapidly, constricting in pain, in want, in need. "Please, Clay," she whispered, "don't leave." But she knew he would go and there was nothing she could do about it.

Clay walked with heavy steps, not liking the disappointment he felt that Lorena had not come to see him off. He told himself it shouldn't matter, but somehow that did not help. When he came to his horse, he looked up to the roof, sensing someone there, as if his name had been called. Slightly disconcerted, he scanned the rooftop but saw no one except the guard. He was strangely disappointed as he turned to Dante and pulled on leather gloves.

"What's keeping you, Clay?" Ben asked from atop a bay gelding he was using for the ride.

Clay glanced back at the rooftop one last time before swinging himself up into the saddle in one swift, fluid motion. Then, without looking back again, he spurred his horse on, under the *torreón* and through the front gate, determined to make the trip as quickly as possible.

* * *

The journey from Paso del Norte to Chihuahua could take as long as eighteen days when traveling with a loaded caravan. But with a small, well-armed contingent of only thirteen men, Clay planned to make the trip in half that time. Nine days there, a couple days to settle Diego's debt, then nine days back. With luck, he hoped to be back in less than a month. That thought made him ride just to the limit of every man's capabilities and each animal's endurance.

After leaving the hacienda, the seven men crossed the ford that took them into town to join the other six who would travel with them. They were all experienced on the trail, and the harshness of it was no surprise.

They traveled southeast, following the river for a few miles outside of Paso del Norte until they veered to the right, taking them south toward Chihuahua. Rocks and sand were interspersed with dunes and scrub brush, monotonous in their regularity. The men traveled in silence, the only sound around them being the regular beat of hooves against the ground, each man concentrating on the trail before him.

A short time later, the sky having lost all traces of black, they came upon a small caravan traveling into Paso del Norte. The caravan consisted of no more than five wagons and, from what Clay could see, carried only men—several hard-looking men of the type who made their living traveling for other men.

"This is not the type of caravan I would like to meet up with in the middle of nowhere if I was unprotected," one man said to Clay and Ben as they rode up to the leader of the meager caravan.

"It looks awfully small for a trade caravan," Ben remarked.

"Small, yes. It is surely not a trade caravan. They could not have enough goods in there to make the trip worth their while. I wonder what they're doing?" Clay wondered out loud, sensing it could be no good.

"Maybe just moving on to bigger and better things," Ben offered.

As Clay and Ben came to the lead wagon, it pulled to a halt, bringing the line to a rumbling stop behind them.

"*Buenos días*," Clay called.

The man who sat in the first wagon looked like a Mexican—thick dark hair and a full face, dark brown eyes that did not show the division between pupil and iris, and a short stocky body. Though his features were like those of many others of mixed Spanish and Indian blood, this man did not look ordinary at all. He was dressed in traditional Mexican garb more suited to a grand fiesta than a two-hundred-mile journey across a barren desert. He wore a large sombrero that was heavily ornamented and intricately embroidered, though it was now covered in dust. He could not have been more than twenty-five years old and was obviously not a veteran of the trail. He had not been smart enough to find out about it before he left. His white shirt was stiff from dried sweat, and rings of salt had formed a crusty brown pattern on the fabric. His face was streaked with dirt, and his dark hair stuck out from under the sombrero in stiff ridges.

Clay disliked him on sight.

Six of Clay's men rode on, back to the wagons that formed the remainder of the caravan. The rest stayed at the front looking on as Clay attempted to talk to the man.

"You up from Chihuahua?" Clay asked.

"*Sí*" was all he said, his brown eyes looking Clay over warily as if sizing him up.

"Where you headed?" Clay persisted.

The man stared at him without answering, then in thick Spanish, said, "Norte."

The one-word answer caused Clay's expression to cloud with concern. It was men like this who caused many of the problems for reputable traders on the trail. And he couldn't shake the feeling that this man was up to no good.

"Now, if you have no business with me, amigo"—the

man paused, his lips spread in a mocking smile—"I will go."

Without waiting for a response, he brutally whipped the mules, the sound as much as the sting frightening the animals into a jerking start. Clay was about to go after the man, his cruel and unnecessary treatment of the beasts the final straw in the man's intolerable behavior. But Ben put his hand out, anticipating his brother's intent, preventing a confrontation. "Don't," Ben said, "you can only make it worse. You know how men like that are. Feeling that they have to dominate, they're cruel to anything weaker than they are."

"I should tear that man out of his wagon and beat him to a pulp," Clay seethed.

Ben looked curiously at his brother. "Granted he's an obnoxious bastard, but why such anger? Do you know the guy?"

Clay looked from his brother to the line of wagons as they moved off down the trail, and shook his head. "Never met him before in my life, but I've met his kind. They're no good."

"Well, for now you have more important problems than getting rid of trail scum. Come on, let's get going."

Clay knew his brother was right. They had to keep going, but he hoped that one day he would find the man again and teach him a well-deserved lesson.

The contingent of men gathered together as the small caravan moved toward Paso del Norte.

"Though I'd like to meet up with that slime again someday, I hope 'norte' means farther than Paso del Norte," Clay said, more to himself than to anyone.

The rest of the men sat watching the wagons pull away, all in silent agreement that a man like that was nothing but trouble.

"What did the men in the back have to say?" Clay asked, pulling his gaze back to his men.

"Not much, just that they had been hired to make the trip

up the trail with that guy in the lead wagon. They didn't appear to like him too much, but you know how it goes. They said he pays."

"Who was he, did they say?"

"No," came the answer. "Just said he was from Chihuahua."

Juan Lopez and his caravan of five wagons arrived at the outskirts of Paso del Norte just hours after they met up with Clay. Juan looked ahead and could see scattered adobe buildings along the river. Much farther away, in the distance, he could make out what appeared to be the bell tower of a church. That would be Our Lady of Guadalupe mission, he reasoned, but even that sight of civilization held no comfort for him as the entire place looked desolate. He was used to the thriving city of Chihuahua with its fine buildings. Though their walls were made essentially of adobe, their cornerstones and doorways were made of hewn stone. This town, what he could see of it, was nothing but mud huts. Surely, Juan consoled himself, it would get better as he drew closer to the mission.

But as the group moved on, the setting did not change. What appeared to most to be a series of plantationlike homes surrounded by sprawling green fields, to Juan was little more than rural peasant farmland in which he had no interest. What of the thriving haciendas he had envisioned, with coffers of riches stored away behind their thick walls? Was that not what he had traveled all this way to find?

Juan's gloomy thoughts were interrupted by a harsh voice. "We want our money, amigo," a dark man with a thick mustache said.

Juan shifted uncomfortably, thinking that the long trip had been nothing like he planned, and to top it off, the small village of Paso del Norte was a huge disappointment. He swallowed down his concerns, his haughty facade swiftly slipping when faced with the band of rugged men. "You will get the rest of your money just as I said, but first I must go to my hacienda."

The group of men laughed and looked around. "What kind of hacienda could be around here? All we can see is small farms, amigo." Though the men were of the trade, they had only traveled from Chihuahua and south to Veracruz, never before having ventured north.

"You better not try to cheat us, señor," the first man said, the laughter quickly replaced with a sneer as he took a menacing step closer.

Juan held up his hand as if to protect himself from the unfriendly men. "Never, never. I would not think to cheat you. I gave you half of your money before we left. You will get the other half when we reach Paso del Norte," he said, visibly shaken.

A short, stocky man with an unshaven face moved closer, holding out a callused hand. "We are here, amigo. Now where is our money?"

Juan took a step back. "But I said it would probably be a couple days after we got here before I could get the money." He looked wildly from one man to the other. "Tell them, Rodrigo."

Rodrigo was a big man who appeared to be in command of the small band of hired men. He looked from his men to Juan, as if debating what answer would best serve his purpose. Finally, after an interminable silence, he spoke, his voice heavy and threatening, slow as though he wanted everyone to understand. "*Sí*, he did tell me this, and I did agree."

When the men began to grumble, he continued. "I say it is worth it, hombres. Our young merchant here pays well." He turned to his men, then back to Juan. "The good money is worth a few days' wait, and if he does not think to pay"—he moved closer until his hot, fetid breath singed Juan's face—"then we will have to convince him of the need. *Sí*, amigos?"

The men laughed in response. "*Sí*, Rodrigo, we will show him."

"And we will make him wish he had never laid eyes on any of us."

"Go to your hacienda, Señor Lopez, and get us our money. We will wait in town for you, and if you do not come soon, we will be forced to come and find you." Rodrigo looked around before he continued. "I do not think it would be hard to find you. Come, men, we will go see what Paso del Norte offers in the way of pleasure."

They left Juan standing in the middle of the road, his dust-covered sombrero clutched tightly in one hand. His mind churned frantically, wondering how he could have been so stupid as to think it would be so easy. But then he thought of Diego Cervantes, and the bloodlust filled his mind, banishing all rational thought. He would pay those men. He sneered, his fright forgotten. He laughed into the air, a high, shrill cackle that sent a flock of birds flying from an overhead tree. Diego Cervantes was going to pay off this debt. Juan would take everything, leaving Diego to wallow in poverty, stricken as he deserved to be. The thought made his heart pound harder, the intense pleasure of a long-awaited goal coming to fruition, the realization of a dream.

He beat his hat against his leg, sending puffs of dust whirling in the air, then wiped the brim with his hand, leaving streaks where his sweat-covered fingers touched, trying unsuccessfully to rid the hat of the many layers of dust that had accumulated. He wiped at his pants and shirt before he spotted an *acequia* that brought water from the Río Bravo del Norte to irrigate the crops. With the handkerchief that was tied around his neck he tried to wash his face and arms but only managed to make the mess worse. Finally he reluctantly stuck his entire head in the water, then pulled it out and shook vigorously, sending a spray of water flying in all directions.

Juan hated being dirty, the feel of grit and grime reminding him all too clearly of another time, another place. Wanting nothing more at that second than a refreshing bath and a clean set of clothes, he looked around for someplace that could accommodate him. The few clothes he had brought were now all dirty, rolled up together in a pile at his feet. Standing by the *acequia*, Juan Lopez debated. He had a few silver coins hidden. How important was it that he present himself as clean and respectable? Did it outweigh the need for the silver? Yes, he finally decided, he would find someplace where he could get his clothes washed and take a bath. He could not make his plan work if he pulled into town and asked questions while looking like an outlaw.

With determination, he walked toward the few buildings he saw in the distance.

At the first adobe house he came to, a woman sat placidly in the front grinding corn into masa while several children played in the yard, chasing chickens and dogs in a whirlwind of dust and feathers. When Juan approached, all activity stopped, the dust slowly settling, feathers seesawing back and forth to the ground. Rarely did these people see others, unless it was a long line of wooden wagons filled with men and goods as it made its way up or down the trail, but then it was only in the distance, the men never making their way to their home. The woman called something Juan could not make out, bringing a man, apparently the father, to the doorway of the small house.

"What do you want?" the man inquired without preamble.

"I would like to eat a meal, take a bath, and have my clothes washed."

The man looked warily at Juan.

"I will pay . . . silver," Juan added, holding up one silver coin.

As he eyed the money, the man's attitude changed abruptly. Life in the river valley rarely involved money, running on a barter system where goods one made or raised were traded for goods one needed. Only the rich had money, and even the landowners' wealth was measured in

possessions rather than actual cash. "*Sí*, Señor, come in."
The man stepped aside to let Juan in. "*Mi casa es su casa.*"

The man pulled out an old copper tub that had seen better days, calling to the children to bring buckets of water from the river. He set a bar of harsh homemade soap next to a rough cloth that Juan assumed he was to dry himself with.

"This is what I get for my silver?" Juan asked in anger. "I could wash myself in the river for free."

The man became flustered, never having thought to wash with anything but river water. But when Juan began picking up his dirty clothes, the man quickly made other arrangements. "No, no, no, Señor. I did not think. Pepe, Jesus," he called to his boys, "bring water from the well, *rápido.*"

Later, after an uncomfortable and cold bath, dressed in a pair of pants and shirt provided by his host, Juan sat down to a simple hot meal. He ate rapidly, having passed up much of the atrocious fare he had been expected to eat on the trail. Beans and tortillas had never tasted so good.

Once his bowl was empty and his stomach full, Juan looked around the small house and noticed only sparse furniture and the familiar religious figures that were found in every home Juan had ever been in. The man, assuming Juan was looking around for his clothes, said, "My wife has gone to the river to wash your clothes."

Juan's look turned to one of distaste as he imagined his clothes, new when he set out for Paso del Norte, being ruined as they were washed in the murky water of the river.

Sensing Juan's concern, the man said, "Do not worry, señor, clothes have been cleaned in the river for hundreds of years, the shirt and pants you have on now were cleaned there. Your clothes will be fine."

With that the man sat down near the table on an adobe bench that was an extension of the wall. He eyed Juan warily and said a silent prayer that this stranger would soon be out of their lives. The man began to regret his desire for the money, sensing they would have been better off without it. "Where you from, señor?" His grammar was poor, Juan thought with disgust. He himself had spent late nights after work teaching himself to read and write, how to speak Spanish like the well educated.

Looking at the man Juan debated before he answered. He did not see how it could hurt to tell the man where he was from. Possibly he could get the information he needed out of the man. Juan felt that the fewer people he spoke with the better off he would be.

"Chihuahua," Juan answered.

"Chihuahua?" The man asked excitedly, forgetting his earlier reservations when he found someone to talk to about the one place he had been in his life. "I been there, too," he said enthusiastically.

When the man smiled his enthusiasm, he revealed several missing teeth. Juan was revolted, anything that bespoke poverty made his skin crawl. Poverty was something he had no tolerance for. But he swallowed his revulsion, hoping for information.

"How long have you lived in Paso del Norte?" Juan asked with feigned interest.

"Many years, I think."

How could any man just *think* many years? Juan wanted to say but managed to hold his tongue. "So you must know Diego Cervantes?"

"*Sí*, I did. He was good man." The excitement left the man's face, replaced by a solemn look.

The man's words confused Juan, making his heart beat faster, causing sweat to break out on his brow. With a feeling of dread Juan asked, "Why do you say 'was'?"

The man looked warily at the stranger he had brought into his home before answering. "Don Diego Cervantes is dead, señor."

Juan sat in disbelief. Surely he would have heard? But he hadn't, and the shock was almost more than he could bear.

The man watched. Death was a regular part of life in this land. Confronting it frequently taught a man to grieve inwardly, not showing his pain. So he did not understand

the emotions that played across Juan's face or the strange
way he acted. But he thought perhaps it was grief, overwhelming grief that the young man was unprepared for, so
he took a step forward to comfort his guest.

Unleashed fury swept through Juan's body. Coming to
his feet, he knocked against the table, spilling the beans and
juice that had been left in the bowl. Juan looked down and
saw the bean juice dripping onto his foot, sending him into
an insane rage. With one hand he grabbed the edge of the
table, pulling it up and throwing it over, sending earthen-
ware bowls and cups flying to shatter against the brown
walls. "How can he be dead?" he screamed, as if blaming
the man who had told him.

The man stood rooted to the floor, paralyzed by the
maniacal behavior of the stranger. His wife and children
came to the door, frightened by the noise, not knowing what
was happening.

Seeing his family propelled him from his spot. "Get out
before he hurts you," he cried, wanting to protect his loved
ones.

Juan stood against the wall, his forehead pressed against
the cool adobe. How was it possible that Diego could have
won? How was it possible that he was being deprived of the
one thing he had lived his entire life for—revenge against
the man who had made his life a living hell? For that small
space of time, as he stood motionless against the wall, Juan
felt bereft of his lifeblood, bereft of the substance of his life,
the very thing that fed his every step, his every thought, his
every waking moment. Suddenly it was gone.

Juan straightened, out of breath, panting. How could this
have happened? It wasn't fair. But he still had the means to
take over Diego's hacienda, he realized as his mind began to
clear. Slowly, reluctantly, he began to steady. He could still
have what had been Diego's. Juan took a deep breath. It
would not be the same. But it was something. Better than
nothing. Juan moved away from the wall, his eyes focusing

on the man. Juan's clothes lay in a pile on the earthen bench.

"Change your clothes and then go, señor," the man said gruffly. "You are lucky I do not send for the authorities." The man turned to leave the room, then hesitated. "You leave the silver or I *will* go to the authorities."

Yes, the money, Juan thought. He would leave the money. Juan knew he had not been wise to make such a scene. He could not afford to draw attention to himself, not when he was soon to become a prosperous landowner in the area. The thought brought a sly grin to his round features. This new plan wasn't ideal, but it was something.

Juan stripped off the borrowed pants and shirt, leaving his short, thick body bare as he crossed the room to retrieve his own clothes. He did not give a thought to the young children and the woman who stood outside the door. Pulling on his still damp clothes, he grimaced at the uncomfortable feeling. His white shirt fit into tightly fitting black pants. He tied his bandanna around his neck and put on his wide-brimmed sombrero. Black boots finished off his ensemble. Dark skin, dark eyes, and mostly dark clothes blended together making him look sinister.

He tossed a piece of silver on the table as he strode from the room only to stop before the older girl child, the father at her side. Juan spoke to the man, though one long finger stroked the girl's chin, his brown eyes boring into hers. "You speak to no one of me, old man, do you understand?"

The man mumbled as he nodded his head in assent.

"Good, I am glad you understand. I am sure you would hate to see anything happen to any member of your family." His threat was clear. Abruptly he turned from the girl, looking at her father, "Do not forget, *comprende*?"

"*Sí*" was all the man said.

Juan Lopez turned from the family and left the quiet yard. Even the dogs and chickens quieted down as the dark stranger strode from their midst. He caught sight of the mission in the distance and began to walk slowly, apparently in no hurry as he made his way toward the tall structure.

Juan was not too far from the house when he got a ride into town. They let him off at the mercantile where he stood outside dusting off his clothes. Juan surveyed his surroundings and grimaced in distaste. Disappointment welled up again. Not only was Diego Cervantes dead, but his only revenge now lay in living in this desolate place. Maybe he would sell. But who would buy out here? Questions raced through his mind.

When he walked into the mercantile, the people inside stopped and stared at him suspiciously. Juan knew that if he was going to get any information out of them he would have to turn on the charm.

"*Buenos días,*" he said as he took off his sombrero.

"*Buenos días,*" Harold Selig replied cautiously. "What can I do for you?"

Juan's smile transformed his sinister face. "I am in need of a few supplies, and directions to the home of Diego Cervantes."

The people in the store looked from Juan to one another, then back to Juan. "What do you want with Diego Cervantes?"

"I am a friend from Chihuahua, and I have come to pay my respects to his family, God rest his soul," he added as he made the sign of the cross over his breast. "He spoke of El Paso often and said anyone could give me directions to his home if ever I came this way," Juan said innocently, not wanting to give away the hatred he felt seething in his body at the mere mention of Diego Cervantes's name. He turned his head away from the many faces who looked at him and added, "I only regret I could not have made it sooner."

"Señor?" Harold asked in concern, having misread Juan's look for one of grief. "You all right?"

Juan looked at the man. "*Sí,* I am all right. It has just been a long trip."

"Why don't I get someone to take you over to the hacienda? You can pay your respects to Lorena."

"Lorena?" Juan asked, surprise written clearly on his face.

Harold looked at Juan suspiciously. "Lorena is Diego's daughter. Surely he told you about her."

His surprise was overcome by a lifetime of self-preservation. Sensing that he had been about to make a major mistake, Juan pulled himself together. "Oh, yes, how could I forget? It has been so long since I saw Diego."

"Well, I guess. Harry," the man called to another. "Can you take this fellow over to Cielo el Dorado?"

"Sure, come on," he said to Juan.

"Much thanks," Juan said to no one in particular.

They rode over in a small cart, the man talking constantly, extracting only grudging responses from Juan. Juan was angry that he was not going to get the full measure of revenge that had kept him going all his life. Now he would have to settle for uprooting some insignificant female. He gave no thought to this girl and her innocence in his scheme against Diego; his only thoughts were of revenge.

The river was low and easy to cross, and it was not long before Juan Lopez caught sight of the *torreón* of Cielo el Dorado. He hated it on sight, as he hated everything about this backwater outpost called Paso del Norte. It was a shame that Diego had not lived in Chihuahua. Selling seemed more reasonable by the minute. But whatever he did, first he would extract his revenge in whatever form he could manage.

19

❦

RIDING THROUGH SAND AND NOTHINGNESS FOR THIRTY miles brought Clay and his men to Los Médanos, a vast expanse of sand hills with an occasional scrub bush to dot its mounded terrain. The deep sand made it difficult to travel, and had their small band of men been a true caravan of wagons filled with goods to trade, Clay and his group would have needed a team of mules to carry the goods across. But with only Clay and his twelve men on surefooted horses and no wagons or goods, they were able to traverse the sand in record time. The road through Los Médanos wound its way between the sand hills, winding around to the lowest points to make the traveling as easy as possible.

Their first sight of water came when they reached the *presidio* of Carrizal, where they would change horses. Carrizal was a small town with a fort to provide protection from the marauding Apaches who had plagued the area in years past. The occasional menacing Indian still plagued the ranchos at will, brazenly within sight of the fort at Carrizal. While there were treaties and an uneasy peace, it was as if the people of the land knew the peace could not last, leaving them wary all the time.

Twelve miles south of Carrizal was a warm spring that would have provided a welcome respite from the barren

desert with a refreshing bath and sparkling water, but there
was no time for comfort on this rushed journey and no man
voiced his desire to linger. At a brisk pace, they rode up to
the water and stopped only long enough to rest their horses.
Clay thought of how he would like Lorena to see this place,
a haven in the starkness that surrounded it. But they
continued. There was no time to dally with one's thoughts.
It was not a land in which to daydream, but one in which to
be on constant lookout. They watched not only for danger
from other men, but also for the dangers of a perilous trail
that could bring a horse down with one misplaced step.

At night they slept under the stars, their guns at their
sides, pitching a tent only when there was a threat of rain.
While Clay had never totally adopted the ways of the
Mexican traders, he had learned a great deal from them.
The dry and salubrious air made perfect weather for
camping, making it rare that much more than a blanket to
sleep on was needed. At night, when the dry air was
sometimes cool, the Mexican trader used nothing more than
his serape, which by day served as his cloak. Even in the
coldest winter weather, he would not add more than one
simple blanket. This made for light traveling, and that was
exactly what Clay and his men were doing.

It was at night that it was the hardest for Clay on this
unusual journey, his thoughts filling with images of Lorena.
He envisioned her as she laughed and teased, remembering
times when she turned on him in wrath, her red hair flying,
green eyes flashing in anger. He was left rigid with desire
when his mind was plagued with visions of her as she lay
beneath him, quivering at his touch, opening to him as he
stroked her body to life. He missed her and wanted to be
done with the trip so he could get back to her, to see her
smiling face and hear her moans of passion. But most of all
her saw her as wife and mother, friend and lover. He wanted
her physically, yes, but like it or not, there was something
more, something that loomed great in his mind, more
pronounced each time it tried to surface, though not yet

there. He wanted to spend his life with her, and the thought of leaving her to go back to Missouri twisted him in a way he did not understand.

His thoughts were interrupted when Ben came to sit next to him. Neither said anything, both merely looking out into the night.

"You love her, don't you?" Ben asked without looking at his sibling.

Clay was startled by the question, shifting uncomfortably at the words. "Love, brother?"

Ben chuckled quietly. "Yes, love . . . brother. I've always heard it was the man who was the last to know."

"I believe you're confusing love with cuckold."

Ben shook his head. "That, too, I suppose, but fortunately, being cuckolded is not one of your concerns."

"Neither is love."

"You're a hard man, Clay Wakefield," Ben said, all traces of laughter gone from his voice. "You had responsibilities too young."

"We do what we have to, nothing more."

"You didn't have to pay for me to go to school, support me all those years, not to mention starting me in my own business."

"Not to mention," Clay said as if trying to stop the conversation.

"No, I think I have to mention it, if not for you, then for me. I owe you and though I can't pay you back monetarily at this point, I can try to make you see some sense."

Clay moved uncomfortably, as if to get up.

"Clay, listen. You have got to go on with your life. You've made your fortune already. When are you going to learn to enjoy it? When are you going to let someone share it with you? And I don't mean people like me. I'm talking about someone to share your life with, to start a family." Ben paused before continuing. "Not everyone is like our ma and pa. I may have been young, but I could see what they were. They were weak. You aren't, Clay. Haven't you proved that to yourself yet?"

Ben wanted to say something about Lorena, about the love he knew his brother felt for the girl, but couldn't. It was one thing to talk about something they both shared, like their parents, but Lorena was solely Clay's, his private affair, and brother or not, Ben could not bring himself to intrude that far.

They sat quietly, Ben hoping Clay would respond, but after a time and still nothing from Clay, Ben pushed himself off the ground. "You know, believe it or not, it's okay to love. Strong men do it all the time." He dusted his pants with a few sharp swats. "It's weak men who can't." Ben walked away, making his way toward the other men, who had already lain down for the night, leaving Clay alone in the darkness.

They traveled through Aqua Nueva, Hormigas, and Pabloblanco, before they made their final descent into Chihuahua. Nine days after leaving Paso del Norte, thirteen tired, dust-covered men rode into the city, knowing their journey had only begun.

Clay sent his men to clean up and prepare to make the trip back as soon as he had taken care of business in the city. Ben led Clay to the store whose owner held Diego's notes. The store was in a part of town that had prospered due to the trade, its streets lined with assorted shops and businesses as well as saloons and houses of ill repute. Unlike the older, nicer parts of town that were built of adobe and rough-hewn stone with ornately carved columns and entryways, the section Clay and Ben arrived in looked as if it had been quickly thrown together to accommodate a need. The buildings were shoddily put together with rough wood and adobe, much in need of repair. The streets were much the way nature made them, and they looked as though they had never been cleaned.

"Why would Diego have come to this part of town?" Clay asked, more to himself than to anyone else.

Ben shrugged his shoulders. "I wondered that myself, but I thought perhaps this was a normal part of the trade."

"I knew that quite a few men came over here. I just never realized Diego was one of them."

They made their way through the streets, careful of ruts and debris, until they arrived in front of a small but well kept store.

"This is it," Ben said.

"It looks closed," Clay said with concern.

Dismounting and tying their horses to a rickety post, the brothers mounted the few steps that led to the storefront and tried the door. It was locked. Impatiently, Clay pounded on the door, but no one came, only a few curious passersby seeming to notice.

"Maybe he's late today," Ben offered, trying to explain away the unease and impatience that he sensed growing in Clay. Ben was afraid his brother would not contain his feelings for long.

"I don't have time to wait around for this Señor Medina to show up. We'll have to go find him."

"How? We don't even know his first name."

Clay looked impatiently at his younger brother before he replied. "Then we must go from door to door until we find the man."

"It would take us months to do that," Ben said in disbelief.

"It won't come to that. We'll start asking around here, and I'm sure we will find Señor Medina in no time."

They walked into the shop next door, its occupants looking suspiciously at the two Americans. Though it was no longer uncommon to see Americans walking through the streets of Chihuahua, it was strange for people to be coming around Señor Medina's store.

"What can I do for you?" asked a short Mexican man in halting English.

"We are looking for Señor Medina who owns the store next door." Clay's deep voice filled the small confines of the room, demanding everyone's attention.

The man moved restlessly, looking from Clay and Ben to the other occupants of the room. The others quickly looked away. "What do want with him?" he asked, clearly nervous.

Clay eyed the man. He knew something was wrong, but he didn't know what. The tingling of apprehension that pricked at his body was not for himself, but for Lorena. He sensed that something was terribly wrong and it had to do with the notes. Clay wanted more than ever to be back at Cielo el Dorado to assure himself that Lorena would come to no harm.

"What do you want?" the man asked again, his unease making it impossible for him to speak English.

Clay spoke calmly and deliberately, trying to calm the man. "We have business with Señor Medina, nothing more. If you could tell us how we can find him, we will be out of your way."

The man wavered, not knowing if he should trust him. "I do not know where you can find him, but possibly the man across the street in the stable could help." The man suddenly felt confident that he had done the best he could. He had not told the Americans where to find Medina, but he had been helpful to them. He had not displeased anyone.

"*Gracias,*" Clay said, knowing that to ask more questions would do no good.

Clay and Ben left the small shop and walked out into the sunshine, which was growing hotter by the hour.

"I think he knew where Medina was but didn't want to tell us," Ben said.

"I think you're right. This is looking worse by the minute."

"What do you suppose has happened?"

"I don't know, but I don't like it one bit." Deep lines of concern were carved in Clay's face.

"Let's go over to the stable."

They walked across the dirt street, dodging piles of manure and ruts that could easily have broken a man's leg.

At first the stable seemed to be empty with the exception of horses, but then from the back they could make out the sound of someone moving around. They followed the sound.

"*Buenos días*," Clay called when they found a young boy putting a saddle on a stand. Clay figured he was about thirteen.

The boy turned around. He seemed surprised but not scared. "*Hola*. Señor Vasquez is not here. He will be back later. But I can help you," he offered proudly, eager to please.

"What's your name?" Clay asked with a rare smile.

"Felipe."

"Felipe, we are looking for Senõr Medina who owns the store across the street."

Felipe's eyes lit up with excitement.

"Do you know where he is?" Clay asked.

"He is at home, señor," he said proudly, excited that he knew something these men did not know. "Everyone thought he was dead, but he was not. Just lots of blood. You should have seen it." Felipe spoke dramatically. "The Federales came, and when they were going to take him away, he coughed. I saw it! I thought the devil had taken over the dead body. The dead Señor Medina coughed. But I am too smart for that," the boy said knowingly. "I figured out he was not dead. I told them. I said, 'He is not dead!' So they took him to his home so Señora Medina could take care of him. That is why he is not at the store."

"What caused the blood, Felipe?" Clay asked, impatient with the young boy as he went on and on with his story.

"I do not know, señor, but there was a lot of blood, it got all over everything. If you look in the window, you can see some of it."

"Felipe, where does Señor Medina live?" Clay pressed
trying to remain calm, eager to find the man.

After long-drawn-out directions, with a few more detai
of the blood and gore, Clay gave the boy a coin for h
efforts and then left, Ben following close at his heels.

Clay considered going to the officials but then thoug
better of it, he wanted to see Medina first. They followe
the boy's directions and, after only a few wrong turns
arrived at a nice but modest home.

Clay knocked at the door. He could hear some murmu
ing from within, but no one answered. He knocked agai
this time louder. Still no one answered. "Damn!" h
exclaimed in frustration. "What is going on around here?

Ben looked at his brother. "Maybe we should go to th
officials. Something has obviously happened."

"The officials will be no help. They tolerate American
only because they have to, because of the goods they brin
in. We need to talk to Medina."

Clay knocked again. This time the door cracked open
bit to reveal a slice of craggy brown skin and one dar
brown eye.

"Señora Medina?" Clay questioned.

The door opened a bit farther, revealing more of th
wrinkled skin and the other eye.

"I am Clay Wakefield. I was told that Señor Medina ha
been hurt."

The woman started to shut the door, but Clay was too fas
for her. He caught the door with his hand. "Señora, I am no
here to hurt anyone. I only want to help."

The woman began to turn as if to run.

"Señora, I am here to pay off Diego Cervantes's debt.

She hesitated for a second, then started to run for the bac
door, but a voice from somewhere in the house stopped her

Clay opened the door and stepped inside.

"I am Hector Medina." He stood in the doorway o
another room, his head swathed in bandages, surveying
Clay. "I hoped you would come."

20

🌢

JUAN LOPEZ ARRIVED AT CIELO EL DORADO LATE IN
the afternoon the same day Clay had left. The sun was huge
in the western sky, and Lorena was crouched in the herb
garden pulling weeds and pruning plants when she heard the
commotion caused by someone approaching. Pulling herself up from the soil, she hurriedly pushed her hair back,
leaving streaks of dirt across her face, but she did not notice
as her heart leaped with excitement, thinking that surely it
was Clay who was approaching. Even though it was only a
few hours after he had left, she imagined that he had gotten
outside of Paso del Norte, then turned around and returned
to her, unable to bear being away from her. He did love her,
she thought joyfully, swiftly wiping her hands on her skirt.
When she looked down, she saw the streaks of dirt left on
her clothes. "Oh," she exclaimed in surprise. Before the
gates were opened, Lorena ran to her room and, in record
time, changed her clothes, washed her face, and ran a brush
through her long hair. Then, tossing the brush on her bed,
she ran from her room, pausing briefly to check her
appearance in the mirror before making her way to the front
gate to welcome back the man she loved.

Juan surveyed his surroundings and was not displeased
with what he saw. Obviously the fields were plentiful as

were the servants. The hacienda was well cared for, and from the looks of things, he was sure he could get a good price for this place called Cielo el Dorado. He smiled as he thought of changing the name to El Rancho Lopez, or maybe El Tierra de Lopez, the Land of Lopez. He chuckled with satisfaction as he imagined the change, and would have rubbed his hands together and jumped for the sheer pleasure of it had he not been surrounded by strangers. He could already imagine the new sign above the entrance. He would tear the present one down with his own hands and replace it, and then all around everyone would know that he was the master of the land. And yes, then he would sell, pack up the things he wanted, take his money, and go back to Chihuahua, or maybe even to Mexico City. He would live the life he was supposed to live, the life he had dreamed about, the life he believed he deserved.

His musings were brought up short when he saw a girl, bright hair flying about her face as she came running toward him as if she felt happy to see him. Was this Lorena, Diego's daughter? But then she stopped, disappointment written clearly across her face. Resentment seethed within him. Who had she expected? he wondered. He obviously wasn't good enough, he reasoned groundlessly, as she had no reason to know him, much less expect him. It did not matter that his thoughts were irrational, they almost always were.

Lorena's excitement turned to surprise when she arrived at the entrance to find two men sitting in a rickety cart pulled by one tired old mule. And then the surprise turned to bitter disillusionment. Had she truly been so naive as to believe Clay would appear when the gate opened? Disappointment rocked her when she realized he had not come back to her. Her eyes closed in pain when she realized what a fool she had been to believe he loved her. Lorena wanted to turn back to her room and shut the door on her pain, but pride surged in as she tried to fill the hole that gaped within. She was mistress of her home, and she would not embarrass

ae memory of Cervantes ancestors by turning her back on
er duties.

With that, Lorena turned her attention to the new arrivals.
On closer inspection she recognized the driver as a man she
ad seen in Paso del Norte. But the other man made her
ead swim, her heart beat as if in recognition as she looked
t him in confusion. Stepping closer, Lorena stared at the
aan, certain if she tried hard enough she would come up
vith an answer as to who he was. She felt certain she knew
im, but when she looked closer she realized that she had
ever seen him before in her life. She felt momentarily
isoriented until she told herself she was being silly; she had
een out in the hot sun too long.

Pedro and Dalia came up behind Lorena, and it was a few
econds before anyone spoke. Pedro finally stepped for-
vard, greeting the man from Paso del Norte before turning
o the stranger. Dalia and Lorena held back and watched,
houghts of welcome forgotten.

Dalia disliked the stranger on sight and was taken aback
t the clear, calculating look that held his features. She was
ot sure, but he looked to her as if he was assessing the
vorth of his surroundings.

The men spoke, but Dalia and Lorena could not hear
vhat was being said. After a few minutes of conversation,
he stranger got out of the cart and the man from Paso del
Norte waved his farewell.

Pedro turned to the women. "This is Juan Lopez." His
one was noncommittal. "He tells us that he was a good
riend of Diego's."

Pedro's ambivalence was lost on Lorena, who was
xcited at meeting a friend of her father's. It never occurred
o her that this man's word might not be good.

"I am so happy to meet you, Senõr Lopez," Lorena said
nthusiastically.

Juan looked at the girl, feeling somewhat mollified by her
aow enthusiastic manner. And suddenly he realized his
good fortune. Where fate had intervened tragically in one

area, by Diego being dead, it had provided for him i
another in the form of a beautiful girl who was Diego
offspring—his heiress. A smile lit Juan's face, banishing th
cold, calculating expression to some hidden recess.

The transformation took Dalia by surprise. Had she ne
seen the other look with her own eyes, she would hav
sworn that the man who stood before her now was a perfe
gentleman. Her dislike intensified.

"I was so sorry to hear of your father's death. It greatl
saddened me." Juan looked truly disheartened, and he wa
for just one second as he remembered again that he woul
never have the true revenge that he wanted, that h
deserved.

But Lorena saw his expression only as pain, which sh
assumed was caused by the loss of a dear friend. "It was
great shock to all of us, and we appreciate your sympathy.

"When Diego left Chihuahua I never would have know
he was so sick," Juan said, thinking that if he had he woul
have killed him on the spot. "I told him at the time that
would be coming to El Paso to visit him soon. I only regr
I am not able to see him again."

Before Pedro or Dalia had a chance to say anythin
Lorena said, "Even though my father is not here, you mu
stay and visit with us just as if he were here."

"I could not do that, Señorita. I could not be such a
imposition," Juan lied, having no intention of stayin
anywhere else.

Dalia looked at Pedro as if to say, I just *bet* he cann
stay. Pedro, sensing his wife's unspoken words, grimace
Something was not quite right about this man, and he di
not like the thought of him being here with Lorena. Sh
apparently did not see through his facade. And Pedro als
knew that, after Clay's sudden departure, Lorena wa
feeling alone, making her vulnerable to deceit and tricker

"You will be no imposition at all," Lorena said sincerel
"Is that not right, Dalia?" Lorena turned to Dalia, the
Pedro.

"If the man does not feel comfortable staying, Lorena," edro said in hopes of getting the man to leave, "then we ould not play on his conscience and force him to stay."

Instantly Lorena felt riddled with guilt. "You are so right. am sorry, Señor Lopez, if you do not wish to stay, I ertainly understand."

Juan shifted uncomfortably, irritated at the old man for nterfering. "Maybe just for a small time I will stay. I would njoy meeting Diego Cervantes's family." Juan inwardly ighed with relief, having come up with a quick answer.

"This is wonderful!" Lorena clapped her hands together. I will have the guest room made up for you now. Pedro, ould you show Señor Lopez to the bathhouse so he can lean up after his long trip? By then I should have his room eady."

Lorena failed to notice the anger that flared when she said uan needed to clean up. The bitch, Juan seethed. She had mplied that he was not clean enough for her! After he topped and bathed at the man's house, paying good silver or it as well. She would learn, he promised himself. She vould learn.

With no choice but to do as Lorena asked, Pedro led Juan o the bathhouse.

"How long did you know Diego?" Pedro asked.

Juan sensed that he was being questioned and needed to e careful of his answers—very careful. "For about four ears," he lied, four years sounding like an appropriate mount of time.

"Then you must know Señor Wakefield?" Pedro probed.

"I have heard of him, but I have never met him," Juan eplied truthfully.

Pedro was sure that Juan must have passed Clay on the oad. "Did you not see him on the road to Chihuahua? He eft just this morning."

Juan looked sharply at Pedro, forgetting his need to be areful. "A group of men with no wagons?" he questioned.

Pedro hesitated. "*Sí*, that was Señor Wakefield. Did you meet him?"

Juan's mind raced. What had Wakefield been doing in Paso del Norte? It was true he had never met the man, but he had heard more than enough about him. Clay Wakefield was not the kind of man to tangle with. But then, Juan reasoned, what could Wakefield possibly do to him?

Seeing Juan's mind race, Pedro did not wait for an answer but plunged ahead, hoping to find out who this man really was. "Clay is in charge of the hacienda now. Diego left it to him."

Juan sucked in air as if he had been punched in the stomach. His mind whirled. How could Diego have left the hacienda to Clay Wakefield, of all people? This could not be happening. But then Juan's swirling thoughts calmed and he took a deep breath, closing his eyes, his nostrils flaring as he pulled the air into his lungs. Cielo el Dorado was his. He would have the hacienda, that was all there was to it. Slowly he expelled the air, gradually opening his eyes, but what he saw did not please him. He saw Pedro looking at him and knew he had made a major mistake. If his plan were to work he could not raise suspicions. His only hope was to lessen the damage. "If I had known it was Señor Wakefield I met," he improvised, "I would have spent some time with the man. I regret not having seized the opportunity to talk to him as I have heard so many things about him."

Pedro eyed Juan suspiciously, wanting more than anything to kick the man out and send him back to Paso del Norte. He knew that Juan had not told Clay his destination. Had he done so, Pedro was sure Clay would have turned around, not allowing such a man to get anywhere near Cielo el Dorado and Lorena.

"In fact," Juan added, knowing that he needed to find out if and when Clay Wakefield was coming back, "I hope Wakefield gets back soon so I will have a chance to meet him." Juan looked closely at Pedro. "When is he getting back?"

"Soon, he is only making a quick trip to Chihuahua. That is why he took no wagons to slow him down," Pedro answered, praying that he was right, hoping that Clay had been telling the truth when he said he was making only a quick trip.

Juan calculated the number of days it had taken him to reach Paso del Norte and was reassured that he had plenty of time, not realizing that the lack of wagons would shorten the trip. "Now, if you could show me where I can clean up."

Pedro bristled at the tone of voice Juan used. If he was not mistaken, the man was acting as if he owned the place. His dislike of the stranger increased, but not knowing what he could possibly do he said, "Everything you should need is in here. When you finish, come back to the courtyard and I will show you to your room." Pedro turned away, preoccupied with concern, leaving Juan at the bathhouse.

Juan walked into the small room that was used for bathing and closed the door behind him. He smiled with relief. The old fool. Yes, he was suspicious, but what could he do? He was only a servant, after all. Sure that Wakefield would not be back for two or three months, Juan was convinced he had no need to worry. He had plenty of time.

Dismissing Clay and Pedro from his mind, Juan looked around. He was amazed to find such a modern convenience as a bathhouse in such a backwater hellhole. Juan began to like his surroundings more and more. Although it was out in the middle of nowhere, Cielo el Dorado offered many of the comforts of Chihuahua—comforts, he reminded himself, that he had not been afforded in his life. He could get used to it all. Maybe he wouldn't sell right away, though he would have to do something before Clay Wakefield got back. But what?

Juan's thoughts drifted to Lorena. He remembered her red hair and green eyes. He stripped away the bandanna that was once again covered with dust and grime from the road.

Her skin was tanned, but even so, she was not nearly as
dark as he. And her body, the lush curves that strained
beneath her clothes . . . Juan tossed the bright-colored
bandanna aside. She was Diego's daughter. A small laugh
surged up in his chest, a low rumbling sound that contained
little mirth, and he could feel the warmth grow within his
loins. Yes, he just might have to change his plans.

His small bundle of clothes sat on a wooden bench, the
bandanna draped across the top. Every garment he owned
was tattered and torn, in need of a good washing and
mending, if not fit to be thrown out altogether. Looking at
the pile, Juan wondered if he would be able to get some new
clothes. The ones he had bought for his journey to Paso del
Norte had definitely not stood up well during the harsh
journey along the trail. It was easier to blame the clothes
than to admit he had made impractical choices when buying
the garments. Juan had spent a lifetime in Chihuahua, never
going beyond its limited confines. He had only imagined
what the trail was like and had never paid much attention to
the stories told by the men who traveled it. To Juan, they
were a bunch of loud, dirty men who were little better than
animals. It never occurred to him that they could be
anything else. Why else would they spend their nights
living out in the open instead of in a home with all the
comforts it would offer? Now he grudgingly admitted he
would have been better off with some of the rugged clothes
those men wore. But for now his clothes would have to do.

A copper tub stood in the corner, and Juan would have
loved to pull it out, fill it up, and soak in it for hours, but
there was no time and he knew that Lorena just expected
him to wash his face and hands. Later he would soak. Yes,
later.

Juan dipped his hands in a basin of cool water and
splashed it on his face and neck. He imagined the day when
he would walk about Cielo el Dorado as lord and master.
The thought brought a smile to his face. He would wear nice
clothes and eat good meals. Maids would wait on him, and

the old woman would mend his clothes. Juan sneered when he thought of the old man. He was a little too suspicious, and Juan made a special note to tread carefully around the man. He would bide his time until he could take his revenge. Then he would make a Cervantes suffer, just as he had suffered all these many years.

Juan pulled a towel from a neat stack on a corner rack and dabbed at his face, being careful of his skin. He grimaced at the thought of putting on his tattered clothes, but with a resigned sigh he left the room, promising himself new garments at the first opportunity.

In the distance he heard voices. One he was certain was Lorena's. Lorena, he smiled, would prove to be sweet revenge. Juan threw his head back and laughed to the sky. Revenge, despite the death of Diego, was turning out to be sweeter than he had hoped.

Dalia returned from the guest room to find Pedro in the kitchen. No one else was there. Pedro poured hot coffee into a cup, and when he saw Dalia enter he poured another for his wife.

"You do not like that man," Dalia stated.

Pedro looked at his wife, ever amazed that she knew him so well. Had he been so obvious? He hoped not, as he sensed that it would not be good if this Juan Lopez realized that he was not welcome.

"No, I do not" was Pedro's simple answer.

"Why not?"

Pedro looked into his cup as if seeking an answer before his gaze drifted to the bathhouse that held the man. "I do not know, Dalia. It is just a feeling about the man that makes me uneasy."

"*Sí*, I sensed it, too. I cannot understand why Lorena does not see it," Dalia said. "She has not been good at determining character since she returned from England."

Pedro looked at her speculatively, knowing of whom she spoke. "I thought that it was I who was wrong about Señor

Wakefield. He left, did he not? I was the only one who
thought he would be good for Lorena."

"You were right, husband, as I tried to tell you last night
before he left," Dalia said, ignoring Pedro's look of
disbelief.

"What are you talking about, Dalia? Clay left, just as you
said he would, just as Diego left his own wife."

Dalia waved her hand as if to dismiss the fact. "That was
different."

"How?"

"Well, I do not know exactly, but Clay did not want to
leave, that much I am sure of. And, Pedro, I cannot get it
out of my head that in some way Clay's leaving and this
Juan Lopez's unexpected arrival are related. Oh, how I wish
Señor Clay were here right now."

"This is true, but he is not, so we must be on our toes to
find out what this Juan Lopez is about."

The days passed uneventfully, Pedro and Dalia on a
constant vigil, watching and waiting for any slipup that
would reveal to them who Juan Lopez really was and what
he truly wanted.

Lorena spent a great deal of time with Juan during the
day, showing him around and talking. One day he asked if
he might go to town to buy just a few things he needed.
"Certainly," Lorena had responded. "I will go with you and
show you where to shop."

As they rode into Paso del Norte, Juan told Lorena that he
had forgotten his money back at the hacienda, but if he
could charge his purchases to her account, he would pay her
when they returned. Of course, she said, and stood skeptically by as Juan bought, in her opinion, enough clothes to
constitute a new wardrobe. She only hoped he had enough
money to pay for them all.

But all of it kept her busy, filling her days, keeping her
mind off Clay. At night, though, she was not so lucky, as
her thoughts were filled with him. She lay in bed night after

night and relived every moment she had spent with the handsome American, the laughter and the teasing, the sharing, and even the anger, and then her thoughts always drifted to their times alone, the times he had held her in his arms, doing things to her body that she did not understand. In her bed, alone at night, she felt her loins grow tight, her nipples harden, as she remembered the things he did to her. Then, in anger over his betrayal, she would pound her pillow and swear not to think of him again.

And then there was Juan, who bided his time, learning all he could about Lorena Cervantes and Cielo el Dorado, and how to make it all his.

Early one morning, after a fitful night of dreaming about Clay, Lorena strode into the kitchen, determined to put the man out of her mind. "Have you seen Juan?" she asked.

"No, *chica*," Dalia said, not liking it that Lorena spent so much time with the man. "Speaking of Señor Lopez, has he told you when he is leaving? I thought he was here to pay his respects and then leave."

"Dalia, he was a friend of my father, and he is our guest. He is welcome to stay as long as he likes." Lorena's voice was impatient, and it surprised both her and Dalia.

Dalia turned back to the tortillas she was making.

Lorena came up behind her, not understanding the way she felt inside, feeling terrible that she was taking her frustration out on the people she loved. "You do not like him, do you?" she asked apologetically.

Dalia turned around, the dough still in her hands. "*Chica*, I do not know what it is, but . . ."

"But what?" Lorena prompted.

"But Pedro and I both feel he is not being honest about why he is here."

"Why?" Lorena questioned, taking a step back.

"Well," Dalia said hesitantly, "we do not know. It is just the way he acts. It is not right."

"Oh, Dalia, I understand. He is a bit harsh. But you have not gotten to know him as I have. I believe he is hurt deep inside and it makes him behave oddly at times." Lorena looked out to the courtyard. "I do not know what it is, but I feel as though I should help him. I feel he needs me, Dalia."

Tossing the dough down in frustration, Dalia wiped her hands on her apron and took Lorena by the shoulders. "Lorena, he is not some stray animal in need of a home. He is a man, and if my guess is correct, he is a dangerous one at that. Do not get involved with him."

"Dalia, you are being silly. Now, come on," she said, determined not to have a confrontation with Dalia. "Let me help you with those tortillas."

Dalia looked into Lorena's green eyes and saw the all too familiar determination there. With a sigh, she turned back to the counter, knowing to push the matter would only turn Lorena away. "No, it is such a beautiful day. Why do you not go for a ride on that horse of yours?" Dalia responded in defeat, but only temporary defeat, she consoled herself. She did not have any real proof that Juan Lopez was bad, but he was, of that she was sure.

"Are you sure you don't need my help?"

"*Sí*, now out with you." Dalia tried to smile. "Go for a ride!"

Lorena left the kitchen looking forward to her ride, already forgetting Dalia's disturbing words. Wanting to forget the relentless images of Clay that haunted her, she welcomed the diversion of riding.

"Juan," Lorena called when she saw him come out of the bathhouse, wondering how any one person could spend so much time bathing. When she told Dalia that he was hurt deep inside, she meant it, and she truly did feel a need to help him. But sometimes that did not make it any easier to be around him. He was a strange sort of fish.

Juan looked at Lorena coming toward him and felt lust rise in his body. He needed a plan, he told himself. He did not want to jeopardize his ultimate goal, but he wanted this girl. He wanted Diego's daughter. "*Sí*, Lorena?"

"I thought we might go for a ride. You have been cooped up inside for days."

Juan fought down the initial grimace that came. The last thing he wanted to do was get on a horse and ride around. Hadn't anyone in these parts heard of a carriage? He had never been one to feel comfortable on a horse and because of that he defensively deemed that the only people who rode were heathens. "You are too kind, Lorena, possibly later," he offered, though he hoped it would be much later, if at all.

Juan had spent much time with Lorena over the past few days, and in that time he had learned a great deal about her. Every little bit helped.

"Yes, possibly later," Lorena said, disappointment written clearly across her face as she wondered if it would be rude to leave her guest to entertain himself. However, before she could decide, Juan spoke, making her decision for her.

"Lorena, would you mind terribly if we just sat here and talked for a while?" Juan asked.

Lorena looked longingly toward the stables before turning back to her guest. "Certainly. That will be fine." She looked around and then said, "Why don't we sit here and talk. You never have told me how you knew my father. I will go get something to drink and you can tell me all about it."

Lorena went to the kitchen to fetch some apple cider. While she was gone, Juan's mind raced. What should he say? What could he tell her? What had he said the day he arrived? He could hardly remember. It was imperative that he keep his stories straight.

When Lorena returned she carried a tray holding two cups and a pitcher. "I hope you like apple cider."

"You know, actually, I would love some of the famous Cielo el Dorado wine."

"This early?" Lorena asked in surprise.

For a fleeting second Juan could not contain the resentment he felt inside, and in that second a look of total hatred

crossed his face. Lorena was confused, seeing the look but
not knowing what it was, never having come in contact with
such intense hatred. But it was gone before her thoughts had
a chance to gel, and Juan hurriedly smoothed over his
mistake.

"Normally I would never think to partake at this hour, but
I feel like celebrating my good fortune in finding someone
as nice and kind as you. Pour me some apple cider. I'll have
wine later."

"Oh, no, Juan, that's all right," Lorena quickly said,
basking in his kind words. "I was just surprised. I will go
get some now." She left once again, this time off toward the
wine cellar to get a bottle of wine.

Juan watched until her slim body disappeared around the
corner, then turned his attention back to his surroundings.
He had memorized every room and each piece of furniture,
thrilled that soon it would all be his. He looked back to
where Lorena had disappeared, wondering if she was worth
the wait. Should he dispense with them all now or savor his
conquest of Lorena—then take the hacienda? He had been
denied the pleasure of breaking Diego Cervantes, and so he
would do the next best thing. He would ruin Diego's
daughter and then take over the hacienda. The revenge
would be sweet, almost better than his original plan. He
would have many kinds of pleasure this way. His laugh
disturbed the birds in the branches of the trees overhead,
sending them into flight, fluttering wildly before calmly
settling down again. Juan's pleasure was imminent. He
would have his revenge, the revenge he had waited a
lifetime for. Mamá, we will win. For a moment despair
engulfed him, before he consciously shook it off. For you,
Mamá.

Lorena came back with a bottle of wine. She poured the
dark red wine into the cup and handed it to Juan.

"Will you not join me?" he asked, taking the cup from
her outstretched hand.

"No, thank you. I am not thirsty," Lorena lied. She sat

down on the grass as there was only one bench on which to sit, and Juan sat there and made no effort to move over. She leaned back against the tree as Juan bent over, picked up the bottle, and poured himself some wine.

"Are you sure?" Juan asked, holding the cup toward her.

"No, thank you. So how did you meet my father?"

Juan shifted. He had not yet come up with his story. He cursed her for asking so many questions. "Diego knew my mother."

"Did he know your father, too?" Lorena asked.

Juan looked at Lorena carefully. "Yes, he knew my father."

"Did he meet them in Chihuahua?"

"Yes," Juan said, looking at her over the brim of his cup.

"What did you do in Chihuahua?"

Juan poured some more wine. "I was a merchant."

"Really? What did you sell?"

Smothering his irritation, he said, "The usual—pots, pans, cloth, almost anything a person needs."

"Did you meet my father through the trade?" Lorena asked, failing to notice his displeasure.

"As a matter of fact, I did." Juan smiled as he thought of Diego when he last saw him. He savored the image as he looked off into the sky, swirling the wine around in the tin cup. He looked at Lorena and wondered if she knew anything. From what he could tell, she did not. But she would, yes, and soon.

Hoping to divert her attention, Juan asked, "Do you like living here?"

"Oh, I love Cielo el Dorado. I missed it terribly the entire time I was away at school."

"Away at school?" Juan was surprised and angry. While he festered in poverty, she was away at school. "Where did you go?"

"England."

"How nice for you."

"Well, I suppose, but I would have preferred to stay

here." Lorena looked around her, loving everything she saw. "I love it so, the land and the animals, I never want to leave it again."

"Really?" Juan said tightly, though the harshness was lost on Lorena. Anyone else would have been charmed by her demonstration of true emotions, the sincerity with which she spoke, but it only infuriated Juan. She should have been left to wallow in the gutter, the little bitch, he thought.

Lorena told him of her feeling about the land and how she missed her father, unintentionally providing Juan Lopez with a crystallized plan for his revenge.

"Men always leave, drawn by the trail," Lorena continued, forgetting that she was speaking to Juan, thinking only of Clay. "Why can't a man be content to stay at home around the family that loves him?"

She had given him an idea: He would persuade her to marry him. That way there would be no doubt that Cielo el Dorado would be his. Yes, he thought to himself, it was perfect. He would marry her, then conveniently get rid of her. She would meet with an unfortunate accident, and then there would be no question about the hacienda being his. Yes, Diego, I will win—and your daughter has made it all the easier.

"You know, I understand what you are talking about. I have wondered many times how the men of the trail can stand being away from home for such long periods of time. I could never do it," he said, planting the first seed of his plan.

Lorena turned to him. "But you are on the trail now," she said, confused.

"No, I am here to find a home, a small farm where I can live and raise a family."

"But why not in Chihuahua?"

"Chihuahua is no place to have a farm and raise a family. I want land to grow crops and raise animals, a place where my children can run and play." He could have laughed to the sky at the look on Lorena's face, the innocent belief that all he said was true, when in fact the last thing he wanted was to run a farm. But Lorena did not need to know that.

"Lorena, if you would not mind, I am a bit tired and would like to rest for a while. Perhaps we could talk more later."

"Oh, of course. How silly of me to go on and on like that! I must have bored you to tears," she said in embarrassment, quickly getting up from the ground, her mind racing, realizing that this was the type of man she should marry. She pushed away the thought that there was something strange about a man who said he was tired before noon, even if he had drunk almost an entire bottle of wine. No, instead she thought of what he had said, a man who wanted nothing more than to live on the land and raise his family. Clay's dark handsomeness loomed in her mind, sending a jolting pain coursing through her. Oh, how she loved him. All the more reason to marry someone like Juan Lopez, someone who would not hurt her.

"Never think you bore me. I was truly enthralled with your stories. In fact, they make me realize how much we have in common. I look forward to continuing this conversation at a later time."

For now, however, all Juan wanted to do was be alone to think through his strategy. Things were working out better than he could have hoped.

21

❦

C LAY LOOKED AT THE MAN IN CONFUSION.

Hector Medina shifted in the doorway, easing his weight against the door frame with a tired sigh, his hand tucking a corner of the bandage back in to secure it.

Ben stepped in behind Clay and recognized the man whom he had confronted weeks before about Diego Cervantes's debt. Now the man wore a mass of bandages around his head and had lost a good deal of weight.

"Come, sit down." Hector motioned to his guests. "Marta, it is fine," he said to his wife, who still stood by as if trying to decide if she should defend her husband or run for help. "They are not here to hurt us." The woman did not move. "Marta, *querida*," Hector said reassuringly to his wife, "go get our guests something to drink."

Reluctantly the woman moved toward the kitchen.

"Do not mind Marta. She has been upset about this scratch," Hector said, pointing to the bandages around his head.

In the distance, the men could hear Marta grumble and snort as she mimicked, "Scratch."

Hector chuckled but quickly stopped as a jolt of pain shot through his head. He looked at his visitors, one hair-covered hand going to his head. "So maybe it was a bit

321

more than a scratch, but that is neither here nor there. What you want to know is how I knew you would be coming."

Clay and Ben followed the man, ready to catch him if he needed assistance. Hector Medina motioned toward two straight-backed chairs that faced what appeared to be the man's bed. "I hope you do not mind if I lie down. I tire quite easily these days." He chuckled, only to be instantly reminded of the pain. He grimaced. "I will be only too glad when this scratch," he said with a smile, "heals and I can get back to work." He shook his head, remembering. "No telling how much business I am losing. But again I digress."

Clay and Ben waited patiently while Hector settled himself in his bed and lay back with a groan. After a few seconds he opened his eyes. "Now tell me, how did you know to come? Was it your brother's insistence?"

Clay leaned forward. "As a matter of fact it was. I knew Diego had been in trouble, but I didn't know the cause until Ben found you. But what has happened since?"

"Well, it was strange, and I do not pretend to understand it all, but I will tell you what I know. After Ben came to see me, I was greatly saddened to hear that my amigo had passed on. I truly liked Diego. I knew him for many years." Hector smiled. "Why else would I lend him so much money? But then, in recent years, I have needed to be paid back." Hector shrugged his shoulders apologetically. "I no longer could spare the money. You understand, no?"

Clay said nothing.

Hector continued. "I told Ben I needed to collect the money. If not, I would have to take over Diego's assets. It was a bad time. I was harsh. I could never have done it, but sometimes a man speaks without thinking. I know that Diego had a daughter," he added, as if explaining why ordinarily he would not have tried to collect.

"But I sent Ben on his way before I had a chance to think clearly. I would have sent word, but as you can see, I met with a bit of misfortune." Hector closed his eyes momenarily before continuing. "And I believe my accident is related to Diego's debt."

"Why?" Clay and Ben asked in unison.

"A man named Juan Lopez worked for me for many years. He was a strange sort, often gave me an eerie feeling, but he was good with numbers," he said with a small chuckle, "and I am not, so, you see, I kept him on, strangeness and all."

Clay listened intently, a feeling of danger beginning to grow.

"Well, soon after Ben came to Chihuahua," Hector continued, "Juan asked a few questions about what Ben wanted. Of course I did not tell him," he said indignantly, "as Diego's debt was a personal matter between Diego and myself. I forgot all about it and went on about my work. I had finally realized that I had been overly harsh about the debt and began to think of the best way to send word to Ben to let him know that I had no intention of collecting. In fact, I went to the store to burn Diego's notes. That was on the same night I was hurt." Hector closed his eyes.

Clay waited, but the man appeared to have fallen asleep. Quietly he said, "Señor Medina, I would not trouble you if this was not so important. Please finish your story. What happened? And how does your injury relate to the notes?"

Hector opened his eyes. "Excuse me. I find that this injury tires me more than a week's worth of hard work. So where was I?"

"You were going to burn the notes," Clay prompted.

"Oh, yes. Well, that is how I came to be in my store so late at night. When I arrived I noticed a light coming from the back room, and fool that I am I did not think to get the officials. Instead I entered quietly, hoping to catch the thief in action. Once inside, I peered into the back and saw that it was Juan. While I thought it strange he was there so late, it never occurred to me that he was up to no good. 'Juan,' I said, and abruptly he turned around. That was when I saw he had the box that contained Diego's notes. When he recovered from his surprise at seeing me, his face relaxed into a smile. I remember distinctly him saying that this would make his revenge all the sweeter. And then he pulled out a gun and shot me. I suppose he thought I was dead. The wound spilled a great deal of blood, although the bullet only grazed my head. *Gracias a Dios* that I am alive today, that I did not bleed to death," Hector said as he made the sign of the cross over his breast. "When I came to, I was here, and it was many days later. I have not been to the store, but I would guess the notes are no longer there. Juan Lopez surely took them."

Clay and Ben sat quietly, assimilating the information. What did it mean? And who was Juan Lopez? Both felt an uneasy foreboding, but neither could find a coherent reason for it.

Hector Medina interrupted. "Go to the store and look for the notes. If they are gone, which I am sure they are, then we know Juan Lopez took them."

"Have you told the officials about this?" It was Clay who asked.

"*Sí*, I have told them, and I am sure they looked around a bit, but"—he sighed—"they are not overly interested in this case. Juan Lopez has apparently gone away and is now out of their district and no longer their concern."

Clay stood up and pulled a packet from his vest. "We're going to search the store then talk to the officials. Here is the money Diego owed you. His debt is now paid in full." Clay set the packet down before the shocked Medina.

The brothers went straight back to the store after receiving a receipt for payment. Clay suspected he would need proof.

They searched every nook and cranny, until Clay was convinced that the notes were not there. Clay lingered over what must have been Juan Lopez's work area. The small cubbyhole seemed somehow familiar, somehow out of place. It was immaculate, unlike the rest of the store, and though the space could not have been more than three feet wide and not much longer, it was reminiscent of a grand study. A fine wooden chair held a red velvet cushion, and the desk had been polished to a high sheen. A gilded retablo hung on the precious wall space, so unlike the usual primitive art that was typically found in the area. The small space in which Juan Lopez had worked was definitely unusual. And there was a small painting. It caught Clay's eye. The image of a man, hard to make out but clear enough that Clay's heart began to pound in his chest.

"It's him!" Clay almost shouted.

Ben turned around, clearly startled by his brother's outburst.

"Juan Lopez—the man we ran into as we were leaving Paso del Norte, the man who looked out of place on the trail," Clay explained. But as soon as his realization sank in, a cold chill spread through his body. "And he must have been on his way to Cielo el Dorado . . . and Lorena."

Ben was taken aback by the look that transformed Clay's face. The realization turned from fear to a deadly rage, a rage so intense and consuming that Ben had never in his life seen such an expression before.

"We ride," Clay ordered as he raced from the store, oblivious to all except the need to get back to Lorena.

The men rode as none had ever ridden before, stopping only to change horses. Clay spoke to no one, intent on the trail, on making the best time, on getting back to the hacienda as quickly as possible. When his thoughts went to Lorena, his chest tightened and his anger rose. If anything had happened to her, he would follow Juan Lopez to the ends of the earth until he found him, and then he would tear him apart, bit by bit, slowly, until the man would wish he had never been born. Juan Lopez would suffer as no one had ever suffered before.

Clay imagined waves of long, soft hair and fiery green eyes, and he knew that whether he liked it or not, he couldn't live without her. He wanted her always, forever by his side. Nothing could happen to her! He had to see her again! And then he knew, beyond a doubt, that he loved her with every ounce of his being, just as she was. He remembered her disobedience and had to smile. Yes, he wanted her even if she disobeyed him for the rest of their lives.

He spurred his horse on, creating a gap between him and his men. Whether it was smart or not, Clay Wakefield knew that he loved Lorena more than he had ever loved anything in his life. He was going to get to Cielo el Dorado in time—he had to.

22

❦

DALIA WATCHED WORRIEDLY FROM THE KITCHEN, her mind racing. What could she do? Things were definitely getting out of hand, and with no hope of Clay coming back in the immediate future, Dalia felt it was time to take matters into her own hands. With a determined sigh, the woman who loved Lorena like her own child decided to search Juan Lopez's room. But how was she supposed to do that when he was always about? Then she remembered the clothes he had ordered. Not all of them had been finished; surely they were done by now. So without thinking about the consequences if the clothes were not ready, Dalia went outside just as Lorena and Juan were getting ready to leave the courtyard.

"Lorena! Juan!" she called.

Both turned around.

"I believe the rest of Juan's clothes are ready. I thought perhaps you could go across to town and get them. It is such a perfect day."

Juan wavered, wary of the old woman's sudden consideration for him, but eager to get the rest of his clothes. The only remaining garment was formal attire that he had been waiting impatiently for. The clothes won out. "This is a good idea," he said to Lorena, ignoring Dalia. "We will go . . . if it would be all right with you."

"Surely, Juan, we can go right now."

Dalia went back to the kitchen and pretended to busy herself with cooking while she waited for Lorena and Juan to leave. The wait seemed interminable, but finally she heard the echo of hooves beating on the ground as the horses made their way under the *torreón* and out into the open. Hurriedly Dalia wiped her hands on her apron and went in search of Pedro. She didn't find him right away, and when she did he was getting ready to leave.

"Where are you going?" Dalia asked, surprised that her husband was going somewhere.

"I am going to the mission. Fray Cristóbal sent word that he needs help with some work. Since he rarely asks, I must certainly go," Pedro answered as he packed a small cart with tools, goods, and anything else he could think of that the priest might need, leaving only a small space for himself.

"*Sí*, this is the truth. You must go," Dalia said distractedly.

Pedro looked closely at his wife. "Is something wrong, Dalia?"

"No, no, nothing is wrong," she answered feeling that it would be unwise to tell him what she was doing. Let her find something first; then she would tell him. "I was just surprised to see you leaving. Now, you go on and help the padre. *Vaya con Dios*."

"I will see you at dinner," he said as he hauled himself up into the tiny wagon. "*Adiós*."

Dalia watched as her husband passed under the *torreón* no more than a few minutes behind Juan and Lorena. Then she went back to the kitchen and waited just long enough to be sure her husband had left and was not coming back for something he might have forgotten, so she could get on with her plan. She had only a short wait before all was quiet, Lorena, Juan, and now Pedro gone to Paso del Norte while all the others were busy with their work. As casually as possible, Dalia made her way to the guest room. When she was sure no one was watching, she slipped into Juan's room and quietly shut the door.

Dalia was frantic. She had searched Juan's room fruitlessly before finally giving up and going back to the kitchen. She had sat at the old oak table for a long while, knowing she had missed what she was looking for. It was there; she was certain.

Then, as if some higher power compelled her, she hurried back to the guest room, unmindful of anyone watching, and went directly to what she had been looking for. She found them in a hidden compartment in his bag. Now she wished the same power that had led her to the papers would lead her Pedro back to the hacienda.

Pacing back and forth, Dalia stopped periodically to peer out the window. When would Pedro be back? Why did he have to go today? Why had the padre called him away on this day of all days, when she needed him? How soon would he be back? But Dalia was afraid she knew. He had said he would not be back until dinnertime. Lorena and Juan had returned only a short time before, and Dalia was frantic. Something had to be done, and soon.

Nervously she pulled several heavy pieces of parchment out of her apron pocket and clutched them to her breast. What was she supposed to do? Sit back and wait for Pedro to come home? Probably, she reasoned. Surely nothing could happen between now and then. And possibly God above would even bring Clay back this day as well.

Dalia unfolded one of the pieces of parchment, already knowing they were all the same, and read it once again, thankful for the first time in her life that the old señor had insisted that all servants be taught to read. Though she was not exactly sure what the document was, common sense told her enough. Diego had owed money to a Señor Medina, and this man, Juan Lopez, held the notes. Who was Señor Medina? Who was Juan Lopez? And why did he have the notes? Her mind whirled with questions, questions that only Juan Lopez could answer. Dalia would have to wait for Pedro to come home and hope that Juan would not notice the missing note beforehand.

Dalia's mind raced as she tried to remember if she had set his room back exactly as she had left it. Surely she had, but doubt filled her. What if she hadn't? Would Juan notice and turn on them all? Had she put Lorena in more danger than she must already be in? Though Dalia did not know for a fact that anything was amiss, the feelings she had had since the very first day Juan Lopez arrived, combined now with the stack of notes, were enough to convince her that she had been right all along: Juan Lopez was out to do no good.

Lorena walked into the kitchen. "*Hola*, Dalia," she said without her usual enthusiasm, but Dalia did not notice the unusual tone of voice as her mind raced with fear.

"*Buenos días*, Lorena," she said, distracted, then turned to the counter and began to chop unwashed vegetables.

"Is something wrong?" Lorena questioned as she watched dirt-covered vegetables being sliced.

"Wrong?" Dalia asked too quickly, with a sharp intake of breath that would have given her away if Lorena had not been so absorbed in her own problems. Instead, Lorena accepted Dalia's hasty reply. "No, no. I am just a bit out of sorts with Pedro, who is gone for the day."

Lorena sighed wistfully, thinking of the two people who after so many years were still so in love that they hated to be apart. She turned to look out the window. "How glorious it must be to be in love, like you and Pedro."

Dalia turned to Lorena, the knife in one hand, a dirt-encrusted vegetable in the other. "You, too, will have a love like that, I am sure." If only Clay would hurry back, Dalia added silently.

"Enough of this silly talk. I came in to tell you that I am going to marry Juan."

Dalia's mouth fell open. The knife clattered to the floor just before the vegetable landed next to it on the blue and white tiles. "*What?*" Dalia cried in disbelief.

Lorena stared at the items that lay forgotten on the floor, not wanting to look up into Dalia's eyes. "I am going to marry Juan Lopez."

"When did this come about?"

"This afternoon when we went into town. I don't know, but one thing led to another until we were talking about marriage. Everything he said made all the sense in the world."

"Lorena Cervantes, that is the craziest thing I have ever heard." Dalia tried to sound severe in hopes of hiding the tremor of fear that threatened to consume her, leaving her helpless to deal with the urgent situation. How could Lorena be so completely fooled by this deceitful man?

"No crazier than marrying someone else who is sure to leave me unhappy. At least in Juan I will have a husband who will stay home and love the land as I do. At least he will not ride off on the trail to find his happiness." Lorena's dispassionate voice gave way to a tremor and then tears. She hated what she was doing, but felt she had no alternative.

Realizing the young girl's heartache, Dalia momentarily forgot Juan Lopez. She went to Lorena and wrapped her tiny body in her welcoming embrace. "You love Señor Clay, do you not?"

"Oh, Dalia," she sobbed, "I love him so much, but I cannot bear to be like my mother, living here all alone, watching the front gate, hoping it will open to admit the man I love, being disappointed almost every time as it would rarely be him."

Dalia was at a loss. How she wished Pedro were here. How she wished Clay were here. "Lorena, you must wait for Señor Clay to come back before you do anything rash."

Abruptly Lorena pulled out of Dalia's arms. "No! I will not wait for Clay to come back, because then I will have no chance. I will be destined to a life of misery!"

"How do you know that, Lorena?" Dalia asked heatedly. "You have not given Señor Clay a chance."

Lorena looked at Dalia as if she did not believe what she heard. "Not given Señor Clay a chance," she mimicked. "I was set to marry the man before he left, thinking he was different. But then he left, just as I suspected he would. I was lulled by his easy charm into believing he was different. How lucky I was that he showed his true colors before I made the fatal mistake of marrying him."

"You exaggerate, I think."

"Exaggerate? Why do you say that?"

"Because you said 'fatal mistake.' I think you are being dramatic."

"Ha! Didn't my mother die from being left alone? Loving and longing for my father killed her!" Lorena shrieked.

Dalia was surprised, though she should not have been, she told herself. All these years she had never realized that Lorena pined for her mother, blaming her father for her death. Now, before Lorena ruined her own life, Dalia had to tell her the truth. "Lorena." Dalia's voice softened as she reached out for the young girl whom she had wronged by not being honest with her about her mother. Lorena pulled away, so Dalia continued from a distance. "Your mother was a very beautiful woman, and there were many good things about her. But you must understand that she was very unhappy at Cielo el Dorado."

Before she could go on, Lorena interrupted. "She was very unhappy here because my father was never around."

Dalia thought about that for a moment before she continued. "Yes, that is true. But she was unhappy when your father was here as well."

"That was because she knew he would only turn around and leave again."

"No," Dalia stated. "That is not true. Your father left because he could not please her no matter what he did."

When Lorena tried to protest, Dalia silenced her, her patience replaced with sternness. "You will listen to me for once. If I had known that you blamed your father for your mother's death, I would have said this years ago: Your

mother did not like Cielo el Dorado; she did not like this
area; she did not like the people or the clothes; she hated the
hacienda because it was rustic, she said, not fit for human
beings, and the mission could never compare to the beautiful cathedral she had attended in Spain. She did not like
the weather, and she hated the desert. She blamed your
father for bringing her here. Over and over again she would
cry about 'this Godforsaken place out in the middle of
nowhere.' It was an arranged marriage, *chica*. Some of
those marriages work out, and the man and woman are able
to find love, but your parents' arranged marriage brought a
pampered young Spanish miss to the rustic desert, and she
hated it before she arrived. Your father tried everything to
make her love him. Why do you think Cielo el Dorado is so
modern?"

"Because he wanted to have the nicest hacienda around!"

"No! Because he tried to please your mother. She made
your father's life miserable, so finally he left. And that just
gave her one more excuse to complain. She poisoned your
mind with resentment of your father. If your father had been
that horrible, you would have hated him as much as she did.
But do you? No! Your father was good to you when he was
here. The only reason he came back at all was to see you."
Dalia's voice began to fade. "Diego loved you very much,
and in the beginning he loved his wife very much as well,
but his life here was miserable."

"Why didn't she go back to Spain?"

"Her family would not take her back. It would have been
a disgrace."

Lorena reeled with the news, but old habits died hard.
Resolutely, she got up. "That does not change anything,"
she said, though not truly convinced. Upset and more
confused than ever, she left the kitchen, wanting, needing,
to get away and think. She had come to accept that she was
not responsible for her father's absences from home. She
knew that her father was not capable of staying. Now she
was being asked to accept that her mother as well had been

to blame for the lonely childhood Lorena had lived, and that she was not sure she could do. How was it possible that both of her parents could have been so . . . so what?

After Lorena left, Dalia did not know what to do. She needed Pedro. Making a decision, she left the kitchen and went to the stables to find Jaime. She would send him to the mission to ask Pedro to come home immediately. But when she arrived, Jaime wasn't there. Thinking he might be in the back, she walked farther into the stables. She heard quiet rustling coming from the back, confirming Jaime's where-abouts. But when Dalia looked into the room she found not Jaime but Juan Lopez, a sickening smile spread across his face. He stood in the tack room fingering solid silver bridles and caressing fine leather. Walking over to finely studded saddles, he inspected them as if trying to determine their worth. Dalia knew in that moment, with sparkling clarity, that Juan Lopez had come to Cielo el Dorado with his stack of hidden notes to take the hacienda away from them. He had never been a friend of Diego's, as he had said, but more than likely a vicious enemy. Without thinking of possible consequences, Dalia confronted him.

"Who are you, Juan Lopez, and why are you here?"

Spinning around to face the door, Juan was momentarily startled. But when he saw who it was, he easily regained his composure. He studied her closely, as if by looking he could tell how much she knew, and he decided that she knew too much, no matter what she knew. He knew she had not liked him since the day he arrived, barely being civil, never making him feel welcome. She was almost as bad as her husband. Now she would pay. Juan shrugged his shoulders. She would have paid eventually anyway. "Old woman," he said with a sneer, "you should mind your own business."

"Anything having to do with Lorena is my business."

Juan smiled then, a full smile across his face, sending a shiver of foreboding down Dalia's spine. That one smile

revealed all the putrid evil Dalia had known was in Juan
since the day he arrived.

Madre mía, Dalia prayed silently, why did I not wait for
Pedro?

As soon as the kitchen door closed behind Lorena, she
forced herself to walk until she was out of sight, not
wanting Dalia to see how the story of her mother had
affected her. As soon as she was around the corner she ran
into the next courtyard and headed straight for the cool
recesses of the storage room. No one would be there, and
she wanted to be alone with her thoughts to try to make
sense of them.

The heavy wooden door creaked open, and Lorena could
smell the fresh hay within. The room was dark and cool,
and for a minute she could not see anything. She pulled the
door shut behind her. Slowly her eyes adjusted to the darkness
before she made her way toward the straw. She walked softly,
sitting down on the piles carefully as if she might break
something, as if possibly she herself might break. Lorena felt
as if she had a tenuous hold on reality, her whole concept of
her parents having been torn to shreds. Was it possible that
what Dalia had said was true? Lorena's thoughts went back in
time. She saw her mother and she saw her father. In the first
image her mother was stretched out on her chaise lounge
sipping cool cider. In the second, she was sitting in a chair
diligently stitching fabric, all the while berating her absent
husband. But now, as Lorena thought about it, she realized
that it was not just her father, but everything around her—the
servants, the weather, the people from town. At the time, the
other things had not mattered to Lorena so she had given them
no heed. Only her father mattered, and those words had cut
deep. Was it possible that her mother was at fault after all and
that her father was more victimized than victim?

It was hard for Lorena to give up what she believed to be
true, especially when the new belief put her mother in the
wrong. But as Lorena pulled her legs up to her chest and

held them tight, she knew that it was not just her mother
and, for that matter, not just her father. Both of them had
been at fault. A marriage needed two partners who were
willing to give, willing to make it work. Lorena felt
suddenly overwhelmed with it all and knew that she had to
go to Dalia and ask all the questions that came to mind. She
had to know; she had to find out the truth, the entire truth
about her parents' marriage. It was important, for her past
and her future.

She jumped up off the pile of straw, giving no notice to
the shafts that had found their way into her hair, and ran to
the door. She pushed it open, eager to find Dalia.

The courtyard was deserted. She ran back to the kitchen
and startled Luz.

"Luz, where is Dalia?" Lorena asked, out of breath.

"I do not know, Lorena. I have not seen her."

Lorena left the kitchen and ran past every room in the
main courtyard until she reached Dalia and Pedro's room.
Still no Dalia. After leaving that room, she headed back to
the other side, but when she did not find Dalia a tremble of
concern stole into her body. Where was she? Something
wasn't right.

Lorena was just about to pass the stables, knowing how
Dalia disliked horses, when she thought to take a peek
inside, sure she wouldn't find the missing woman. It
occurred to her that she had not seen Juan either in all her
searching of the hacienda. Before Lorena had a chance to
think about this fact, she opened the stable door and stuck
her head through. She almost did not hear the murmur of
voices that came from deep inside the stable. She was so
sure she was not going to find Dalia within that it took a
moment for her to realize that it was indeed Dalia's voice.
Lorena started to call out, but the hushed tones made her
stop. She walked inside and quietly stepped toward the
voices.

They were in the tack room, Dalia, clearly upset, and
someone else. It took a moment for Lorena to realize the

ther person was Juan. Could that voice possibly belong to their easygoing guest? At the realization that it was indeed his voice, Lorena knew that something was very wrong. Cautiously, she moved closer until she could make out their words.

"I think you need to explain yourself, Juan Lopez." Dalia's voice was strong, but Lorena recognized the fear that underlined her words. Her heart began to pound. More than ever, she wished Clay were home.

"As I said, old woman, this is none of your business." Venom dripped from Juan's voice. "You should have kept your nose out of this, because now you have caused yourself many problems."

"What are you talking about?" Dalia demanded.

Juan sensed her fear, though he admitted she was doing a remarkable job of hiding it. But fear was an emotion Juan knew well, and he recognized it in its many forms. He thrived on others' fear. It gave himself a sense of power, a feeling he craved.

"Now that you have gotten involved in something that has nothing to do with you," he said, "I will have to kill you to teach you a lesson."

Dalia's heart raced, but caution was not with her. "To keep me quiet, do you not mean? I know your type, Juan Lopez. You prey on those who are weaker than you. You gain a feeling of power from plaguing women and children, and if they get in your way or become a bother, you resort to killing."

Her words were a caustic barb, cutting deep to the core of his corrupt soul. "That is not true," he said, his eyes growing large.

Dalia sensed her advantage. "Yes it is, Juan, you are a coward." Her voice was calm, all traces of fear gone, and her words sent Juan into a rage.

"That is not true." He raised his voice. "Diego Cervantes was not weak, and I killed him—if not by my hand, then by my words."

Dalia suddenly felt sick, as if she had been punched in th
stomach. Things were more serious than she had imagined

Lorena stood outside the room, anger welling up insid
her.

"What are you talking about?" Dalia questioned frant
cally.

Juan regained his composure at the sight of Dalia
reoccurring fear. A sinister smile found his face. "You see
I am Diego Cervantes's son."

"Diego has no son."

"Oh, there you are wrong. I am Diego's son, only fro
the wrong side of the sheets."

"You are his bastard?"

Juan's control slipped slightly at the crude word she use
to describe him, the word that had made his whole life on
long misery. "Bastard, maybe. But that does not matte
now. I will have what is rightfully mine—Cielo el Dorado.

"That's what the notes I found were all about, is it not?
Dalia asked.

Juan smiled. "*Sí*, I have all the notes that Diego signed
Cielo el Dorado is mine."

"Cielo el Dorado is Lorena's. That is why you said yo
wanted to marry her."

"No, the hacienda is already mine because of th
notes. I just wanted to taste the pleasures that her youn
body offers, and"—he shrugged his shoulders—"it woul
strengthen my claim to what is rightfully mine. I wi
destroy the remaining Cervantes as Diego Cervantes de
stroyed my mother."

"But if what you say is true, Lorena is your half siste
How could you possibly conceive of marrying her?"

"I would not keep her, woman, only teach her a lesso
And now, since you have gotten in the way, I must remov
you so you cannot ruin my plans."

Lorena was shocked by what she had heard. How was
possible that her father had had another child and never tol
anyone about him? But as Lorena was about to call o

npulsively to the half brother she never knew she had, uan reached for a heavy piece of wood, banishing all amilial thoughts from Lorena's mind, knowing she must ave Dalia from this crazed man. Without thinking, she :aped into the room.

"Stop!" she screamed, startling both Dalia and Juan.

"Lorena, run! He is crazy. Go get help!" Dalia cried.

But before Lorena could do anything, Juan stepped in ont of the door blocking her escape.

"So it comes to an end so soon," he said. "Fortunately, have the notes, so it is not essential that I marry you to get hat is rightfully mine. But," he added as his eyes traveled e length of Lorena's body, "I will taste the pleasures you ave to offer." Then, swiftly, Juan swung the board, hitting alia in the head, causing her to fall in a heap on the floor.

Lorena lunged toward Dalia, but Juan knocked her away.

"I am sure that only knocked her out. I will have to get d of her later. But first I will have you."

Juan started toward Lorena, and she moved away until er back was against the wall. She started to scream when e lunged at her. He covered her mouth with his hand, then rew her to the floor. He was on her in a second, covering er mouth again before she had a chance to call for help.

Lorena kicked and clawed, then bit his hand.

"You bitch," he screamed as he drew back his hand. He aught a glimpse of blood before he swung his hand in a igh arc and hit her with resounding force. Lorena was nocked back down, and Juan pinned her firmly to the oor. She kicked and scratched and managed to get loose, rawling swiftly to the other side of the tack room. Slowly, uan got up, never taking his eyes off her as he came closer.

"You will pay, Lorena Cervantes. You will pay for verything Diego Cervantes did." He came closer. "But I ink you will die slowly, as my mother did. You will suffer or a great length of time, as I have over these many years. es, Lorena Cervantes, sister," he sneered, "you will die."

And then, just as he lunged for her, a shot pierced the air. Lorena's eyes widened, not comprehending the sound.

Juan's face stretched in a startled grimace before he fell to the floor, red blood forming a puddle around his chest.

Lorena was startled as well, not knowing what had happened. She turned to the door, and there stood Clay, the gun still smoking in his hand.

His eyes met hers, clouding with relief. He had made it—but only barely.

Lorena looked at Clay and knew she had never loved anyone more in her life. Without hesitating a second longer, she flew into his arms. "Clay!" she cried into his chest.

"It's all right now," he soothed.

"Don't ever leave me again."

"I won't, little one, I won't."

Lorena held fast to his massive body, blocking out the horrible events of only a few moments before, blocking out the reality of the situation, her only thought being that he had come back to her, that he had come home.

23

🎔

LATER THAT SAME DAY, AFTER DALIA HAD AN-
nounced emphatically that she was perfectly all right, Clay and
Lorena found each other in the courtyard. They stood some
distance apart, she at one end of the courtyard, he at the
kitchen door. When defenses were down and lives were at
stake, everything had seemed quite clear. But now that the
shock of the earlier events had died down, neither knew what
to say.

Clay moved across the grass and stepping stones, then
under the huge trees, until he came slowly to a stop before
Lorena.

"What do you say to starting over?" Clay asked, a half
smile bringing a gleam to his dark eyes.

Lorena looked up at him. "What do you have in mind?"
Her heart pounded, but she controlled her features. She was
not about to throw herself at Clay one more time.

"Come on, I'll show you." Clay grabbed Lorena's small
hand and pulled her toward the stable.

"Where are you taking me?" she demanded as she tried
to keep up with him, having to run every few steps to keep
from falling.

The horses were readied in record time, and before
Lorena knew it, she and Clay were riding through the front

gate. He led them to the swimming hole, where Lorena had
first seen him. She didn't know what to do or what to say,
only looked warily at Clay. She couldn't imagine what he
could possibly want.

Clay dismounted, but when Lorena tried to follow, he
stopped her. "No, stay where you are." The devilish half
smile was still mischievously in place.

"Clay, what are you up to?"

"Now ride in circles and laugh at Miss T."

"What?" Lorena cried in confusion.

"You know, when I first found you that day"—Clay's
devilish smile turned to a glower—"when you were out here
all alone and could easily have been found by a man who
did not have the same respect for an unprotected female as
I do."

Lorena's confusion turned to her own devilish smile. "As
I recall, I had to draw a knife on you!"

Clay's good humor instantly returned. "Not that it could
have done any harm."

"You—"

"I believe it was 'overconfident cow.' "

"And that's the truth, Clay Wakefield, you are!"

"But"—Clay looked deep into her eyes, only a hint of the
teasing left—"it seems to me you also called me . . .
Now, wait. Let me see. I want to get it exactly right."

Lorena sat on her horse, a crimson blush creeping up her
cheeks as she remembered that day so long ago when she
had been so naive, filled with visions of knights in shining
armor. "Don't bother going on. I well remember the day
and am not likely to forget it in the near future."

"But I would like to remember it. 'A god sent down from
the heavens to play havoc with my heart,' I believe you
said."

"Maybe so," she conceded haughtily, "but I also recti-
fied my dreadful error by changing that to 'wretch.' "

Clay's booming laugh filled the air. "Yes, and you have

called me just about everything else since that day I met you."

Gradually Clay's laughter subsided. And then he looked up into Lorena's eyes all traces of teasing gone. "I was afraid I wouldn't make it home in time."

Lorena felt as if her world had tilted. One minute he was laughing at her; the next he was revealing a side of him she had never seen. He seemed like a small boy now, unsure of himself, as if he might lose something he held dear. Was it possible? She held her breath, scared that at any second he would turn back into a demanding tyrant.

When Lorena didn't respond, and only looked down at him, Clay continued. "I thought of you constantly from the minute I left and every second after that until now."

Lorena's heart was at war. She knew she loved him with all her heart and soul, and part of her cried that it didn't matter if he left her regularly. She wanted whatever time with him she could get. But she also couldn't forget the loneliness and sorrow he would cause her when he went away time and time again, and she wasn't sure she could live a lifetime of such pain.

Clay saw the emotions race across her features and knew that she was torn. "I will not leave you again."

Lorena looked at him closely, wanting to believe what he said.

"If I have to go, you are going with me."

Lorena's heart skipped a beat. She had never thought to go with him anywhere.

Clay moved closer to the horse until he almost touched Lorena's leg. "I love you, Lorena Cervantes," he said, his voice deep with emotion, "and as God is my witness, I will never leave you alone again."

Unshed tears glistened in her eyes, and with a groan, Clay reached up and pulled her down into his fierce embrace. Lorena wrapped her arms around him as if she would never let him go, so tight that she could feel his heart pounding in his chest.

"I love you, little one," he mumbled into her hair.

"Oh, Clay, I love you so much."

And then they both started to speak, relief washing away the tension and uncertainty.

They sat next to the water and Clay began to tell Lorena about her father's debt and why he had not told anyone of his suspicions. He told her of Hector Medina and how they had met Juan just as they were leaving Paso del Norte.

"You were a fool, Clay Wakefield. You should have told me."

"Maybe, but it's over now. All that matters is that you're safe."

"And Cielo el Dorado is secure!"

Clay laughed, pulling her down beneath him. "Yes, Cielo el Dorado is secure and will be passed down from generation to generation of our family."

Lorena looked up at him, green eyes glistening with all the love she felt. "There will be more generations of Cervantes children!" she said, almost in disbelief.

"They'll certainly carry Cervantes blood, but they'll have the Wakefield name."

Then she punched him playfully in the arm. "You are the most arrogant man I have ever met. For tradition's sake, I think we should keep the Cervantes name."

"Oh, no," he responded as he lowered his lips to her forehead. "Wakefield," he said with a kiss. "And I think it might be wise if we start trying to produce an heir right away." His kisses were followed by tantalizing caresses.

"Not until we're married."

"It seems that it's too late to make that demand at this point."

Lorena blushed as she remembered their night of wild and intoxicating passion.

Clay pulled back and looked down at her, the humor sparking back to life in his eyes. "Besides, I thought you said you would never marry me."

"Too late. You're stuck," she said with laughing eyes.

"I guess you're right. I am stuck," he said in playful lament.

So when Clay leaned back down to find her lips, Lorena caught his between her teeth.

"Ahggh," he bellowed, his lip firmly caught.

"Who's stuck?" she mumbled, not letting go.

"No one!" he mumbled back.

"Good."

"Actually, you're stuck," he said pulling her close in his arms. "With me." He dipped his head to kiss her, a long, leisurely kiss, before he pulled back and looked into the depths of her green eyes. "I plan to spend the rest of my days showing you just how much I love you, Lorena."

Her green eyes shone with unshed tears of happiness and love. Not knowing the words to express all the feelings she held inside, she pulled Clay down to her and kissed him with all the love and passion she felt.

*If you enjoyed this book, take advantage
of this special offer. Subscribe now and . . .*

GET A *FREE*
HISTORICAL ROMANCE
—— NO OBLIGATION(a $3.95 value) ——

Each month the editors of True Value will select the four best historical romance novels from America's leading publishers. Preview them in your home Free for 10 days. And we'll send you a FREE book as our introductory gift. No obligation. If for any reason you decide not to keep them, just return them and owe nothing. But if you like them you'll pay *just* $3.50 each and save at least $.45 each off the cover price. (Your savings are a minimum of $1.80 a month.) There is no shipping and handling or other hidden charges. There are no minimum number of books to buy and you may cancel at any time.

send in the coupon below

THE TENDER TEXAN

by Jodi Thomas

Anna Meyer dared to walk into a campsite full of Texan cattlemen...and offer one hundred dollars to the man who'd help her forge a frontier home-stead. Chance Wyatt accepted her offer, and agreed to settle down and build a home with the lovely stranger. They vowed to live together for one year only. But the challenges of the savage land drew them closer together and although the boy in him never considered the possibility of love, the man in him could not deny the passion . . .

__ THE TENDER TEXAN 1-55773-546-8/$4.95